"TELL ME MORE," SHE WHISPERED.

His dark eyes gleamed and his hand caressed the nape of Linette's neck. "These are your cervical vertebrae—seven in all." His fingers brushed across her bare shoulder and followed the line of bone across the front. "This is the clavicle—your collarbone. I can tell you're not a laborer," he teased.

Stephen traced the line of her jaw and under her chin. "The inferior maxillary—what you call the jawbone."

His breath was warm against her cheek, and Linette could barely breathe. As his fingers brushed softly over her lips, she shut her eyes.

He was going to kiss her. The thought was barely formed when he touched his mouth to hers.

His kiss was soft, caressing, and achingly sweet. When he pulled away, Linette found herself looking into the dark brown depths of Stephen's eyes.

"I shouldn't have done that," he said in a hoarse voice.

"Why?" she whispered.

"Because I want to do it again."

Stolen Hearts

Melinda McRae

A TOPAZ BOOK

TOPAZ
Published by the Penguin Group
Penguin Books USA Inc., 375 Hudson Street,
New York, New York 10014, U.S.A.
Penguin Books Ltd, 27 Wrights Lane,
London W8 5TZ, England
Penguin Books Australia Ltd, Ringwood,
Victoria, Australia
Penguin Books Canada Ltd, 10 Alcorn Avenue,
Toronto, Ontario, Canada M4V 3B2
Penguin Books (N.Z.) Ltd, 182-190 Wairau Road,
Auckland 10, New Zealand

Penguin Books Ltd, Registered Offices:
Harmondsworth, Middlesex, England

First published by Topaz, an imprint of Dutton Signet,
a division of Penguin Books USA Inc.

First Printing, October, 1995
10 9 8 7 6 5 4 3 2

 REGISTERED TRADEMARK—MARCA REGISTRADA

Printed in Canada

This book is dedicated to the librarians and libraries who have helped along the way.

Special thanks to the Seattle Public Library, for their eagerness to help, free interlibrary loan services, and the Internet access.

Thanks also to the University of Washington libraries, particularly Health Sciences, for having such an amazing cache of material on nineteenth century medicine.

And, of course, many grateful thanks to the usual suspects for their support, encouragement, and willingness to listen—and advise.

Author's note:

The medical procedures described in this book were accepted practice in the late 1820's. Early 19th century medicine was primitive, and often misguided.

Medical practitioners in early nineteenth century England were divided into three groups: physicians, surgeons, and apothecaries. Each was licensed by a separate governing body, and training requirements varied widely. Physicians held university degrees, and were called "doctor," but they often had little formal medical education. Physicians concerned themselves with internal disease; they diagnosed and medicated.

Surgeons and apothecaries had more formal medical training, including anatomy. Surgeons could not prescribe medicines, but often earned an apothecary license so they could. Surgery was still viewed as a "trade" and surgeons were addressed as "Mister." Surgery was the more "modern" discipline; operations for kidney stones, gall stones, and tumorous cancers were routine. Of course, these were all performed without anaesthetic.

Medical education in England was a combination of loosely organized hospital instruction and private medical schools. St. Bartholomews (St. Barts), St. Thomas, and Guys were the main teaching hospitals of the time. Students had the opportunity to walk the wards and observe surgeries and dissections. According to student complaints, instruction from the staff doctors was often minimal. At the private schools, they took instruction in anatomy, chemistry, and general medicine. Teaching could be a lucrative venture for a well-known practitioner.

Doctors and surgeons were appointed to the hospital staffs. Influence with the voting boards of governors was the major qualification for a post, and nepotism was rife within the system. All the positions were unpaid, but the resulting status and the ability to take on pupils more than made up for the lack of salary.

Prologue

A tall, hawk-nosed man, bundled against the night cold, peered down at his companion, busily shoveling away the rich dirt.

"Ain't you reached it yet, Bill?"

A muffled thunk of metal against wood brought a smile to the digger's grizzled face. "I thinks we got it, boys." He didn't pause, continuing to shovel aside the last few remaining clods of earth from the lid of the box.

" 'And me the 'ooks, George," he said at last.

A third man stepped out of the shadows and handed him two stout iron hooks, attached to separate lengths of rope. Bending over the hole he'd just dug, Bill worked the hooks under the lid, then tossed the ropes to his companions before scrambling out of the way. The lines grew taut as the two men pulled with all their strength, until the wooden lid splintered with a loud crack.

"Bloody hell! Watch the noise."

" 'Ow we supposed to be quiet *and* get this done, I'd like to know?"

Ignoring the complaints, Bill worked quickly, clearing away the splintered pieces of wood and removing the hooks. Taking one of the ropes, he wrapped it securely about the contents of the box and handed the line off again.

"Pull on it now, lads. And be careful! Damaged goods don't help us none."

Exerting themselves, the two men pulled and hauled until the white bundle came free of its container. They hastily stripped off the wrappings, tossing them back into the empty box while Bill started to refill the hole.

While he worked, George and the other man stuffed the unearthed treasure into a long canvas sack, securely tying the top end. Then they turned to help their comrade finish with his job.

"That looks good, lads," Bill said when the hole was filled again. He bent and cautiously slid open the side of a shuttered lantern. With a trowel, he smoothed over the heaped dirt with painstaking care, stopping at times to inspect his work. Finally satisfied, he stood up.

"That's it, then," he said, shutting the lantern with a snap. He picked up the shovel and the hooks, coiling the ropes, while the other two men struggled with their burden. Swiftly, silently, they passed through the gate in the high stone wall and walked toward the cart waiting in the lane.

"Give us a 'and 'ere, Bill," said one of the men carrying the bundle. "This is a heavy 'un."

They struggled to lift the load into the back of the cart. While George spread straw over the sacking, Bill hid the tools beneath the wagon seat, then climbed up to take the reins. George jumped into the back and the third man melted into the darkness.

"A good night, tonight," said Bill, slapping his companion on the thigh.

"I can't complain," George agreed. "We should get a good price for this 'un."

They drove along in silence. Traffic was light this time of night, and they made quick progress across the city. Once or twice, at the sight of an approaching carriage, Bill guided the cart down a deserted side street, not wanting to take any chances. There'd be no profits for a night's work if they didn't deliver the goods.

At last, the cart turned down a narrow, crooked lane running behind a row of nondescript buildings in Clerkenwell. One door, halfway down the alley, was marked with a lamp.

"Looks like the man's a-waitin'," Bill said with a grin.

"I still says we oughta take advantage of the situation. Charge 'em more, see? If 'e's so eager, let 'im pay for it."

Bill shook his head. "Now, George, we don't want to upset a good customer. 'E's willing to pay what we ask without complainin', which is more 'n I can say of some of them other blokes. No need to cause trouble."

Bill reined in the horse and the cart halted a few steps past the door. George got out and pounded on the wood. For some minutes there was no response, then the sounds of bolts unlatching echoed in the quiet night. A sandy-haired young man peered out the door.

" 'Ere now, you're not our man!" George stepped back as if preparing to flee.

"It's all right, I'm Ashworth's assistant," the young man said. "You have something for us?"

"I'm deliverin' it to Ashworth and no one else," George said.

"Good grief, what difference does it make?" But seeing the determined looks on their faces, the assistant relented and turned back into the building. In a moment, a tall, dark-haired man in shirtsleeves came to the door.

"Brought ye 'nother one, Mr. Ashworth," Bill said. "A right nice one, too."

"Bring it in," Ashworth said curtly, turning back inside.

"We need another hand."

Ashworth turned and yelled down the hall. "Mathers! Get out here and help these gentlemen with their delivery."

With a grim expression, Mathers stepped out into the alley, helping the others lift the sack out of the cart and through the door. Making a sharp turn to the left, they entered a small anteroom, bare except for a long, scarred table. They plopped the heavy bundle down with obvious relief.

Ashworth followed behind them. "Well, let's see it."

The tall man eagerly undid the rope at one end of the sack and pulled the material back. "A prime 'un, he is."

Ashworth peered at the contents. "Hmm."

"Yep," said Bill. " 'E's worth his weight, this 'un is.

Ashworth glanced warily at the two men. "Let's see the whole thing."

The men stripped off the canvas cover and stood back while Ashworth carefully inspected their offering. Then his face broke into a satisfied smile.

"Gentlemen, you've done well this evening." He reached into his pocket and pulled out a handful of golden coins. "Six guineas."

"This is an arful nice 'un," George began.

"*Six* guineas," Ashworth repeated. "As we agreed."

Bill grabbed the money and stuffed it into his pocket. " 'N when will you be needin' another?"

Ashworth glanced back at the table. "Oh, give it a few days. Unless you find something exceptional, of course."

The man nodded. Ashworth escorted them to the door, saw them out, then bolted it again. He stepped back into the room and turned to his assistant.

"Well, Mathers, looks like we've got a busy day ahead of us. I'm off to get some sleep. Prepare the specimens for tomorrow—we'll do the arm, first, I think. Then you can go home."

Mathers nodded.

With a final, relieved glance at the male body lying on the dissecting table, Stephen Ashworth, surgeon, grabbed his coat and headed out the front door of the Great Howard Street School of Anatomy, heading toward home. Hands stuffed in his pockets, his collar turned up against the cold, his face held a satisfied expression as he strode along the deserted street. His students would have ample opportunity to practice their dissecting skills tomorrow.

Chapter 1

From his position at the front of the tiered lecture room, Stephen looked up at the faces of his students. Several looked more bleary-eyed than usual, and he didn't think it was from studying too intently. They would soon wish they had.

"We're going to examine the structure of the shoulder joint today." He looked directly at Smith, slouched in the back row. "Mr. Smith, would you care to review what we've learned so far?"

Smith turned beet red. "We have not studied the shoulder yet, sir."

"I realize that, Smith." Stephen hid his amusement. "But the shoulder doesn't float about in space—it's connected to other parts of the body. Would you care to tell us what those parts are?"

"Ah . . . um . . . the arm?"

"The arm." Stephen nodded. "Very good, Mr. Smith. And which part of the arm connects to the shoulder?"

"The ulna?"

The more enlightened members of the class laughed.

"An interesting anatomical phenomenon, Mr. Smith." Stephen directed a withering look at the hapless student. "Would someone like to tell Mr. Smith exactly why that is so?"

"The ulna is the large bone in the forearm, you dolt," Chance shouted. "The humerus fits into the shoulder socket."

"Very good, Mr. Chance. Now let us examine this socket joint . . ."

At the conclusion of his lecture, Stephen looked up. "Any questions?"

No one broke the silence and in a moment he nodded. "Very well, then. Mr. Mathers will guide you through your efforts in the dissecting room this afternoon and see how well you've been paying attention. I'll see you again on Friday."

Stephen hurried out of the room and was back in his office before the students had filed down the stairs.

Stripping off his soiled demonstrating coat, Stephen scrubbed his hands in the washbasin. As he dried them, he frowned.

He wanted to be across the corridor, in the dissecting room, supervising the students. Mathers knew his anatomy well enough, but Stephen hated to be away when the students were cutting. Not only did they work better in his presence, he was also able to gauge their skills. Ah well, Mathers could handle things for an afternoon.

Stephen grinned ruefully. With this new group of students, it wasn't going to make much difference. He couldn't force them to become good surgeons—although if he knew how, he might try. At least there were two or three lads in the class this term who looked promising.

Actually, he didn't mind missing the dissecting session. He just didn't want to attend this stupid afternoon tea. Standing around an elegant drawing room, trading social conversation with men who couldn't tell the difference between a trephine and a bullet extractor, was not Stephen's idea of a good time.

But when he'd taken the position of head surgeon at the Barton Dispensary, he'd known he would have to attend these things. Working at the Dispensary was a key step toward his major goal—an appointment at one of the major London hospitals. He hoped working at the Dispensary would bring him the connections which could bring him that coveted appointment. Stephen enjoyed teaching, was buying the Howard Street School for that very reason, but he knew he'd never receive the respect and acclaim he wanted until he had one of those prestigious hospital positions.

This tea was his first experience dealing with the men and women whose charitable donations paid for the medical care he would provide. Stephen hoped they wouldn't ask a lot of stupid questions. Trying to explain surgical procedures to laymen was a daunting task. Either they didn't understand, or the specific details were too bloody.

What did they expect—that surgery was a clean and pristine occupation? Cutting into people was a messy business, but it was necessary to save lives, and to learn.

Mathers peered around the door. "Any last instructions?"

Stephen shook his head. "Just keep those miscreants from tearing the building apart." He set the towel down. "And keep a close eye on Tomlinson and that Walker fellow—they seem to treat this as a lark."

"I've got just the thing for them." Mathers gave him a knowing grin. "There's a particularly ripe specimen they can have."

Stephen laughed. "Good. That will teach them to mind their manners in the future."

"I see that the tenon saw's missing."

"Again?" Stephen scowled as he rummaged through the jumble of papers on his desk, looking for the scrap of paper with Mrs. Barton's address. "What would anyone want with a tenon saw? No, let me guess—they're practicing amputations on each other. I can see it now, we'll be flooded with one-legged students in a few days' time." Mathers snickered.

"Order another one," Stephen said wearily. "And take it out of the student fund this time. They can share an arm or a leg to make up the cost."

Mathers guffawed and returned to the dissecting room.

Stephen grimaced with weary resignation. Maybe it would be a relief to deal with sensible Dispensary supporters instead of mischievous students. He didn't think the guests at this tea were the type to steal the furniture. As long as he praised them for their farsightedness and charity, they'd be happy. These people enjoyed flattery and Stephen knew how to appear properly grateful for the great opportunities they provided.

If he was lucky, the tea wouldn't last more than an hour. He'd have just enough time to check on the progress in the dissecting room before he started work for the night on his own research.

Stephen reached for the cravat he'd tossed carelessly atop his disordered desk after lecture this morning. It wasn't exactly in pristine condition, but then, he wasn't going before the governing board of St. Barts or Guys, either. He hastily tied it into an indifferent knot and grabbed his coat from the peg by the door.

He looked about for his hat, then realized he hadn't worn one that day. Running a hand through his hair, he straightened his coat and stepped outside. He decided to allow himself the luxury of a hackney this afternoon; the weather looked ominous and he didn't want to arrive on the doorstep soaking wet.

His curiosity got the better of his displeasure as he neared the home of Mrs. Amelia Barton, widow of the Dispensary's founder. The neighborhood around Fitzroy Square was indistinguishable from all the other new ones that had sprung up on what had once been the fringes of the city, by Regent's Park. New houses. New money. Solid, respectable money from trade.

In his one interview with her, Mrs. Barton had struck Stephen as a most unusual woman. Unusual, because she took such an active interest in the dispensary founded by her late husband. He didn't know of another medical facility in the city where a woman played such a significant role.

But there was more than that. He'd been surprised by

her willingness to give the medical staff a free hand with their work, even allowing them to bring students to observe. It had been an even greater surprise to find that as chief surgeon, he could refer his own patients. Usually, the privilege of recommending patients was reserved for the financial supporters. But Mrs. Barton was a shrewd woman, and knew that she could afford to extend a few favors to her unpaid medical staff.

And if things progressed as he hoped, he would acquire a few paying patients in the process, through his contacts with the governing board and subscribers. It was a good arrangement all around, and the main reason Stephen had jumped at the chance to be the Dispensary's surgeon. It would mean more work in his already crowded schedule, but the potential benefits made it worth his while. There was a good chance some of the Barton Dispensary supporters had connections to the bigger hospitals, or knew people who did. That was important to him.

By the time the hackney stopped in front of the Barton town house, Stephen had convinced himself that he looked forward to the afternoon.

Yet he ran a nervous hand through his hair as he mounted the steps.

A stiff-faced butler met him at the door, then led him down a wide hall to the rear of the house. The place fairly reeked of money, from the gilded picture frames on the wall to the thick carpet beneath his feet. Stephen smiled. There were bound to be influential people here.

The butler threw open a gilt-trimmed door and Stephen stepped into a large, airy drawing room. He eyed the knot of people gathered at the far end of the room, his apprehension growing when he didn't see Mrs. Barton. Should he walk up and introduce himself to these strangers?

His dilemma was solved when a rotund, jovial man stepped forward and held out his hand. "You must be Ashworth."

Stephen grabbed the proffered hand with relief.

"I'm Hartwell, Jonathan Hartwell. Barton and I were partners—Barton and Hartwell, Victuallers, that's us. 'Cept now it's just me and my lad, but we kept the name."

Stephen smiled politely, wondering what role Hartwell played in the Dispensary. Mrs. Barton hadn't mentioned him. "Are you a partner in the Dispensary as well?"

Hartwell shook his head, grabbing Stephen's arm and leading him across the room. "I don't involve myself much with the Dispensary as a rule—that was Barton's pet project—but I lend a hand when I can to Mrs. B. Can't tell you how glad we were to find a man with your qualifications to help us."

Stephen ducked his head with feigned modesty. "I'm very pleased to be part of the staff."

They reached the circle of well-dressed guests. "Ladies, gentlemen, allow me to introduce Mr. Stephen Ashworth. He's the new surgeon at our little enterprise and comes well recommended."

Stephen smiled with confidence as all eyes turned to him and Hartwell hastily made introductions. The names and faces meant nothing to Stephen, but he tried to remember them. One never knew which person would prove the most beneficial.

He chatted with the guests, enduring an endless string of inane and silly questions. As he'd suspected, no one was much interested in the medical side of things. They wanted to talk about the wonderful work of the Dispensary, or their own *modest* contributions to its success. But at least one person inquired about a consultation "for a friend." Stephen had no objection to that—any paying patient was welcome.

As Stephen turned to respond to a question from a plump matron, he caught a glimpse of a striking young woman standing beside the tea tray. Slim and golden blond, she was a delightful contrast to the middle-aged ladies who surrounded him. He hadn't expected anyone quite so young—and attractive—to be here. Her dark blue frock set off an impossibly small waist and Stephen's eyes widened in appreciation.

Someone's daughter no doubt, recruited to pour tea for her elders. Stephen made a few glib remarks to his audience while he cast admiring glances at the girl. He wouldn't mind attending more Dispensary functions if she was going to be there.

She glanced up and caught his gaze, responding with a dazzling smile that erased any lingering trace of the autumn chill outside. Stephen suddenly wished he'd spent more time on his cravat.

He turned to Hartwell. "I think I'll get myself a cup of tea." Before the man could respond, Stephen started across the room toward the young lady.

Linette Gregory watched with amusement as the tall, dark-eyed surgeon came toward her. She knew who he was without having been introduced; she'd been looking forward to meeting him ever since her aunt first recruited him for the Dispensary. Surprisingly, he looked more like a medical student than one of the rising surgeons in London. He certainly dressed like a student; his coat looked as if it had been slept in, his limp cravat was a disgrace, the knee of his trousers sported a suspicious stain, and his thick, chocolate brown hair needed more than a trim.

But she saw no sign of student innocence and frivolity in his intense gaze. Those dark eyes were well acquainted with the grim side of the trade he practiced.

Hartwell was suddenly at her elbow, making introductions. "Ashworth, this is Linette. Linette Gregory. She takes a very active role at the Dispensary, holding sewing classes for the ladies in the neighborhood."

Ashworth lifted a skeptical brow. "I am surprised, Miss Gregory. The Dispensary is hardly the place for a genteel young lady."

Linette waved away his concern. "I feel it is my duty

to serve where I am needed, regardless of the circumstances."

Handing him a cup of tea, she regarded him with avid curiosity, eager to learn more about him. "I understand you also teach."

"Yes, I do. At the Great Howard Street School. In fact, I was lecturing earlier today on the muscles and bones of . . ." His smile oozed condescension. "I'm certain you're not interested in that."

Ashworth's patronizing look annoyed her. "Oh, but I am," she said pointedly.

"We were studying the shoulder. I was explaining to my students that it's the perfect example of a socket joint."

"Do you enjoy teaching, Mr. Ashworth?"

"Enjoy?" He laughed. "My students are a bunch of undisciplined idiots. I hate to think of the chaos they're causing my poor assistant right now in my absence."

Linette frowned. "One would think that they'd be grateful for the good fortune that allowed them to study the honorable art of medicine."

Ashworth shrugged. "Students are students. A few of them take great interest in their work, but the vast majority do only what needs be done—if that."

"And which type of student were you, Mr. Ashworth?"

An arrogant smile spread over his face. "Why, the former, of course. There is nothing to compare with the study of medicine, Miss Gregory. *Nothing.*"

She bristled at his misplaced enthusiasm. "Oh, I suspect there are those who would disagree with you. Painters, who believe art is man's greatest achievement, for example, or writers, who would argue that words are the sublime reflection of the soul."

His dark eyes narrowed. "Words and pretty pictures don't save lives. Medicine does."

Linette eyed him with growing unease. "Is that why you practice medicine—to serve mankind?"

"I serve *medicine*," he said. "And if, in the process, I can help a patient, I'm grateful."

"What if your patient dies? Does the fault lie within you, or medicine?"

"One learns something from every case—even if the outcome isn't successful. That's why I chose to work at the Dispensary—to take advantage of the opportunities to practice my surgical skills. I anticipate many interesting cases."

Dismay washed over her. This wasn't the kind of surgeon she wanted at the Dispensary. She wanted a man who was caring, compassionate. He sounded aloof, cold. "Is that all patients are to you—interesting cases?"

He gave her a mocking smile. "I forget that the language of medicine doesn't always sound humane to the general populace. Of course I value each and every patient who comes under my care."

The arrogance of his expression belied his words. She didn't think he believed any such thing. Linette opened her mouth to deliver a blistering set-down when she felt a hand on her arm.

"Linette, dear, are you trying to frighten away our surgeon before he has even begun to help us?" Mrs. Barton came up beside Ashworth. "I am sure the others would like to have the opportunity to chat with this nice young man some more. That is the reason for this little gathering, after all."

"Of course," Linette replied, trying to look more chastened than she felt. She was beginning to think it might be a good idea if Mr. Stephen Ashworth didn't work at the Dispensary.

Mrs. Barton held out her hand to Stephen. "I'm sorry to have kept you waiting so long. And I hope my niece didn't overwhelm you with questions. She can sometimes be most persistent."

Ashworth stared at Linette. "Your niece?"

Linette smothered a smile at the dismayed expression on his face. He hadn't known who she was! That would teach him to be so outspoken about his views. She gave him a dampening look.

Mrs. Barton nodded approvingly at her niece. "Linette takes a deep interest in the Dispensary. She has been such a help to me since my dear husband passed on." A smile brightened her face. "She has organized a training program for the ladies who live near the Dispensary. Linette believes very strongly that the poorer classes should learn to help themselves."

Ashworth cast a doubtful look at Linette. "Surely, you must have some concerns about her working in such a neighborhood."

Mrs. Barton laughed softly and took his arm. "My dear Mr. Ashworth, I fear that what I think does not matter very much. Linette does what she pleases."

Aunt led the surgeon back toward the knot of guests and Linette watched him go with a mixture of relief and concern.

The new surgeon had been much as she would have imagined—brash, arrogant, and supercilious in his dealings with the nonmedical world. That was no surprise; she had met enough medical men to know the type.

But for some reason she had expected more of this one. Partly because he'd been so eager to work at the Dispensary. Linette had no illusions; she knew that it was a small facility and not able to attract a major practitioner. Stephen Ashworth's interest had been a pleasant surprise. He was reputed to be a skilled surgeon, a talented teacher, and ambitious and eager to rise in his profession. He would be a great asset to the staff.

Yet after talking with him, she knew that he realized the same thing. He expected them to be grateful to have a man of his talent working there, and that troubled her. She wanted him to be someone who genuinely cared about the patients he treated.

Still, she might be attaching too much importance to a few words uttered at a casual meeting. Over time, she might discover that Mr. Ashworth was really the type of surgeon she wanted working at the Dispensary—caring, considerate, and concerned.

And if he wasn't . . . well, she would take that up with Aunt Barton when and if the problem arose.

The guests left soon after five and Linette breathed a sigh of relief. She'd much rather be working at the Dispensary itself than entertaining its supporters. But these affairs were important to her aunt, and ultimately to the Dispensary, so Linette attended, albeit with reluctance.

"Goodness, that went well, don't you think?" Aunt Barton beamed with pleasure as she surveyed the disarray in the drawing room. "What do you think of our new man?"

"I am sure he is very capable," Linette said coolly.

Her aunt wrinkled her nose. "That almost sounds damning."

"It is difficult to gauge a man's abilities until he has started work," Linette replied. "I shouldn't like to judge him merely on his drawing room manners. It's his performance as a surgeon that counts."

"True, true." Mrs. Barton took a seat on the plush velvet sofa. "Remember, tomorrow night we are dining at the Richardsons'."

Linette looked at her aunt with a suspicious glance. "Will Frederick be there?"

Her aunt shook her head. "Why you are not fonder of that nice young man, I cannot understand. I begin to see why your father grew so irritated with your headstrong nature."

"Now, Aunt, you wouldn't wish me to give encouragement when it isn't due? Frederick is a very nice man, but he isn't for me."

"I begin to wonder if any man is."

Linette laughed. "Perhaps that's so. But it's not a tragedy. Goodness, with a husband and a family I wouldn't have the time to do half of the work I do now."

Aunt Barton waggled a warning finger. "That is part of the problem, my dear. You spend far too much time

worrying about those students of yours. Young girls your
age should be more concerned about enjoying
themselves."

"I find it hard to enjoy things when I know so many
others are suffering."

"You can't save all of humanity, my dear. You do
quite enough as it is. Why, you even make me feel as if
I am not doing enough."

Linette took a seat next to her aunt and slipped an
arm about her waist. "Now, Aunt, you know you do a
great deal. Your decision to keep running the Dispensary is most admirable and you look after the subscribers
very well. That is what you do best."

"While you are not content unless you are actively
helping each and every person who comes across your
path."

Linette smiled. "I can't help it. These poor women
have so little. If I can teach them something that will
improve their position, I am happy."

"But a husband who could finance such a venture
would not be such a terrible thing, would it?"

Linette sighed. "No. Perhaps there is a man out there
who would like to have a wife with such interests. But
that man isn't Frederick Richardson!"

"That still doesn't mean you cannot enjoy his
company."

"I promise you I shall try."

"Good." Mrs. Barton rose and left the room.

Linette turned her gaze to the glowing coals on the
hearth. Aunt meant well, but she did not understand.
Linette wouldn't be content until she found a man who
cared as much as she did about helping others, and
among Aunt's circle of friends that was an unlikely hap-
penstance. Most of them were more concerned with in-
creasing their wealth. Oh, they participated in "good
works," but only on a financial level. How many of the
Dispensary sponsors ever actually came to the facility?
A rare few.

No, she wanted someone who would do more than merely fling money at the problems in society. A man committed to helping people at the basic level—helping them to help themselves. A man who could not walk down the streets of London without seeing the suffering all around him and wanting to alleviate it.

A man willing to devote his life to helping others— and who wanted a wife who could be at his side, helping, encouraging, supporting.

And she wasn't going to find a man like that at the Richardsons' tomorrow night.

For an instant, she remembered the flashing intensity in Stephen Ashworth's dark eyes when he talked about medicine. There was a man with a calling, a crusade.

But from his remarks she could tell that it wasn't people he wanted to help, but medicine. And if their interests conflicted, she knew exactly which side he would choose.

Stephen Ashworth was definitely not a man dedicated to helping people. He was out for personal glory, in the name of medicine. Sick and injured people were only a means to an end.

Compassion had no part in his life.

And it was everything in hers.

Chapter 2

Linette had no time to think about Stephen Ashworth
when she arrived at the Dispensary in the morning. She
gathered her sewing supplies and went to the small room
on the first floor that served as her classroom.

Linette looked forward to meeting with her advanced
group, where they could sit and sew and chat. She preferred these informal sessions to the regular classes. It
gave her the opportunity to learn more about these
women, their concerns, and their needs.

She smiled a greeting at Mary Cummins, who waited
outside the door.

"I finished the shirt last night," the girl announced
proudly.

"I'm sure you did a wonderful job." Linette opened
the door. "Perhaps you can help one of the others today.
I think Amy is a bit behind in her work."

"She'd be finished like me if she spent more time
working in the evening 'stead of a-flirting with Jimmy
Boggs," Mary said with a disparaging toss of her head.

"You might remind her of that," Linette suggested.
She wondered if she should speak to Amy, as well. It
was difficult to know when guidance was necessary.

Over the next five minutes, the other ladies arrived,
carrying baskets with their sewing projects.

Linette had started her sewing classes over a year ago,
when she first moved to London. Appalled by the lack
of domestic skills among the wives and daughters of the
local workers, she'd decided to teach them a few basic

skills. And from simple sewing lessons her project had grown to include reading, and writing, and even some mathematics. The women were eager to learn, and more and more students appeared each session. A teacher had even been hired to handle the formal schooling.

Several of her students had found employment after acquiring their new skills, which spurred Linette to work harder. If people were willing to work, they should have the opportunity. She wanted every one of her students to have that chance.

In other cities, the women would have gone into the factories, but there was little manufacturing work in London. Linette had no illusions; these women could not aspire to be more than seamstresses or maids. But for families teetering on the edge of poverty, any source of money was welcome.

Eventually, she wanted to expand the school to include the younger children. They could have so many more opportunities if they began their education sooner. But within the limitations of the present setting, she could only accomplish so much.

Someday ... Linette envisioned a complete facility, which provided medical services, schooling, training, and even jobs. A place where people could learn how to pull themselves out of poverty by their own efforts.

She thought back to Aunt's words. A husband with money could finance the kind of venture she planned. Perhaps she should take out an advertisement in *The Times:* "Young lady seeks husband who wishes to finance charity school." Would she have any offers?

Linette glanced up as one of the women asked her a question. Setting down her own sewing, Linette went over and guided her student through the difficult part of the armhole seam. The stitches were a bit uneven, and the thread tangled several times, but Linette didn't wish to discourage her. In time, with practice, she would do better.

Linette smiled fondly as she watched Mary busily

helping Amy with her project. Linette vowed to give Mary some extra instruction. Her sewing was so good that she should learn the finer techniques that could get her a job in a fancy shop. The work would be hard, but the pay better than in an ordinary seamstress's. She made a mental note to bring some embroidery patterns with her next time.

The hour passed quickly, and soon the women filed out of the room. Linette was surprised to see Amy lagging behind the others.

"You are making good progress with your shirt." Linette tried to sound encouraging.

"Can I ask you a question, miss?"

"Certainly, Amy."

"It's about a friend of mine . . ." Her voice broke with reluctance. "I was wonderin'—that is, she was wonderin'—when that new doctor's gonna be here."

"I believe Mr. Ashworth will be on duty tomorrow. Is your friend ill? Dr. Hooper is here today."

"No, no, it can wait. It's probably nothin' anyway." Her smile was nervous. "You know how some girls are, always imaginin' something's wrong."

"Well, if she thinks she needs to see the surgeon, it must be serious. Tell her to come in tomorrow."

"I will."

Linette carefully locked the door behind her and made her way to the cramped cubbyhole that served as the Dispensary office. It was hard for her to understand, this reluctance to seek medical treatment. She hoped that as the Dispensary became a respected part of the neighborhood, that view would change.

When she reached the office, Linette sat at the desk and pulled out the large green ledger. There had been some question about the costs for medical supplies last month; Aunt Barton wanted her to take a look at the account books.

The problem, Linette decided, after she'd looked through the long columns of figures, was that everything was so expensive. The amount of money spent on leeches was atrocious! She didn't like to tell the doctors and surgeons how to conduct their business, but surely they could make do with a little less. Minor economies could make a big difference over time; had not her mother taught her that? She made a note to speak with the board.

Taking up her bonnet, she tied it in a bow beneath her chin and fastened her cloak before leaving the building. She would have time for a quick cup of tea at her aunt's before they attended the meeting of the bazaar committee. Linette would rather have remained at the Dispensary, but Aunt Barton insisted that her niece spent too much time there as it was. And in her never-ending campaign to make Linette a respectable marriage, Aunt considered committee activities far more important than actually working with the recipients of that charity.

Linette sighed. Someday, she hoped to make Aunt Barton understand.

With a loud oath, Stephen leapt across the dissecting room. "MacNeil! You are not carving the Sunday roast! That is a human arm you are dissecting, not a piece of meat. If you want to be a butcher, you should be down at Smithfield. Delicacy and light-handedness is the key." Grabbing the scalpel from the student's hand, Stephen nudged him aside.

"You cut like this." He made a neat incision in the pallid flesh. "Go with the line of the muscle, not against it. How are you going to recognize any part of this if you hack it to pieces?"

He handed the scalpel back. "Now you try it."

Shaking with tension, the student made a wobbly cut next to Stephen's.

"Good." Stephen stepped aside, arms crossed over his chest. "Now make your crossways cut, and peel back the skin." He watched intently while the rattled student did as directed.

"That's an improvement." Stephen turned away and walked over to the next table, where Mathers supervised another group of students.

"A little rough on MacNeil, weren't you?" the assistant inquired.

Stephen snorted. "Better I'm a little rough on him now than having him kill a patient later through cow-handed clumsiness." He ran a hand through his hair. "God, why am I always saddled with one of these every term? Why do they always pick this school? Why can't they enroll at Guys?"

With a loud laugh, Mathers cuffed Stephen on the shoulder. "Because they all want to learn at the feet of the brilliant Mr. Ashworth."

"With such fulsome compliments, you must want another evening off, Mr. Mathers."

Mathers grinned. "Next Friday, if you please. I'll take Sunday night in return."

"Good. That will give me time to prepare for next week's work." Stephen shook his head. "This Dispensary position is going to take more time than I thought."

"Too many patients?"

"Too many extra duties. No one mentioned that I'm expected to attend all the charity functions. That tea yesterday was only the beginning."

Mathers fingered his stained coat. "Show up in your work coat one or two times and they'll gladly ask you to stay away."

Stephen grinned at the idea. "Believe me, I've thought about it. Nothing like a dose of reality to send them dashing back into their safe, comfortable world."

With a nod, Stephen allowed Mathers to go back to his work and he prowled about the dissection room, peering over the student's shoulders as he evaluated their work.

Someday, he thought, he would have his own private

students, and he would only take in those pupils he wished to teach. No bumbling idiots who didn't know a leg from an arm, no ham-handed butchers who hacked and sawed their way through their work.

And no ghoulishly minded souls who thought it a great joke to prop up a cadaver in their teacher's chair.

Although that incident had *almost* been amusing.

No, he would only take on dedicated students who wanted to learn medicine. They were the men the field needed; farsighted men who weren't afraid to observe, to learn, to try new things. Unlike the hidebound rulers of the Royal College of Surgeons, who wouldn't recognize a new surgical technique if it hit them on the nose. And unlike those who thought hospital appointments should be doled out under the ancient practices of nepotism and favoritism, rather than on skill and talent.

It galled him to have to rely on connections and support to gain a position he was more than qualified for. And it wasn't merely the prestige he wanted, but the acknowledgement that he was successful at his calling. The opportunity for his opinions to be heard and respected. To be in the forefront of the latest surgical techniques and developments.

Instead, he was forced to deal with clumsy idiots like MacNeil, who would probably kill as many patients as he saved. And Stephen agreed to do it, because MacNeil paid him sixty guineas a term. Until Stephen had a reliable source of income, he needed every paying student he could get. Otherwise, there was no money for the supplies and bodies and materials he needed to carry on his own studies.

But someday . . .

A loud shriek, followed by raucous laughter, caught his attention. He turned around—and swore. Bryant stood on top of a dissecting table waving a flaccid penis at his fellow students.

"Get down from there this instant," Stephen roared.

Bryant hastily jumped to the floor as Stephen stalked

over to him. "Well, Mr. Bryant, you must have a particular fondness for this part of the human anatomy. Perhaps then, you won't mind if I assigned you the task of preparing the drawings for the lecture on Monday?"

"Yes, sir," Bryant stammered. "I mean no, sir."

"Good. I want a transverse view, a side view, and a longitudinal presentation."

"Yes, sir."

Stephen turned on his heel and left the room.

Outside, he leaned against the wall, smothering a grin. There was always one joker every term. What was the name of the fellow who'd pranced around with a breast on his head last year? Simmons?

Students would always be students. But couldn't he be spared their idiocy just once?

In the office, Stephen sat in his chair, propping his feet up on the desk. There was an interesting case at the Dispensary—a kidney stone in an awkward presentation—and he wanted to refresh himself on the procedure before he operated tomorrow.

Mathers quietly slipped in and grabbed his coat from the wall, nodding a silent farewell. Stephen continued reading, pausing now and again to thumb through the stack of books on his desk until he found the relevant passage.

It was dark outside when he finally stood up and stretched. He felt confident now that he could perform the operation with the minimum of fuss. Tomorrow, he'd show those Dispensary people just what kind of surgeon they'd hired themselves.

Stephen gratefully accepted the mug of ale handed to him by the Dispensary porter in the small room behind the operating chamber. It had been a successful surgery, but that didn't make the process any simpler. While he usually displayed icy calm before an operation, Stephen felt drained and exhausted afterward. The ale restored him.

At least the remainder of the day would be easy, barring any accident cases. There were the usual minor ailments to examine and treat, but no more complicated cases faced him. Stephen was glad. One operation like that a day was enough.

It was a rare thing here at the Dispensary; usually, the more serious cases went to the hospitals. But he'd argued loud and forcefully for the privilege to perform the necessary surgeries here. They had the room to handle a few in-house surgical patients.

Resting his feet on the table, Stephen took another sip of ale, mentally reviewing the entire operation, but he couldn't find any flaws in his procedure. A nice piece of work.

"Do you always drink while on duty?"

Stephen froze at the words. Glancing over his shoulder, he saw the look of scathing irritation on the face of Mrs. Barton's niece.

"Only when the operation has been a success," he said curtly.

Linette Gregory glared at him, hands fisted on her hips. "I hardly think it inspires confidence in the patients if the doctor has ale on his breath."

Slowly, Stephen lowered his feet to the floor and twisted around to face her. She was dressed in plain, serviceable gray today, and although it didn't dampen the golden glow of her hair, her delicate features were not enhanced by the scowl she wore. He felt a flicker of annoyance at her interference.

"If the board of governors sees fit to serve ale to the patients, I don't think there will be objections to serving it to the medical staff." He lifted his mug in mock salute. "And I daresay there will be more than one patient who'll feel better knowing the surgeon enjoys a little ale now and then."

She gave him a withering glance. "I understand you performed a complicated operation this morning. Did it go well?"

"The man's still alive, if that's what you mean. Now, if you don't mind Miss—ah—Gregory, I'd like to have a few moments of peace before I see today's new patients."

She pulled a white vellum note from her pocket. "I fear Aunt Barton forgot to mention this to you when you were at the house. We're having our first fund-raising musicale of the fall on Tuesday next and she wants you to attend."

"Can't," said Stephen, with deep relief. He didn't relish being trotted out again for another group of supporters. "I'm presenting a paper to the Chiurgical Society."

Her expression turned smug. "Oh, Aunt's already taken care of that. You've been moved to next month."

Stephen leaped out of his chair. "What? She can't do that."

Linette smiled. "Aunt considers Dispensary business to come first, before anything else. She's a close friend of the president of the society, you know."

Stephen leaned back against the desk. No, he didn't know. And that meant it wouldn't do any good to protest; Miss Gregory was merely presenting him with a fait accompli.

With marked reluctance, he took the invitation from her. "Where is this grand event to be?"

"At the Dorchester Rooms. Evening dress, if you please." She eyed his rumpled coat. "You do have evening clothes, don't you, Mr. Ashworth?"

"Is supper going to be served?" That would save him the cost of a meal, at least.

"This is a fund-raising venture, Mr. Ashworth. Refreshments cost money that could be better used to purchase supplies for the Dispensary." She eyed him with curiosity. "Do you use leeches often?"

"Leeches?" It was the last thing he'd expected her to ask. He gave her a puzzled look. "Why, do you want one?"

A faint moue of distaste crossed her face. "I've been

examining the Dispensary accounts, Mr. Ashworth. An atrocious amount of money is spent on leeches."

Stephen shrugged at her pronouncement. "Take it up with the physicians. They overprescribe leeches, along with everything else."

She smiled. "I've heard that the surgeons don't always think highly of physicians, and vice versa."

Stephen laughed heartily. "It's hard to have much respect for a profession that's filled with incompetent providers and antiquated theories."

"And what is it that they say? That the motto of the Royal College of Surgeons is 'When in doubt, cut it out.'"

"It's better than poisoning the patient, which is what most of the physicians do." He stepped away from the desk. "I would love to continue this conversation, Miss Gregory, but I do have patients to see."

She smiled blandly. "I look forward to seeing you at the musicale on Tuesday."

"I will be delighted," Stephen drawled sarcastically, brushing past her as he headed for the examination room.

A musicale. Just what he needed. His paper on the gluteal muscles, on which he'd been working for the last month and a half, was to be postponed because he had to attend a blasted musicale. He was a surgeon, for God's sake, not a zoo specimen. Why would anyone think that his presence at a stupid musical evening would make a bit of difference in the donations to the Dispensary? What did she expect him to do, stand up and give a surgical lecture between the performances?

With his luck, he thought glumly, she probably did.

If he'd known what demands would be made on him, he might have turned down the position. The contacts he gained here were simply not worth this much trouble.

Then he remembered who'd agreed to change the presentation date on his paper. The Dispensary supporters might not be significant people, but they knew ones who were. No matter how little he liked the situation, he didn't dare complain.

No, she had him there.

Striving to suppress his irritation, Stephen marched off to the examination room. He treated the new surgical patients, wrote out his orders, and was off to check on his recovering patient before he left for the night. He was going to need every spare minute he could squeeze out of his schedule to get his own work done. And now there was that blasted musicale. . . .

"Damn."

"Excuse me?" Jenkins, the porter, glanced at him, not a little alarmed.

"I'm a fool, Jenkins, a real fool." Stephen clapped the man on the shoulder. "Next time you're made an offer that looks too good to be true, be wary, for it probably is."

"Wimmen troubles?" Jenkins asked hopefully.

Stephen laughed. "You could say that. One woman in particular."

But when he thought of a nemesis, it wasn't Amelia Barton who came to mind, but her niece. She might appear slim and delicate, but it was a deceiving picture. That blond-haired miss had the heart of a tyrant. And he wasn't merely attacking the bearer of bad tidings. There'd been a note of glee in Linette Gregory's voice when she'd told him how neatly her aunt had rearranged his schedule. She enjoyed seeing him at the beck and call of Mrs. Barton.

There must be something he could do to let Miss Gregory know how much he appreciated her sensitive feelings. Some way he could show her that he realized how much she enjoyed telling him the unpleasant news.

He ran a hand through his hair. He'd find some way to get back at her for this. Plotting her comeuppance would be the one thing to make that musicale endurable.

Chapter 3

"I do have great hopes for Mary," Linette told her aunt that evening as they shared tea in the parlor before dinner. "She has a real talent for sewing. I thought I would take in some special projects for her to work on, to teach her some fine work."

"Your little school is becoming quite a success, isn't it?" Her aunt smiled fondly. "I own I had my doubts when you first proposed the idea, but I cannot see anything but good coming of it now."

"There have been a few stumbles along the way. Not all the women are willing to work hard. But those who do make it all worthwhile."

"Mrs. Miller was asking me about your project just yesterday. There was some talk among the ladies of trying to establish something similar in their parish."

"I think it would be a worthy project for every parish," Linette said, with emphasis. "There are so many women who could benefit. I only wish we could reach more people at the Dispensary."

"Expansion will come with time. Goodness, when dear George started up the Dispensary, it was only open two half days a week. Now look! We have a doctor there every day, and the surgeon comes in three times a week."

"And someday, it will be the Barton Hospital." Linette grinned at her aunt's doubtful expression. "Oh, I know that I'm impatient. But there are so many people who need our help."

"We cannot help everyone, and we spread ourselves too thinly if we try. With a small group, you can know everyone you work with, and can be sure that their efforts are serious. All the work we do is of no good if the people do not desire to help themselves."

"I know I can't force anyone to better their situation; they have to want to do it." Linette became thoughtful. "I should be pleased that I do have such a wonderful group. Although I am beginning to wonder about Amy."

"Oh?"

"She was such an industrious girl last spring, but now she does not seem interested in her work. Mary says she is flirting with the boys far too much."

"She better watch herself, lest it lead to unfortunate consequences," Aunt said with a warning shake of her head.

"Oh, I cannot believe it will come to anything." Linette laughed off her concern. "Amy is a levelheaded girl after all, and she does want to work. If I think it necessary, I shall have a word with her."

Aunt Barton patted her hand. "It is commendable that you have such a care for your students."

Linette smiled ruefully. "It comes from looking after everyone at home. I don't feel like I'm being useful unless I am helping someone."

Aunt directed her a pointed look. "That's all well and good for a young unmarried girl like yourself. But remember, once you marry and have a family of your own, they will take a good deal of your time. Your first obligation is to your husband, and children."

"But if I never marry, I won't have to worry about that, will I?"

A look of dismay crossed Aunt's face. "Do not say such a thing! Even if you do not like Frederick Richardson, there are other nice men who would love to have a wife as sweet and caring as you."

"Yes, but would they also agree that the work I do at

the Dispensary is important, and encourage me to continue it?" Linette shook her head. "I think not."

"There are other ways you can help the less fortunate."

"Heading committees and hosting luncheons is not the type of thing I wish to do." She lay a hand on her aunt's arm. "I know you enjoy those things—and you are so good at it. But I am not. There are plenty of ladies who are willing to do that sort of thing, but not nearly enough who want to work directly with people."

"I hope you will not suggest that to Lady Howell at the musicale tomorrow night."

"Aunt!" Then Linette saw the teasing look in her eyes. "You know that I will treat Lady Howell with the utmost deference."

"She is an important sponsor. It is a coup for our group to have drawn her in."

"I wonder who makes her dresses," Linette mused. "Do you think she might be persuaded—?"

"Linette!"

She smiled impishly. "I only thought to ask the name of her modiste. I shall wait until I am better acquainted before I ask her to recommend someone for a position. Besides, Mary still has much to learn before she could work at an establishment that caters to the likes of Lady Howell."

"Remember that tomorrow night," Aunt Barton said warningly.

A guilty flush crept to Linette's cheeks. "I forgot to tell you. I did speak to Ashworth and he'll be there."

"I hope he did not mind the change to his schedule, but it will be most helpful if he is there."

Linette suppressed a smile. "Oh, he didn't mind in the least."

"Wasn't he performing an operation today? Did it go well?"

"He seemed to think so." Linette wrinkled her nose.

"But then, I doubt any patient would have the audacity to die on Mr. Ashworth. He'd be far too angry."

"Why do you not like the man? He is an excellent surgeon."

"That does not mean he is an excellent human being. He was actually having a tankard of ale after the surgery!" Linette twined her fingers together. "I can't help but think he is more interested in the art of medicine than the welfare of his patients."

"Medical men must learn to control their compassion—their work has so many unpleasant aspects. It does not mean he is heartless."

Linette considered her aunt's words. Did Stephen Ashworth casually down a tankard of ale after a bloody surgery to hide his dismay at what he had to do—or simply because he had no feelings at all?

"Perhaps I shall discuss that with him tomorrow night," she said slowly. "He may set my mind at rest."

Aunt Barton nodded. "A good idea. It is important that you maintain good relationships with the staff at the Dispensary. I have no illusions as to why that young man is helping us, but we must do our best to make sure he is comfortable during the time he is with us."

"You don't think he will stay long?"

"A man like that? Goodness, no. He will jump at any new opportunity to further his career. He is quite ambitious." She tapped her temple. "But smart. He knows the value of the useful connections he can make even in such a small facility as ours. Our only hope is that no hospital surgeon in London dies soon, 'else he will be a prime candidate for the position."

"I should think he would have some loyalty to the Dispensary."

"We can't expect him to forget his own career merely to keep us happy." Aunt smiled wistfully. "I am only glad he is helping us now."

Linette bit back an acid remark. Managing the Dispensary was her aunt's concern, after all, and if she was

aware of the surgeon's motives, it wasn't Linette's place
to turn her against the man. But she vowed that Mr.
Ashworth was not going to make callous use of any Dispensary patients to further his single-minded climb to
the top.

The man was not long for this life.

Stephen frowned as he stepped back from the bedside.
He wasn't even supposed to be at the Dispensary today,
but he'd come by to pick up some papers and the matron
grabbed him. Now he was faced with this awkward situation. Should he send for the physician—or deal with the
situation himself? Although consumption wasn't a surgical matter, he'd seen enough of the disease to know this
patient was in the final stages.

He drew the matron aside.

"I doubt he'll last the night," Stephen said, shaking
his head. "I'll increase the dosage of laudanum—it can't
cause him any harm now."

The matron's face darkened. "Dr. Hooper ain't goin'
to like it."

"By the time Dr. Hooper comes back tomorrow he
isn't going to have a patient to worry about," Stephen
snapped. "The least I can do is make the poor man
comfortable."

The matron nodded reluctantly. "But if the doctor
says anything . . ."

"Send him to me," Stephen said, and headed for the
apothecary's room to get the medicine.

That was *one* advantage to working at a small dispensary. Even though he held an apothecary's license, he'd
never be able to concoct his own medications in a large
hospital. Of course, in a large hospital, he wouldn't dare
go near a physician's patient, either. There, the line between physic and surgery was strictly drawn—and jeal-
ously guarded. At the Dispensary, the lines were often
blurred.

Stephen made up the medicine, gave it to the ward

matron, and hastened toward the front door before he was called back for something else. They needed someone here in the evenings to deal with these emergencies. Maybe he could find a few students willing to sit in the wards on alternating nights. They knew enough to recognize a dying man when they saw one.

Stephen halted suddenly at the door and spun around. This was too good of an opportunity to miss. He didn't know if Dr. Hooper wanted the body, but Stephen wanted to put in his name now, just in case. Having treated the patient this once, Stephen could rightfully make a claim to the corpse.

The porter wasn't in, but Stephen left a note, explaining he would send a student over in the morning to check on the patient's condition. He fully expected the man to be dead, and if all went well, Stephen could have the corpse and save the school six guineas.

Then, at last, he left the Dispensary and walked briskly toward his rooms. It was early; he could take time for a decent meal and still get some work done tonight.

Since he wasn't going to get any work done tomorrow night with that blasted musicale.

"Mr. Ashworth?"

Stephen swiveled in his office chair, impatient at the interruption. It had been a busy morning, lecturing and demonstrating. He'd just sat down to review his notes for tomorrow's lecture and glared angrily at the intruder. Smith. The student he'd sent to the Dispensary to check on that consumptive patient. "Well?"

Smith smiled faintly. "As you predicted, the man died during the night."

Stephen nodded. "They have that certain look when the end is near. Did you bring the body back with you?"

A panic-stricken look passed over Smith's face and he swallowed nervously. "They said you can't have it."

Stephen groaned. "Damn. That blasted physician beat me to it."

Smith studied his toes. "Not exactly."

"Well, what's the problem? The poor fellow didn't have any family. He's headed for the paupers' pit."

Smith continued to stare at the floor. "No one is allowed to have the bodies for dissection."

Stephen wondered if he'd heard correctly. "What did you say?"

"Apparently it's a policy at the Dispensary. If there aren't any relatives, they see to a burial."

Stephen threw down his pen and stood up. "I don't believe this. You mean they plan to bury a perfectly useful body?"

"That's what the porter told me. Says Miss Gregory wants it that way."

"Miss Gregory." Stephen clapped a hand to his forehead. "God, I knew that woman was going to be trouble. Someday, we'll have medical facilities run by doctors instead of lay persons, and that day can't come too soon. " 'No dissection' indeed!"

He turned his angry gaze on Smith. "And why, for God's sake, didn't you have the sense to ignore those fools and take the body anyway?"

Gulping nervously, Smith stared at him blankly. "I wasn't thinking, sir."

Stephen paced the tiny room. "That's right, you weren't thinking. You followed the rules like a well-trained sheep." He waved an angry hand. "How do you ever expect to be a decent surgeon, Mr. Smith, if you aren't willing to think independently? Or do you only intend to follow the dictates of those fools at the Royal College?"

"No, sir."

"A perfectly good body in my grasp, and now I can't have it. Do you know what this means?" He pointed an angry finger at Smith. "If those blasted resurrectionists don't come up with enough bodies next week, we can't study the thoracic cavity."

"Yes, sir."

Stephen stared unseeing at Smith, his brain whirling as he made new plans. "Tell Mr. Mathers—he was planning a special demonstration for tomorrow. Tell him he'll have to use the models again."

Smith hastily slipped out of the office.

Stephen let out a long, discouraged sigh. He shouldn't have taken his anger out on the student. In his place, Stephen doubted he would have had the nerve to take the body, either. But it didn't hurt to keep the students wary of his temper. It made them work all the harder.

And he knew if he ever sent a student for another body, they wouldn't come back empty-handed, no matter what they had to do to get it.

Stephen pulled out his watch. Half past five. There wasn't time to confront Miss Gregory before the musicale, but, by God, he'd corner her there. Then he would tell her precisely what he thought of a medical facility that put up such barriers to research. All those promises of freedom for the medical staff meant nothing, after all.

He'd brought his evening clothes to the school, so he wouldn't have to go home. After a quick dinner at the tavern, he'd come back here to dress. And all the while he could think of exactly what he wanted to say to the interfering and annoying Miss Gregory.

His mood hadn't improved by the time he reached the Dorchester Rooms. The man at the door asked for his ticket, and it took Stephen several long minutes to explain that he wasn't a subscriber, but a member of the Dispensary staff. For a moment, Stephen feared he might have to suffer the humiliating experience of asking Miss Gregory to vouch for him, but the recalcitrant old man finally allowed him to enter.

Stephen followed the other guests into the music room, where a semicircle of chairs faced a piano and several music stands. Stephen pushed his way through

the throng, looking for Miss Gregory. As soon as he
talked to her, he was leaving. He wasn't going to stay
here to please anyone.

But before he found her, Mrs. Barton spotted him and
motioned for Stephen to join her. With an inward groan,
he did as he was bid.

"I am so glad you are here with us tonight, Mr. Ashworth." She turned to the thin, turbaned lady beside her.
"Lady Howell, may I present Mr. Ashworth, our new
surgeon. He is reckoned to be a very promising practitioner of that art."

Stephen bowed. "Lady Howell."

"It was good of you to postpone your talk to the society so that you could come tonight," Mrs. Barton said.
"Dr. Wilkins was able to join us also."

Stephen wondered what threat they'd used to drag
Wilkins here. "It's a pleasure to attend." He craned his
neck, scanning the room for a sign of Miss Gregory.

"Are you fond of music, Mr. Ashworth?" Lady Howell asked.

"Alas, it's a rare treat for me. I fear my schedule
doesn't allow for much leisure time." He smiled politely,
although he really wanted to tell the both of them that
he despised music and despised the way he'd been
forced to attend tonight.

"Then I am doubly glad you are here," Mrs. Barton
said. "You will enjoy yourself, I'm sure."

Stephen shifted impatiently. There was still no sign of
Linette Gregory and those blasted musicians were going
to start at any moment. He smiled blandly at Mrs. Barton. "Is your niece joining us tonight?"

Mrs. Barton waved her hand vaguely. "She's here
somewhere. Probably attending to a last-minute detail.
Honestly, I do not know what I would do without the
girl. She is such a help."

Stephen thought of numerous things he could accomplish without Miss Gregory's annoying interference, but
he held his tongue.

The sound of a violin being tuned drew their attention to the front of the room, where the musicians had begun their preparations. Before he could flee, Mrs. Barton took Stephen's arm and drew him to the seats.

So much for a chance to talk to Miss Gregory before the performance, he thought glumly. Now he'd have to stay at least until the intermission. But he wouldn't go home tonight without confronting her, even if he had to remain for the whole blasted evening.

From the corner of his eye, he caught a flash of blue, heard the rustle of silk as she slipped into the vacant seat next to him. Before he could utter a curt admonition, the musicians took up their instruments and he didn't dare speak.

Stephen settled back in his chair and schooled his features into what he hoped was an appreciative expression. The musicians could have been playing out of tune and in the wrong key for all he could tell. For him, music was a painful reminder of one more way he hadn't measured up to his father's exacting standards.

Musical talent was expected of an Ashworth; without any, Stephen was the outcast in the family. No manner of lessons, practice, icy displeasure, or physical punishment had ever changed that. It was one more way his parents considered him unworthy.

Like taking up the study of medicine.

In the overheated room, the cloying scents of the ladies' intermingled perfumes gave him a headache. It didn't help that he was angry with the high-handedness that had brought him here, and wanted to wring the neck of the woman sitting next to him.

When the interval came, Stephen quickly turned to Miss Gregory. "Come with me into the hall," he said curtly. "I need to talk with you."

"Do bring me a glass of ratafia when you return, dear," Mrs. Barton said with a sly smile.

Stephen grabbed Miss Gregory's elbow and steered her into the hall.

"Where are we going?" she asked in confusion, when he sped her past the refreshment tables.

"What I have to say isn't meant for the ears of others."

He drew her down the corridor, looking in every doorway until he found a small, empty antechamber. He pulled her into the tiny room and closed the door behind them before he turned to confront her.

"Are you aware that Mr. Tompkins died this morning?"

She nodded. "I understand you looked in on him last night and made him more comfortable. That was good of you."

"He's slated to be buried tomorrow."

She smiled. "We give all our patients a decent burial, if the families cannot afford it."

"Mr. Tompkins doesn't have a family. Or, as near as I can tell, a friend in the world." Stephen glared at her. "Why then, do you insist on tossing his body away when it could be put to greater use?"

Her face paled and she stared at him, her eyes narrowing with suspicion. "You want his body! Is that why you checked on him last night—to see how close to death he was?"

Stephen ran a hand through his hair. "I treated him as a patient. But now that he's gone, yes, I would like to have the body. I have fifty medical students who are studying human anatomy and they need practical experience."

Linette crossed her arms and gave him a challenging look. "You can't have any Dispensary patients for that purpose. I simply will not allow it. Dissection is a horrible process, fit only for animals, and criminals."

He grabbed her wrist. "And if it weren't for dissection, where do you think we'd stand? Do you think I could have performed that operation yesterday if I hadn't practiced on human tissue? How would I have known what to do if the organs and veins and nerves hadn't been mapped out by anatomists?"

She jerked her hand free. "But that has already been done."

"Do you think we've learned all there is to know about the human body?" Stephen gave a short laugh. "For everything we do know, there are probably ten more things we don't. And without bodies to study, we will never know."

"Mr. Tompkins suffered greatly. He deserves to rest in peace."

"Good God, the man is dead! He doesn't care what happens to his body." He clenched his fists at his side. "You're the one with the objections. You're no relative; you can't claim to speak for him."

"Someone has to speak for those who can't defend themselves," she said heatedly. "The poor and the destitute are as entitled to a proper burial and the same undisturbed slumber as the wealthiest man in the country."

"Do you think it is only the poor who end up in dissecting rooms?" Stephen's harsh laughed echoed in the small room. "Astley Cooper once boasted that he could have any corpse he wanted, for a price, and he is right."

She took a step back. "That is horrible."

"It is reality, Miss Gregory, and your objections won't stop the practice." He moved closer and glared down at her. "Meanwhile, your refusal to let me have the body is costing me money."

She looked at him with a puzzled expression.

"You know that we have to pay for every cadaver we use. Mr. Tompkins would have been a welcome gift."

Color rose to her cheeks. "That is what you think this is all about—money? We are discussing a human *life*."

"No," he said. "We are talking about a *dead* body. A dead body that is worth at least six guineas on the open market."

Her gray eyes widened. "Six guineas?"

"The Dispensary could make more money selling bodies than they could from a month of fancy musical evenings," he said with a cynical smile.

"How could you even suggest such a thing?" She shuddered. "The whole idea is immoral."

He shrugged. "It's your choice, of course. But I won't hesitate to bring up the issue before the board of governors. It's in the Dispensary's financial interests to make use of all available resources."

She gave an arrogant toss of her head. "You forget, Mr. Ashworth, that it is my aunt who has the final voice in the running of the Dispensary. And I assure you, she will never agree to such a thing. She shares my views on the sanctity of the human body."

Stephen looked at her coldly. "And the next time a patient dies because the surgeon didn't know enough to save his life, you can console yourself with the thought that the *sanctity* of Mr. Tompkins' body is intact. What is life, after all, compared to that?"

"You medical men are all alike," she said, her voice rising. "You think you are gods, and anyone who doesn't agree with you is hindering the march of scientific progress. Yet some things are more important than pure science, Mr. Ashworth."

"I've yet to find anything that was."

"Then I feel sorry for you." She turned toward the door. "I think we should go back to the music room, Mr. Ashworth. I am sure the second half of the program will be starting soon."

Stephen brushed past her and pushed open the door. "I've lost interest in listening to music this evening, Miss Gregory. Give my regrets to your aunt."

With a sense of satisfaction, he noted the look of stunned surprise on her face before he turned and strode toward the exit. She hadn't expected him to walk out. Cramming his hat on his head, he stalked down the front steps.

Oh, he'd met many like her before. Those who were glad to accept the medical benefits of a surgeon's knowledge, but who disdained the source of that knowledge. You couldn't have one without the other, but there were still people who didn't understand that. They wanted everything in their world to be neat and tidy. These were the same people who didn't see the poverty of the people around them, who deplored the acts of criminals while they cared little for the environment that bred them. They lived in a dreamworld, sheltered in their little cocoons, oblivious to what went on around them.

They expected men like him to deal with these unsavory aspects of life, but then deliberately put obstacles in their way, and didn't give them credit when they were overcome.

They were fools, all of them.

But he would show them. Someday, the name Ashworth would be as well known as Cooper or Bell. And then he wouldn't have to put up with people like Linette Gregory.

And in the meantime, he would do his very best to see that their paths didn't cross.

Of course, it would be amusing to send her a rendering of the school's monthly accounts, showing her exactly what he had to spend for dissection subjects. Just to remind her that there was a practical use for the human body after the death of its owner, and that she was throwing away six guineas every time she insisted on a burial. It probably wouldn't do anything to change her mind. But it would give him a smug sense of satisfaction to know that she knew the facts.

The thought cheered him so much that he stopped at the Three Swans and treated himself to supper before he returned to his rooms.

Chapter 4

Linette stood in the hallway, staring after Ashworth's retreating form.

She had never met such an outrageous man! Pretending solicitude yesterday for poor Mr. Tompkins when he only wanted the body for his horrible anatomy school.

Linette didn't think she would ever understand surgeons. Ostensibly, they practiced medicine to save mankind, but they were more concerned with the heartless pursuit of medical knowledge. They didn't care if the patient lived or died, only what they learned in the process.

And in her eyes, Ashworth was one of the worst offenders. Behind that handsome facade stood a man with a heart of stone. He only thought about the success of his school, and whether his students had enough bodies to perform their violations on. He would never care that this patient's brother was out of work, or that his sister couldn't read, or that the entire family didn't have enough to eat.

No, when he looked at a patient all he saw was a collection of blood, bones, and tissue. Together, they formed a living human being, but to a surgeon they were only separate parts to be studied, dissected, analyzed, and discarded.

He was as lacking in humanity as any cold-blooded killer.

And this man was Aunt's choice for surgeon at the

Dispensary? An institution that had been founded on the principle of helping people lead a better life?

Stephen Ashworth didn't give a fig for what happened to these people after he treated them. Unless, of course, they died. Then he wanted their corpse.

Six guineas. The price of a human body.

Shuddering, Linette hugged herself against the sudden chill that swept over her.

Strains of music drifted into the hall and she realized the concert had resumed. Aunt would wonder where she was, but Linette didn't care. She wasn't ready to go back into that room yet.

Entering the deserted refreshment room, she poured a cup of punch. Sipping it slowly as she walked about the room, Linette wondered what she would do about Ashworth.

Was there any hope for a man like him? Could he be made to see that it was life he should glorify, not death? It was a challenge she couldn't ignore.

If she could convince a man like Ashworth, she could convince anyone.

Hearing muffled sounds of applause, Linette set down her cup and waited outside the music room. She could slip in now, between pieces. Trying to remain unobtrusive, she opened the door and walked to her seat, certain the entire room was staring at her.

"Where have you been?" Aunt Barton whispered loudly when Linette slid into her seat.

"Having a discussion with your new surgeon," she replied tartly.

Shaking her head, Aunt looked pained. "Did you chase the poor man away already?"

"Hush!" a voice behind them commanded.

Mrs. Barton patted Linette's hand. "We will discuss this later."

Linette barely listened to the rest of the music. Aunt had every right to be angry with her; she had driven Ashworth away. But when Linette explained the circumstances, she knew her aunt would be sympathetic. Perhaps she would have some suggestion on how Linette could change Ashworth's views.

But Linette still didn't have a plan when she went to the Dispensary in the morning. She'd have to wait until class was over before she could think more about Ashworth. Today, she'd brought the latest edition of *The Ladies Magazine* for Mary and planned to work with her on the complicated embroidery patterns.

As soon as she entered the building, the rector of the parish came toward Linette, a frown on his face.

"Really, Miss Gregory, I am terribly disappointed by this new turn of events." The rector clutched his prayer book. "I thought you and I were of the same mind regarding the fate of the unfortunate patients who die without friends."

Linette looked at him in total confusion. "What do you mean?"

"I am speaking of that detestable practice of the medical profession—dissection of human subjects."

"You know that the Dispensary doesn't allow that."

"So you say. But I came here this morning, prepared to speak the last words over—" he consulted the paper in his hand—"Mr. Josea Tompkins, only to discover that the body had been taken away."

"What?" Linette ran down the hall toward the dead room. Flinging open the door, she saw the bare table, where poor Mr. Tompkins should have lain while awaiting his final resting place.

It didn't take much imagination to guess where he was now. Linette shook with fury.

"How dare he! He knew perfectly well that it wasn't allowed and he did it anyway! This time he has gone too far."

The rector peered over her shoulder at the empty table. "You did not permit this defilement?"

"Permit it?" Linette whirled to face the rector. "I specifically forbade it. I suspect that our new surgeon is trying to show me that he doesn't care what I say."

The rector bowed his head. "The poor man. I can only hope that someday the eyes of these unfortunate medical men are opened to the wrong that they do."

"It will be sooner than someday," Linette muttered. "Ashworth is going to be very, very sorry that he did this."

His eyes widened. "You think that the new surgeon . . . ?"

"That's precisely what I think."

"Perhaps if I spoke to him . . . "

Linette shook her head emphatically. "No, I want to. And I will get poor Mr. Tompkins back. You will still be able to hold your funeral."

The rector took her hand. "Miss Gregory, please, let me take charge of this matter. Such a mission will cause you too much distress."

Linette wasn't about to let anyone else go. She wanted to see the look on Ashworth's face when she confronted him with his perfidy. "It won't be as distressing as losing Mr. Tompkins. You have your own duties to attend to. I'll deal with Mr. Ashworth."

He eyed her doubtfully. "Do you think you will be safe?"

"Safe?" She laughed. "He won't attack me with a scalpel; he knows he's in the wrong. I only intend to take back what he stole."

"If you are certain . . ."

She clasped the rector's hand. "I'll take Nate Hawkins with me. He'll provide ample protection."

"Let me know when you wish to hold the funeral, then." With a bow, the rector went off to his duties.

Linette ran back to the office and retrieved her cloak. It shouldn't take her long to find Nate. And then Mr. Stephen Ashworth was going to discover that it didn't pay to cross her.

Nate and Jimmy Boggs were in the basement, sitting

atop some wooden crates and looking as if they didn't have a care in the world. They jumped to their feet with guilty looks when Linette found them.

"We was just takin' a break," Nate said.

The two men should have been attending to their work around the Dispensary, but Linette chose to ignore their dereliction of duty. "I need you to accompany me on an errand," she said.

Jim grinned widely.

"Where we be goin'?" Nate asked as he trailed behind her up the stairs.

"To the Howard Street Medical School."

"Ain't that where the new surgeon comes from? Why we be goin' there?"

Linette halted and turned around. "Because I want to see if our new surgeon took a body from the dead room during the night."

Nate stared at her, his face darkening. "Tompkins? The bloke what died t'other night?"

Linette nodded.

"The surgeon's gonna be cuttin' 'em up," Jim said and started toward the door. "Come on, Nate, let's go."

Linette grabbed his arm. "I plan to deal with this. I only want you two along as escorts."

"You gonna have the man arrested?" Nate asked hopefully.

The thought hadn't even crossed her mind. Linette only wished to get the body back. But as she considered the idea, she realized that going to the authorities would only generate bad publicity for the Dispensary.

"No," she said. "I want the matter settled quickly." She gave them each a sharp look. "And that means I don't want you talking about it, either. We will get Mr. Tompkins back and that will be the end of it."

"No better'n murderers," Jim mumbled under his breath as he followed her into the carriage.

Linette thought he wasn't far wrong. The thought of poor Mr. Tompkins lying on a table, being subjected to all sorts of indignities at the callous hands of medical students was almost more than she could bear.

Ashworth would pay dearly for this abomination.

Righteous anger overcame any trepidation Linette might have felt as she marched up the steps of the Howard Street School. Nate and Jim's presence also bolstered her courage.

The entry hall was deserted, but she heard the faint hum of voices coming from the top of the interior stairs. Linette hastened up them and peered through the open doorway.

Rows of chairs descended in a steep slope to the front of the room, where Ashworth stood beside a table. Over it lay a sheet, covering an ominous shape.

Linette swallowed nervously and stepped into the lecture hall. A quick whispering arose among the students.

Ashworth glanced up, his eyes widening when he caught sight of her. Linette straightened her spine and marched down the aisle, Nate and Jim at her heels. A few catcalls and snickers erupted from the students.

She stopped a few paces from Ashworth. "I would like to have a word with you, Mr. Ashworth."

"I am in the middle of an anatomical lecture, Miss Gregory." He waved an arm at the class. "These young men have paid money to hear this talk and I don't think it fair of you to cheat them of their due."

She darted an apprehensive glance at the lecture table, its display hidden by that draped sheet.

"This involves Mr. Tompkins," she said with quiet determination.

"Well, unless I'm mistaken, he isn't among my students today." Stephen looked up at the class with a smirk. "Do any of you happen to have a dead, consumptive laborer sitting next to you?"

Loud laughter rang out and Linette raised her voice to be heard above the din. "That is not what I meant." She pointed at the table. "Is that ... him?"

"Well, let's have a look." Before she could move to

stop him, Ashworth whipped back the sheet, revealing two torsos—one bare bones, the other with muscle and tissue still attached.

Linette felt the blood drain from her head and she swallowed quickly. She could not faint—not in front of all these students.

Ashworth grabbed her arm and pulled her toward the side door. "Mathers, get her out of here."

Linette shook off his hand. "No, I am all right." She averted her eyes from the table and focused instead on the surgeon's face. The amused glint in his eyes fueled her anger. "Mr. Tompkins' body was taken from the Dispensary during the night. Do you have any idea how that happened?"

"I can assure you that this fellow"—Ashworth pointed to the model on the table—"isn't he."

She looked at him coldly. "Did you take the body?"

"No, I did not," Stephen said wearily. "If you recall, Miss Gregory, you told me very emphatically that I couldn't have it."

Anger coursed through her. "I didn't think *that* would stop you."

Laughter erupted from the students, who were following the confrontation with rapt attention. Ashworth quelled them with a furious look, then turned back to Linette.

"I don't have Mr. Tompkins here and I don't have any idea what happened to him. Mathers, take Miss Gregory to the dissecting room and let her examine the subjects. She'll see that I'm speaking the truth."

Mathers looked hesitant. "Are you sure—?"

"Yes, I'm sure," Stephen snapped. "I have a class to teach and I mean to teach it." He turned back to the students and took a deep breath. "Now, as we were saying . . . the humerus fits into the cavity of the scapula. Who can tell me . . . ?"

Trembling, Linette followed Ashworth's assistant into the corridor.

She feared she'd made a fool of herself, but she hadn't stopped to think in her white-hot anger over Mr. Tompkins' disappearance. Ashworth was the obvious culprit.

Now, his denials made her less certain. But she wouldn't leave until she knew for sure.

The smell assaulted her the moment she walked into the dissecting room. Strong chemicals, mixed with something fetid and sweet. Wrinkling her nose, she peered about the room. Tall cabinets and shelves lined the walls, filled with vials, jars, and books.

Five long tables ran down the middle of the room. One was empty; the others were covered with sheets but there was no doubt what lay beneath. Gasping, Linette clasped a hand over her nose and stumbled backward.

A strong hand grasped her elbow and Ashworth's assistant pulled her out the door. He dragged her across the hall and into a cramped, dimly lit room. She sank down into the first chair she spotted.

A sharp, astringent odor filled her nose and Linette coughed, her eyes burning from the smelling bottle he held.

"Will you be all right?" The assistant looked at her with concern.

She looked up with a wan smile. "I . . . I think so."

The man pocketed the bottle and sat down in the other chair. "Most people react the same way the first time they step into the dissecting room," he offered cheerfully. "Why, I fell over in a dead faint my first time."

Linette shivered. "How unfortunate."

"You get used to it." He examined her curiously. "You're from the Dispensary?"

She nodded, fumbling in her reticule for a handkerchief. Linette blew her nose and wiped her eyes.

He smiled with encouragement. "We really didn't take your body; believe me, I know. Ash—Mr. Ashworth— was roundly cursing you for its absence just this morning."

"That is a comfort," she retorted with as much sarcasm as she could muster.

He grinned.

Linette looked away, studying the small room. It was a picture of chaos. Papers, books, journals were strewn about the scarred desktop. Odd items of clothing—waistcoats, scarves, even socks—hung from every perch. Surprised by the disorder, she glanced at the assistant.

"Is this Mr. Ashworth's office?"

He nodded cheerfully. "Bit of a mess, isn't it? He'd probably have straightened it up if he'd known you were going to visit."

It was shocking to think that a surgeon with such a reputation for meticulous detail worked amid such disarray. Linette stood abruptly. "I must be going. Please apologize to Mr. Ashworth for the intrusion—and the accusation." She edged out the door and walked down the corridor with measured, deliberate steps. Nate and Jim waited for her at the entrance.

Pushing open the heavy door, Linette stepped out into the fresh air. She took a deep breath, fighting to keep her knees from collapsing beneath her.

She turned to the two men. "I am sorry to have brought you here unnecessarily. It appears I was mistaken."

Nate glowered back at the door. " 'E might not 'ave Tompkins, but 'e's got some other poor coves in there. Me 'n Jim looked."

"Butcherin' bodies and callin' it medicine." Jim spat. "I'd like to cut some of them doctors up."

Linette sighed. "I don't approve of what he's doing with them, but those poor men aren't our concern." She handed them each a silver coin. "When you get back to the Dispensary, check with the porter and see if he has any more duties for you today. I'm going home."

"You shouldn't be goin' alone," Nate grumbled. "Not after what happened in there."

"I'll be fine. It is only a short distance in the carriage."

Shrugging, Nate and his companion turned and sauntered away.

Linette took another deep breath, reveling in the fresh air that filled her lungs. She glanced warily at the building behind her. How could anyone live and work in such a house of horrors? What kind of man was Ashworth? His assistant said they grew accustomed to it, but Linette couldn't imagine how anyone could become used to *that*.

Shuddering at the very memory, she hastened down the steps and climbed into Aunt's coach. She wanted to put as much distance as possible between herself and that awful place.

Her horror made her realize that she was far from understanding Ashworth, yet that was the key to finding a way to change him. But was it even possible to change a man who was so lost to all human notions of decency? For the first time, she wondered at the impossibility of her task.

But Linette wouldn't give up so easily. She'd find some way to get through to Ashworth. It would be her personal crusade.

She sighed with relief when the coach pulled up in front of the Barton house. Inside, it was safe and warm.

Linette removed her bonnet and placed it on the table in the entry when she heard Aunt's voice.

"Linette, is that you?"

She groaned inwardly, feeling close to tears. She didn't want to see anyone now, particularly her aunt. "Yes, Aunt."

Mrs. Barton stepped into the hall. "Goodness, you're home early today. I thought you were going to stay behind and help Mr. Henderson."

"There was a problem." Linette's eyes filled with tears. "Oh, Aunt Barton, it was dreadful. First Mr. Tompkins disappeared, then there was that horrible dissecting room, with all those bodies . . ."

"Good gracious, girl, what is going on? Where have you been?"

Linette took in a big gulp of air. "Mr. Tompkins was the poor man I told you about; the one whose body Ashworth wanted. When the rector came in this morning to perform the service, the body was gone."

Aunt's hand flew to her cheek. "Oh, how dreadful! Who would do such a thing to a poor soul?"

"I thought it was Ashworth," Linette said. "At least, I thought it was, at first. I went to his school to find out. They had plenty of bod ... bodies, but not Mr. Tompkins." She burst into tears.

Aunt Barton enveloped her in comforting arms. "There, there, my child. You have had a shocking experience, to be sure." She led Linette into the parlor and sat her on the sofa before ringing for tea.

"I feared something like this would happen when you chose to involve yourself so deeply with the Dispensary. A gently bred woman shouldn't expose herself to the distasteful side of medicine."

"It has nothing to do with the Dispensary; it's that terrible school." Linette shook her head. "And the worst thing ... was that they didn't even care! Ashworth insisted, even dared me to look at the ... at the ..."

Aunt patted her hand. "Now, my dear, you can't expect a surgeon to be aware of your gentler sensibilities. He's grown accustomed to that kind of thing."

"How could he stand to work in that atmosphere? The smell alone ..."

"Perhaps it would have been better had you sent him a note, rather than going yourself."

"But I had to know for certain," Linette protested.

"Then you should have sent one of the men from the Dispensary, or the rector. You need not do everything yourself, my dear."

Linette sighed. "I was so angry when I found that Mr. Tompkins was missing. I thought Ashworth took the body for spite, since I told him he couldn't have it. It never occurred to me that someone else might have done it. And I still don't know what happened to the poor man!"

"I know you meant well," Aunt Barton said, in a tone that caused Linette to look up, "but I do think you owe Mr. Ashworth an apology."

Linette bowed her head. "I know. I feel so embarrassed now. I interrupted one of his classes! Please say I can send a note. I don't think I could face him again today."

Aunt studied her thoughtfully. "A note will suffice. And perhaps you should stay away from the Dispensary for a few days. You need a chance to forget this unpleasant incident."

"Goodness, Aunt, I am not so fragile as all that." Linette looked up as the maid entered with the tea tray. "A cup of tea will make me feel much better."

Aunt peered at her doubtfully, but said nothing while Linette poured.

"I had a lovely visit with Mrs. Branby this morning," Aunt said, declaring the subject closed. "They have invited us to join them at the theater on Thursday."

Linette eyed her aunt warily. "Does she have a son?"

Mrs. Barton laughed. "You are the most suspicious girl! Yes, she does have a son, and I have no idea whether he will be joining us or not. I merely thought you would enjoy the performance."

"Do you know what the play is?"

Mrs. Barton sipped her tea. "She didn't say. I only hope the audience is more well behaved than the last time we attended. Something really must be done."

Linette giggled, remembering how those in the cheaper seats had tossed fruit at the stage and the audience. "You must admit that sometimes the show in the pit is better than the one on the stage."

"Wicked girl!" Aunt regarded her fondly. "Shall I tell Mrs. Branby that we will attend?"

Linette nodded. "Yes, I would like that." She set

down her cup with a smile and stood. "It will give me something to look forward to—after I write an abjectly apologetic note to Mr. Ashworth."

Aunt gave her an approving smile.

But despite her best intentions, the note was not easy to write. Linette was truly embarrassed over her false accusation. Thank goodness Aunt had been polite enough not to point out the sheer irresponsibility of her invading Ashworth's school.

Still, Linette was glad she'd gone and experienced the horror firsthand. It made her more determined than ever to bring Ashworth around to her point of view.

She also vowed to ask him to find out what had happened to Mr. Tompkins. Linette doubted she'd ever recover the body, but she would feel better knowing what had happened. If anyone from the Dispensary had been involved, she wanted to know.

Linette crumpled several sheets of paper before she finally had a note that satisfied her. After sealing it, she put it in the hall for the post. At least she would be able to hold up her head when she next saw Ashworth.

When his last lecture of the day ended, and the students dispersed to their afternoon pursuits, Stephen retreated to his office, pulled off his coat, and flung it into a corner.

What a way to start the day. Confronted by a slip of a girl in front of the entire class. The students would be whispering about that unexpected disruption for weeks. Was Miss Gregory always so impetuous in the cause of righteousness? Lord, he hoped not. She'd make life miserable for any number of people.

Mathers said she'd nearly keeled over in the dissecting room, which would have served her right. Stephen might bemoan the waste of a good body, but he would not blatantly disregard her wishes. It irked him to think that she thought so poorly of him. She'd told him he couldn't have Tompkins, and that was that.

He did wonder who had taken the body. Was some-one at the Dispensary in the pay of the resurrectionists? Miss Gregory would be horrified to learn that. Stephen smiled at the thought. He'd make a few inquiries.

Pulling a bottle of brandy from the bottom drawer of the desk, he looked about for a clean glass and poured himself a drink. He was just raising it to his lips when Mathers sauntered in.

"Your timing is impeccable," Stephen said with a wry grin. "If you can find another glass, you can join me."

Mathers rummaged through the mess until he un-earthed a battered tankard, which he held out to Stephen.

"Quite a girl, that Miss Gregory," Mathers said re-flectively, as he sat down.

"Quite an *annoyance*," Stephen added with a scowl.

"Oh, I don't know." Mathers grinned annoyingly. "I rather admire her for what she did."

"I hope you're the one lecturing the next time she decides to burst in. Then we'll see how well you like it."

"You have to admit that she carried the whole thing through with aplomb. The woman has nerve, she does."

"I'd say it's more a lack of brains than anything else," Stephen said sourly.

Mathers snickered. "I haven't seen you so bedeviled by a female since that corpse last spring—the one with the missing arm."

Wincing at the memory, Stephen shook his head. "We never did find out who took that arm, did we? Truly, I prefer my ladies dead than alive. Dead ones are a lot less bothersome—even if they don't have all their appendages."

Mathers slapped him on the back. " 'T'will do you good to have your assurance shaken—and by a mere female, at that. This one could lead you on a merry dance, if she wanted, I'll wager."

"I'm not dancing with anyone," Stephen grumbled. He drained the last of his glass and stood. "I want nothing more than a good hot meal and a plain, quiet evening. I've got Brock's new treatise and I intend to finish it tonight."

"Good. Then I can take a look at it tomorrow."

Stephen shrugged on his coat. "There's no need for you to stay here this evening—unless you're working on a project."

"Not tonight." Mathers' eyes gleamed. "I plan to be completely irresponsible once I leave. It's a night of wine, women, and song."

Laughing, Stephen shook his head. "Your student days aren't far enough behind you, I see. Just make sure you're still standing by morning—we've got work to do. I want them to start cutting on the shoulder."

"I'll be here."

Stephen waved farewell and stepped outside into the cool air. With winter fast approaching, it was already dusk.

Mathers was a decent sort—even if he was less serious than Stephen would like. He was a skillful cutter, and had a good deal of patience with the students—far more than Stephen did. When the school had grown big enough, Stephen would appoint him head lecturer. Mathers would never be a brilliant surgeon, but he was competent—and reliable.

And obviously more well equipped to handle interfering females.

Thank God he wasn't scheduled to work at the Dispensary tomorrow. Perhaps by the next time he crossed paths with Linette Gregory, he could look back on this incident with less anger. Tomorrow was too soon.

Then again, Miss Gregory wasn't stupid. She'd have enough sense to stay out of his way for a while. When they did meet again, he could behave with a modicum of civility.

That would probably cause her more consternation than if he railed at her. The thought amused him. There was a way to keep Miss Linette Gregory off-balance. If he did the opposite of what she expected, he'd have her thoroughly confused. And a thoroughly confused woman wasn't going to cause him nearly as much trouble.

Why couldn't she merely stand about and look pretty, without forcing her opinions on others? He could willingly admire her looks, that deceptively fragile blond beauty. It was her ideas he couldn't appreciate.

He'd seek her out his next day at the Dispensary. That would surprise her and it was important that he made the first move. Stephen tried to picture the exact expression on her face when he greeted her, all smiles and politeness. He'd thank her for visiting the school and taking an interest in his students. He'd suggest she visit anytime she wished, and offer to set aside a seat for her, assuring her she would find the lectures most illuminating.

She would never accept, of course. According to Mathers, she'd been violently distressed at what she'd seen today. But by forcing her to refuse his offer, Stephen would achieve a small victory.

A victory over an unctuous busybody who sought to interfere where she was neither needed nor wanted. Medicine could get along very well without her, and other "well-meaning" ladies. Let them put their time and money into founding hospitals and clinics and dispensaries, and leave medicine to the professionals.

Linette Gregory should spend her time worrying about her sewing circle, instead of interfering with scientific progress. The sooner she understood that, the sooner she would leave him alone. He didn't need accusing glances from those soft, gray eyes.

Chapter 5

Stephen awoke abruptly, jolted from sleep by loud pounding on his door. He blinked in the dim predawn light.

"Ashworth! Wake up!" Mathers' cry was followed by more loud pounding.

Bleary-eyed, Stephen crawled out of bed and stumbled toward the door. It must be some kind of medical emergency if Mathers was here.

Jerking open the door, Stephen peered into the dark hall. "What?"

Mathers stood in the corridor, wide-eyed and out of breath. "The school," he gasped. "You've got to come."

Stephen felt as if he'd been dashed with a bucket of cold water. "What's wrong?"

"Someone broke in during the night—the place is a shambles."

Stephen grabbed Mathers' arm and dragged him into the room.

"Robbery? Who'd want what we have, apart from another surgeon? No one can be that desperate for a few saws."

Mathers looked at him uneasily. "I don't think it was a robbery."

Stephen pulled on his trousers. "Well, what was it then? Gin-soaked young lords out for a spree?"

Mathers cleared his throat. "I think it was an antianatomist group.".

"What?" Stephen gave him an incredulous stare. "In

London? That kind of thing never happens here. Who would dare—?'' He shut his mouth with a snap.

He knew exactly who would dare. Someone who actively objected to the practice of dissection and anatomy study. Someone with a personal grudge against the Great Howard Street School. Someone who was angry with *him*.

Miss Linette Gregory.

Stephen quickly finished dressing, hardly daring to believe that this had happened.

First, he needed to inspect the damage. Thank God it was a light day—no dissecting time scheduled at the school and only an early evening lecture at one of the small hospitals. He and Mathers should be able to set things to right before the full day of classes tomorrow.

That was critical. He dreaded having to close even for one day—that type of thing could severely damage a school's reputation. He'd make sure they were ready if he had to stay up all night.

But when everything was settled, he was going to pay a visit to Miss Linette Gregory and have a little chat with her. If she was in any way responsible for this, he'd make sure she paid.

He didn't even try to find a hackney. Walking—nearly running, with Mathers trailing along—was a way to keep his anger from overpowering him. Stephen wanted to keep his energy focused on repairing the damage. There'd be plenty of time to be angry later.

And he was going to be angry. Very, very angry. If he ever got his hands on the people responsible . . .

Mathers led him up the alley. "They broke the window here"—he pointed to the missing panes—"and climbed in."

Stephen made a mental note to reinforce every ground floor window with iron bars, despite the expense. No one was going to break in here again.

He held his breath as he stepped through the alley door and bounded up the stairs to the lecture room.

Mathers hadn't told him the details of the damage, and Stephen hadn't asked. As a surgeon, he'd learned to rely on his own observations. He wanted to see everything firsthand.

The place was a mess. Chairs were overturned, leaning against each other at crazy angles. A few lay in splinters on the floor and the lecture table was tipped on its side.

For a moment, he felt an unexpected sense of relief. Surely, no lady had done *this*. Miss Gregory wasn't responsible after all.

Then he remembered those two hulking brutes who'd accompanied her yesterday. Just the kind of men who could carry out such destruction with great ease.

He shut the door and walked back to the dissecting room with a deep sense of foreboding.

"My God," he whispered as he surveyed the damage from the doorway.

The five dissecting tables, with their sheet-covered corpses, stood untouched. Apparently the marauders wanted to show their respect for the dead. But as for the rest of the room . . . broken jars, papers, and medical instruments lay scattered across the floor. A piece of glass crunched beneath his heel as he crossed the floor. Stephen bent down and picked up a trepan, which had been broken neatly in two. He scuffed his foot at a pile of bow saws, their blades and frames bent and twisted.

His face darkened with anger. This had been intentional, malicious destruction, directed at the men who strove to unlock the secrets of the human body. Directed at *him*.

He turned to Mathers, hovering at his elbow. "Find a few of the students—the more responsible ones—and get this mess cleaned up. We need to inventory all the instruments; find out which ones are damaged beyond repair and which ones we can still use. I don't want to replace anything we don't have to—I can't afford it."

With a disgusted shake of his head, he turned on his heel and marched toward the office. He'd have to go through the account books and see how much money he had.

"Ashworth?"

Mathers' voice held an apprehensive note. Stephen gave him a questioning look.

"They were in there, too."

Stephen nodded curtly and pushed open the door.

Pure, hot rage filled him. Out there, in the other rooms, it had been furniture, or instruments of wood and steel that had taken the brunt of the marauders' anger. But here ... this was his office, with his papers, his books, his work, scattered across the floor. This was a deliberate, personal attack on him. No one had the right.

"By God, those bastards are going to pay for this."

Stephen stepped back and pulled the door shut behind him.

"Well," he demanded of Mathers, who stood looking at him, "why are you still standing there? Didn't I tell you to get someone to help clean up this mess?"

"Yes, right away." Mathers darted into the dissecting room.

Stephen perched on the edge of the stairs, running a hand through his hair. God, he still didn't know what time it was. Past dawn, he knew, but not by much. Most of the city was still abed. Linette Gregory would still be.

He would shatter her peaceful sleep like she'd shattered his. She wouldn't expect him to know about the damage yet. If he hurried, he could confront her at home, before she'd had a chance to prepare herself. He didn't care what time it was, didn't care if he had to wake the entire household. He was going to deal with the matter *now*.

The long walk to the Barton house only fueled his anger. Hatless, he didn't even feel the cold. With each step, Stephen relived the pictures in his mind: the overturned table, the smashed glass bottles, the bent and twisted probes.

His office, the floor hidden beneath torn and ink-splattered papers. Six months' work on his book, thrown about like so much garbage. He hadn't had the heart to see what, if anything, had survived the rampage. Stephen didn't want to know how bad it was. Not until he'd confronted Linette Gregory.

Oh, he didn't think she'd actually been there. No, she'd had her helpers do the dirty work for her. A "lady" wouldn't want to sully her hands with the actual deed. To Stephen's mind, that made her a coward of the worst sort—the kind who didn't hesitate to voice a strong opinion, but didn't have the nerve to act on it.

The residential streets surrounding the Barton home were nearly empty in the early morning gloom. A well-bundled maid scurried about on some errand, a groom led a string of horses toward the park, and a street sweeper guarded his corner. But the residents were still tucked snugly in their beds.

Stephen smiled grimly. One of them was going to be awakened in a few more minutes. With a firm step, he walked up the stairs and pulled the bell.

It was some minutes before the door was opened by a rosy-cheeked maid.

"I wish to speak with Miss Gregory," Stephen said.

The maid looked back at him in goggle-eyed surprise. "Miss doesn't receive callers this early."

She tried to shut the door but Stephen stuck his foot in the gap. "She will want to see me. Tell her that Stephen Ashworth is here to speak to her—and it's urgent."

The maid led him to a small room at the front of the house. He ignored the comfort of the upholstered chairs and paced back and forth across the patterned carpet, his impatience growing with each length of the room. He'd be lucky if she appeared in the next half hour, and he needed to get back to the school. Mathers could take care of the classrooms, but Stephen wasn't going to let anyone else touch his office. Sorting through that mess would involve hours of long, painstaking work.

When the door opened five minutes later, he didn't

even bother to turn around, assuming the maid had brought tea. The universal answer to every problem in the world.

"There is an emergency? At the Dispensary? What's wrong?"

Whirling about, Stephen stepped back in surprise at seeing Miss Gregory standing in the doorway, protected from the chilly morning by a quilted wrapper. She'd obviously come straight from bed. And for one instant, his anger faded at the tempting sight. With her soft gray eyes misted with sleep and her golden hair tumbling about her shoulders, it was an enticing display. Stephen wondered if she looked this alluring every morning.

Then he recalled his purpose.

"Wrong?" He arched a brow. "Why should you think something is wrong?"

"The maid said it was urgent."

Stephen picked up a porcelain figurine from the table and weighed it in his hand. "I had a rather rude awakening this morning, Miss Gregory. There was a break-in at the school during the night."

Her hand flew to her mouth. "How dreadful! Was anything stolen?"

He set the figurine down. "I don't think theft was the aim. The intruders merely tore the place apart."

"Why would anyone do such a thing?"

"I asked myself that." Stephen eyed her coldly. "And the only reason I could think of is opposition to the work we're doing there."

She looked at him, a puzzled expression on her face. "You might be right," she said at last. "Some people do have strong feelings against what goes on at medical schools."

"I fully intend to prosecute the culprits."

"As well you should." Linette brushed back a lock of hair. "There will be no problem at the Dispensary; you can have as much time off as you wish."

Stephen wanted to reach out and shake her and struggled to control himself. "Damn it, this isn't about the Dispensary. This it about you."

"Me?"

"Don't you remember the irate female who stormed into the school yesterday, accusing me of stealing a body?"

"I'm still mortified at my behavior, but—" Her eyes widened in surprise and she took a step toward him. "You think that I was responsible?" Her surprise changed to anger. "How dare you imply that I would do such a thing?"

"You made your feelings about my work very clear when you marched into my classroom yesterday, Miss Gregory. I don't underestimate your determination."

"But to accuse me of wanton destruction is beyond all reason. I would never do anything of the sort."

Stephen sneered. "Oh, I don't think you were actually there. Breaking chairs and smashing glass is not your forte. But you know the type of men who could do the deed—men like those two fellows who accompanied you yesterday."

"You certainly have a low opinion of me, Mr. Ashworth. I would never ask anyone to commit a crime."

"Oh, I don't think you'd have to ask. A few hints . . ."

"I never hinted anything to anyone."

"They knew why you were at the school."

"I told them I was mistaken, that you hadn't taken Mr. Tompkins." Her eyes grew troubled and her hands flew to her cheeks. "Oh, dear. Nate and Jim. They just might do something like this."

Stephen relished the prospect of dealing with the culprits. "Tell me where they live. I'll find out what happened."

"Let me go instead," Linette said quickly. "They'll talk more freely to me."

He gave her a look of pure loathing. "Haven't you done enough already?"

She stood up to his anger. "Mr. Ashworth, if Nate or

anyone else I know did this because of something I said, I want to know about it."

"And you can conveniently help them disappear, as well." Stephen shook his head angrily. "You've caused enough trouble already."

Linette put her hands on her hips and gave him a stern look. "Mr. Ashworth, if I do find who is responsible, I assure you I won't do anything to help them evade punishment."

"Fine, then." He brushed past her and reached for the door. "I'll have my hands full cleaning up the mess."

She pulled gently at his sleeve. "Was the damage very bad?"

He looked down at her. She looked genuinely regretful, but that didn't soothe his anger. "It's bad enough. I can lecture in the street if I have to, but the dissecting room is in complete chaos." His expression hardened. "I hope we can find enough instruments to work with by tomorrow."

"Mr. Ashworth, please believe that I had nothing to do with this. I may not agree with your medical principles, but I would never stoop to wanton destruction to express my displeasure."

Ignoring the soft pleading in her gray-blue eyes, Stephen gave her an icy glare. "The fact is, Miss Gregory, if these men caused the damage, you're as guilty as they." He shook off her hand. "But I'm sure you can find some way to soothe your conscience. After all, they were acting in a *worthy* cause."

Her lips compressed into a thin, angry line. "You have no right to say such a thing. Had I known of this mischief beforehand, I would certainly have stopped it."

"And if you hadn't made such rash accusations about the fate of Tompkins, it wouldn't have happened, either," he retorted. Without giving her time to reply, he turned and walked out the door. The maid, hovering in the hall, dashed before him, barely reaching the door in time. Stephen gave her a curt nod and hastened down the front steps.

So. His theory had been right. Linette Gregory was ultimately responsible.

Oddly, the thought didn't give him much satisfaction. It would be a hell of a lot easier to remain angry if she hadn't been so apologetic. He'd expected vehement denials, or smug satisfaction. Instead, she'd sounded nearly as outraged as he, and accepted her role in the whole affair with such contriteness that he almost felt guilty for dragging her out of bed at such an hour.

Then he shook himself. How could he feel sorry for her? No one needed to feel sorry for Linette Gregory; it was her victims who needed compassion. She had more determination than a company of soldiers. If you stood in her way, she would run right over you.

He'd been run over once, but he'd be wary from now on. Stephen knew enough to jump out of the way when he saw her coming.

Linette sank down into the upholstered armchair as soon as Ashworth left.

His news appalled her. How could Nate and the others have done such a thing? There was no doubt in her mind that they had, in the misguided belief that it would please her. She shook her head. If she hadn't been so angry yesterday, so eager to accuse Ashworth of going against her wishes, this never would have happened. But it had, and she must accept the responsibility.

Linette jumped up. She had to talk with Nate. Linette vowed to be certain of the facts this time, before she marched into action. But then she would do all she could to set things right.

She ordered the carriage brought round, then dashed upstairs to dress, wanting to get out of the house before her aunt awoke. Hopefully, she'd think Linette had merely gone early to the Dispensary.

Ashworth hadn't detailed the damage, but Linette

guessed that it would be costly. She had some money of her own, set aside for her school, which she would gladly turn over to him. Nate and the others, of course, had none, but they could work at cleaning up.

Remembering Ashworth's threats to prosecute, she hesitated to drag the men into this. Nate and the others couldn't go to jail. *If* they were guilty, she'd find a way to persuade Ashworth not to bring charges. Surely, if they cleaned up the mess and she paid for the damages, he'd be willing to let them go.

Climbing into the carriage, she directed the coachman to one of the dingy streets near the Dispensary. Linette had been here often enough, but she still couldn't shake off the sense of despair that clung to these buildings. Yet the people living here were better off than so many others. . . .

She climbed the dark steps to the third floor room, her nose wrinkling at the smells that permeated the very wood beneath her feet. Beer, sweat, cabbage, and urine. The odors of poverty.

At first she rapped tentatively, then with more confidence, at Nate's scarred door. It was finally jerked open by a thin, hollow-eyed woman.

"Hello, Mrs. Jenkins. Is Nate at home?"

The woman nodded and stepped aside so Linette could enter. "Nate! Miss Gregory's 'ere to see ye."

Nate came bounding out of the other room, a crooked grin on his face. "Got another job for me today?"

Linette shook her head. "Nate, I need to speak with you about something—about something that happened last night."

He jerked his head at the woman and she disappeared into the other room.

"Did you . . . were you involved in breaking into the Howard Street School?"

"Me?" Nate's grizzled face was a picture of innocence. "Why, Miss Gregory, what gives you the ide—"

She waved a warning finger at him. "Don't play the

innocent with me, Nate Hawkins. Were you there last night?"

"I was with Jimmy Boggs all evening, miss."

"That doesn't give me much confidence." Linette frowned. "You better tell me the truth now, or I'll see that you never work at the Dispensary again."

He hung his head. "We didn't think you'd mind."

"Mind?" Linette strove to keep her voice under control. "Of course I mind. Breaking into a building is against the law."

"Me and the boys was sittin' around and I got to talkin' about what happened yesterday—with Tompkins disappearin' and that dreadful dissectin' room, with all them bodies. 'T'wern't a fit place for any body."

Even though she agreed, Linette regarded him sternly. "Mr. Ashworth wants to go to the magistrate and you are in a great deal of trouble, Nate. A great deal of trouble."

"How's he gonna know who did it?" He smiled. "We was real careful, like."

Linette's expression grew sterner. "Ashworth will know because I will tell him."

"What? You wouldn't be sendin' us to jail, Miss Gregory."

"I'll try to persuade Mr. Ashworth not to make a complaint. But he isn't going to feel generous after his school was torn apart."

"He only got what he deserved," Nate said sullenly. "Cuttin' up bodies. It ain't right."

"What you did wasn't right either." Linette gave him an encouraging smile. "But I know how you can make things better."

Nate regarded her suspiciously. "How?"

"Come with me to the school and help clean up the damage."

"And put myself in 'is 'ands? Not bloody likely. If he don't give me over to the magistrate, he'll probably try to cut me up."

"Oh Nate, he wouldn't do any such thing."

"I've 'eard stories about them doctors. Killin' patients to get the body."

"Mr. Ashworth is a reputable surgeon, Nate. You'll be safe."

"What about the magistrate? I could be transported for this."

"You should have thought about that before you acted," Linette said dryly. "If you offer to help, I'm sure Ashworth will be reasonable."

"Promise?"

Linette sighed with exasperation. "This is your chance to make things right. You have to do this."

Nate hung his head.

"You won't have to go alone—I will come with you."

Nate's expression brightened. "I kin get Jim and some of the other lads to help."

Linette smiled. "Good. I have the carriage—you can ride with me."

Nate looked uneasy. "Best if we meets you there, miss. It won't take long."

She looked at him carefully. "You won't try to run away, will you, Nate?"

He shook his head.

"Very well, then. When you get there, tell Mr. Ashworth I asked you to come and help with the cleanup. Don't tell him that you were responsible—I'll talk to him about that."

"We'll do a real good job cleaning, we will." Nate bobbed his head. "Here, let me walk you down the stairs. This ain't no place for a lady."

Linette smiled wryly. "And what of your sister?"

"She hain't a lady," Nate announced, then reddened. "She's brought up here; she be used to it."

"I do wish you could persuade her to come to school," Linette said as they walked down the narrow steps. "We could teach her so many things."

Nate shook his head. "She don't want to have anything to do with it. Says what was good enow for her mam is good enow for her."

Linette sighed. It was an old argument among many of the people she wanted to help. They didn't understand that things were changing, and they would have to change with them—and that they needed education to do that.

Nate stood back while she stepped into the carriage.

"Don't you fret now, missy. Me 'n the boys will be there real soon. I'll tell the doctor man that we'll fix things up right and tidy."

Linette's misgivings rose again as the carriage pulled away. Yesterday, she'd vowed never to set foot in Ashworth's school again, yet here she was, returning the very next day, hoping to beg a favor from a man she'd falsely accused of theft.

She could only pray he'd be mollified when she offered to pay for the damages. That, coupled with Nate's offer to help, should be enough to persuade Ashworth not to go to the magistrate. She couldn't bear the thought of Nate, or any of the others, languishing in prison, or worse, being transported, because they had tried to please her.

Because if anything happened to the men, it would be her fault. She'd swallow her pride and grovel on her knees before Ashworth if that was what it took to persuade him not to press charges.

Linette was certain he would enjoy the sight.

Chapter 6

By the time Stephen returned to school, Mathers and some of the students were already cleaning the dissecting room. Stephen was glad to see Smith and MacNeil here; he hoped Mathers had given them a particularly disgusting job.

Mathers glanced up when Stephen walked in, greeting him with a broad grin. "Good news—it looks like they damaged fewer instruments than I first thought."

Stephen looked about the room, assessing what still needed to be done. "Just get that inventory completed as soon as possible. I need to buy the replacements this afternoon."

Steeling himself, Stephen headed for his office. He hesitated for a second, then pulled the door open.

He looked—really looked—at the destruction this time. Even with the evidence before his eyes, it was unbelievable.

With a muttered oath, Stephen bent down and snatched up the nearest sheet of paper, scanning its contents. Notes from last week's lecture. Wonderful. Why couldn't he have found tomorrow's instead? It would take days to get his papers back into some semblance of order, let alone trying to piece together the torn scraps. And as for replacing his books ... more than one lay in a ruined heap on the floor, the spine broken, pages torn out.

Grabbing a chair from the hall, he propped open the office door and knelt down. He had to start somewhere.

Stephen shoved papers onto the chair without bothering to look at them; sorting could come later. He had to clear a path to his desk before he had a place to work.

"Damn!"

He looked down with dismay at his fingers. A pool of ink lay hidden under that last sheet of paper and he'd stuck his hand in it. Rummaging in his pocket for a handkerchief, he tried to keep the dripping ink from staining any more pages.

Stephen angrily slapped more pages on top of the unsteady stack, then watched with dismay as the whole pile toppled off the chair.

"Damn and blast!"

He threw the papers aside, stomped out of the office, and climbed the stairs to the lecture hall. If he didn't rein in his anger before he dealt with those papers again, he'd have a worse mess than he did now. He'd work in here for a while. Starting at the back of the tiered room, he began to right the furniture.

After finishing the back row, he sat down on the end chair, gazing down at the toppled lecture table. He couldn't wait to get his hands on the men who'd done this.

"Ash?"

Mathers stood at the front door, three roughly dressed men beside him. They looked vaguely familiar. Stephen frowned as he tried to place them.

He jumped to his feet as the memory washed over him. Yesterday. That tall fellow had been here with Miss Gregory.

Were these the ones responsible for last night's rampage? Stephen raced down the aisle, determined to find out.

The tall man pulled his cloth cap from his head as he spoke. "Miz Gregory said we was to come by and help you clean things up." His eyes darted nervously about the room. "Looks like you had a right good brawl in here."

Stephen eyed them with growing suspicion. "And I suppose you know nothing about it?" The men remained silent.

Shaking his head, Stephen pointed to the upended chairs. "Set them back into rows on the tiers and pile the broken pieces down here. You can haul them away later."

The tall man picked up a broken chair leg, turning it over in his hands. "I got a friend 'oo mends chairs," he said. "He ought to be able to fix this up right enough."

For an exorbitant price, no doubt. "Clean up this room first and then we can worry about the chairs." Stephen couldn't believe this. First they broke his furniture, now they offered to fix it. And who was to say they wouldn't be back to break everything again in a few days? He turned and marched back to his office.

Snatching up the fallen pile of papers, he shoved them back onto the chair, then surveyed the room again, running a hand through his hair as he thought.

He needed to proceed in a logical manner. Clear a path to the desk first, then work back across the room. There was no telling where those lecture notes might be, but he'd find them faster if he made a more organized search.

Stephen had managed to clear a narrow path to the desk when he heard a light rap on the door frame. "What?" he demanded, without bothering to look up.

"I see the men I sent to help have arrived."

Stephen stood slowly and turned around, fixing a baleful gaze on Linette Gregory. "What a generous gesture on your part, Miss Gregory, to provide me with such willing helpers. I suppose they're the ones responsible for all the damage?"

"Do you intend to report this to the magistrate?" she asked.

He laughed harshly. "Is there any reason why I shouldn't, now that I know who the culprits are?"

She remained silent for a moment, then turned pleading eyes upon him. "I ask you—beg you—not to press charges against the men. They're truly very sorry for what they did and they're willing to make amends."

"Are they?" Stephen asked dryly. "Or did you persuade them that they should be?"

She caught her lower lip between her teeth. "A little of both," she admitted finally. "But they really are good men. Nate willingly works at all sorts of odd jobs to help support his sister and her family, and Jimmy—"

Stephen held up his hand. "Spare me the sad tales, Miss Gregory. I am sure they are the *most* honorable of men and half the widows and orphans of the city are dependent on their support."

"Quite right," she said with a trace of a smile.

"Why I am doing this, I don't know," he muttered to himself. "All right, I won't bring this matter before the courts."

"Oh, thank you." She grabbed his hand. "I promise you, Mr. Ashworth, they will work hard."

For an instant, he was entranced by the look of joy that lit her soft gray eyes. Then he remembered that she was the one behind this all and his pleasure faded.

"Ash?" Mathers peered around the door. "I need you in the dissecting room."

"I'll be there after I see Miss Gregory to the door," Stephen said, waving his assistant away.

"But I wish to help, also," Linette said.

Stephen gave her a weary look. "Frankly, Miss Gregory, you are the last person I wish to have in this building. Haven't you caused enough trouble as it is?"

"Will you be able to hold classes tomorrow?"

He shrugged. "Maybe. It depends on the extent of the damage in the dissecting room. Which is where I need to be right now. So if you will excuse me . . ."

"All the more reason why you can use another hand," she said, a look of determination on her face. "I can sweep, or make lists of damaged items, or anything else you would like."

Stephen shrugged. "I don't have time to stand here and argue with you." He gestured at the office. "See if you can create some semblance of order in here. Don't worry about the torn papers—I need someone who knows what they're doing to match them together. If you can stack everything in piles, that'll be enough."

"Thank you." She flashed him a grateful smile and knelt to pick up a sheet of paper.

Stephen sighed inwardly as he crossed back to the dissection room. The word "nemesis" came to mind. His life had been so uncomplicated before Linette Gregory had stepped into it. Why had he ever consented to take the position at the Dispensary?

Because he was impatient and ambitious. He'd hoped that the Dispensary position would provide a boost for his career. Instead, it had only brought him trouble.

"Pride goeth before a fall." His father, of course, would say that Stephen was being punished for his arrogance. He knew it was human interference rather than divine providence, but it rankled just the same.

Mathers sat on the floor in the dissecting room, a jumbled heap of twisted and broken instruments next to him.

"I put the usable ones back in the drawers." Mathers pointed to the pile. "These are all beyond repair. Those fellows must have had a thing against trepans. Every single one of them is broken."

Stephen bent down and picked up one of the broken skull drills and tapped it against his hand. "I'm tempted to put this to use on the ones who did this . . ."

Mathers looked at him curiously.

"Those are the culprits out in the lecture room," Stephen explained.

Mathers jumped to his feet "What? What are you going to do?"

"According to Miss Gregory, they've been persuaded of the error of their ways and they're here to make amends." Stephen said. "I trust them with the chairs but

I don't want them back here. Let them haul away the rubbish when you're done."

Mathers looked at him, an idiotic grin on his face.

"Is something wrong?" Stephen asked crossly.

"And here I thought you were impervious to female charms," Mathers said. "She has you going in circles."

"This has nothing to do with Miss Gregory," Stephen snapped.

"Oh, certainly." Mathers smothered a laugh and handed the list to Stephen. "This is still partial, but it'll give you something to start on."

Stephen glanced down at the long list of instruments and sighed. "Looks like we'll have to ask Weiss to extend us credit again."

"We could get them cheaper at Cobb's," Mathers suggested.

"And watch them break after a few months' use? No, Weiss might be more expensive, but his instruments hold up better under those cowhanded students."

Stephen started back to his office before he remembered that Miss Gregory was there. The one person he didn't want to see.

He had half a mind to go back and upbraid Mathers for his ridiculous insinuations. But he had to replace these blasted instruments, and the account book was in the office—hopefully still in the top drawer of the desk. If he was going to haggle with Weiss over the price of new instruments, Stephen needed to know how much he could afford.

With resignation, he crossed the corridor, than halted in midstride at the doorway, staring into his office.

Miss Gregory sat on the floor, surrounded by neat stacks of papers. A wisp of hair straggled from her tidy coiffure, but otherwise she looked as composed and elegant as if she were pouring tea in a drawing room. Was she always so at ease in any situation?

He surveyed the results of her work and scowled. In mere minutes she'd accomplished more than he had in

three times as much time. Soothing her guilt with industrious labor. It was an uncharitable thought, but he
couldn't help himself. He shouldn't have given her the
opportunity. But then, he shouldn't have allowed those
men to escape justice, either. She'd talked him into dropping those plans as easily as she'd persuaded him to let
her help.

He seemed to have a real problem saying no to Linette Gregory.

She glanced up as he stepped into the room. "It was
a dreadful mess, wasn't it?" she said with a rueful expression. "I'm so very sorry this happened. I'm glad I
can do something to help."

"Humph." Stephen picked his way across the floor to
his desk. Sweeping aside the few sheets of paper that
still covered his chair, he sat down and pulled open the
top drawer. Thank God the account book was still there.

He flipped it open to the last entry page and ran his
finger down the long list of figures. What he saw gave
him little comfort. He'd raised school fees this term, but
prices had risen as well—especially for cadavers. Even
this early in the session, money was tight. Yet somehow,
he had to squeeze out enough funds to replace what had
been damaged.

He wished he had more money of his own. . . . But
every spare penny was tied up in this school, in the payments he had to make to buy out Grosse, the former
owner. Stephen barely had enough money for his own
bills; he couldn't afford to replace school supplies out of
his own pockets as well.

Stephen sighed heavily. It looked like he would have
to put off buying that new microscope until next term.
He needed the money now, to buy trepans and bone
saws.

If only he had more paying patients . . . But there
wasn't enough time to teach, research, write, and solicit
patients. He'd hoped that his work at the Dispensary
might bring more his way, but so far there had been

only a few referrals—not enough to make a drastic improvement in his finances.

Shaking his head, he picked up the list Mathers had given him. If he bought carefully, and the students shared, he could almost afford to replace most of what had been destroyed.

Of course, he might have to give up eating.

"Mr. Ashworth?"

Stephen turned wearily toward Miss Gregory.

"Is that the list of damages?" she asked.

Stephen nodded.

"I want to pay for what has been broken. I feel it is my responsibility."

A wave of relief washed over Stephen. Suddenly, the situation looked brighter. "For once, I am not going to argue with you, Miss Gregory. You've just freed me from having to make some disagreeable choices. Do I buy scalpels for the students or eat?"

A frown creased her brow. "Is your situation really that desperate? I thought this was a successful school."

Her sudden concern brought forth a laugh from Stephen. "Matters aren't critical—yet. But I run this school on a pittance. There's no extra money for *unexpected* expenses."

"Surely, with the high fees you charge the students, you must be making a great deal of money."

"Those fees go back into the operating costs of the school—instruments, chemicals, Mathers' salary. I told you what I have to pay for cadavers."

She lowered her gaze.

"There are only a few lecturers who can command astronomical fees. The rest of us charge what we can get. Remember, I'm also buying this school. I'll be lucky to have a ha'penny in my pocket at the end of the term."

"Couldn't you take on some private students?"

"I'd love to, Miss Gregory, but I barely have enough time for my own work."

She rested her chin on her hand, a thoughtful expression on her face. "Then why are you working at the Dispensary? I would think you'd gain more by seeking out private patients."

"I wanted the variety of cases that I'd see at the Dispensary," he said. "Private patients might pay, but their ailments are usually minor—and similar."

"So what you need," she said, a thoughtful expression on her face, "are fee-paying patients with interesting cases."

"Exactly." Stephen leaned forward in his chair. "And they aren't that common. If I had the money, I'd do like Cooper, and hold open office several days a week. But I can't afford to do that until I've built up a clientele of paying patients—and I don't have time to do that."

"There must be something we could do."

Stephen arched a brow. "We?"

She flushed. "The Dispensary should help you. After all, you're not being paid for your work there. The least we could do is find you patients who can pay for their treatment."

He gave her a wry look. "I'll start looking for a grand consulting room, and hire a porter to keep the throngs in order while they wait to see me."

"And you will command the highest fees in the country and even kings and queens will stand in line to see you."

Her left cheek dimpled as she smiled. He admired the sight until he realized what he was doing and shut the account book with a snap. "Hand me that stack of papers. I need to find my lecture notes for tomorrow."

Linette handed him a sheaf of papers and turned back to the loose papers still littering the floor.

Rubbing her aching neck, she bent to the task. It felt as if she'd been sitting on the floor for hours, reaching to pick up and stack paper. How much paper did Ashworth have in his office? She remembered the chaos she'd seen in the room yesterday, and groaned inwardly. A great deal.

Linette watched him surreptitiously while he sorted through the papers on his desk. At least now she understood why he looked so rumpled—he probably couldn't afford to dress better. All the more reason to find him more patients.

To ease the monotony of her task, she began glancing at each paper before she set it down. Most of the words were meaningless to her—medical terms—but occasionally a few lines caught her eye.

She couldn't suppress her surprise when she found a bundled sheaf of papers, all in French. She held them out to Ashworth. "What are those?" she asked.

He glanced at them. "Medical papers from France. Damn! Mathers was supposed to get those translated for me."

"You don't read French?" Linette asked, surprised.

"No, Miss Gregory, I do not." His eyes darkened ruefully. "It was all I could do to muddle my way through Latin."

"I am proficient in French." An idea quickly formed in her mind. This was a way to *really* help him. "I could translate these for you."

Setting down his pen, Stephen turned to face her, a look of skepticism on his face. "These aren't romantic poems or silly novels, Miss Gregory. These are medical reports, full of technical terms and anatomical descriptions. You wouldn't understand a word of them."

"I might not understand what they mean, but at least I can read them—which is more than you can do."

He gave her an exasperated look. "Tell me, Miss Gregory, has anyone ever accused you of being interfering and pushy?"

She bit back the angry retort that sprang to her lips. "Many times," she said with a forced smile.

He shook his head begrudgingly. "I should have known. It probably did no good then, either. Fine, Miss Gregory." He shoved the papers back into her hands. "Take these home and translate them into English for me. Perhaps you will gain a better understanding of the work we do here."

"Are the French making great discoveries in medicine?"

He nodded. "They're ahead of us in many ways. Probably because they don't have to go around digging bodies out of graveyards for study."

"What do they use, then?"

"Bodies, Miss Gregory. Just like we do. The difference is that they're given them by the hospitals and infirmaries."

"Indigent paupers, with no one to care for them," she said bitterly. "Does their poverty make them any less valuable as humans?"

"As medical subjects, they have great value."

She set her lips in a thin line. "I'm not going to be drawn into another argument with you on the subject. You know very well how I feel."

"Thank the Lord," Stephen muttered, loudly enough for her to hear. "This must be a first for you, Miss Gregory. Backing away from an argument, I mean."

"It's because I know how obstinate and pigheaded you are on the subject. There's no point in belaboring the issue with you."

"Me obstinate and pigheaded?" Stephen tipped back his head and laughed. "This is a fine case of the pot calling the kettle black. If you weren't so outspoken on the subject, you wouldn't be sitting here now, trying to repair the damage done by your friends."

"I've never advocated violence or destruction of medical facilities," she said. "I merely said that it's wrong to cut up human bodies for study."

"You'd prefer that we cut up living people?"

She saw the teasing gleam in his eyes. "You know that's not what I mean. You have the most annoying habit of twisting everything one says."

"Only because your words are so easily twisted." Stephen turned back to his papers. "Keep to your fund-raising and your ladies' sewing circle, Miss Gregory. They are occupations best-suited to the fairer sex. Leave medicine to the experts."

Linette refused to be patronized. "I shudder to think where we would be if everyone thought the way you do. You would probably cut up the entire population for 'research' and then complain when you ran out of subjects."

Stephen laughed aloud. "It's a tempting thought, Miss Gregory. May I start with you?"

She tossed the papers she held into the air. "You are the most odious man! If you are this rude to your patients, I can see why you don't have many."

"Patients come to me for medical help, not platitudes or jokes," Stephen said. "If I'm cutting for the stone, no one cares what I say if I get rid of their pain."

"Unless, of course, they die later," she muttered.

He grinned. "I've never yet had a patient come back from the grave to haunt me."

"They should! Perhaps it would bring you a bit of humility—a characteristic you are sorely lacking."

"But how can I be humble when I'm saving mankind?"

She glared at him. "Look at me. I daresay I have done as much good as you and you don't see me running around bragging about it. A true servant is modest about his work."

His grin widened. "They why are you telling me about it?"

"Because I am *trying* to make a point. Although with you, that's a difficult task."

He smiled with irritating cheerfulness. "My teachers used to say the same thing."

"No doubt because you argued with them constantly." Linette shook her head in mock horror. "I declare, if I said that your eyes were brown you would probably say they were blue, just to be contrary."

"I admit they're brown. I don't argue about *facts,* Miss

Gregory. Only opinions. Particularly when they're as narrow-minded and obstructionist as yours."

"Excuse me." Mathers stood in the doorway, an amused look on his face.

Stephen tilted back in his chair. "What new disaster has befallen us?" he asked.

"Those men want to take the chairs to be mended. Should I allow it?"

Stephen stood up. "Let me talk to them."

Mathers gave Linette a sympathetic grin before he turned to follow Stephen down the hall.

Linette grabbed a handful of papers and threw them on the nearest stack.

How could one man be so irritating? It was as if he tried to be deliberately obnoxious—and he succeeded very well at the task.

Reaching for another sheet of paper, her hand paused in midair.

Was he doing this on purpose, baiting her for his own amusement? It seemed a purposeless exercise. Was it because she was the one person around him who dared to call any of his opinions into question? She doubted that his nice assistant ever dared to contradict the mighty surgeon. And the students, of course, wouldn't dare to question their teacher.

Someone needed to point out to Mr. Stephen Ashworth that he wasn't the only person on earth whose opinions mattered. He needed to learn that there were other points of view, and his was not necessarily the right one every time.

Thoughtfully, Linette began stacking the papers with more care. How could she hope to succeed at such a monumental task? She suspected more forceful personalities than hers had fought against Ashworth, and lost.

But she had a few advantages. First, there was the matter of those French articles. She'd translate those foreign medical terms if it killed her, showing him that she could understand medical language as well as any trained person. He'd be bound to respect her opinions more when she could talk knowledgeably about his profession. Linette knew a great deal about medical matters from working at the Dispensary. How much more would she really need to learn?

Then she'd show him that she was not an inconsequential female, with no head for medical matters. And once he started listening to her, there was no end to the things she could tell him.

A slow smile crept over her face as she resumed her work. Stephen Ashworth would get his comeuppance at last. And it would be her doing. She couldn't hide her pleasure at the thought.

Chapter 7

Two hours later, Linette stood in the doorway and surveyed Ashworth's office with a sense of satisfaction. The papers that had covered the floor now sat in neat piles, the books were stacked on the desk, and she'd even managed to match some of the torn and damaged pages together.

Heaped in a box were a jumble of dirty dishes, medical instruments and assorted items of clothing. Not knowing what to do with them, she went in search of Mathers.

She found him in the lecture room, sweeping up broken glass.

"I've finished straightening up the office. I stacked up all the papers and books, but there's a box of odds and ends that I don't know what to do with."

Mathers set down the broom. "Ash will be amazed that you've accomplished so much."

"Because he thinks I couldn't do it?"

"Because it took nothing short of a miracle to bring order to that room."

Entering the office, he peered into the box. "I don't know what he wants to do with these. We can put them in the storeroom for now."

"Where's that?"

He hefted the box. "I'll show you."

Linette followed him to the front of the building and into a room opposite the lecture hall.

She stared at the room in surprise. This was a store-

room? Tall windows overlooked the street, and an ornately carved mantel stood over the fireplace. Boxes of
rubbish were piled along the wall, but even so, this was
a far grander room than the hole Ashworth called an
office.

"Why isn't Ashworth using this for his office?" she
asked.

Mathers shrugged. "I think he likes being close to the
dissection room."

"But look at the advantages." She rubbed a clear spot
in the begrimed window. "The room is well lit and with
that fireplace, it could be downright warm in the winter."

"Ashworth doesn't spend that much time in his office," Mathers replied. "I don't think he cares about his
comfort that much."

"Well, he should." Linette circled the room, inspecting
it closely. The wallpaper was stained in several spots and
the entire chamber needed a thorough scrubbing, but
under the layer of dirt and dust was an elegant room.

And a much more impressive office that the dark
hidey-hole at the back of the building.

She tossed a speculative glance at Mathers. "Just how
long do you think Ashworth will be gone?"

"Oh, several hours at least."

Linette smiled. "Good. There will be time enough to
switch things around."

"Switch things—?" Mathers looked at her with alarm.
"You aren't planning to . . ."

Linette nodded emphatically. "Oh, but I am. And if I
want to have things ready when he returns, I need to
get to work."

She dashed into the hall, calling for Nate. She'd send
him for Mary and Amy and some of the other girls.
With all of them working, it shouldn't take too long to
scrub out the front room. Then they could move Ashworth's furniture and have the whole thing done before
he came back.

He would be surprised—and pleased. Linette hoped

that this would go a long way toward enabling him to forgive her for what had happened last night.

After dispatching Nate, she went back to the front room and looked around again. The room really needed a carpet, and there was plenty of room for more furniture. A sofa would be good, for visitors, and Ashworth could certainly use another bookcase.

Linette rolled up her sleeves. There was a great deal of work to be done and not very much time to do it.

With Mathers' list tucked in his pocket, Stephen set out for Weiss's. He needed to replace as many instruments as he could today.

He walked several blocks before he found a hackney to take him to the Strand. Hopefully, Weiss had everything they needed in stock; Stephen didn't relish making the rounds of every surgical instrument maker in the city in order to resupply the school.

Thank God Miss Gregory was paying for it all. He'd be able to buy that new microscope after all—and replace his ruined books. If only he could replace his lost time as well.

The clerk at Weiss's gave him a curious look when he handed over the lengthy list, but Stephen didn't bother to explain. The fewer people who knew about what had happened, the better. Word was bound to leak out, of course, but as long as things were back to normal tomorrow, it wouldn't matter. In fact, the whole incident might even enhance the school's reputation.

As he feared, Weiss didn't have everything he needed, so Stephen was forced to visit some of the other instrument makers. By the time he finished, he was still short a few items, but he had the important ones. He'd send Mathers over to Southwark tomorrow to look for the rest.

Since he found himself near St. Barts, Stephen stopped and browsed through several bookshops, remembering the damaged volumes back at his office. He purchased a new copy of *Bell's Surgical Anatomy* and decided to stop for lunch. He deserved a decent meal after this morning.

It was late afternoon when he returned to the school. He'd no doubt have to spend the rest of the afternoon sorting through his papers, putting them back into order, and finding his lecture notes for the next few days. The talk at Middlesex Hospital wasn't until seven, so he'd be able to get some work done beforehand. Then he'd come back here and finish the job.

When he stepped into the building, an unfamiliar odor assailed his nose. It smelled like a mixture of beeswax and ... strong lye soap? Puzzled, Stephen followed the smell up the stairs and into the lecture room.

There, at the front of the room, two ladies were on their knees, vigorously scrubbing the floor, while a third washed the walls.

Stephen cleared his throat. "What is going on here?"

One of the women looked up and gave him a saucy grin. "We be cleaning for you, Mr. Ashworth." She looked around the room and laughed. "Looks like you needed it, too."

He retreated out the door.

Linette Gregory was behind this, of course. What else had she been up to while he was gone? Quickly, he hurried down the stairs, dreading what he would find in his office. He shouldn't have left her here alone.

Nervously, he pushed open the door and peered inside. There wasn't a single scrap of paper on the floor; everything was neatly stacked along the far wall. She'd done a damn fast job of that, he had to admit. Once they were sorted, he could—

Stephen's mouth sagged open in mute surprise. There wasn't a single stick of furniture in the room. The desk, his bookcase, the chairs, everything was gone.

A loud thump sounded from the front of the building and Stephen ran back into the hall. Mathers stood by the front door, straining to hold up one end of a large,

upholstered sofa while two red-faced students brought
the other end. Stephen strode toward them.

"What are you doing?" he demanded, his voice taut
with anger.

"One side, if you please," gasped Mathers. Stephen
barely had time to press himself against the wall when
they swung the sofa around and carried it into the empty
room facing the street. Following closely behind them,
Stephen stopped, stunned, on the threshold, eyeing what
had been an unused, dust-filled chamber the last time
he'd looked.

His missing desk stood against the interior wall,
flanked by two chairs, with the bookcase at the far end
by the fireplace. A worn but serviceable carpet covered
the center of the floor, giving the room a formal air. It
almost looked like the retreat of a learned medical
man—not the harassed director of a financially strapped
medical school.

He watched with growing confusion as Mathers and
the others positioned the sofa beneath the tall windows.

Stepping back, Mathers dared a grin. "Not bad, eh?"

Stephen glared at his assistant. "What the hell is
going on?"

Mathers bowed low. "Your new office."

"And whose brilliant idea—" Stephen clapped a hand
to his forehead. "Don't tell me, I can guess. Miss Gregory. And why didn't you put up any objections?"

"She thought you needed a bigger office. This room
is much larger," Mathers said.

Scowling, Stephen pulled one of the chairs in front of
the desk. "I don't need a bigger office. The old one was
closer to the dissecting room."

"The old office was a rat hole and you know it." Miss
Gregory stepped into the room.

Stephen fought hard not to stare at her. The once
impeccably dressed Miss Gregory was wrapped in a voluminous apron, streaked with dust. Wisps of blond hair
straggled from beneath a mobcap and there was a

smudge of dirt on one cheek. She looked no different from one of the ladies scrubbing the lecture room.

With a sudden shock, Stephen realized that he'd misjudged her. She wasn't playing at being Lady Bountiful; Linette Gregory wasn't afraid to get her hands dirty. He felt a grudging sense of respect for her, and her principles. How many ladies would deign to dirty their hands in the cause of helping others?

He just wasn't sure he wanted her helping *him*.

She eyed him coolly. "However do you intend to impress patients and patrons if you don't have a presentable office?"

Stephen scowled. "No one ever comes here to see me."

"Well, they should. As head of the school, you need an office more befitting your station. Mr. Mathers can use your old one."

Stephen swing his gaze back and forth between them. "It's a conspiracy, isn't it? You two are working together to drive me insane."

"I can't imagine how anyone would mind an improvement in his working conditions." Linette pointed toward the tall, multipaned windows. "Look at all the light that comes in. I don't see how you could work in that dark hole at the back."

" 'That dark hole' suited me just fine," Stephen said, his irritation rising. "I don't recall asking you or"—he glared darkly at Mathers—"anyone else to change it."

"I finished stacking your papers," she said, blithely ignoring his complaint. "Would you like to start going through them now? I can help you."

Stephen sank into his chair. Her question reminded him that he didn't have time to argue about her high-handed interference with his life. Moving his office again would be a waste of precious time. Until he finished sorting through that mountain of papers, he was stuck here.

"Miss Gregory, you've done *far* too much already."

Stephen gave her a bland smile. "If you would be so kind as to bring the papers here, I will sort through them." He tossed a vindictive look at his assistant. "I'm sure Mr. Mathers will be *more* than willing to help me."

She darted out the door.

Mathers gave him an apologetic look. "She's a difficult woman to dissuade once she gets an idea in her head."

"I assume those washerwomen in the lecture room were her idea, too?"

Mathers nodded. "She said it was obvious the place hadn't been cleaned in years and she wondered how anyone would want to study amid such filth."

Stephen laughed sourly. "They should be scrubbing out the dissecting room. Now *there's* the place that could use it."

"She refuses to set foot in it," Mathers said. "Can't say that I blame her after yesterday."

Stephen glanced out the window, his attention caught by the action of a carriage and dray maneuvering to pass each other on the narrow street. Then, with a muttered oath, he turned away. He didn't need any more distractions.

Surveying the room with a critical eye, Stephen turned a pleading look on Mathers. "Do I really need all this space?"

Mathers shrugged. "It wasn't as if we were using this room. Your office would make a good closet; we could move some of the extra specimens out of the dissecting room. It'd be a lot more convenient than having everything upstairs."

Stephen grinned wryly. "I thought you wanted the room for *your* office."

"That was *her* idea. I'm content with my little nook upstairs," Mathers said with a self-effacing look.

Stephen glanced at the sofa again. The ornately carved gilt frame looked totally out of place in this room. "What is this for? And where the hell did it come from?"

"A bargain from the chair man," Mathers said, not bothering to hide his grin. "He said he'd have the chairs patched up in a day or two."

Stephen shook his head. "What did it cost?"

"I didn't ask. Miss Gregory paid for everything. Did you find what we needed at Weiss's?"

"Almost. They'll send them later." He handed the list back to Mathers. "I need you to go to Southwark tomorrow and look for the last few things."

Mathers drew a folded paper from his pocket. "Miss Gregory said to give you this—it's a list of the books in your office that were damaged. She says she'll replace them, as well."

"It's a damn good thing, too," Stephen grumbled as he sat down. "I already picked up a new copy of *Bell's*. Twelve shillings!"

Mathers perched on the edge of the sofa. "You know, you might say that this whole episode worked to our advantage."

"Oh?" Stephen raised a skeptical brow. "And how is that?"

"Look at all the new equipment we're getting—instruments, furniture, books. All at someone else's expense. You can't complain about that."

"You're right," Stephen said sarcastically. "Maybe I'll hire her lackeys to destroy my rooms and have everything there replaced as well."

"At least talk her into lending you her scrubwomen." Mathers snickered. "I know what your rooms look like."

"I like them just the way they are." Stephen leapt to his own defense. "I don't need anyone poking about in my things. I know exactly where everything is."

"For a man who constantly upbraids the Royal College for their hidebound ideas, you're certainly resistant to change in your own life." Miss Gregory, her arms full of papers, chided him from the doorway.

"You would be, too, if someone went about rearranging your life without permission." He stood and crossed the room with long steps, snatching the papers from her hands. "Mathers, help the lady with the rest of these."

Mathers heaved himself off the sofa and trotted obediently behind her.

Stephen leaned back in his chair with a sigh. He had the uneasy feeling that once Miss Gregory set her mind to something, it would take an entire regiment of British cavalry to drag her away. Right now, he wished he'd never heard of the Barton Dispensary, Linette Gregory, or that blasted dying Tompkins. All he wanted was to be left in peace.

He didn't need his school transformed into an ornate palace. What was next? Framed paintings of eminent surgeons in the lecture hall? Wallpaper in the dissecting room? If she *really* wanted to make their surroundings more pleasant, she'd fill the cellar with coal. He'd rather have a roaring fire than a sofa in his office any day.

But he didn't have time to deal with her anymore today. Once he'd restored order here at the school, he'd talk with her, informing her that he didn't want her interfering with his school, his patients, or his work. He would discuss Dispensary matters with her, but beyond that, she was to keep her interfering nose out of his life. He didn't need her help.

Stephen looked up as she returned with Mathers, watching impassively as they set their armloads of papers on the sofa.

"That's the last of it," Miss Gregory said with a cheerful smile. "Now, are you sure you don't want me to help? The rest of my day is free."

Stephen found her cheerfulness grating. "*Quite* sure, Miss Gregory. You may go."

"I found a few more French articles while I was cleaning in your office. I'll take them with me, along with the others."

"You're most welcome to them," Stephen said, hiding a smile. He couldn't wait until she was forced to bring them back, admitting she couldn't make any sense of them.

"I'll check on my ladies, then. They should be finished soon." With a swish of her skirts, she slipped out the door.

Shutting the door firmly behind her, Stephen turned back to the desk.

Mathers shot him an inquiring look. "French articles?"

"That's one more thing I'm holding against you, Mathers." As he sat, Stephen glared at his assistant. "*You* were supposed to find me some student to translate those articles. I foolishly mentioned the matter to Miss Gregory and she immediately offered to do it."

"She reads French?"

Stephen laughed. "Oh, she can probably understand drawing room French, but I doubt she'll be able to make head or tails of a medical treatise."

"Then why did you let her take them?"

He tipped back in his chair. "To prove my point—that she won't be able to do it. You've seen the woman—do you think she'd believe me simply because I told her that? No, she'll have to learn it on her own."

"She's a bit overbearing, but she's been a great deal of help today," Mathers said. "I could barely believe my eyes when I saw her down on her knees, scrubbing the floor."

Stephen shook his head. "I wish she'd confine her good works to her own projects and leave me alone."

"You're starting to sound like a hardened misogynist."

"Her being female has nothing to do with it," Stephen insisted. "If you weren't my assistant, I'd be just as irritated with you for helping her." He gave Mathers a dark look. "In fact, I think I'm irritated anyway."

Mathers shrugged. "Someone has to look out for your interests."

"And I'm the best person to do that," said Stephen

with a pointed look. "Now, help me sort through these papers. I need to have my lecture notes for the next few days."

In silence, they settled down to work, Stephen at his desk and Mathers on the floor by the sofa.

They'd been working in silence for about half an hour when a light tap sounded on the door.

"Enter," Stephen called, not looking up from his task.

"We've finished cleaning the lecture room," Miss Gregory announced. "There's just the front hall left, and then we'll be done."

Stephen knew if he looked at her one more time, he would explode, but he couldn't resist the impulse to tweak her sensibilities one more time. He kept his gaze focused on the paper in front of him. "If you really want your ladies to be useful, have them scrub out the dissecting room. The glass has been swept up, but the room is still a mess."

"As long as you persist in mutilating the bodies of the deceased, I will not set foot in that room," she announced.

Stephen stretched lazily and stood, regarding her with a cool glance. "Then why don't you take your ladies and go home? I'm grateful for your help, but now I want you to get the hell out of here and leave me alone."

She drew herself upright. "Really, Mr. Ashworth, you don't have to curse. I'm more than willing to leave if that's what you wish."

"It is."

Her lips compressed into a thin line. "Very well, then, we will go. I'll have Nate deliver the chairs when they're ready."

"Fine, fine." Stephen took her arm and guided her firmly to the door. "Goodbye, Miss Gregory. Give my regards to your aunt." He shut the door none too gently behind her.

"You're a rude bastard," Mathers observed.

"That's the only way to deal with people like her."

Stephen sat down and turned his attention back to his papers. He had to leave for his talk in a few hours; he needed to make good use of the time.

He *had* been unconscionably rude to her, but he didn't care. He'd learned long ago not to rely on anyone, yet here he was, indebted to her already, and he didn't like the feeling. However much this destruction had been her fault, she'd done more than enough to make up for it. She'd gone well out of her way to be helpful, which only made him angrier.

Like moving his office. He'd never admit it to her, but this was a better room. Those tall windows meant fewer candles, and he wouldn't lose track of time as easily as in that dark hole at the back. And if anyone ever did come to see him, he'd be able to host them in tolerable surroundings.

He'd let her have her way with this. But no more. He wasn't going to become her pet project.

The front hall was dark and empty when Stephen let himself back into the building at eleven. His lecture had gone well, thank God. He desperately needed sleep, but he still had a mound of paper to sort. He'd found most of his lecture notes late this afternoon, at least, and a good chunk of his book. And he'd been able to piece together some of the torn pages. All in all, he'd made good progress. He *could* let the rest sit for a few days. But if he didn't sort them now, it would become harder and harder to find time to finish the task. Already, he'd lost a day of his own time—a day when he'd planned to work on his book. Now he'd have to wait until Saturday, and if he wasn't caught up by then, he'd be hopelessly behind forever. A few hours of lost sleep didn't mean much compared to that.

The smart thing would be to forego his next session at the Dispensary, but a streak of stubbornness made that idea untenable. He'd be there as expected. Linette Gregory would have no cause to claim that he wasn't properly executing his duties. No, he'd be a model surgeon.

He'd walked halfway down the corridor when he remembered his office was now at the front. Drat that woman, he thought as he retraced his steps.

At least Mathers had remembered to leave a candle burning in the office. It shouldn't take more than an hour or two to finish and then he could go home to sleep. Stephen thought longingly of a cup of tea, but he was too tired to take the time to heat the water.

The mere thought of hot tea made him shiver and he pulled his coat closer. Winter was closing in and that meant more money keeping the building warm.

Sometimes he wondered if it was worth the trouble and expense to buy the school. It was going to take years for him to complete the purchase, and in the meantime, his finances teetered on the edge of disaster. If the school failed, he would lose his entire investment.

But if it succeeded ... he'd be closer to having the success he wanted. A hospital position was key. Once he had the prestigious appointment, the school's future was secure. If the Royal College of Surgeons and the hospitals again colluded to control medical education in London, he wouldn't have to worry because he would be part of the system. Then he could be the senior instructor and devote his time to research.

He sighed. Unfortunately, that could take years. Once again, he wished a thousand plagues on every surgeon with a hospital position. Until one of them quit—or died—Stephen was forced to play a waiting game that grew more frustrating with each day.

Hospital surgeons didn't have to worry about the cost of heating the building, or how many saws they could afford, or the number of corpses they could obtain. Hospital surgeons could command any price for a consultation, and students flocked to their classes. All because of their position. No matter that he was a better surgeon, or teacher. He didn't have a big enough name, and until he did, no one cared about his skill. Stephen would continue to toil in an obscure school, treating patients in a minor dispensary that was run by a woman who knew nothing about the practice of medicine.

If he was totally honest with himself, Stephen would admit he was grateful for what Linette Gregory had done today. Without her money, Stephen would have been hard-pressed to repair the damage and replace the supplies. Now, only the most observant student would notice anything different when they came to class in the morning.

But she'd done more than merely pay for the damage. She'd bullied the guilty men into helping with the clean up, brought in her cleaning ladies, scrubbed floors herself, and tried to make his work area more comfortable.

That puzzled him the most. Why should she care about his comfort, or whether he had a suitable place to host visitors? One would almost think she had an interest in promoting his career, which was laughable. If she was truly concerned, she wouldn't put up such a fuss about dissection. No, she had other plans; he just couldn't fathom what they were.

His eyes scanned the unfamiliar room and lit upon the sofa. Unconsciously, he yawned. A short nap would be refreshing. Then he would finish his work, head back to his rooms, and have a few hours of uninterrupted sleep in the comfort of his own bed.

Stephen sat on the couch, testing the softness of the cushions. It wasn't too uncomfortable. He stretched out, his hands behind his head, and stared at the dark ceiling. After lecture tomorrow, he'd pick up the rest of the medical instruments, while the students moved supplies into his old office. There would be time later in the afternoon to . . .

A merciless bright light penetrated Stephen's closed lids. Covering his eyes, he groaned and rolled over. It couldn't possibly be time to get up yet, even if the room was as bright as midday. . . . He must have forgotten to close the curtains when he'd gone to bed last night.

Bed. Stephen sat up with a start and stared about him in sleepy confusion. The curtains weren't closed because there weren't any on these particular windows.

"Damn!"

Rubbing his stiff neck, Stephen swung his feet to the floor. The light streaming through the tall windows assured him that it was, indeed, morning. He'd slept the entire night on that blasted couch.

Slowly he stood and peered outside. A carter's dray drove by, and he counted at least ten people on the street. It must be even later than he thought!

Damn and blast. He fumbled in his pocket for his watch and flipped it open. Half past eight—and he had a lecture to give at nine. There was barely time to grab some breakfast before the students arrived.

As he dashed out the door, his wrath centered on Linette Gregory. This was all her fault for putting that blasted sofa in his office. One more crime he could lay at her feet.

She'd soon be knee deep if she wasn't careful.

Chapter 8

Linette had never before wanted a morning to go so quickly, yet today her sewing class seemed to last an interminable time, and then several pupils wanted to speak with her after. She endured their questions with a patient smile, but inwardly she seethed with frustration. She still had to pick up Aunt Barton's new muff and take the Dispensary ball invitations to the printer. Only then could she start searching for a French medical dictionary.

Last night she had sat down confidently with the first French article, certain she would have something to show Ashworth in the morning. But after a painstaking struggle with the first two pages, she realized the task wasn't going to be so easy. And she desperately wanted to show him that she was as serious about her work as he was about his. She was under no illusions—Ashworth would never think well of anyone who wasn't practicing medicine. But he could hold her in higher regard.

Linette wanted his respect. Because despite everything—his brash manner, his smug arrogance, and his revolting support of dissection—Stephen Ashworth was a man she admired. They were, ultimately, engaged in the same noble cause. They should be on the same side, working together. She intended to show him that was possible.

And once he began to respect her, there was no telling how she might be able to influence him.

But first, she had to translate these articles. Ashworth

had been right—they were full of medical terms she didn't know, in French or English.

Still, she would show him. There had to be books—dictionaries, or lexicons—that would list and explain all those terms. She merely needed to find one.

At last, Linette was free to look, but her hopes plummeted again after she left the first bookshop. They didn't have what she needed, and couldn't tell her where to find one. She tried another bookseller near St. Barts, but they were of no help either. She would have to try in Southwark, by the Borough hospitals.

Aunt's coachman tried to dissuade her when she instructed him to drive across the river, but Linette would not be deterred. A French medical book she wanted, and a French medical book she would have, even if she had to send to Paris to get one.

Once they reached the Borough High Street, she rapped on the window and told the coachman to drive slowly while she looked for a promising shop.

The carriage turned down the street that ran between St. Thomas and Guys. Spotting a group of young men who looked like medical students, Linette lowered the window and called out.

"Excuse me, could you tell me where I might find the nearest medical bookseller?"

They stared at her, dumbfounded.

Linette eyed them more doubtfully. "You are medical students, aren't you?"

One of them sketched an elegant bow. "May I be of service, madam?" He turned and grinned at his fellows. "I'd be more than willing to examine you *thoroughly* for any sort of illness."

Linette flushed crimson, then grew angry at their impertinence. "I am executing a commission for my father, Dr. Barnes." *That* name stifled their grins; he was head of the Royal College.

"Try over in Tooley Street," one offered, his demeanor now polite.

"Thank you," Linette replied with the haughtiest air she could muster. She pulled the window closed with a snap.

The coachman had to stop and ask directions several more times before he finally found Tooley Street.

"There's one!" Linette called out and the carriage creaked to a halt. Without waiting for assistance, she jumped down and dashed into the cluttered shop.

At the sight of the skeleton hanging on one wall, she skidded to a halt. With a shudder at the macabre sight, Linette hastily turned away, reminding herself that a shop catering to medical men wasn't going to consider normal human sensibilities.

Linette rapped on the counter several times before the stooped proprietor appeared.

"Yes?"

"I am looking for a dictionary of French medical terms," she said.

The man gave her a searching look. "What would you want that for?"

Linette sighed with exasperation. "It doesn't matter why I want it. Do you have such a thing?"

"I might." The man made no move to look.

"Do you think you *might* check?" Linette asked, her irritation growing. "I don't have all day."

"I'll have to search in the back," he said. "We don't get much call for that sort of thing."

"I'll wait." Linette hoped the blasted man would hurry. If he didn't have what she wanted, she would have to ask at each and every bookstore until she found one that did. If they all had skeletons propped in the corner, it would be an unnerving task.

The man shuffled off toward the back of the store and disappeared behind a curtain. Linette walked about the small shop, careful to keep her back to the skeleton. A jumble of books rested on the nearest shelf and she scanned their titles.

Picking one out, she opened it at random, then quickly

slammed it shut again. She had not expected to find a picture of *that,* even in a medical text.

Hastily she turned and scanned another shelf, sighing with relief when she found pharmacological titles. Medicines were a safe topic. But the first book she looked at was filled with long formulations in Latin. Now she knew how Ashworth felt when he looked at French.

She glanced back at the curtain. What was taking that blasted man so long? Was he sending to Paris for the book?

Browsing though another shelf, Linette started at the sight of a familiar name. Carefully, she pulled the book out and examined it. *A New Technique of Lithotomy* by Stephen Ashworth, RCS.

It was a small volume, bound in boards. Not a cheap chapbook, but not an expensive one, either. The kind of thing a student, or a newly licensed surgeon could afford.

Ashworth had written a book. The thought shouldn't surprise her; it seemed that nearly every medical man in the country had done the same. But finding it here, like this, was oddly comforting. Was it a sign that she was doing the right thing, trying to gain his confidence and respect?

Or did it mean that she was on a fool's errand; that a surgeon such as he would never bother to pay attention to the trifling opinions of a nonmedical person?

The shopkeeper appeared silently at her shoulder and she jumped. He held out a dusty, leather-bound volume. "Is this what you want?"

Linette glanced quickly at the book. *Encyclopédie de Medécine.* "This will help in translating medical articles from the French?"

The man peered at her over his spectacles. "Who's doing the translations?"

Linette glanced down at the book clutched in her hand and smiled. "I am," she said with a smug look. "For Stephen Ashworth." She handed the small book to the shopkeeper. "I should like to have this volume as well."

The man looked at her with a curious expression. "I've had the man in my shop once or twice," he said as he wrote up the bill of sale. "Can't say I've sold many copies of his book."

"I believe he is working on a new one," Linette said with the ghost of a smile. Wouldn't Ashworth be surprised, to hear her promoting him like this?

The man bundled the two books together with string. Linette paid, and he handed them to her.

"One thing, miss."

"Yes?"

"You might want to bring in those translations when they're done. Could be there's a few students that might want them."

Her eyes widened. "Someone might want the articles?"

He nodded. "In English. Not all these chaps read the French, you know."

Linette gave him a shrewd look. "And how much would you be willing to pay for these translations?"

His expression grew guarded. "Depends on the length, and the topic."

Linette smiled inwardly. In order to repair the damages, she'd given Ashworth nearly all her money. Now she had a way to earn it back.

"I'll bring in the first one when it's finished and we can discuss the cost then," she said. "I bid you good day, sir."

Settling back into the coach for the long ride back to town, Linette felt a sweet sense of success. She'd found her book and perhaps had found a way to earn some money.

When she had the articles translated. There were still many hours of work ahead of her. But once she grew familiar with the strange terms, the translations should proceed quickly. She ought to have something for Ashworth in the next few days.

* * *

Three days later, she found herself perched nervously on the sofa in Ashworth's office, waiting for him to finish his morning lecture. Already, papers covered every surface in the room—indeed, she'd had to move a stack before she could even sit down. Soon, this office would be in the same deplorable condition as the last.

He needed a work table, and a cabinet to store his papers, she thought while looking about. And another bookcase—the shelves in the existing one were already overflowing. Aunt might be willing to help; surely there were a few pieces of furniture in the attic Ashworth could have.

And curtains ... Lincttc's mind raced. That would be a good project for her advanced class. Not only would they have to do the sewing, but they would have to measure, calculate the needed yardage, and buy the fabric. A very practical project.

She heard a step in the hall and the door flew open. Ashworth stormed into the room and tossed a sheaf of papers on the desk. He stripped off his stained coat, hung it carelessly over the back of the chair, then swung the chair around to face her before he sat down.

"Good morning," she said, smiling sweetly.

His expression didn't soften. "To what do I owe the honor of this visit?"

She handed him a stack of papers. "Here is the first article I translated. I wanted you to look at it."

Ashworth tilted back in his chair. "Ah yes, Montclair's work on the spinal column. Well, Miss Gregory, let's see just how good your command of the French language is."

Perching on the edge of the sofa, Linette nervously clasped and unclasped her hands as she watched him read. If he found her efforts inadequate, she'd be hard-pressed to ever gain his respect.

But the sight of his long, tapering fingers against the white pages distracted her attention. He had such beautiful hands. Hands that were made to perform the delicate magic of surgery.

Or to caress a woman.

Yet she doubted he ever concerned himself with that.

This wouldn't take long, Stephen surmised. He'd discover her mistakes readily enough, see what bizarre misconstructions she'd made of the thing, thank her for her efforts, and send her on her way.

The further he read, the deeper his brow furrowed. Instead of the errors he'd anticipated, the damn thing read perfectly. He shot a quick glance at her, sitting patiently on the sofa, hands moving restlessly in her lap.

Good God, she actually knew what she was doing.

He began reading in earnest, and was soon engrossed in the detailed explanations.

"Mr. Ashworth?"

Startled, Stephen looked up. "What?"

"The translation. Is it all right?"

He turned and looked at her, surprised by the eagerness in her face. He cleared his throat. "It appears to be *adequate,* Miss Gregory."

"Oh, good." She reached into her voluminous bag. "I have another one that is finished, if you would care to look at that as well."

Stephen stared at her.

When she'd offered to help, he'd accepted without thought, fully confident that she wouldn't be able to complete the task. She would soon see how ridiculous the whole idea was and eventually give up, full of apologies for wasting his precious time, and he could dismiss her from his life.

Instead, she'd given him a work as well done as anything he'd seen.

His eyes narrowed with suspicion. "Who helped you with this?"

She drew herself erect. "I did both of these myself,

Mr. Ashworth. And I think I did them rather well, if you must know."

Stephen met her gaze and in that instant, he knew that she realized what he had expected. Knew that he'd given her the articles with the express anticipation of her failure. And he knew that she'd worked hard to make certain that he'd have no cause for complaint.

Grudgingly, silently, he acknowledged her determination, and her success.

Flipping through the pages, Stephen tried to marshal his thoughts. He couldn't lie—these translations *were* good. Yet he hated to admit it to her. It was like being forced to admire the surgical mastery of a man whose ideas you despised.

Stephen acknowledged the mean-spiritedness of his attitude. He was reacting out of pure spite and he knew it. But damn it, Linette Gregory had been a thorn in his side since the day they'd met. He wanted her out of his office, out of his life.

Yet if she could translate articles like these, she was a godsend. He thought longingly of those two texts he was dying to read ...

Glancing up, Stephen saw her watching him with a knowing smile. He set the papers on the desk, taking great pains to square the corners neatly while he planned his words.

"Well?" Her eyes danced eagerly.

Stephen shook his head. "You've done a damn good job," he admitted reluctantly.

He saw the relief in her face and for a moment he half feared she would spring from the sofa and hug him. Instead, she restrained herself to a broad smile. Only the deep gleam of pleasure in her eyes showed how much his words pleased her.

"Thank you, Mr. Ashworth. I wasn't certain you would admit it."

"Did you think I wouldn't acknowledge your efforts?"

Her smile widened, revealing the dimple on her left

cheek. "You seemed less than appreciative of my efforts the other day."

Sighing, Stephen considered his behavior. He had been rude, true, but he had certainly been provoked, as well. "I was under a great deal of strain that day, as you well remember. I assure you, your efforts were very helpful."

Linette smiled. "How do you like your new office, now that you've had time to accustom yourself to it?"

"It's all right. Except for that blasted sofa." He glared at the offending piece of furniture. "I lay down for a quick nap and slept the whole night."

She burst out laughing. "You poor thing!"

Stephen grinned wryly. "I sound ungrateful, don't I? But I'd intended to sleep in my own bed that night."

Her gray eyes twinkled impishly. "Perhaps I should find you a more uncomfortable sofa. One that you can't possibly fall asleep on."

He laughed at the absurdity of his complaint. "No, I'll merely have to exert more willpower over myself in the future."

Linette stood and walked to the windows. "You will need draperies for these, of course. I meant to get the measurements the other day."

Stephen was on his feet quickly. "Please, don't trouble yourself about that. You've done so much already."

Laughing, she turned and caught his eye. "You mean you wish I would take my papers and go."

"I didn't say that! I really don't need any draperies."

"I'm not thinking of you, but of my sewing ladies. This would be a marvelous project for them. You wouldn't begrudge them the opportunity, would you?"

Stephen knew when he was beaten and held up his hands in defeat. "Whatever you wish, Miss Gregory. I cannot say no to such a benevolent project."

"Good. I'll try to work around your lecture schedule, so we won't bother you while you're working here." She picked up her bag from the sofa. "I must be going."

Stephen grabbed her cloak off the chair and held it out to her. He waited patiently while she fastened it, then extended his hand.

"A truce, Miss Gregory?"

She took his hand. "A truce, Mr. Ashworth."

He followed her to the door and helped her into the carriage, then stood watching as it lumbered down the street, turned around the corner and drove out of sight. Slowly, he walked back up the stairs.

He didn't know what to think anymore about Miss Linette Gregory—and not just because she could translate medical articles from the French. All in all, she was a surprising lady. He remembered his first glimpse of her, in the drawing room at her aunt's house, when he'd paused to admire her. He'd been drawn to her golden blond looks and slim figure. Before they'd argued about the role of medicine and society, and he'd discovered just how opinionated she was.

Now, he had a better understanding of her. She was a woman who believed sincerely in what she was doing, and who wasn't afraid to follow her convictions. She wasn't the grand dame dabbling in good works that he'd first thought her. Her desire to help people was sincere, and her compassion was threaded with practicality—like putting curtains on his windows so her sewing students could have a project.

More surprisingly, she was a woman who had the honesty to admit when she was wrong—and a sense of responsibility that forced her to make amends for her errors. He couldn't remember meeting another woman like her.

She'd make the ideal wife for a medical man—a woman who was interested and cared about her husband's work.

A flush crept over him and he stopped in midstride. The ideal wife for some men, but not for him. She had no understanding of *his* work, why it was necessary and important. She only saw mutilation and defilement, where he saw all the wonders of the human body, and the enormous potential for surgery in the future.

Most people weren't that sincere in their motives or beliefs, and could be easily swayed or cajoled with the right words. Linette Gregory wasn't one of those. Stephen knew she would hold on to her tenets in the face of spirited attack, and likely convert the opposition in the process.

If only she weren't so wrongheaded, he would admire her.

But as it was, he merely wished that she would leave him alone. He didn't have time to wonder what life with a woman like her would be like. He had his work to do.

Chapter 9

Linette's pleased smile didn't fade during the carriage ride back to Aunt's

She had done it. She'd translated those articles skillfully enough to please Ashworth. And he'd admitted it to her, as well.

Her plan was a smashing success.

She tried to stifle her excitement. It was merely the first step, after all. She'd only managed to alter his opinion about her ability to translate French, not his opinion about her work. That was a far more monumental task.

But one that didn't seem quite so out of reach now as it had two days ago.

At the theater that night, with Aunt and Mrs. Branby, Linette found herself too distracted to take any enjoyment from the play. Her thoughts kept straying back to the brick building on Great Howard Street, and the man who worked inside it.

She knew that he firmly believed in his work, and the value it held for humankind. But somewhere, somehow, he'd lost his sense of humanity—if he ever had one. Patients weren't people, but "subjects" to be treated and hopefully cured. If they died, they were fodder for the dissecting table, where he could study them in even greater detail.

Nowhere in that attitude was there a place to regard a patient as a *person*, a human being with hopes, dreams, goals, needs. Patients with families and relatives who loved them, cared for them, rejoiced if they lived and wept if they died.

Was it a result of his upbringing? Had he been raised in a "modern" home, where science and progress were emphasized over compassion and understanding? He must have, in order to think the way he did. It was no wonder then, that he acted as if the quest for knowledge justified any action.

But she knew how wrongheaded that idea was. She didn't argue against medical progress. It was nothing short of a miracle that doctors and surgeons were able to treat diseases and conditions that had once killed thousands of people. But that didn't mean they could overlook the purpose of life—honoring and improving the lives of everyone around them. Men like Ashworth only wanted to improve their own medical knowledge, bettering the lives of future generations without a thought to today's. That wasn't right.

Yet she truly wondered if anything she could say or do would have an effect on his firmly held convictions. They'd reached a truce of sorts, today, but that didn't mean she had any influence over him. He might appreciate her ability to translate French, but he wouldn't listen to her on medical matters, she was sure.

Why then, was she so determined to try? Despite her aunt's reservations, Linette didn't enjoy the pursuit of lost causes. There was no point in wasting energy where one wasn't wanted. Yet she was willing to waste a great deal in order to get Mr. Stephen Ashworth to change his mind. Why?

Linette fingered the lace on her sleeve, not wishing to admit it, even to herself. But the truth was, she liked him. In Ashworth, she saw a dedication and purpose that few people had. Despite his complaints about money, he wasn't practicing surgery to become rich. Fame he might want, but fame for his medical skills. He truly wanted to improve his profession and alleviate the suffering of others. A goal that paralleled her own.

There must be some way she could show him the value of helping others for their own sake, not just for the betterment of science. To look upon his patients as individuals, and not merely cases to be treated and forgotten. Like old Dr. Emory, at home, who knew all his patients by name, knew the histories of their families, the names of their children, their hopes, their fears.

If Ashworth had been trained in one of the London hospitals, it was easy to understand why he had such a cold attitude. He hadn't seen the other parts of his patients' lives, their homes, their families, their work. What he needed was to deal more closely with patients instead of seeing them only in the Dispensary setting. It was difficult to develop a relationship with a patient you only saw once. Trust and rapport required repeated visits.

But the people who used the Dispensary weren't those who could afford frequent medical treatment either. If Ashworth was going to take the time to see more patients, he needed ones who could pay for his services. She could help him with that by talking to the Board and the subscribers.

Linette smiled. Until then, she could afford to subsidize some patient visits, at least at first, until he built up a more affluent clientele.

The problem would be to encourage more of the neighborhood people to go to Ashworth. There was still a lingering reluctance among many of them—like Nate's sister—to have anything to do with the Dispensary. The Dispensary was seen as a measure of last resort and the unfortunate loss of Mr. Tompkins wouldn't help. But once people saw they could safely have Ashworth treat their minor ailments, they would go.

But where would he see them? The school was the ideal place, but it was too far away. And she doubted whether Ashworth had space in his own living quarters for a consulting room.

He could still work at the Dispensary; only in a different setting. Space could be found in the building for a separate consulting room. They would limit the nature of ailments treated, and the hours, so it wouldn't interfere with the daily working of the Dispensary.

Now, she had to convince Ashworth that it would be worth his while.

Surely he would see the sense of the idea. He'd have to spend a few more hours every week at the Dispensary, but he'd be paid for his trouble. If he was as desperately in need of money as he claimed, he wouldn't turn down such an opportunity.

And through these new patients, he would begin to realize that he was treating human beings, not just diseases or injuries. Once he began to look upon his patients as individuals, he would be less willing to look upon dead bodies as mere commodities. He would recognize that they had once been living, breathing people, and the thought of cutting into them would no longer seem palatable.

Linette felt a gentle nudge and turned toward Aunt.

"It is intermission, my dear," Mrs. Barton said with a fond smile. "Goodness, I've never seen you so absorbed in a play."

Smiling guiltily, Linette fumbled with her fan. If anyone asked, she couldn't have told them a thing about what had transpired on stage.

But what she had been thinking about was far more important than an evening of casual entertainment.

Aunt Barton eyed her shrewdly. "You've been acting so mysterious this week. Is anything amiss? I heard that Mr. Ashworth was at the house at some dreadfully early hour the other day."

Linette had never told Aunt what had happened at the school. There was no reason to upset her, and everything had been taken care of.

"It was merely a minor Dispensary matter," she lied. "I'm afraid he doesn't realize that the world keeps a different schedule than his."

Mrs. Barton tittered. "These medical men. Always so

wrapped up in their work, they never know the time of day or night."

Linette nodded in agreement. "I think that aptly describes Ashworth's habits."

"Still, he is doing a good job at the Dispensary, from all I hear. Do you still find him so objectionable?"

"Oh no, not at all," Linette said hastily. "I think he's a very dedicated surgeon. Do you realize that he is buying the Howard Street School? It's unfortunate that we can't pay him a salary at the Dispensary. It would make his life more comfortable."

Aunt looked thoughtful. "Hmmm. That is something I have never considered. But don't you fear that the medical men would be insulted at such a thing?"

"I think that most of them would be glad to have a few extra coins in their pocket."

"Perhaps I shall discuss this with the board at the next meeting."

"I've been giving thought to some other ways we can help the doctors," Linette said. "Many people have medical problems that aren't serious enough to be treated at the Dispensary, but are still bothersome. What if we established a time each week for the doctors to treat these minor ailments? It would do much to improve the general health of the community."

"Do you think the doctors would be willing?"

"If they were paid for their time, I don't think they'd have any objections."

"Can the Dispensary afford such a thing?"

Linette leaned forward eagerly. "I'm sure the money can be found. And this would do so much to expand the good work of the Dispensary."

She watched with growing assurance as her aunt considered the matter. The Board of Governors would have to give final approval for the project, but if Aunt was behind it, approval was a foregone conclusion.

"I think," Mrs. Barton said, at last, "that you should

discuss the matter with the doctors and surgeons. If they show an interest, I will pursue this."

Linette barely restrained herself from hugging her aunt. In no time at all, she'd have Stephen Ashworth face-to-face with the kind of people who could convince him that there was more to medicine than pure science. That it was the patients, after all, who were the most important part of medicine.

In the morning, Linette took the carriage to the Dispensary. She'd arranged for Mary and Amy to meet her and together they would go to Ashworth's office, where she'd show them how to measure the windows. Then they'd go to the drapers' warehouses and buy the material. Everything could be cut by this afternoon and be ready to sew.

They were both waiting for her when she arrived at her small office.

Linette smiled at their eagerness as she unlocked her office door. "I have a sewing project for the both of you. We'll be making draperies for the windows in Mr. Ashworth's office."

"Ashworth doesn't have an office," Amy said.

"I meant his office at the medical school."

Mary looked reluctant. "The school where they cut people up?"

Linette felt sympathy for her distaste. "Unfortunately, they do use human subjects for dissection. I'm as appalled by the prospect as you are. But we won't go anywhere near that room. We'll measure the windows as quickly as we can, and be gone."

"I don't know ..."

"This will be a valuable experience," Linette said with an encouraging smile. "I don't want just any pupil to help me with this special project. I know you two are the best."

Amy gave her a sly glance. "Will we be getting paid for our trouble?"

"Goodness, yes. That was my purpose." Linette smiled. "Think of it as your first job."

"We'll go then," Mary said, linking arms with Amy.

Grabbing her basket of sewing supplies, Linette led them outside, where the carriage waited. They climbed in and drove off toward Great Howard Street.

Linette knew Ashworth would be lecturing until eleven, so they wouldn't encounter him. She didn't want to challenge their newfound truce too strongly yet. He'd agreed to the project, but she didn't want to test his enthusiasm.

She had no intention of mentioning her new plan to him until the Board of Governors approved the idea. She didn't want Ashworth to raise any objections ahead of time. It was better to take him by surprise.

Amy and Mary followed Linette into the building with marked disquiet. She ushered them into Ashworth's office and closed the door.

"Here we are," she said brightly, pointing to the windows. "There is our project."

Amy looked about the disordered office. " 'Tis not so grand a place for a doctor."

"Surgeon." Linette sighed. "I fear Mr. Ashworth isn't a very tidy man, and he doesn't pay much attention to his own comfort. If I hadn't proposed putting up draperies, I doubt he would have thought of such a thing."

Amy squinted at the books in the case. "Look at the size of these. D'you suppose 'e's read 'em all?"

Linette set out her supplies. "I am certain he has. Medical men must be very learned, you know." She picked up her measuring tape and handed it to the girl.

They completed their work in a short time and Linette was packing up her materials when the door opened and Ashworth strode in. He stopped suddenly at the sight of them.

"What are you doing here?" he demanded, his dark eyes examining Linette with his customary penetrating look.

She stared back. "You're supposed to be in lecture now."

"I stopped early, to give them more time in the dissecting room today." He gave Mary and Amy a curious glance. "Are you planning to clean the dissecting room after all?"

Linette smiled. "We are here to measure your windows. For the curtains."

"Ah, yes, the curtains." He sat down at the desk and pulled out some papers. "You can get on with your work; I have plenty to keep me busy."

His abrupt dismissal irritated Linette. "We wouldn't dream of disrupting you."

He gave her a sharp glance and set the papers on his desk. "All right, Miss Gregory, what is the problem now?"

"Have you given any consideration to a color?" Linette looked dubiously at the dull, faded walls. "Something less in keeping with the character of the room. Bright yellow would be cheering."

"I hate that color."

"What about red? A deep, scarlet red would look nice."

"To remind me of the blood I deal with elsewhere?" Ashworth laughed. "No thank you, Miss Gregory."

Linette flushed. "Green?"

Ashworth looked thoughtful. "Green. Yes, I think that might do. But dark green, not some hideous, fashionable color."

"I would never think to give you *fashionable* draperies, Mr. Ashworth," she replied tartly.

He laughed again. "You are learning, Miss Gregory, you are learning. Now, what else can I help you with? You must need to hang the blasted things from something."

"I'll take care of that." Linette smiled with sweet sarcasm. "I don't want to cause you any inconvenience. We will do all the work when you are gone."

"I appreciate that." He pulled open a drawer and drew out a thin book, holding it out to her with an apologetic smile. "If you would be so kind . . . ?"

Linette took the volume from him. Another French work. "I'll add this to my stack."

"Now, I don't want this to be an imposition . . ."

Linette gritted her teeth, knowing he didn't worry about that in the least. He could keep her as busy as he wished, but it wouldn't discourage her from her main goal. "Oh, I enjoy the challenge. In fact, my French will be so improved that I think I will suggest to my aunt that we visit Paris in the spring."

"I'll give you a list of books to purchase for me," Ashworth said, and stood. "Since you are finished, let me walk you and your lovely assistants to the door."

Amy giggled and Linette shot her a dampening look. Ashworth followed them to the door and down the steps. Linette wondered if he planned to hold the door open for them as well, but the coachman was there before him.

She wished Ashworth would decide whether to be rude or gallant. His changing behavior rattled her, for she never knew what to expect.

Except that he would keep surprising her. Well, she had a few surprises of her own planned. She would see how well he dealt with *those*.

By Saturday, the draperies were finished. While Ashworth worked at the Dispensary, Linette sent Nate and Jim over to the school with a ladder to put up the curtain rods. Then, as Amy and Mary helped, they hung the dark green velvet curtains.

Stepping back, Linette admired their work. "They look perfect," she exclaimed. "You two ladies did a wonderful job."

Mary beamed at the praise.

" 'T'weren't nearly so hard as sewin' a shirt," Amy said. "I'd rather make draperies any day."

That gave Linette an idea. "Perhaps that's what we should do for our first commercial venture."

"But what about bein' a fancy dressmaker?" Mary asked.

"Oh, that is still a good plan. But those who have trouble with the fancier stitching can probably manage draperies. We can approach the subscribers first, then gain recommendations to their friends . . ."

"You think enough people are gonna want curtains?" Amy looked doubtful.

"Everyone needs curtains," Linette said firmly. She smiled at Nate and Jim. "Now, you two take the ladder back to the Dispensary in the cart. We'll follow in the carriage."

"We'll be takin' the ladies with us," Jim said, putting an arm around Amy's waist. She didn't pull away.

Linette frowned. "I really think—"

"It's all right," Mary said quickly. "I'll keep an eye on them two."

Jim snickered and Mary turned on him. "You watch yourself, Jimmy Boggs."

Suppressing a smile, Linette watched as Nate took down the ladder and the two men carried it out to the cart.

Walking back into Ashworth's office, Linette inspected the curtains again. Did one side seem a trifle longer than the other? She looked up to see if the problem lay with the curtain pole, or the hem, but she couldn't tell. And the clatter of hooves from the street outside told her that Nate and Jim had just driven off with the ladder.

Perhaps if she climbed up on Ashworth's desk, she'd have a better perspective.

Moving the chair over, she used it to climb onto Ashworth's desk, but the angle was still wrong. With an unladylike oath, Linette scrambled down, dragged the other chair over and hefted it onto the desk, and climbed atop it.

The pole was slightly atilt. But if she adjusted the hem she doubted Ashworth would even—

"What in God's name are you doing?"

She stared, horrified, as Ashworth stood framed in the doorway, looking at her with such a shocked expression that she felt like the bearded lady at the fair.

"I was examining your curtains," she replied with as much dignity as she could muster.

"Get down before you kill yourself."

Hopping down to the desktop, Linette put out a foot to step onto the chair. But in her haste, she came down too far to one side and the chair toppled over, tumbling her onto the floor. She fell with a thud, cracking her elbow and landing on her stomach.

"Don't move!" Ashworth sprang to her side. "Are you hurt?"

Stunned, Linette tried to take a breath but she couldn't. Her panic rose as she gasped for air.

"Relax," Stephen said. "You've just knocked the wind out of yourself."

Struggling to calm herself, Linette sucked in air and soon the terrible ache in her chest went away. She tried to roll over but he put a hand on her back, pinning her to the floor.

"I said don't move. I want to make sure you aren't injured."

"My elbow hurts," she said.

She felt the gentle touch of his hands as he carefully probed her arm.

"Did you hit your head?"

"No."

He touched her left elbow. "Is this the one that hurts?"

"No, it's the other—Ow!" She twisted her head and gave him a baleful stare after he touched the sore joint. "You're supposed to be helping, not hurting."

"I want you to roll over, but very carefully."

Linette rolled to her left and struggled into a sitting position.

Ashworth knelt at her feet, rotating her ankles. "No pain here?" he asked, without looking up.

"No. I told you before, it's my elbow that hurts," Linette snapped. Was the man deaf?

"You can't always tell," he said, and ran his hands slowly up her calf.

Even padded as she was by skirt, petticoat, and stocking, the intimate touch still sent a delicious tingle up her spine. When he reached her knee and flexed first one and then the other, she had to bite down on her lip to suppress her reaction.

But as his hand inched up her thigh, she jerked away. "What do you think you're doing?" she demanded heatedly.

"Ascertaining whether you have any broken bones," he replied.

"Well, I don't. Unless it's my elbow. Kindly confine your inspection to there."

He sat back on his haunches, an inscrutable look in his dark eyes. "Do you think I'm trying to take advantage of you in this situation?"

"I don't know what to think," she said.

Ashworth laughed. "I assure you, Miss Gregory, I have better things to than to fondle a foolish young lady who's tumbled onto my office floor."

"It's a pity I didn't kill myself. I know you'd enjoy exploring my *dead* body."

He arched a brow. "My dear girl, I may be a surgeon but I still prefer my women warm—and breathing."

Her cheeks flamed and Stephen grinned at her embarrassment. "Now, let me see that elbow."

She held her arm out stiffly.

He pinched the merino fabric between his fingers. "I'm afraid I can't tell much with all those layers of cloth in the way. I shall have to cut your sleeve off."

"No! That's a criminal waste of a gown."

"Well, there is an alternative, but I didn't want to offend your gentler sensibilities."

She looked at him, her eyes widening as she caught his meaning. "I am not going to take off my clothes," she said with marked indignation.

"Did I ask you to?" His grin widened. "I merely want you to slip your arm out of the sleeve."

"No."

"Good God. I'm a surgeon. Your elbow is the only part of your anatomy I'm interested in and I can't examine it when it's swaddled in layers of clothing."

She nibbled her lower lip nervously. "Promise?"

"Promise what?" he asked with growing exasperation. "That I won't be so inflamed by the sight of your naked arm that I'll fling myself upon you?"

Linette looked at him, then smiled. "I am being foolish, aren't I?"

"In the extreme," he replied. "Now, can you unfasten your gown one-handed, or will you need my help?"

"Your help," she whispered in a throaty voice.

Chapter 10

Linette sat in frozen silence as Stephen fumbled with the tiny buttons on the back of her dress. Not from excessive modesty, or fear of jarring her injured elbow, but to suppress the delighted shivers that ran down her spine each time he touched her.

"Can you pull your arm out now?" he asked when he'd reached the buttons at her waist.

Linette tried to slide her arm from the sleeve, gasping involuntarily at the stabbing pain in her elbow. "No," she said, her voice barely a whisper.

Stephen brusquely pushed the gown off her left shoulder. "If you pull this arm out first, it should be easier to free the other."

With his help, she struggled out of the first sleeve, tensing each time his fingers brushed against her. She didn't care if he was a surgeon, he was also a man. A very attractive man, who was assisting her in removing her clothes. The thought was both thrilling and frightening.

Stephen must have seen some of the confusion in her eyes, for he gave her an encouraging smile as he reached for her right hand. "I'll try to be as gentle as possible," he said.

He lifted her arm, halting immediately at her soft gasp.

"Go ahead," she said with a wan smile. "Too late to turn back now."

Stephen carefully pulled her arm free of the sleeve. The bodice of her dress fell forward, puddling in her lap.

Truly embarrassed now, Linette kept her eyes lowered, jumping when she felt the warm heat of his fingers on her shoulder. Glancing up, she saw the look of concern in his dark brown eyes.

"I need to examine your arm," he said, his voice sounding strangely thick to her ears. "I'll be gentle."

Sitting up straighter, Linette closed her eyes and took a deep breath, fighting against the tempting thrill of his touch.

He ran his hand down the curve of her shoulder, sending her skin tingling. As his fingers brushed her bare arm, a sharp jolt of electricity shot through her body. Biting her lower lip, Linette tried to distract herself from the pleasurable onslaught. She didn't want to feel this way, didn't want to respond to Stephen's touch.

But she couldn't help herself, couldn't deny what she felt. Stephen ran his fingers lightly down her forearm and Linette bit down harder on her lip to keep from crying out. Not from pain, but from pleasure. Never could she have imagined that he would make her feel like this.

He clasped her elbow, flexing it carefully, and she sucked in her breath at the sudden pain. That stab of discomfort broke the spell and she was in control of herself again.

Frowning, he gave her a cautious look. "Does it hurt to move your fingers?"

Linette wiggled them carefully, and shook her head. She stifled a sigh of relief when he gently set her hand back in her lap.

"I don't think anything's broken," Stephen said at last. "You may have chipped the bone, but it's more likely a severe bruise, possibly with some strained ligaments."

"Is that bad?" she asked anxiously. "Will it take long to heal?"

"I haven't heard of anyone dying from this yet," he

said dryly. "Your elbow may be stiff for a few days, but there shouldn't be any lasting damage."

Linette bowed her head thankfully. She could imagine what Aunt would say when she heard about this incident. At least the damage was temporary. "What should I do for it?"

He shrugged. "Not much. You can put it into a sling if you find that more comfortable, but it's not necessary."

Linette's laugh was shaky. "In other words, we've both made a fuss over nothing."

An odd expression crept over his face. "Oh, I wouldn't say that. One can't be too careful." He gave her a stern look. "Which you certainly weren't when I came in here. What in God's name were you doing?"

"The draperies were crooked."

"Idiot," he mumbled softly.

The warm expression in his eyes held her still for several long seconds until she dropped her gaze in confusion. If she hadn't known better, she would almost think he felt more than a medical concern for her. But that was impossible. . . .

Looking down, Linette was reminded that she was still sitting here, half dressed, in front of him. She grabbed for her sleeve. "I need to get dressed."

"I'll help you," he said, and before she could protest he lifted her injured arm and drew the sleeve over it again.

Hastily, Linette pulled on her dress, but she was helpless to fasten it by herself. Mutely, she turned her back to him.

"Is there a reason these blasted buttons are so small?" he demanded crossly as he worked to refasten her dress.

"Not many men act as ladies' maids," she retorted, trying to mask her nervousness. Every time his fingers brushed against her back she reveled at the warm, gentle strength of his hands.

He finished the last button and gave her a pat on the

shoulder, then helped her to her feet. "There you are. All respectable again."

Linette blushed and turned away, seeking to regain her composure. "I would appreciate it greatly if you say nothing of this. . . ."

Stephen laughed wryly.

"This was such a trifling injury, Miss Gregory, that I would be embarrassed to admit that I was called in. Consider the matter forgotten."

Not sure if she was pleased or annoyed by his words, Linette reached for her cloak, only to be caught up short by the pain in her elbow.

Stephen grabbed the heavy garment and set it around her shoulders. "I'll get the rest of your things. That's your aunt's coachman outside, isn't it? I'll have a word with him—I want you to go straight home."

"You don't need to talk with him."

"Oh, but I insist." He smiled widely. "You're my patient and must follow my orders."

"I thought you said this was a 'trifling injury'?"

"Only for *my* medical skills. A pity it didn't require amputation . . ." His eyes brightened mischievously. "Although it would be a shame to ruin such a shapely arm."

Linette felt her cheeks flame. "You said you wouldn't notice anything except my elbow!"

"I may be a surgeon, but I'm not dead, Miss Gregory." He held the office door open, a wide grin on his face. "Believe me, I know the difference between an attractive arm and an ugly one."

She flounced past him into the hall. He dashed to open the front door, then hurried down the steps to hand her into the waiting carriage.

"There is no need for you to accompany me," she said when he put his foot on the step.

"How else will I know that you followed my orders?"

"You'll just have to trust me," she said. "Good day, Mr. Ashworth."

He started to shut the door but she suddenly cried out, "Wait!" and he pulled it open again.

Linette leaned forward. "What do I owe you for your services?"

Stephen shook his head. "Consider it a professional courtesy, Miss Gregory."

"I insist on paying for your time." She reached for her reticule. "What do you charge your patients?"

Ignoring her, he firmly shut the door and motioned for the coachman to drive away.

Linette leaned back against the cushions, more shaken by the afternoon's events than she wished to admit.

She didn't want to be attracted to Stephen Ashworth, but her reaction today showed her how futile that wish was. She'd practically melted beneath his fingers.

What would happen if he ever kissed her?

Linette was afraid to find out. She knew she'd be hopelessly lost if he did.

Taking a deep breath, Stephen slowly walked back inside the building.

He hadn't lied to her—completely. He *had* needed to examine her arm, needed her clothing out of the way.

But he had lied in telling her that he wouldn't be affected by the sight of her in that delightful state of undress. From the moment she'd agreed to the examination, his pulse had been racing.

He'd never responded this way to a patient before.

Of course, he wasn't accustomed to treating attractive young ladies. The patients he'd seen as a student, and those he saw at the Dispensary, came from the poorer classes. It was easy to maintain a clinical detachment when you were treating a blowzy matron with a suppurating sore.

It required more concentration than even he possessed to ignore the smooth, shapely flesh of Linette Gregory. Just the remembrance of the feel of her soft, silky skin sent his blood boiling.

It had been a monumental struggle to keep himself detached, aloof. Thank God he'd been able to keep his urges in check. She didn't know how much he'd enjoyed touching her heated skin, how his gaze had wandered to the gentle swell of her breasts.

He shouldn't have been affected so. Any evening gown uncovered more skin, and as an anatomist, he was familiar with all the parts of the female form.

But for the first time ever, he had lost his ability to be objective about a patient. He was acutely aware that it was Linette's skin he examined for bruises, Linette's bones he felt for breaks. There had been a moment, when he clasped her tiny wrist in his fingers, and traced the delicate bones in her hand, that he almost forgot to breathe.

She was the last woman on earth he wanted to be attracted to. Yet he was forced to admit that he was, and the realization didn't please him. There was no place for her in his life; he didn't need the distraction or the drain on his precious time.

And he didn't need her objections to his work.

It was clear he needed to see less of Linette Gregory. He didn't want to be tempted like this again.

A strange restlessness plagued Stephen the following morning. He needed to work on his book—the sooner he delivered it to the publisher, the sooner he would be paid—but he simply couldn't concentrate. Instead of focusing on leg dissection techniques, his mind kept picturing other, more pleasing images: ridiculously small buttons running down the back of a dark blue dress, the white lace edging around the sleeve of a chemise, the feel of soft, warm flesh beneath his fingertips.

Stephen slammed his pen down with disgust and pushed back his chair. At this rate, it would take years to finish the book. Maybe a brisk walk would clear his head. He could go as far as Spa Fields and come back refreshed and ready to work.

Pulling on his coat, he hastened down the stairs and stepped out into the biting November air. He might even treat himself to coffee and a bun when he reached the Spa.

He fully intended to do that. But at each street crossing, he was drawn inexorably westward, until he'd passed the Fields entirely and found himself on the edge of Somers Town. He was a few streets away from Fitzroy Square, and the Barton house.

He had not intended to see her today—in fact, he had resolved to keep away from her. But as a conscientious practitioner, he should look in on his patient, making certain that the elbow was as lightly injured as he'd first thought. Sometimes, with joints, it was difficult to tell for a day or two. If it had grown swollen and tender during the night . . .

They would call in their own medical man if it had.

Stephen didn't relish the humiliation of discovering his diagnosis had not been correct. If he looked in briefly and made certain that nothing untoward had developed, he would still have time to stop at the Spa on his way home.

In scant moments, he found himself lifting the brass knocker on the Barton door. He remembered the last time he'd called, when he'd confronted her about the break-in at the school. She'd come straight from bed, her soft gray eyes still filled with sleep. The sight had taken his breath away.

The butler ushered him into the hall, took his coat, and led Stephen back toward the rear drawing room, where he'd attended the Dispensary tea on the day he met Linette.

"Mr. Stephen Ashworth," the butler intoned in a somber voice, holding the door open for him.

Linette sat in a chair near the window, a warm shawl about her shoulders, a book on her lap, and a cup of tea on the table beside her. At her look of pleased surprise,

Stephen felt an unexpected surge of pleasure, which he quickly dampened.

"Mr. Ashworth, how nice of you to call." She held out her hand—her left one, he noticed.

Stephen stood awkwardly, just inside the doorway. "I thought to inquire about your health."

"Then the least I can do is offer you a cup of tea." She looked past him to the butler. "Tea, Mallon."

"Yes, ma'am."

"Please, sit down." Linette pointed to the chair next to her. "I appreciate your concern."

Feeling more foolish with each passing moment, Stephen perched gingerly on the edge of the mahogany chair. "How is your elbow today?"

"Most vexatious, I assure you. I cannot sew, or write, or even lift my teacup." Laughing wryly, she pointed to the book in her lap. "I fear reading is the only thing I can do."

"Is it bruised? Are there any signs of swelling?"

She shook her head. "No, it merely hurts whenever I move it. I will be of little use to my sewing class tomorrow."

"It should feel better soon," he said and tried to look encouraging.

Coming here had been a big mistake. Seeing her again, so soon, brought all those enticing images flooding back into his brain. He couldn't look at her without envisioning the soft curve of her nape, or the gently rounded slope of her shoulder.

Thank God she appeared perfectly calm. If she had displayed any trace of embarrassment, Stephen would have fled the room. She was reacting in the way he should, treating the incident as a medical examination, nothing more.

"Did you decide if you like the curtains?" she asked.

Puzzled, Stephen stared at her for a moment until he remembered. She had been checking the curtains when she'd fallen. He couldn't even recall what they looked like. He'd been too concerned about her to even notice.

An accusing look crept over her face. "You didn't even look at them, did you? And to think I nearly killed myself trying to make them hang perfectly."

"I promise to examine them with great care tomorrow," he said.

To his relief, the butler arrived with the tea tray. Stephen's eyes lit at the sight of the biscuits and tiny cakes as his stomach reminded him that he hadn't bothered to eat that morning.

"Hungry?" she asked in a teasing tone.

"Starving." Without hesitating, he crammed one of the tea cakes into his mouth. "I forget to eat when I'm working."

"Dare I ask what you were working on—although if it involves dead bodies, I don't want to know."

Stephen reached for another cake. "I'm trying to finish the draft of my book."

"I would think an anatomy guide for students would sell well."

He grinned. "I hope so. As does my publisher."

A shy smile crossed her face. "I bought a copy of your work on lithotomy."

Stephen laughed. "Are you planning to take up surgery?"

"Not at all." She took a sip of tea. "I was interested because you wrote it."

"Have you read it?"

She blushed a becoming shade of pink. "No."

"Don't. You'll find it excruciatingly boring."

He saw her stiffen at his words. "Because I wouldn't understand it?"

"Because it's poorly written."

She gave him an arch look. "I find it hard to believe that you would allow yourself to do anything poorly."

Laughing, Stephen refilled his cup. "My attempts at modesty won't wash with you, eh?"

"Modest is the *last* word I would use to describe you."

He raised a brow. "Oh? What would you say?"

"Confident—to the point of being arrogant. Determined. Dedicated. Hardworking."

"You flatter me."

She smiled. "I could add opinionated, stubborn, and abrasive, but I wouldn't want you to think I was being critical."

Leaning back in his chair, he eyed her carefully. "While you would describe yourself as compliant, demure, submissive, and dutiful?"

Her eyes crinkled with laughter. "Touché. I fear we have more than a few traits in common."

That beguiling smile hit him like a sharp blow to the chest. Draining the last of his tea, he sprang to his feet.

"I have work to do." Giving her a curt bow, he turned to the door.

"You wouldn't accept payment yesterday," she said. "But perhaps you will allow me to reimburse you in another manner. Is there a piece of equipment or a book you need?"

"I'll accept the curtains as payment, since they were the cause of your injury."

"But I've already given you those. It must be something else."

"The curtains will do."

Linette smiled ruefully. "I see you are as stubborn as ever." She held out her hand. "Thank you for coming."

He took her hand briefly. "Good day, Miss Gregory."

Stephen let out a low moan of frustration when he stepped into the street. It was becoming increasingly impossible to maintain his emotional detachment in her presence.

All the more reason to avoid her as much as possible. Now that the curtains were hung, she had no reason to be at the school. And now that he knew her elbow was not seriously hurt, he had no reason to see her. Unless they had business to discuss at the Dispensary, they had no reason to meet.

Except when she brought him her translations.

Stephen was glad she could read French.

Linette felt sadly deflated after Stephen left. His visit had been a pleasant surprise. She'd feared he would be as embarrassed as she about what had happened yesterday. But his cool demeanor today showed that he didn't give a thought to the incident.

Unlike her. It had taken all her willpower to appear calm before him, when she wanted to blush crimson and race from the room. Even now, she could feel those strong, warm fingers caressing her arm, sending sensations that she didn't wish to acknowledge racing through her body.

If she'd known the result, she never would have let him touch her. And worse, he obviously had not been affected in the same way.

Or had he?

He might have been making a simple, professional call, making certain that she hadn't suffered any ill effects. It was a considerate thing to do—more considerate than she would have expected of him. Perhaps Stephen Ashworth wasn't as unfeeling as she'd first thought. It showed he *did* care about his patients.

Did he care about her?

She suddenly wished he hadn't come. The turmoil that she'd struggled against during the night returned full force. How could she be attracted to a man whose philosophies she abhorred? A man she disagreed with on the most elemental aspects of medicine, and life.

Yet she couldn't get him out of her mind. Stephen could be brusque and arrogant, yet his touch was gentle and tender. He trafficked with resurrectionists, yet stuffed tea cakes into his mouth like a sweets-starved child. He labored daily over dead bodies, yet was human enough to have admired the shape of her arm.

Stephen Ashworth had no place in her grand plans. The schools and clinics that she wanted to fund required money, and he'd cheerfully confessed he had none. Yet no wonder his finances were in such dire straits; he'd refused payment for treating her.

She determined anew to find him more paying patients. Stephen Ashworth would never be a wealthy surgeon, but the least she could do was steer him toward a more comfortable existence. It was one way she could thank him for treating her.

If only she could deal with her reactions so neatly.

Chapter 11

[faded text from previous page bleeding through, partially legible]

Three nights later, Stephen sat hunched over the table in his rooms, rewriting his chapter on the arm, when a furious pounding sounded on his door.

Instantly, he jumped to his feet, remembering the last time he'd been so rudely interrupted. Pray there wasn't a problem at the school again. Jerking open the door, he saw Smith standing before him, and Stephen's heart sank. The lad was on night duty at the school; something must have happened.

The boy was red-faced and gasping for breath. "You've got to come right away. The lady says she's dyin'."

Stephen grabbed Smith by the coat and hauled him into the room. "Who's dying?"

Clutching the door frame for support, Smith struggled to speak. "I don't know. But Miss Gregory wants you—she sent this note. I ran all the way."

He shoved a crumpled piece of paper into Stephen's hand. Unfolding it, he quickly scanned the contents.

Ashworth—come at once. I think Amy's dying and you must save her. Linette

An address was scratched at the bottom. Stephen recognized it as being a few blocks from the Dispensary.

Dying. Stephen scrambled to get his instruments together. Why couldn't Linette have been more specific? He didn't know if he needed an amputation saw or opium, and he wasn't certain he had either one here. He wasn't often called out on emergencies and most of his equipment was at the school.

After tossing what medical supplies he had into a bag, Stephen grabbed Smith's arm and pulled him out the door and down the stairs. "You're coming with me—I might need you to run back to the school for more instruments."

"But I'm supposed to be on guard tonight."

Stephen gave him a dark glare. "What's more important, Smith—a young lady's life, or a building?"

"A life," Smith stammered.

Stephen clapped him on the back. "Now you're thinking."

It took only scant moments to hail a hackney and in less time than he could have imagined, they arrived at the address on Linette's note. Stephen flung a coin at the driver, and raced into the building, Smith a few steps behind him.

A young girl—five or six at the most—stood on the stairs. "Be you the doctor?"

Stephen nodded and the girl pointed a finger up the stairs. "Second floor, to the right. They's waitin'."

As he bounded up the rickety stairs, Stephen felt the familiar mix of anticipation and dread rising in him. He didn't know what awaited him, but it certainly wouldn't be the orderly procedures of the operating theater. There, he was in control. Here . . . he could only guess at what he'd have to do.

A door on the landing stood ajar and he peered inside. An elderly lady grabbed his hand and drew him in. "The doctor's here," she called.

Linette Gregory came out of the back room and raced toward him, grabbing his hand as she drew him toward the far door. "Stephen, thank God you came. Amy's bleeding and I can't stop it. You've got to help."

Hearing the desperation in her voice, Stephen gently squeezed her hand, seeking to reassure her. "I'll do whatever I can," he said softly. Then he glanced down. The hand he clasped was covered in blood.

She drew him into a dimly lit bedroom, where an ashen-faced girl lay on a lumpy mattress. Stephen recognized her as one of the girls who'd helped with the curtains only a few days ago.

There was blood everywhere, on her nightrail and the sheets, and crimson-streaked cloths littered the floor. Amy was obviously bleeding badly. He clenched his jaw. This was not going to be a pleasant evening.

He took her limp hand in his. "What happened?" he asked.

"The baby . . ." she whispered.

Stephen swore under his breath. The girl was pregnant and this was a uterine hemorrhage. "How far along?" he demanded.

Linette leaned over his shoulder. "She says four months."

"Did she try to get rid of it?"

There was a feeble wave of protest from Amy. "I din't, 'onest."

Linette lay a soothing hand on her forehead. "We know you didn't, Amy. Mr. Ashworth is here and he'll make things better."

Wishing he shared Linette's confidence, Stephen stepped away from the bed and beckoned to Smith, who lingered in the doorway.

"I need ergot, fast." He looked at Linette. "Is there a chemist anywhere near?"

She shook her head. "I don't think so."

"Go to the Dispensary then—there should be some in the apothecary's room. *Ergot of rye*. Bring the entire bottle. I also need some rum—is there any in the house?"

"You want a drink?" Linette's shocked voice echoed through the room.

"It's for the patient," Stephen snapped. "Rum, gin, anything you can find." He glared at Smith, who stood uncertainly at the door. "Well, go, man. This girl's not going to wait."

"I don't know where the Dispensary is."

Stephen gave an irritated snort. "Oh, for God's sake. Who can take him to the Dispensary?"

"I'll do it." Linette moved toward the outer door.

"No, I need you here." Stephen remembered the woman who'd let him in. "Is that Amy's mother out there?"

"A neighbor," Linette replied. "Her mother is next door."

"Well, have her find someone to take Smith to the Dispensary—and bring him back as well. I don't want him wandering lost around Shoreditch for hours. I need that medicine."

Smith had started down the stairs with the recruited escort when Stephen dashed after him. "Opium. Don't forget the opium."

"What preparation?"

"I don't care what kind—bring whatever you can find."

He reentered the apartment. Linette clutched at his sleeve, her face drawn and pale.

"What can I do?"

"Get me those spirits."

"Can you stop the bleeding?"

Stephen sighed. "I don't know," he said, being brutally honest. But it was best she know, from the start.

Her mouth sagged open. "You mean she might . . . ?"

"Get me the liquor," he said, pushing past her into the bedroom.

Amy's pulse was rapid and her breathing shallow. Bending down, he examined the bed and towels, trying to judge how much blood she'd lost. If he could stop the bleeding, she *might* have a chance. But he had to work fast.

Pray that Smith returned quickly with the ergot.

He didn't attempt to examine her further, fearing that

it might increase the bleeding. All he could do right now was watch and wait.

Watch and wait. He itched to leap into action, but he was as helpless here as Linette. There was no procedure he could perform, no surgery he could undertake that was going to help this girl. The ergot was the only thing that would do the trick, and right now even that looked doubtful.

If he had more experience with childbirth . . . but Stephen doubted even a trained *accoucheur* could do anything for this girl. Surgeons could excise tumors, and remove kidney stones, and even diseased gall bladders, but with the other internal workings, they were helpless. Surgery here would only hasten Amy's death.

Linette thrust a bottle into his hand. "Gin. It's all I could find."

"Pour some in a cup and try to get her to drink a little," he said. "Use a spoon to administer it—I don't want her to even move her head."

After running to get a spoon, Linette sat on the side of the bed and carefully dribbled the liquid into Amy's mouth. Stephen watched her intently, making certain that she swallowed and didn't choke. The alcohol would stimulate her system and give her strength.

Smith had to get back here soon with the medicine.

Stephen cautiously checked the bloody cloths wadded between Amy's legs. He thought the blood looked darker, as if it were drying. Good. Maybe the bleeding had stopped on its own. He prayed it was true.

"What else can I do?" Linette leaned close.

"Hold her hand," he replied in a low tone. "There isn't anything more I can do until the medicine arrives. You could mix up some sugar water—two teaspoons or so in a cup."

"Shouldn't we change the cloths?"

He shook his head. "If the bleeding's stopped on its own, that might start it again. Later, after the ergot's had time to work, I'll check."

She gave him an anxious look. "Can she afford to lose this much blood?"

Stephen didn't answer. Linette turned away and gave Amy a few more spoonfuls of gin.

Running a hand through his hair, Stephen tried to quell his rising frustration. He was a surgeon; he was used to taking action. Sitting and waiting was more than he could bear.

But there wasn't anything a surgeon could do for this girl.

He watched as Linette tenderly held Amy's hand in her own. She looked exhausted and Stephen wondered how long she'd been here before he'd arrived. "Does your aunt know you're here?"

She shook her head. "I left immediately when Amy's brother came. But I did leave her a note."

"There should be someone at the Dispensary during the night, for emergencies like this," he said. "I meant to suggest that to you. Some of my students might be willing to do that."

"But that won't help Amy tonight, will it?"

"No." He watched her for a moment, then put a hand on her shoulder, giving it a light squeeze. "She has the best nurse in the city. It will help."

Linette attempted a weak smile. Stephen was here now, he was taking action, and as soon as that student returned with the medicine, Amy would be better.

She *had* to get better.

Stephen had stripped off his coat and now sat across the bed from her, his sleeves rolled up, checking Amy's pulse.

Just his competent presence made Linette feel better. She'd felt so helpless to staunch the flow of blood, helpless to offer any comfort to Amy's distraught mother. Linette's first thought had been to send for Stephen. Somehow, she'd managed to remain calm until he arrived and took the burden from her shoulders.

With a start, Linette realized just how relieved she was to have someone else take charge. It was an odd sensation; she prided herself on her independence, her ability to deal with any situation. But Linette knew she was helpless here; only Stephen could make a difference.

And surprisingly, she didn't mind relying on him. There was something comforting in that knowledge, leaving a warm feeling inside her despite the agonizing worry over Amy.

It was almost as if—Linette shoved that thought from her mind. She should concentrate her attention on Amy. Linette poured a few drops of rosewater on the handkerchief and tenderly wiped Amy's brow.

She glanced up and saw Stephen watching her with an unfamiliar warmth in his dark eyes. Hastily, Linette lowered her gaze as a blush crossed her cheeks.

Amy, she reminded herself. We are here to save Amy.

It seemed like hours before Smith returned, the precious bottle of ergot tucked under his arm. "I've got it," he gasped. "And the opium."

Stephen jumped to his feet, relieved he could at last take some action. Measuring out twenty grains of the powder, he stirred it into the sugar water Linette had prepared.

"She needs to drink all of this. Do you want me to give it to her?"

"No, I will." Linette took the cup from him and began spooning the mixture into Amy's mouth.

Clasping Amy's wrist lightly between his fingers, Stephen checked her pulse. It was weakening; the ergot hadn't arrived a moment too soon. But if all went well, the contractions it promoted would halt the bleeding.

Once again, he had to wait. He racked his brain to remember the exact interval between doses. Half an hour? An hour? He'd only had one class in midwifery, and even that was more training than most surgeons received. There had been a slew of ergot articles in *The*

Lancet during the last year, but he couldn't recall the details. He'd have to rely on his observations, and Amy's condition.

Stephen clenched his fists as he stared down at the deathly pale girl. Should he admit defeat and call in a physician? But what else could anyone do? The ergot was the only treatment available. It *had* to work.

He checked Amy's pulse again but noted no change. Linette finished administering the last of the medicine and stepped away from the bed. Stephen slid forward and put his hand on the girl's forehead. It was cool. Deathly cool.

Her eyes flickered open.

"The medicine will take effect soon," he said, trying to sound encouraging. "Everything will be all right."

Amy nodded faintly at his words and closed her eyes again.

Stephen motioned for Linette to follow him and stepped onto the landing.

She eagerly scanned his face. "How is she?"

He shook his head. "Not good, but there's nothing more I can do. You're welcome to send for a physician, but I fear he'll tell you the same."

"But once the bleeding stops she will be all right, won't she?"

"She's very weak from blood loss," Stephen said slowly. "She may not have the strength to survive."

"There must be something else you can do!"

"The one thing she needs is blood and I can't give her that."

"Why not? You take blood out, can't you put it back in?" Her voice rose in anguish. "Surely, there must be a reverse procedure."

Stephen put his hands on her shoulders. "I can't do that, Linette. No one can. There have been one or two—*one or two*—documented cases of successful blood transfusions. I've never done one; I've never even seen it done. The procedure is far too dangerous."

Tears started rolling down her cheeks. "Amy is dying. You have to help her."

Stephen looked away. Linette needed to help him; she didn't have time for this display of emotion. Reaching in his pocket, he pulled out a handkerchief and handed it to her.

"I can't play God, Linette," he said roughly. "I don't—medicine doesn't—know enough to keep her alive."

She turned away. "If only she hadn't become pregnant ... How could Amy be so foolish?"

Stephen stepped up behind her. "Human nature is what it is. Do you know who the father is?"

"I'm not sure ..." Linette hesitated. "I think it's Jimmy Boggs."

"I suggest you send someone to find him."

Leaving her alone on the landing, Stephen went back into the front room.

He wished he could send Linette home. Stephen wanted to spare her what was coming. Death wasn't a part of her world; she didn't belong here like he did. Yet he knew it would be a hopeless task to convince her of that. But stubborn as she was, he knew she would refuse to go.

Yet he couldn't help but admire Linette's devotion to her student. Another woman would have felt that sending for him fulfilled any obligation, and would have left as soon as he arrived. Instead she had stayed, and helped, and done what she could to comfort the poor girl. Unfortunately, it wasn't going to make a bit of difference.

He shared her despair. He'd never felt so helpless dealing with a case. If it was merely a difficult labor, he'd chance a caesarian. Women survived that. But his surgical skills were useless now.

Stephen sat down and ran a weary hand over his face before pulling out his watch. Ten minutes. He should be seeing some results from the ergot by now. He heaved himself out of the chair and returned to the bedroom, hoping against hope that his patient was responding to the medicine.

He didn't know what he'd do if she didn't.

Chapter 12

Linette remained on the landing, too frozen with grief and despair to move.

Amy—impish, smiling, joking Amy—was going to die. Stephen had virtually said so, admitting he couldn't do anything to save her.

Clenching the worn railing until her fingers hurt, Linette raged at the God who would allow this to happen. It was not fair. Amy was only sixteen. She might not have been the best pupil, but her cheery outlook brightened every class. How could that youthful joy be stilled forever?

Linette felt more than a twinge of guilt as she thought about Amy and Jimmy. She had ignored the situation, thinking it a harmless flirtation. If she had intervened, could this tragedy have been avoided?

Perhaps not. Linette knew how easily the heart led the head. Unbridled passion could lead even the most carefully raised girl astray—and Amy was hardly that.

It didn't matter that she wasn't married. Marriage wouldn't have saved her from this fate, it would only attach the label of respectability to her death.

Respectability. What good was that when a sixteen-year-old girl lay bleeding to death on her bed? Respectability was something that only mattered to others. It was absurd to think that a few words spoken in church made a difference between Amy's death being a terrible tragedy or a sad disgrace.

Brushing back a tear, Linette stared down into the

pitch black stairwell. She didn't want anyone condemning Amy for the manner of her death.

At least the condemnation wouldn't come from this neighborhood. There would be head shaking and admonitions to daughters—and perhaps sons—but no one would think the less of Amy for what had happened. Among her friends, the people who mattered to her, there would be only sadness.

No, the type of people who would condemn her were Aunt's friends, the Dispensary supporters and contributors. She knew how quickly they leaped to condemn those who strayed from their standards.

Standards that were for outward show only. At least in this part of the city, people were more honest.

Sighing, Linette went to find Amy's brother. She'd send him to look for Jimmy.

After dispatching the boy, Linette stepped silently into the bedroom. Stephen perched on the edge of the bed, holding Amy's wrist between his fingers.

His expression was drawn and weary. A lock of dark hair fell down over his face and he brushed it back with his free hand. He needed a haircut, a shave, and a clean shirt, yet Linette thought he'd never looked more handsome. He was here, doing all he could to save a young girl's life.

Turning, he caught her gaze and gave her an encouraging smile. "She's sleeping."

"Is that good?"

Stephen rose and stretched. "It can't hurt—she's exhausted."

"Is the medicine working?"

His expression clouded. "I'm not sure. There should be significant uterine cramping by now, but she isn't showing any sign of pain. I'll wait another five minutes and give her another dose. You might want to get more sugar water ready."

Linette left the room. She'd seen the bleak expression

in his weary eyes and knew he wasn't hopeful. Knew that he fully expected to lose this patient.

How ironic. All her grand plans to provide him with patients and the very first one was dying. If she'd known the situation was so hopeless, she would have called in someone else. But when she had seen Amy, scared and pleading, Linette's first thought was that Stephen could save her.

But however much she wanted him to be, he wasn't a miracle worker. Linette couldn't expect him to achieve the impossible, no matter how skilled and talented he was.

He was right; there were still too many limitations in medical knowledge. Would they ever know enough to save someone in Amy's condition? Or would death and dying always be a part of life, especially a woman's life? Babies would be born and die; women would die birthing them. Both thoughts made Linette sad.

"Where's that water?" she heard Stephen call from the bedroom.

Quickly, she took it to him. She watched as he measured out the powder and stirred it into the cup. Amy's faint chance at life lay within that cup.

"Do you want me to give it to her again?" she asked.

Nodding, Stephen stepped aside to allow her past. Lifting the spoon, Linette poured the liquid into Amy's mouth, but it dribbled down her cheek.

"She can't swallow!"

"Damn." Stephen grabbed his medical bag and pulled out a long brass syringe. Plunging it into the cup, he sucked up a quantity of medicine, then inserted the tube into Amy's mouth, depressing the plunger and releasing the liquid. She gasped and choked—and swallowed. Linette watched in rapt fascination as he squirted the rest of the liquid down Amy's throat.

"Give her a few sips of gin, if she'll take it," he said, turning to put his syringe away. "We need to keep her system stimulated."

He left the room and Linette was able to get a few spoonfuls of gin into Amy before the girl sank back against the pillow. Linette watched anxiously for some sign that her condition was improving—or even changing. How long would it take for the medicine to work—if it ever did?

Linette's eyes were drooping shut when she heard a soft moan, then a startled cry. Amy sat up and grabbed her abdomen, her face contorted in pain.

"Stephen!" Linette shrieked.

Dashing into the bedroom, he pushed Linette aside and placed his hand atop Amy's lower abdomen. Then, with a frown, he reached down and pulled away the cloths bunched between Amy's legs. The blood was dried and brown along the edges, but the center was a bright, brilliant red. Clamping her hand over her mouth, Linette turned from the sight.

Stephen didn't move, but kept his hands on Amy, who moaned constantly, rolling from side to side.

"It 'urts," she moaned.

"Keep her from moving," Stephen barked out. Linette grabbed Amy's hand and smoothed back the hair on her forehead. "Hold still, Amy dear," she murmured soothingly. "You musn't move."

"It 'urts so bad," Amy gasped between moans.

Linette turned pleading eyes on Stephen, but he shook his head. "It's uterine contractions," he said. "It means the ergot's working."

She started to speak, but then closed her mouth. She didn't want to question him in front of Amy; she shouldn't know how dire the situation was. Linette gave the girl's hand a comforting squeeze and wiped her brow with a damp cloth.

The minutes crawled by. Linette darted anxious glances at Stephen, but his expression did not change. At last, he bent over and stuffed more toweling between Amy's legs, and then sat down in a chair to wait.

Pounding footsteps sounded on the stairs and someone dashed into the other room.

"Where is she? I've got to see her." Jimmy Boggs started to run into the bedroom, his face a picture of anguish, but Stephen grabbed him and pulled him back. Linette heard them talking in low tones, then Jimmy came in again, slowly.

Linette got to her feet. "You can take my place," she said, relinquishing Amy's hand to his and stepping out to join Stephen.

In the front room, Stephen paced the floor, his brow furrowed in concentration.

Linette plucked at his sleeve. "How is she?"

He shook his head. "The contractions are a good sign, but she's still bleeding heavily. If it doesn't stop soon, I . . ." He spread his hands in a helpless gesture.

A loud scream came from the other room and Stephen raced into the bedroom, Linette dashing behind him.

Amy writhed on the bed, arms wrapped about her stomach. "Oh, God, I'm dying, I'm dying."

Linette believed her. Amy had kicked the towels away and bright red stains streaked the bedcovers.

"Hold her down," Stephen yelled, grabbing Amy's thrashing legs while Jimmy put his arms around her shoulders, forcing her onto the mattress. "Linette, shake Smith awake and have him make up a draught a quarter grain of acetate of morphine. It's in my bag."

Dashing into the other room, Linette grabbed the sleeping Smith and shook him awake. He hastily made up the medicine and she took it to Stephen.

"Make sure she takes it all," Stephen warned, still firmly holding the girl.

Linette tried to speak in a soothing tone while she held the cup to the girl's lips. "Amy, you must take your medicine. It will make you feel better."

Moaning softly, Amy drank the liquid in slow, gulping motions, draining the cup.

"Wot's that gonna do?" Jimmy demanded.

"Ease the pain and calm her down," Stephen said. He looked sternly at his patient. "Amy, you have to lie still. Every time you move, you start the bleeding again."

She nodded wearily and sank back against the pillow, closing her eyes. Relaxing his hold, Stephen nodded to Jimmy to do the same. Amy remained quiet.

Shaken, Linette dabbed the sweat from Amy's brow, then stumbled back into the front room and sank down onto a chair, burying her face in her hands.

Feeling a hand on her shoulder, she looked up into Stephen's face. His concerned expression warmed her. "You should go home," he said. "You're exhausted."

"I can't leave now." Linette shook her head emphatically. "I wouldn't sleep; I'd be too worried. I'll stay out of the way if you want, but please don't send me away."

Stephen knelt beside her chair, clasping her hand. "I don't want to send you away; you've been a marvelous help. But your aunt must be worried."

"She knows I will stay here."

Patting her hand, Stephen stood and yawned. "Stay then. Amy should sleep now—maybe you can try to do the same."

Linette closed her eyes, knowing she couldn't sleep, but wanting to rest all the same. She would check on Amy again in a few minutes. . . .

Her eyes snapped open when someone squeezed her hand. Blinking in the dim light, she saw Stephen standing beside her.

"She's going," he said softly.

Linette was out of her chair in an instant, brushing past him as she dashed to the bedroom. Jimmy sat at the bedside, holding Amy's hand, while her mother sat on the far side of the room, weeping silently.

"No," Linette whispered, almost to herself. "Oh, please, no."

Stephen's hand on her elbow steadied her.

Linette approached the bed and reached past Jimmy to gently stroke Amy's waxen cheek. Already, the girl felt like death. Sinking to her knees, Linette tried to mumble a few words of prayer. But the words would not come—all she felt was a growing anger at the tragedy.

Stephen must have said something, for suddenly Jimmy cried out and flung himself across the bed, gathering Amy up in his arms. Hardly daring to breathe, Linette glanced at Stephen, who nodded. She bowed her head, the hot tears dripping onto her clenched hands.

Sidling toward the door, Stephen sought to escape the oppressive atmosphere of the death room. He wasn't needed here anymore.

He would have preferred to have left long ago, when he knew there was no more he could do, but he stayed because of Linette. Since she insisted on being here, he was not going to let her go through this alone.

He wasn't accustomed to these lingering deathbed farewells, and he didn't like them. Surgery was quick, fast, and precise. It was usually the physician who stood the deathwatch.

Oh, he'd seen death before—on the wards in his student days, mostly. But for the last year, until he'd started at the Dispensary, he had dealt mainly with the dead. It was easy to view them with clinical detachment—they were no longer living, breathing human beings.

But this girl, who'd flashed him her saucy grin a few days ago in his office, was different. With a shock, he realized that this was the first time that he'd presided over the death of someone he'd known as more than just a patient. Someone who'd been alive and vibrant only days before.

And he didn't like knowing her; it made his failure all the more painful. Linette had expected him to save Amy, and he hadn't been able to. If only he could have done something more for her. No matter that no one else could have saved her, Stephen wanted to, to prove that he had the knowledge and the skill to beat death.

He'd lied to Linette earlier—he wasn't God, true, but he wanted to be like Him in this case, wanted to cheat death and revel in his success. Someday, medicine would have the answers to do that. And he wanted to be one of the men who found them.

Instead, his patient lay dead in a blood-soaked bed, mourned by her family, her lover, and a teacher and friend who'd tried to bring comfort to her dying moments.

Hearing a noise, he looked up. Linette stood in the doorway, looking ashen and shaken. Stephen took her hand and led her to a chair. Grabbing the bottle of gin, he filled a glass and shoved it into her hand. "Drink this."

Like an automaton, she obeyed, taking a huge swallow. Sputtering, she gasped as the cheap alcohol burned her throat. Stephen pounded her on the back until she regained her breath.

"Slower this time," he said, holding the glass to her lips. She tried to push it away but he persisted, knowing she needed something to combat her shock. He made her take two more swallows before he set the glass down and sat beside her.

"I can't believe she's gone," Linette said. She covered her face with her hands, her shoulders shaking as she sobbed.

Awkward in the face of her grief, Stephen hesitated, then put his arm about her shoulder. She turned toward him, burying her face in his chest. The muffled sound of Linette's sobs tore at him. He wanted to ease her hurt, wanted to hold her and soothe her until she smiled again.

Wrapping her in his arms, he held her close, feeling her tears dampen his shirtfront. He felt as helpless now as he had in his futile attempt to save Amy's life, yet he could no more walk away from Linette than from a patient. She needed him just as badly. He only wished he knew what to do.

Over her shoulder, he saw Jimmy Boggs stagger from the bedroom. Going straight to the table, he grabbed the bottle of gin, holding it to his mouth and drinking with such haste that it dribbled down his chin and shirt. Stephen said nothing. It was probably the best thing for the lad.

Linette sobbed quietly in his arms. Stroking her hair, her back, Stephen tried to calm her, soothe her, feeling his own inadequacy. Once again, she was looking to him for help, and he couldn't provide it.

He felt Linette stirring in his arms and she raised her face, looking at him with tearstained cheeks. He reached for the glass and gave her another drink of gin. She took it, then pushed his hand away.

"That's enough of that awful stuff."

"Take another," Stephen insisted. "It will dull the pain."

"I don't want the pain to be dulled. I want to feel it, hurt with it. Amy is dead."

"I know," he said gently. "But you're exhausted and upset. This will help you sleep."

"It tastes horrible," she said, but took another drink.

"That it does," he agreed. "I'd rather it was brandy, but I'll work with what I have." He didn't think it would take long for her to grow tipsy and then he'd take her home, confident she would quickly go to sleep. "Finish this and we can leave."

"Oh, but there is so much to do! The body must be laid out, and there are funeral arrangements to make."

"The family can do that," he said firmly.

"Not the funeral," she said, and rose unsteadily to her feet. She gripped the edge of the table, swaying slightly, then she wobbled off to the bedroom to consult with Amy's mother.

The gin was obviously working.

A few minutes later, she returned. Reaching for the glass on the table, she drained what was left.

Stephen frowned. She was at least two sheets to the wind, judging by her unsteady gait. Time to take her home.

"Any idea where to find a hackney at this hour?" he asked.

"We'll have to walk a ways," she said. "Get closer to the Dispensary."

He searched the room for her coat. She stood docilely as he slipped her arms into the sleeves and buttoned up the front.

"Did you know, Mr. Ashworth," she said, enunciating her words slowly, "that you are in need of a shave?"

Stephen rubbed his roughened chin. "Yes, Miss Gregory, I believe you are right."

She ran a wavering finger across his stubble before he captured her hand and tucked it into her pocket. He led her out into the hall and closed the door behind them, shutting the family up with their grief.

The stairs were dark and steep, and Linette's unsteadiness made the descent even more difficult. He should have gotten her downstairs before he forced the gin on her, Stephen thought when she stumbled against him for the umpteenth time. He took a firmer grip on her arm and guided her down the stairs and into the street.

The first rays of dawn streaked against the low clouds. Another gray winter day. There would be no sun to mark Amy's passing.

Taking Linette by the hand, Stephen led her down the street, hoping they would find a hackney before he had to carry her.

He thought they might have to walk the entire way when he finally spotted a carriage. The driver gave them a doubtful look, but Stephen quelled him with an icy glare. He pushed Linette into the coach and plopped down beside her, wrapping an arm about her waist. She'd fall over for certain if he didn't hold her up.

Linette looked at him with bleary eyes. "Am I drunk, Stephen?"

"Most assuredly."

"I thought so."

She slumped against his shoulder and he thought she'd

fallen asleep. But her eyes flew open when the carriage hit a bump and she looked at him with a startled expression.

"You're almost home," he said quietly.

Linette squeezed his arm. "Thank you, Stephen." She leaned over and planted a crooked kiss on his cheek. "For everything." She lay back against his shoulder again and did not stir.

Chapter 13

When the hackney halted in front of the Barton household, Stephen tried to rouse the sleeping Linette. She mumbled something unintelligible and snuggled closer against him.

Stephen shook his head. He'd been too generous with the gin and she'd have the devil of a headache later. But at least she wasn't crying now. With a sigh, he moved his arm from her shoulder and eased himself off the seat, gently laying her back against the cushions. Stepping down, he paid the driver, then climbed back inside to get Linette.

When he took her arm, she toppled sideways onto the seat. With a muttered oath, Stephen grabbed her hands and pulled her upright, slipping his hands beneath her arms. Her head lolled to one side.

Maybe he shouldn't have given her quite so much gin.

Slowly, carefully, he inched his way backward, pulling her along the seat toward the door. Finally, he positioned her in the doorway and unceremoniously slung her over his shoulder. Staggering for a moment while he gained his balance, he started up the stairs and banged the knocker.

He waited several minutes before the door opened. The startled butler's eyes grew wide as he stared at Stephen and his burden.

"Miss Gregory is indisposed," Stephen announced calmly.

"I'll get Mrs. Barton at once."

"Don't!" Stephen gave him a conspiratorial wink. "All she needs is a good sleep."

"Can you carry her up the stairs?" the butler asked dubiously.

"I'll try." Stephen took a deep breath, resettling Linette over his shoulder, then followed the man up the stairs.

Fortunately, Linette's room was on the first floor and he was able to make it there without collapsing. A maid held the door open and Stephen strode into the room, dumping Linette none too gently on the bed.

"She smells like gin!" the hovering maid exclaimed.

"Medicinal alcohol," Stephen said curtly. "The patient she was tending died and Miss Gregory was very upset."

"Poor lamb." The maid turned a dark look on Stephen. "Now you take yourself out of here and let me tend to her."

Stephen eagerly retreated. The butler hovered anxiously at the top of the stairs. "Can I get you some tea, sir?"

He started to decline, then changed his mind. It would still be hours before he could crawl into his own bed. A cup of tea would be welcome. Stephen nodded.

"I shall bring it to you in the morning room."

"Don't bother," Stephen said. "I'll just come with you to the kitchen."

"But, sir . . ."

Realizing his proposal violated a rigid rule, Stephen acquiesced. If the butler wanted to maintain formality, who was he to challenge the man?

As he settled wearily in a chair, Stephen tried to empty his mind of the night's events. The dying patient. A grieving Linette. He hadn't been much help to either. Amy had died. Linette was dead drunk.

Could he have saved the girl if he'd arrived sooner? Would a transfusion have helped? Tomorrow, he'd look up those articles in *The Lancet*. He was not going to be caught unawares again. If he didn't perform a transfusion in the future, it would be because he didn't think it would work, not because he didn't know how.

The butler arrived with the steaming pot of tea and some slices of buttered bread. Stephen gulped down the scalding brew, suddenly impatient to be on his way. Mathers could find the articles for him. If the procedure really worked, Stephen wanted to learn how to do it as soon as possible.

The hackney still waited outside and Stephen told the driver to take him to Howard Street. Inside, he sprawled across the seat. Linette would be all right now.

But as the carriage took him through the nearly deserted streets, he couldn't stop thinking about her. He'd been surprised by her calm competence in caring for Amy, touched by her genuine grief when their efforts had failed.

He felt more than admiration for Linette. Stephen admitted he cared about *her,* cared whether she was happy or sad.

And he didn't want to care. It was too dangerous to his peace of mind.

Stephen felt an overwhelming sense of relief as he stepped into the hall at Howard Street. Here, he knew what he was doing. Here, he was firmly in control.

Revived by the tea, and the security he felt in his own domain, Stephen busily tackled the stack of paperwork on his desk. He barely noticed when Mathers entered.

"You're here early," he commented.

"It's more a matter of being here late—I was up all night with a patient."

Mather looked surprised. "That's unusual for you."

"A favor for Miss Gregory," Stephen said.

"Ah." Mathers smiled knowingly.

"Don't look so smug. The poor girl died. Uterine hemorrhage—a second trimester miscarriage. Two doses of ergot and she still bled to death."

Mathers shivered. "One of the reasons I never wanted

to be a man-midwife. But that's not exactly your line, either."

"As I said, it was a favor. Still, it gave me an idea. I want you to find the articles on that transfusion process in *The Lancet*. It might prove useful in other cases."

Mathers grimaced. Stephen knew he hated doing paper research.

"And since you're here, I'm going home to get some sleep." Stephen stood up. "I'm canceling today's lecture so you can hold a double session in the dissecting room."

"Will you be back later?"

"Probably." Stephen pulled on his coat and headed for the door. "And don't forget those transfusion articles. I want them on my desk by tomorrow."

He stopped for breakfast on the way home, and it was nearly ten when he finally lay down on his bed. Stephen closed his eyes, expecting to fall asleep immediately, but his mind was still racing.

He didn't ponder his own actions—he'd analyzed and reanalyzed them so often he had nothing more to consider. No, it was Linette he thought about; Linette, and all the different facets she'd displayed during the night.

She'd been an invaluable assistant during the long struggle, showing real skill at tending her patient. Her strength amazed him. If Amy could have been saved through sheer determination, Linette would have accomplished it. Then, when it was all over, when her strength was gone, she'd collapsed in his arms and bawled like a baby.

That was the worst part. She'd expected him to deal with her grief, just as she'd expected him to help Amy, but the only thing he'd known to do was to get her drunk, to swap oblivion for sorrow. No doubt she would be furious with him when she awoke today.

Yet Linette's surprising fragility stirred something in him, some long-buried emotion that made him want to shield her from pain. And responding to her vulnerability forced him to acknowledge that the same weakness lurked within him, held back only by training and sheer will. He'd fought long and hard to achieve his emotional detachment, and he wasn't going to lose it now.

Linette Gregory was challenging his hard-won peace of mind, and he had to fight against her influence. If, in the future, he refused to participate in her well-meaning projects, he'd be protected against these threats to his peace of mind.

He'd pay her one more visit, to assure himself that she had recovered from her ordeal, and that would be the end of it. The next time she wanted a surgeon, he'd send Mathers.

Grabbing her aching head, Linette tried to sit up, but the motion only increased the throbbing. She lay back against the pillow with a groan. What was wrong? What had she done?

Memories came flooding back. Stephen—and gin. Amy. Blood. And death.

Linette bit her pillow to keep herself from screaming. It all came back to her; the horrible events of the previous night. Their frantic efforts to save Amy; her still and waxen face as she'd lain dead on the bed in the tiny, cramped bedroom.

Lifting one eyelid, Linette glanced warily about her, half surprised to discover she was home, in her own room. How had she gotten here?

Dimly, she recalled stumbling about the gray London streets with Stephen, looking for a hackney. He must have brought her home, but she couldn't remember a thing about the journey.

But she had no trouble remembering Stephen. He'd tried so hard to save Amy and had been shaken by his failure. That endeared him to Linette more than anything else. It meant he was human, he did have emotions.

And in her grief, she'd turned to him gratefully, needing his comfort, the security of his arms around her. He had been there, warm, and solid, holding her tightly while she released her grief and frustration.

Linette would never forget how close she'd felt to him at that moment.

Glancing at the clock on the dressing table, she saw that it was half past three. She'd slept nearly the entire day! Linette sat up quickly and fell back on the pillow with a moan, clasping a hand to her forehead. She felt abominable. Finally crawling from her bed, Linette rang for the maid.

The tisane the maid brought did little to ease her headache, but Linette bathed and dressed and went downstairs anyway. She must tell Aunt what had happened. But to Linette's disappointment, Aunt was out, making her afternoon calls.

Linette wandered listlessly through the house. It was hard to believe that Amy was gone. Only yesterday, she'd sat in Linette's class and joked with the other girls. Now she was dead, betrayed by the tiny life inside her.

Burying her face in her hands, Linette wept. Wept for all that might have been and wasn't. She cried until her throat was raw and her eyes swollen, cried until no more tears came.

Slowly, she returned to her room. Wetting a washcloth, she lay down on the bed, cooling her flaming face and composing her shattered emotions. Then she rose and went back downstairs. Grabbing her cloak from the hall, she stepped outside and hailed a hackney. She needed to help Amy's family with the arrangements for the funeral. It was the final thing she could do for her student.

Linette was glad she'd undertaken the task, for Amy's family was too grief-stricken to take care of any of the details. It also enabled Linette to pay most of the funeral costs without the family knowing.

She'd barely stepped through the front door on her

return when Mrs. Barton bustled out to greet her. She took Linette's chilled hands in hers.

"Oh, my dear, I had no idea you would even try to go out this afternoon. Come, you must sit and rest. I can't imagine how you found the strength to even leave your bed."

"Arrangements needed to be made," Linette replied dully.

"Yes, but you don't have to be the one to do them. I always said you take too much on yourself, and this is a perfect example. Why, I was just telling Mr. Ashworth—"

Linette's eyes widened. "Ashworth is here?"

"He came to check on you, my dear. Such a conscientious young man. Come, hang up your cloak and join us in the drawing room for tea."

Her heart leapt at the thought. During the long night, she'd watched Stephen closely while they struggled to save Amy's life. She had seen his determination, his unwillingness to give up the fight; and her admiration for him had grown. He was a man for whom medicine was a crusade.

A man she could admire. Respect.

And wanted to know better.

Yet at the same time, she was afraid to see him so soon. This morning, she'd eagerly clung to him, seeking his solace and comfort. She had needed him then, needed his arms around her and needed to hear his soothing words.

And that was what frightened her. Linette didn't want to need anyone, least of all a man like him.

But she couldn't forget how gentle and tender he'd been with Amy, how hard he had worked to save her life, his disappointment and anger when he failed. Linette now knew that there was a caring and compassionate man behind that chilly exterior.

That was the man she wanted to know.

Stephen jumped to his feet as she entered the room

and Linette thought his eyes brightened at the sight of her.

"You should be in bed," he said in a chiding tone.

"If that is the case, then so should you," she replied with a warm smile. "I imagine you've had even less sleep than I."

He bowed his head in agreement.

Linette sat down and took the cup of tea Aunt offered.

"I had to visit Amy's family, and help them with the funeral arrangements. The burial will be tomorrow at Christ Church." She glanced at Stephen. "You will come, won't you?"

"I'm not sure if the family wishes me to intrude . . ."

"Of course they will want you there. They know you did everything you could."

"I'll have to check my schedule," Stephen said.

Aunt gave Linette's hand a comforting pat and stood. "I must check with Cook about dinner." She looked at Ashworth. "You will join us, won't you?"

Stephen's expression turned uneasy. "Thank you, but I have a previous engagement this evening."

Mrs. Barton sighed with disappointment. "How unfortunate. You will have to dine with us at another time."

She went out, leaving Linette to appreciate her aunt's tact at leaving them alone.

"I was worried about you," Stephen said. "I'm pleased to see that you're looking better."

"Better than this morning, you mean? I can't say, as I have no recollection of how or when I entered this house." She darted him a chastising look. "I believe it had something to do with the gin you gave me."

"I did what I thought best. You were very upset."

"Of course I was upset—Amy died. I'm not going to deny what I felt," she said. "Feelings are what make us human, what separates us from the animals. By ignoring them, we only lessen our humanity."

"One can experience feelings without losing control," he said curtly.

Linette felt a twinge of uneasiness at his words. "Is that what you think—that I was behaving like a hysterical female?"

Stephen looked uncomfortable. "You were not reacting well."

She recoiled at his words. Last night, she'd sensed a new closeness to him, a sense of shared mission as they struggled to save Amy. Now, she wondered if she'd been wrong. "Not everyone is able to repress their emotions as well as you."

He stood and walked toward her, anger flooding his face.

"I'm a *surgeon.* I have to keep my feelings under control, else I can't do my work. That doesn't mean I feel nothing when a patient dies."

Linette appraised him coolly. "You have an odd way of showing it."

"Do you think I enjoyed what happened last night? Watching that girl's life slip from between my fingers and not being able to stop it?" His eyes darkened. "Good God, you must be mad to think I wasn't affected. The death of any patient disturbs me."

"A 'patient,' " she mimicked sarcastically. "That wasn't a *patient,* it was *Amy.* Amy Dawlings. A sixteen-year-old girl who died because she was pregnant."

Stephen looked away, his hands clasped behind his back, as if he were deep in thought. Then slowly, he faced her.

"Linette, I can't say that my grief is as deep as yours. You knew Amy much better than I. But I assure you that her death hurts me grievously. As does your unwarranted anger."

She averted her gaze. "I don't wish to discuss it further."

"Fine." Without taking a backward glance, he walked out of the room.

Linette listened to his steps in the hall, heard the front door open and close. Then, and only then, did she release her sobs.

He hadn't changed at all. What she had seen last night was merely the determination of a surgeon not to lose a patient. He cared no more about Amy than he would about an unknown vagrant who came to him off the street.

She was angry. Angry that, despite all their efforts, Amy had died. And angry at Stephen, for not feeling the same pain she did.

The surgeon with a heart of ice. He was as incapable of caring as the cold cadavers he cut into. It only showed how desperately out of her mind she'd been this morning when she'd clung to him for comfort.

What a foolish mistake that had been. The only thing he'd thought to do was get her drunk so he wouldn't have to deal with her grief. A thoroughly *sympathetic* reaction on his part.

What a fool she'd been.

Well, she knew better now. Knew that Stephen Ashworth wasn't the man she thought he was. The man she wanted him to be.

Yet Linette felt a twinge of sadness at the thought.

The next afternoon, Stephen stood, hesitating, under the portico of Christ Church.

He wasn't entirely certain why he was here. Partly to spite Linette Gregory. She wouldn't expect him to be here and he felt the need to show her she was wrong. He did care about Amy and her sad death.

She'd accused him yesterday of having no emotions. It was a ridiculous charge. He had plenty of emotions; he'd merely learned how to control them. The sharpest lesson of his youth was that emotions were a dangerous thing; feeling strongly about anyone, anything, only opened you up to hurt and pain.

No one expected barristers and solicitors to care about

their clients. Why was Linette so insistent that he show such depth of interest in his patients? He was here to treat their ills; he didn't want to become intimately involved with them. That could be left to people like her, who enjoyed meddling in other people's lives.

Still, he was here now, so he might as well go in. Sighing, he pulled open the heavy wooden door to the church and stepped into the dark interior.

The mourners stood in a small cluster at the front of the cavernous basilica and he walked down the nave, his steps echoing loudly in the high-ceilinged church. He took a seat some distance behind the group.

A black-swathed woman in the front sobbed gently— Amy's mother perhaps? He'd only spoken to her briefly that night so he wasn't certain. Stephen recognized the grief-stricken young father who'd flung himself across the bed. Linette stood behind them, the elegant lines of her black mourning clothes marking her from the plain garb of the others.

The service had already begun and Stephen listened absently to the minister recite the office. He couldn't remember exactly when he'd last attended a funeral— his grandfather's perhaps, many years ago. He tried to concentrate on the unfamiliar words, but funerals were not something he had much interest in. They were designed to comfort the living, while he was more concerned with the dead.

Then, hearing the word "resurrection," he sat up straighter. What was the man saying? "It is sown in weakness; it is raised in power; it is sown a natural body; it is raised a spiritual body. There is a natural body, and there is a spiritual body."

A slow smile crept over Stephen's face. That was as good an argument as any as he'd heard for the support of dissection. If the physical body and the spiritual body were two different things, then after death, it did not matter what happened to the physical body.

He wondered if Linette was paying close attention to the words.

Stephen stood quietly as the coffin came down the aisle and the mourners filed past, on their way to the churchyard. Linette's eyes widened with surprise when she spotted him and he nodded briefly, glad that he had decided to come. She couldn't label him an unfeeling monster now.

With the biting December wind, the ceremony in the churchyard was mercifully short. Amy's mother stood with a stoic expression on her face; Jimmy Boggs looked as if he might collapse at any moment. Stephen half expected him to fling himself on the coffin when it was lowered into the ground.

Behind the mourners, sheltering against the church, stood the gravediggers, waiting to finish their task. Stephen wondered idly if they were in the pay of the resurrectionists. Could Amy's body be brought to him that very night?

He'd never before cut into the body of a person he'd known, but he didn't think it would be all that different. He admitted he would like to get a look at that uterus, to discover why the girl had bled so badly. Perhaps he could learn something that would help another woman.

But Linette would never see it that way. To her, it would be a blasphemous desecration to even think of using Amy's corpse for research. No matter that the knowledge learned might save countless other women from the same fate.

The service ended and he forced himself to move, to walk up to Amy's mother and offer his sympathies. Stephen clapped Jimmy on the back and the man clutched at his arm with a pathetic expression, professing his grateful thanks for all Stephen had done. It was more than he would do in the same situation—the girl had died, after all. As far as Stephen was concerned, he had failed.

Then he turned and walked slowly toward Linette.

"I had not expected to see you here," she said stiffly.

"I know. That's why I came."

"At least you're honest."

He shrugged. "Do you think that it makes the least bit of difference to anyone that I'm here?"

"Only to you."

Puzzled, he looked at her closely. "What does that mean?"

She began walking across the churchyard and he followed beside her. "It is good for you to see the final episode in Amy's life. Perhaps you'll remember the experience better."

He laughed mirthlessly. "I'm not likely to forget it soon. Despite your assessment of me as a heartless bastard, I hate to lose a patient. *Any* patient."

She stopped and gave him a searching look. "Sometimes it is difficult to know what you are thinking."

He took her arm and they continued across the churchyard. They reached the far end and turned back toward the entrance gate. Already the small group of mourners had dispersed and the gravediggers were at their work.

Stephen scanned the churchyard with a practiced eye, noting the height of the wall and the position of the gates. Surrounded as it was by buildings, it wasn't the most private of locations, but he didn't think that would stop a determined resurrectionist.

"Will someone be watching the grave tonight?" he asked quietly.

"Watching the grave? For wh—oh!" Linette clapped a hand over her mouth. "Oh dear God. How could anyone think of doing such a thing?"

"Six guineas are a powerful incentive," he replied.

She glanced nervously at the gravediggers. "Do you think if I paid them to stand guard . . . ?"

"It might work—if they aren't working hand in glove with the body trade already."

"How could they?"

Stephen laughed. "You don't think the resurrectionists work all on their own? A few well-placed payments to sextons and gravediggers helps their task considerably."

A look of grim determination crossed her face. "I'll hire my own guards, then. Nate and his friends will do it."

"You probably wouldn't even have to pay *them,*" Stephen said with a mocking laugh. "Tell them it's less work than tearing up an anatomy school—and accomplishes the same thing."

Linette shook her head. "I'll speak to them immediately. How many nights do they need to watch?"

"She's probably safe after a week."

"A week?"

"It's winter; the ground is cold. In summer, it wouldn't be above a few days."

"Why don't you write a book on the subject?" she said sarcastically. "I'm sure the public would be most interested in the sordid details."

"It's reality, Linette."

She glanced down, then looked at him. "If . . . if something goes wrong and they somehow . . . Would you buy the body?"

Stephen hesitated, weighing his reply. As a surgeon, he wanted that body. Wanted to know exactly how and why Amy had died. But he knew how important this was to Linette and he did not want to see that flare of disapproval in those pale gray eyes. Suddenly, it was important to Stephen that she held him in admiration. He conceded defeat. "No."

She wrapped her hand about his arm. "Good."

As he walked her to her carriage, Stephen contemplated his decision with growing dismay. He was actually willing to compromise his principles for her.

The thought troubled him all the way back to school. He wanted to get a look at that uterus, to see if he could learn something that would help another woman. Yet he'd pledged not to because he wanted to please Linette.

Never before had he allowed anyone to influence his actions like this and it was a dangerous precedent. One he could not afford to permit again.

Once again, he realized how often Linette Gregory managed to disrupt his carefully laid plans.

In the privacy of Aunt's carriage, Linette let out a long breath. She felt as if she'd been holding her breath ever since she spotted Stephen in the church.

Why had he come? Had her accusations hit home the other day? Had she realized how hard-hearted he'd become, and was he trying to change?

Or had her judgment been too harsh? Perhaps Amy's death had affected Stephen more than she'd thought. What looked like indifference might have been his own sense of failure. If so, she had misjudged him.

Was that what he meant, when he'd said he was there because she hadn't expected him to be? Was it his way of showing her that she was wrong?

Linette hoped so. Because that meant he did care what she thought of him. And that was merely a step away from caring for her himself. Linette realized that was what she wanted most of all.

Stephen might appreciate her translations and admire her determination in the sickroom. But that paled to insignificance beside his feelings for her as a woman.

Somehow, she must find a way to penetrate his reticence and discover exactly what he thought of her.

Chapter 14

The following week, Linette stood on the Dispensary steps and wrapped her cloak closer around her. The weather was cold, but dry, and she decided to walk home. It would give her time to think.

It had not been an easy day. Her sewing class had met for the first time since Amy's death, and everyone had been subdued and teary. Poor Mary was still too upset to even attend, and her absence made everything worse. Linette had been relieved when class ended.

There were more French medical articles waiting for her at home and she could use the money they brought. She had given Amy's mother a generous sum to pay for the funeral, and now Linette needed funds to pay the men who stood watch over the grave every night. Soon, her money would be gone again.

Aunt would of course give her anything she needed, but Linette didn't want to ask; it was enough that Aunt provided her with a home. Linette disliked being dependent on anyone; she would make her own way without anyone's help. Her father had taught her to be self-sufficient.

Linette was glad she hadn't seen Stephen in the days since the funeral. Her feelings about him were too confused, too unsure. He was not the idealized healer she'd imagined him to be at Amy's, but neither was he the ogre she had painted him later, either. Every time she thought she understood him, he did something to surprise her. Linette wondered if she would ever truly understand him.

She reached the corner of Old Street and started to cross when two roughly dressed men stepped in front of her.

"Excuse me," she said calmly. "Please step aside."

"Be you Miss Gregory?" the taller man asked.

"Who wishes to know?" Linette felt a twinge of apprehension.

"We've got a message for you, missy." The shorter man grinned at her with an evil leer. "There's them that thinks you're messin' about in things wot don't concern ye."

"Oh?" Linette felt no alarm. There were still some people in the neighborhood who didn't approve of her school, or her presence at the Dispensary. She'd dealt with these complaints before.

"Have you been to the Dispensary and seen the work that we do?" she asked calmly. "It is all for good, I assure you."

"You're interferin' with jobs. Peoples gotta work, y'know."

She regarded him with puzzlement. "Jobs? What are you talking about?"

The first man grabbed her arm. "We're talkin' about you hirin' them men to watch the churchyard."

Linette stared at them in shocked horror. "You're resurrectionists!"

"Businessmen," the shorter man said. "We provides a service for the community, so to speak, and you're not doin' us any good. If everyone started hirin' guards, you'd put us right out of business."

"As you should be," she said, her voice rising. "How dare you even show your face to the light of day? You are filthy beasts!"

The man shook her roughly. "You watch who you're callin' names, missy. The boss don't take kindly to your activities and we're here to give you a warnin'."

Linette jerked her arm free. "I don't care what your *boss* says. I abhor what you do and I will fight you any way I can. I hope that everyone hires guards and puts you out of business."

"Look, lady . . ."

The tall man raised his arm in a threatening manner and Linette ducked.

"Hey there! What's going on?"

A carter who'd been unloading his wares across the street ran toward them.

The tall man gave Linette a violent shove, knocking her to the ground, then he and his companion fled around the corner.

"Are you all right?" The carter bent over her.

Linette lay sprawled in the street, too stunned to even move. Everything had happened so quickly! Instinctively, she'd broken her fall with her hands, but she was still too numb with shock to tell if she'd hurt herself. Gingerly, she sat up and ruefully surveyed her palms. Both were scraped and the left one bled a little.

"Are you all right?" the man asked again.

She nodded, although she felt a strange, queasy sensation in her stomach.

"A young lady like you shouldn't be out here all on your own," the man said. He reached under her arms and drew her to her feet. "Where you going?"

"I'm from the Dispensary," Linette said, pointing down the street. "And I was on my way home."

"Better go back and have 'em look at them hands. That's a nasty cut. I'll walk you there."

"I can manage on my own," Linette said with a grateful smile. "Thank you so much for chasing those men away."

"Are you sure you'll be all right? They might come back."

"I don't think they will," Linette said. Now that her initial shock had worn off, her anger grew. "They're the type who usually rely on the cover of darkness to hide their foul deeds. I'm sure you frightened them thoroughly."

The man's eyes widened in apprehension. "What kind of men are they?"

"Resurrectionists," Linette replied.

The man's expression darkened and he scowled. "Devils, that's what they are. You should've said something earlier, I'd a gone after 'em." He grunted in disappointment. "They're probably long gone by now."

"Don't worry, I will talk with the authorities." She bent down and picked up her bag. "Please, if you ever need the services of the Dispensary, do come. Tell them Miss Gregory sent you."

The man tipped his cap. "I'll do that."

Linette walked the short distance back to the Dispensary. She maintained her composure as she went up the steps, but once she was behind the door she sank down on the long bench in the hall. Suddenly, Linette couldn't stop shaking. She relived the terrifying moment when the man had pushed her down, the jarring pain when she hit the ground.

Linette didn't think those men wanted to cause her serious hurt, but she was glad they had been chased away before she could find out. Any man who wouldn't cavil at digging up a dead body wouldn't think twice about hurting a woman.

She was sure they had merely been sent to warn her, to frighten her into calling off the guard over Amy's grave. But the laugh was on them, for this blatant attack only made her more determined than ever to fight their activities. Linette would see that there was a double guard on duty at Christ Church tonight.

She would show those detestable men that Linette Gregory couldn't be frightened away from doing what was right.

The porter came running down the hall. "Miss Gregory, what is wrong?"

Linette laughed lightly, determined to make light of

the incident. She didn't want everyone at the Dispensary worrying about her. "Silly me. I tripped and fell and scraped my hand."

The porter bent over and she held out her injured hands for his inspection.

"Ought to have one of the medical men look at this," he said. "Don't want to scar up your pretty hands."

Linette stood, surprised at how wobbly her legs still felt. She hoped she could walk to the medical room. "I'll see to it."

Her destination was at the far end of the building, just above her office. Slowly, she climbed the stairs. One knee was already stiffening and the other felt bruised. She dreaded having to explain to Aunt about the probable bandage on her hand. Linette dared not tell her what had happened. If Aunt knew the truth, Linette would not be allowed out of the house.

Reaching the top of the stairs, she walked into the examining room and came to an abrupt halt at the sight of Stephen Ashworth.

"What are you doing here?" Dismay filled her. She didn't want to see him. Not now, when she was shaken and hurt and her emotions were in a turmoil. She felt too much like she had the night Amy had died, when she'd turned to him for comfort.

Linette didn't know what to say, what to do. A part of her wanted to fall into his arms, where she knew she would feel safe, warm, and secure. Her more practical side told her that he would be furious when he learned what had happened, saying it was her own fault for angering the resurrectionists. Quickly, Linette shoved her injured hands behind her back, but it was too late.

Stephen dropped the pan he held and grabbed her wrists, inspecting her bruised and bloody palms. "What have you done?"

"I fell," she said. That wasn't a lie, after all. She wasn't going to give him the opportunity to gloat over what had happened.

"Off a chair again?" He shook his head. "You really should stop your habit of climbing onto furniture. Some-day, you'll break your neck."

"It wasn't my fault," she retorted without thinking. "I was pushed."

Stephen froze and his eyes narrowed. "Who pushed you?"

Linette colored guiltily. "Well, bumped is a better term. There was a crush—"

"Who pushed you, Linette?"

She took a deep breath. "A man."

"A man?" Stephen's expression darkened. "A total stranger walked up to you and gave you a shove?"

Linette laughed nervously. "He wasn't precisely a stranger. That is, I didn't know him, but he knew who I was."

"Whose feathers have you ruffled now?" Stephen dampened a cloth and gently wiped the blood from her hand.

His fingers on her wrist were warm. Linette wanted to snatch her hand away but she dared not. Despite his anger, he regarded her with a surprising tenderness, treating her wounds with the utmost care.

It was this side of him that she longed to see, to know, to understand. If only she could find a way to break past his reserve, to show him that he could be this way all the time; that caring for others would make him a better surgeon.

Swallowing nervously, Linette decided to tell him the truth. "It was some resurrectionists."

His fingers tightened around hers. "What?"

"They knew I was responsible for the guard on Amy's grave and they wanted to frighten me into canceling it."

Stephen frowned as he continued cleansing her hand. "They obviously don't know you."

"Not at all—ouch!"

"Sorry." He wrapped the injured palm, then carefully

examined her other hand. "I think your right hand is fine. Any other damage?"

The touch of his fingers sent a wave of dizziness through Linette, destroying her concentration. "I . . . I think I'm all right."

"Give me a few minutes to put things away and I'll take you home," he said.

Linette jumped to her feet. "That's all right, I'll take a hackney. I want to talk with Nate, to tell him to be extra careful at Christ Church tonight and—"

Stephen whirled around and glared at her. "You're not going anywhere by yourself, is that understood? Until this business has been cleared up, you are not to set foot outside your aunt's door without an escort."

Linette was stunned by his imperious demands. Who was he to tell her what to do? She bristled at his interference. "Don't be silly. I'm in no danger."

"I've never been more serious in my life. You aren't going to take any more chances."

"Stephen, I—"

He gave her a threatening look. "I'll tell your aunt what happened."

Linette shut her mouth on her protest. She didn't doubt that he would carry out his threat if she didn't obey, and she didn't want Aunt Barton to worry.

"I don't want to have to wait for someone every time I go out." Linette gave him an imploring look. "I will take the carriage everywhere; that will be enough."

His mouth was set in a grim line. "The carriage and an escort. I'll put some of my students at your disposal."

"You're being overly protective."

Stephen's frown deepened. "If those men are worried enough to frighten you, they're worried enough to try something more serious."

"And that is why I need to talk with Nate," Linette said. "I think there should be extra men at the churchyard tonight."

"That's a good idea." Stephen nodded his approval.

"But I will escort you to Nate's and then home. No arguments."

"Yes, *Mr.* Ashworth." Linette realized it was easier to give in than to argue further. And in truth, his deep concern pleased her. Linette dared to hope it meant he had some feelings for her. Why else would he act in such a protective manner? It was so unlike him that it must mean something. She smiled to herself. Maybe she had broken through that icy wall of indifference after all.

"I have a few things I need to get from my office. I shall meet you back here in ten minutes."

Stephen glared at her in warning. "And if you try to run away . . ."

"I *will* be back. I promise."

After she departed, Stephen dropped all pretense of calm and soundly kicked a pan across the floor.

He wanted to take a scalpel to the men who had done that to Linette. To think that they would dare assault her, practically on the front steps of the Dispensary. His hands clenched in anger. At them, and at her.

This was what came of her infernal meddling. Now she'd angered one of the resurrection gangs and put herself in danger. Wouldn't the chit ever learn?

Stephen gave a rueful shake of his head. No, she probably wouldn't. Linette Gregory was a born crusader and wouldn't let anyone intimidate her into backing down from a stand. He had to admire her for that. Someone just had to make sure she didn't get hurt in the process.

And with a pang, he realized he wanted to be the one to do that. Wanted to protect her and hold her and keep her safe. The thought of anything happening to her left a sick feeling in his stomach. When he'd first seen her scraped and bloody palm, he wanted to press his lips to it, to kiss the hurt away.

It was a totally irrational reaction. And he was a rational man. What was this woman doing to him?

He sighed heavily. No matter how hard he tried to

avoid her, Linette and her problems had landed in his lap once again. If he had any sense, he would leave the job to another. Linette was far too dangerous to his piece of mind. She had a knack for getting past his carefully constructed barriers. An emotional involvement with her was the last thing he wanted.

Just as strongly as he wanted to be with her every chance he could.

He truly was worried. He knew that the resurrectionists could be ruthless in eliminating competition; they might be equally ruthless in challenging their opponents. He had to let them know, in no uncertain terms, that the medical profession in London wouldn't stand for any more incidents like the one today. Let them fight and squabble amongst themselves; Stephen didn't care. But when they resorted to physical violence against women, something had to be done.

No one was going to hurt Linette and get away with it.

Tonight, after he'd seen her safely home, he would talk with one of his contacts and tell him to pass the word. Stephen didn't want to irritate his suppliers in an already tight market, but there were some things that couldn't be ignored.

And Stephen could back up his warning with threats of his own. If they dared to bother Linette again, he would make the resurrectionists exceedingly unhappy— even if he had to destroy the medical body trade in London in the process.

He half thought to talk with her aunt, to warn her to keep a closer eye on her niece. He hadn't promised not to, after all. But he knew Linette would never forgive him if he spoke without her permission. It was the one guarantee he had of her willingness to cooperate, and he needed her cooperation now. He had a school to run, a book to write, patients to see. He didn't need the added worry about her safety as well.

But even as he knew that she was distracting him from his work, and creating havoc with his mind, he couldn't stop thinking about her. And couldn't stop wanting to help her. He still remembered the tearful vulnerability he'd seen in her eyes the night Amy died, and the strange satisfaction he'd felt when she had turned to him for comfort.

They were all feelings he could not afford to have. Yet he was incapable of ignoring them.

Stephen knew he was in deep trouble.

That evening, instead of eating dinner at the tavern near his rooms, Stephen walked purposefully toward a less salubrious establishment in Spitalfields. The man he wanted to speak to was likely to be there.

Stepping through the door into the smoky, overheated room, Stephen allowed his eyes to adjust to the dim light. He didn't spot the fellow he was after, but it was early. He could wait.

Ordering dinner, he sat down at a table near the door, where he could watch the comings and goings easier. The barmaid brought him a greasy meat pie, and a tankard of ale. Stephen glanced dubiously at his dinner, then decided he'd seen worse and ate it without a qualm.

He had just ordered a third tankard of ale when his quarry entered. Stephen waited until the man took a seat near the rear, then grabbed his mug and sauntered over, slipping into the opposite chair.

The man looked up, his startled expression fading as he recognized Stephen.

"Well, well, it's a surprise to see you 'ere. Got a special request, do ye?"

Stephen smiled tightly. "In a manner of speaking." He paused while the man's dinner arrived at the table. "I have a little message I would like you to pass on to your confederates."

The man took a long drink from his mug then wiped his mouth on a grimy sleeve. "And wot might that be?"

Stephen leaned across the table. "There was some trouble in Shoreditch this afternoon—some street toughs accosted a lady friend."

"Pity. No one's safe on the streets these days."

"Except this was a deliberate attack. The lady has irritated some of the local merchants." Stephen leaned closer. "Merchants in *your* trade. I want to make sure that it doesn't happen again."

"Don't know nuthin' about it."

"I merely want you to talk with your ... associates. Tell them I am most displeased."

"So?"

"I don't make idle threats. If there are any more attempts to bother Miss Gregory, or to cause any trouble at the Burton Dispensary, I have no qualms about having a chat with the authorities about certain nocturnal activities."

"Wouldn't do your school no good." The man sneered.

"I'm more concerned about Miss Gregory's safety. I know many of my medical colleagues would be distressed to hear that such a thing had happened. They might decide to look elsewhere to purchase their supplies."

The man looked around uneasily. "I could talk to a few people."

"You do that." Stephen's smile was cold. "I'd watch my step if I were you. My students would love to get their hands on a fine specimen like you."

He felt a wicked sense of satisfaction at the man's shudder. Stephen rose and strode out of the tavern.

Outside, he mopped his brow. He wasn't accustomed to threatening resurrectionists; in his profession, they were a necessary evil. But this was an exceptional circumstance. And from the flicker of fear in the man's eyes, Stephen thought his words would be listened to. Most resurrectionists had a deep fear of dissection.

Linette would be safe, now.

But it wouldn't be too far out of his way to stop by Christ Church on his way home. He could reassure Nate that he'd sent out his warning. Stephen didn't think the resurrectionists would try to subdue the guard and dig up the body; that action would draw far too much attention. No, they'd made their move earlier today and he doubted anything else would happen. But it wouldn't hurt to be sure.

The gate to the churchyard was locked. Stephen peered through the bars, trying to make out any signs of life in the darkness.

"Nate? Nate Hawkins? Are you there?"

No one answered. For one panicked moment, Stephen feared that something *had* happened, that the resurrectionists had indeed attacked the watchers and subdued them. Then out of the shadows, a man approached the gate.

" 'Oo's that callin' for Nate?" the man growled.

"Ashworth. Is he here?"

"Yeah, I be 'ere." Nate stepped forward and peered through the gate. "Wot you want?"

"Everything quiet?" Stephen asked.

"Like a tomb," the first man said, and laughed uneasily.

"I talked with a representative of the . . . businessmen involved in that incident today. I don't think they will try anything else."

"They better not." Nate's tone was menacing.

"I don't think they'll come around here, either, but it won't hurt to keep an eye out."

"We intends to. They ain't gettin' our Amy."

Stephen nodded. The absurdity of the situation struck him—the anatomist in league with the men who abhorred his work, the men who'd wrecked his school. Yet they'd come together now because of Linette.

It was amazing the things that woman could get him to do. Somehow, whenever she needed him, his resolve to resist her pleas drifted away. And he suspected that she realized it, too.

Stephen wondered if he would ever have the strength to resist her. So far, his efforts had been a dismal failure.

He would have to work much harder in the future.

Chapter 15

A rare, clear sky greeted Stephen when he stepped outside in the morning. He took a deep breath, the cold air filling his lungs. It would be a pleasant walk to school.

His good mood lasted until he rounded the corner of Howard Street and saw the people clustered in front of the building halfway down the street. Something was wrong at the school.

Stephen broke into a run. Plunging into the crowd, he pushed his way to the front of the throng.

He smelled it first—the sickening odor of decaying flesh. There, on the steps, lay an oozing pile of something that had once been alive. A thin stream of yellowish liquid trickled down the steps and into the street.

He prayed that it wasn't human.

Angry murmurs came from the crowd and he whirled about, staring them down with an icy glare. Several students hovered on the fringes of the group.

"Get this mess cleaned up," Stephen ordered. "And the rest of you, on your way, before I call the watch."

Skirting the edge of the mess, he marched into the building.

Those arrogant bastards! How *dare* they do this to him. Stephen was white hot with anger. He knew this was a warning from the resurrectionists, a tit-for-tat response to his own threats last night.

But he hadn't been the one to start this game and he wasn't going to let them make the last move, either.

The Dispensary. Had they struck there as well?

If they'd threatened Linette again ...

Stephen raced back out the door, barely noticing the students who were busily scraping the muck off the stairs. He took off down the street at a run and his sides were aching and his chest heaving when he arrived at the Dispensary.

The front steps were bare.

Stephen muttered a relieved oath. He wanted to make sure Linette was kept out of this. It was a personal fight between him and the resurrectionists now.

He had an hour still before lecture; since he was here, he should check on his two surgical patients. They might be well enough to go home today.

Reaching the bottom of the main stairs, he looked up and frowned darkly when he saw Linette coming down them.

Stephen glared at her. "I thought I told you to stay away from here for a few days."

"I came in the carriage and I'll take it home. I am perfectly safe."

He grabbed her arm. "This isn't some game, Linette. Those men can be ruthless when crossed."

"What are they going to do—complain to the authorities?" She laughed. "I'm sure they won't bother me again."

"They have other ways of making their displeasure known," he said grimly. "There was a 'present' from them at the school when I arrived this morning."

She looked at him anxiously. "Did they cause any damage?"

"Only to my name. The neighbors didn't take kindly to finding a pile of rotting flesh in front of the school."

Linette clapped a hand over her mouth, her eyes filling with disgust. "Those horrid men dumped a corpse on your doorstep?"

"I don't think it was human—more likely it came from the knacker's yard. But I don't think that it makes much difference to the average person."

"What a terrible thing to do. I hope you're going to file a complaint."

Stephen laughed. "And what do you expect anyone to do?"

"Well ... something. The resurrectionists can't go about dumping things like that in front of someone's place of business. If you don't stop them now, what might they do next?"

"At least I know my warning was received."

She regarded him suspiciously. "What warning?"

"You don't think I would let what happened to you yesterday go unchallenged? I told them to leave you alone."

"I find it hard to believe that they should be so worried about a lone female," she said with a toss of her head. "They risk jail every night—why should I pose such a threat?"

"Because if everyone put up guards in the church-yards, the body trade would dry up." Stephen glared at her. "I know that's what you want, but with it would go any hopes of medical advances. You'd have every physician and surgeon in the country after you then, as well."

She took a deep breath. "I only wanted to keep them from getting Amy. I didn't mean to cause you any trouble, Stephen."

"That I find hard to believe." Stephen gave her an exasperated look. "You're an endless source of it."

Linette's expression turned indignant. "That's right. I lie awake at night thinking of ways to make your life more difficult."

"I never said you did it on purpose," Stephen said, seeking to unruffle her feathers. "But no matter how well meaning your intentions, something always goes wrong."

"Well, I certainly don't intend to have anything more to do with those nasty men. Anyhow, you said you told them to leave me alone."

"That doesn't mean they'll listen to me."

"What, you doubt the power of your influence?" She arched a brow. "I'm shocked, Stephen."

He threw up his hands. "If you don't want to take this seriously, fine. But don't expect me to save you again." He brushed past her and started up the stairs.

"Stephen?"

He turned back and looked at her.

"I will be careful." She gave him an encouraging smile. "I won't take any chances. I promise to take the carriage home."

"When is it coming?"

"Two."

He pointed a finger at her in warning. "I'll be here to see that you get in it." He turned and headed up the stairs.

Damn that woman. He should be more worried about his own problems, but instead, in a few short minutes, she'd managed to twist his insides into knots again with her stubbornness. Why couldn't she simply take his advice and try to avoid trouble for a few days? Was that too much to ask?

He would be back here at two to make damn sure that she was in that carriage, whether she wanted him to be or not.

She probably had no idea what she was doing to him, either. Linette Gregory was the most infuriating, irritating, stubborn, and intractable woman he had ever met. Why couldn't he get her out of his mind? She was there constantly, taunting him with her face, her words, her actions. There were times when he wanted to turn her over his knee and give her a good spanking.

Or else kiss her into insensibility.

And he wasn't sure which one would give him the most pleasure.

By the time he returned to the school, the front steps were spotlessly clean. Stephen hoped this would be the end of things; he didn't relish an all-out war with the resurrectionists. When provoked, they could do much worse than they had today.

Still, he wasn't going to let this action go unremarked. But he wanted to handle the situation with subtlety. The fall term was almost over. When the new term started next year, he might look for another source of corpses for his students.

As he mounted the steps to Linette's office, Stephen checked his watch one more time. Two minutes past two. And there was no carriage awaiting her out front. She had no intention of complying with his order. He pushed the door open without knocking.

"Where's the carriage?" he asked gruffly. "I didn't see it in front."

"Good afternoon," she said, deliberately ignoring his question. "Is the weather still pleasant outside? One can hardly believe it is December.

"You said you would leaving at two."

Slowly, she turned around to face him. "If the carriage is not here, I can hardly leave, can I? I would be deliberately disobeying your orders."

He ran a hand through his dark hair. "Is it even coming?"

"As far as I know. Why don't you station yourself at the front door and inform me when it arrives? I can get some more work done while I wait."

"I'm going to look in on a patient. Don't you dare set foot outside this office before I get back."

Linette smothered a laugh. "Yes, sir."

Stephen stomped down the hall. She *was* trying to make his life miserable.

At least she was waiting for him when he returned. He helped her into her winter cloak and followed her silently down the stairs. The carriage must have arrived by now.

Linette paused at the front door. "If you're so concerned, perhaps you should escort me home. Otherwise,

I might decide to stop the carriage a few blocks from here and get out."

He gave her a dark look. "I don't think you're that foolish."

She smiled impishly and took his arm. "You'll never know unless you come with me. Besides, Aunt's been begging me to ask you to tea."

"I have work to do," he said with surprising reluctance.

"Which, of course, is why you took the time to come here." Her blue eyes danced impishly.

He gave her a weak smile. "All right, I will have tea with you."

"Good." She flashed him a radiant smile. "Wait until you see all the goodies. There will be enough for even your sweet tooth."

Following Linette into the Barton house, Stephen felt foolish. Foolish, because he shouldn't be here; he had too many things to do. Foolish, because despite everything, he wanted to be here and was pleased that she'd asked him.

Linette led him to the drawing room. "Aunt, look who I persuaded to join us for tea."

Mrs. Barton gave him a welcoming smile. "Good afternoon, Mr. Ashworth. How nice of you to come."

"I promised him that there would be tea cakes." Linette tossed Stephen a teasing look as she took her seat. "I hope Cook has been baking today."

"That she has." Mrs. Barton looked at Stephen. "You are making a favorable impression at the Dispensary, Mr. Ashworth. Everyone speaks highly of your work."

Stephen turned and winked at Linette. "I try to do my best."

A maid brought in the tea tray and Stephen saw that Linette had not exaggerated. There were two heaping plates of delicacies: frosted tea cakes, three different kinds of biscuits, and glazed buns. Enough food for three times as many people.

Linette held out the plate. "Take as many as you like."

Embarrassed, Stephen took only two cakes.

"Only two?" Linette stared at him. "Are you feeling all right today?"

"Stop teasing the poor man," Mrs. Barton chided her niece. "He will not wish to come back again."

"Exactly," Stephen said with a smile. "Even for food as delicious as this. You are an excellent hostess, Mrs. Barton."

She beamed at the compliment. "You must come to dinner soon, and sample Cook's other talents." Aunt turned to Linette. "I spoke with Mrs. Davis today. She asked about you."

Stephen sat back and listened as the two women chatted, grateful he wasn't expected to converse. He preferred sitting here, watching Linette. She wore a plainly styled gown in some light shade of green and it gave her light gray eyes a greenish tint. He suddenly realized that her eyes took on the color of her dress when she wore blue as well.

Once again, he was struck by the contrasts within her. A beautiful woman who wasn't afraid to help others. She was equally at ease in the drawing room as she was in the sickroom. A fascinating lady; one he wanted to know better.

Except that he should not.

"Stephen?" Linette's voice broke into his thoughts. "Did you receive your invitation?"

"Invitation?"

"For the Dispensary ball?"

Stephen vaguely recalled seeing a thick velum envelope on his desk. He hadn't opened it.

Linette looked at him with accusing eyes. "You will be attending?"

He smiled weakly.

"It's our gala festival for the year," Mrs. Barton explained. "This year, Lady Howell has generously allowed us to use her home."

"And you need to spend at least one evening without thinking about medicine," Linette added

He laughed. "You're far too optimistic. I find it impossible not to think about medicine."

"A grand supper will be served. You will be able to eat to your heart's content." Linette's voice was cajoling.

"Are you trying to bribe me, Miss Gregory?" He arched a brow.

"Most assuredly."

"Then of course, I will be there." Stephen grinned widely. "You know I would never miss the opportunity to eat."

Linette beamed at him. "And I shall save you the supper dance."

Stephen's smile wavered. Dance. Of course, one danced at a ball. Everyone except him. But he wasn't going to tell her that. There were a few things he didn't want to admit—and she didn't need to know.

Stephen decided to walk home from Mrs. Barton's. Despite Linette's teasing, he'd enjoyed having tea with her. Until she'd mentioned the ball.

He'd known he would be expected to attend the various Dispensary functions; that had been made clear to him at that very first meeting. He'd never bothered to consider just what that might entail.

He'd never imagined they would have a ball. With dancing.

What would Linette say when she learned that he couldn't dance?

It didn't matter. She would probably have more partners than she could count. He wasn't there to dance with her, he was there to represent the medical staff at the Dispensary. The guests wouldn't care whether he danced or not.

Except for Linette.

For a moment, he wished that he did dance, so he could spend time with her, be a part of the other world that she belonged to, the one of wealth, and society, and privilege. But it was a pointless wish. He had no role to play in that world, and better uses for his time than learning how to dance.

And better uses for his time than thinking about a woman he did not need in his life. One who, no matter how much he thought about her, wasn't the type of woman who belonged in his life.

But since he didn't dance he wouldn't have an excuse to hold Linette in his arms again.

After Stephen left, Linette continued to sit with her aunt in the drawing room.

"I am glad to see you so enthusiastic about the ball," Aunt said. "I do wish you would allow me to buy you a new gown."

Linette smiled at Aunt's persistent attempts to turn her into a fashion plate. "With all my work, I don't have time for any fittings."

"One can always make the time to be fashionable," Aunt remarked. "It will be an opportunity to dazzle the eyes of all the young gentlemen."

"I don't wish to dazzle anyone," Linette said firmly.

"Not even our young surgeon?"

Linette flushed. She would like to dazzle Stephen; to have him look at her with admiration and desire in his eyes. But it was a foolish thought. Colorful silks and satins meant nothing to him. He'd be more impressed if she brought him a new patient.

"He has been most solicitous recently."

"It means nothing," Linette said quickly. "Only that he is not as unfeeling as I thought. He does care for his patients."

Aunt gave her an odd look. "And is that why he accompanied you home today? You are not his patient."

"He came because I invited him—because you wanted me to."

"Are you being wilfully blind, or merely ignorant?"

"Ignorant of what?"

"That young man has a definite interest in you, my dear. Don't you notice the way he looks at you?"

"He doesn't look at me in any way."

Aunt smiled. "I own, he is not exactly what I would have wanted for you, my dear. But you persistently reject all my choices. Perhaps this is for the best."

"Aunt! You talk as if he has offered, when most of the time he barely tolerates me. The only way Stephen Ashworth would look upon me favorably is if I were dead and laid out on his dissecting table."

"I think you give the man too little credit. He knows an attractive woman when he sees one."

Linette remembered the day he'd examined her elbow. He'd said virtually the same thing then.

Was it true? Did he think she was attractive? Did he actually look on her like a man looked at a woman?

"I think you are making far too much out of nothing," she said at last. "Mr. Ashworth is not interested in me— or anyone else, unless they have an interesting surgical problem. Or are dead."

She ignored her aunt's smug smile.

That evening, sitting at her rosewood desk, Linette tried to concentrate on her French translations, but she couldn't focus her thoughts.

Aunt's comments about Stephen distracted her. Despite her denials, Linette wished Aunt's words were true, wished Stephen did care for her, admired her. But she knew it wasn't true. It *couldn't* be true. He'd made it very clear that he thought her a silly fool.

But there were other times, when she saw a gleam of appreciation in his dark eyes, when he expressed his concern for her safety, that she thought he just might have some fond feelings for her. Not that he'd ever admit it.

Linette wasn't sure she wanted to know how he felt. Her feelings for him were so confused. She admitted to a physical attraction; she found his touch both comforting and thrilling. But they continued to argue about nearly everything, his work and hers. She could not envision them ever being comfortable with each other.

But perhaps the ball would be a place to find out. It provided a neutral ground where topics like medicine and anatomy wouldn't be discussed. They could have one night to forget who they were, and what they did, and merely enjoy each other's company

It would be a perfectly normal evening. The kind her aunt wanted her to enjoy more often—with proper young men of her set. The very men Linette wanted nothing to do with.

Stephen was so different from them; it made him difficult to understand. There were times when she thought he might care for her—when he'd so carefully examined her elbow, when he'd comforted her after Amy's death, when he'd insisted on escorting her home yesterday. But at other times, he barely tolerated her, and she didn't know which feeling was the strongest.

Perhaps, in the gala atmosphere of a charity ball, she could find out.

Chapter 16

Stephen fully intended to be on time for the Dispensary fund-raiser. But engrossed in his reading, he lost all track of time and was shocked when he finally glanced at the clock. He was due at the ball in an hour! There was barely time to dress, and no time to eat. Thank God they were serving supper.

Swearing under his breath, Stephen pulled off his shirt and tossed it into a corner. Poking his head into the clothespress, he finally unearthed his last clean one. Somehow, on top of everything else, he needed to remember to send out the laundry tomorrow. He hastily drew on his pantaloons, mumbling epithets as he fumbled with the buttons on the legs. Now, if only he could find his dress shoes . . .

This whole evening was foolish. He didn't need to be there, didn't belong there. No one cared if the Dispensary surgeon attended. He was only going because Linette wanted him to, and he was incapable of refusing her anything.

Or so he told himself. But deep down, he knew he was going because he wanted to have the excuse to see her.

He finally unearthed his shoes from under the bed. Rummaging through a drawer, he found one white glove, but despaired of ever finding the mate. Who was the idiot who decreed this was the proper dress for a gentleman? He discovered it at last, buried in the bottom drawer beneath some old amputation saws and a pair of trousers. Stuffing the gloves into his pocket, he grabbed the cravat hanging on the back of his chair and draped it around his neck. He'd tie it later, on the way.

A quick glance at the clock showed him he didn't have any time to waste. He struggled into his overcoat and took the stairs two at a time, knowing he'd have to walk a few blocks to find a hack.

He was lucky, and only had to go halfway down the second block before he found one. Stephen gave directions to the driver and sat back with relief against the seat.

There were a great number of carriages pulled up in front of Lady Howell's house in Grosvenor Square, disgorging their inhabitants in a swirl of cloaks and finery. As he watched the elegantly dressed gentlemen and their bejeweled ladies enter, Stephen realized this was going to be an even more elegant affair than he had thought. His immediate inclination was to order the driver to pull out of the line and take him home. He didn't belong here; no one would notice if he didn't appear.

Except Linette.

When the hack reached the door, Stephen stepped down, paid his fare, and strode up the steps. He straightened his cuffs and brushed a speck of lint off his jacket. He was as presentable as he could be.

Unlike at the musicale, no one stopped him at the door, questioning his presence. Stephen stepped into the brightly lit hall and looked around him. A glittering chandelier cast its glow over the marbled floor, illuminating the guests who drifted up the massive twin staircases. He heard the faint strains of an orchestra playing.

No, he didn't belong here. A nervous tremor raced up his spine.

He started to remove his coat and found himself entangled in the untied ends of his cravat. How in the blazes was he going to deal with that now, with everyone watching? He skirted the edge of the left stair, looking for an exit from the massive hall. He only needed a few moments of privacy.

"May I take your coat, sir?" A liveried footman appeared before him, holding out his arm.

"Can you tie a cravat?" Stephen blurted out.

He saw the superior look on the man's face. "I believe I have some talent in that area, sir."

"Good." Stephen pulled the man toward a side door.

"I would be careful of him if I were you." Linette came up behind the footman. "He's a surgeon. An anatomist."

The footman stared at Stephen with widened eyes and mumbled a hasty farewell.

Stephen glared at Linette. "What did you do that for?"

She laughed. "You looked so dreadfully serious, as if you were calculating how many students could make use of his body."

"I thought no such thing!" he snapped until he saw the teasing look in her eyes. "If you must know, I was trying to get him to tie my cravat for me."

Linette eyed his dangling cravat with undisguised amusement. "Yes, it does appear you have a problem there, doesn't it?" She motioned for him to follow her and led him into a small anteroom to the left of the stairs, which was crammed floor to ceiling with paintings.

"A minigallery," she explained. "For those pictures which are out of favor at the moment." She inspected a pastoral scene. "I rather like this one."

While Linette examined the paintings, Stephen examined her. Her blond hair was piled atop her head in loose curls that made him want to reach out and touch them—and then run his fingers along the shapely neck below. In her low-cut ball gown, she was displaying almost as much skin as she had that day in his office. His fingers tingled at the memory of the feel of her.

It was hard to believe that this elegant-looking lady was the same one who'd stayed at Amy's side all night, tenderly caring for a dying girl in a shabby room. And though she would deny it, Stephen knew the woman he

looked at tonight was the true Linette, a woman who
belonged to a world he could never be a part of.

She turned from inspecting the picture. "Take off your
coat. I can't deal with your cravat otherwise."

Stephen complied. Linette took the two ends of the
cravat, looking dubiously at their limp condition. "Does
your laundress know about starch?"

"It doesn't matter." Stephen felt embarrassed by his
predicament. He wanted to get out of here, wanted to
get away from her as quickly as possible. His heart
pounded at her nearness. "Tie the blasted thing in a
semblance of a knot so I don't look the perfect fool."

"Hold still, then." She stripped off her gloves and
flung them onto the table.

Her fingers brushed against his neck as she adjusted
the cravat around his collar and Stephen tensed at her
touch.

It was an action fraught with intimacy, the type of
favor a wife would do for her husband. He kept his gaze
fixed on the far wall, but he didn't need to see her to
be acutely aware of her presence. The delicate fragrance
she wore tantalized his senses. It was so different from
the smell of decay and preservative that permeated his
daily existence. Soothing. Enticing.

"Quit fidgeting," she said crossly as she struggled with
the limp material.

He tried to distract himself with the reminder that he
didn't want to be here. He could have stayed home and
worked on his book, organized his instruments, anything,
to keep away from her.

"There," Linette said, patting the knot. "You will do."

Stephen instantly stepped back. "Thank you," he said
stiffly, both relieved and dismayed that she had finished.

Her lips curved into another teasing smile. "Why, Mr.
Ashworth, what a generous response! You will acquire
a reputation for friendliness if you persist."

"I said thank you," he grumbled, looking uneasily
about the room. He wanted to be out in the hall, with

people around them. Here, in the small confines of this chamber, it was far too difficult to ignore the enchanting picture she presented. He was shocked at how badly he wanted to touch her.

She tilted her head to one side and examined him with a critical eye. "You look very nice tonight."

He ran a finger under the cravat, which felt as if it were choking him. "I still don't know what I'm doing here."

"You're here to enjoy yourself—as are we all." She displayed the small card that hung from her wrist. "I saved the supper dance for you. Would you like a waltz as well?"

He stared at her.

"You did intend to dance with me tonight, didn't you?"

He flushed. "No."

Now it was her turn to color. "Well, thank you very much." She grabbed her gloves and started for the door but Stephen reached out and grabbed her arm.

"It's not you," he said, reluctant to make his confession. "It's just . . . I don't dance."

She stared down at his feet. "You look like you have two good feet."

"But they don't know what to do on a dance floor," he said ruefully.

Linette looked up at him, astonishment in her face. "You really mean it, don't you?"

He shrugged. "Dancing isn't a requirement for either a surgeon's or apothecary's license."

"Then why did you even come?"

Stephen eyed her coolly. "I didn't think I had a choice."

Linette nibbled her lip. "I'm sorry, Stephen. I never meant for you to be uncomfortable."

"Not everyone is as talented as you."

"Talented?"

"Languages, music, dancing. All the accomplishments I lack."

"Many of the guests won't dance. No one will even notice."

"I am so relieved."

She put her hands on her hips and said reproachfully, "If you'd told me about this earlier, we could have done something about it."

Stephen laughed, trying to ignore how her hands accentuated her tiny waist. "Now, that I doubt. You can't know how impossible a task that would be."

"Why? If you can learn to amputate a leg, surely you can learn to dance."

He shrugged. "I detest music, for one."

"You do? Why?"

"Because I don't have an ear for it."

Linette waved off his explanation. "Lots of people don't. It's of no consequence."

"Unless you come from a family that lives for music."

Her eyes widened. "Did yours?"

He avoided her gaze and nodded. "I'm their one failure."

"I would hardly call being a noted surgeon a failure. Look at the difference you make in people's lives. You chose to engage yourself in a noble cause."

Stephen gave her a wry glance. "I decided to became a surgeon to spite my father."

She stared at him. "What?"

"Ironic, isn't it? I didn't think I would enjoy it this much. But I do; I can't imagine doing anything else."

Linette's eyes widened. "Your family doesn't appreciate your work?"

He shrugged, trying to appear indifferent, then reached out and fingered the card dangling from her wrist. "If you are not on the dance floor soon, they will come looking for you."

"Stephen . . ."

"It doesn't matter, Linette," he said softly.

She looked up at him. "Will you take me into supper, at least? I know you can eat."

He bowed. "That I will do." He held open the door and followed her into the hall.

She put her hand on his arm and they walked up the stairs. "I do mean to introduce you to some of the guests. There are several who want to meet you."

"How do you know I want to meet them?"

"You do, I assure you." She bent her head closer. "Money and hospital connections. Aren't those the two things that interest you the most right now?"

"You forgot dead bodies," he said with a teasing smile, then patted her hand. "I will be *delighted* to meet anyone you care to introduce me to."

Linette squeezed his arm. "We both know what a lie that is. But I am glad you are willing to pretend, tonight."

The moment they entered the ballroom, she was snatched from his arm by her partner and whirled out onto the floor. Stephen retreated to a far wall and leaned against it, watching the dancers. Eyeing them intently, he sought a glimpse of Linette. He caught a flash of blue that looked like her gown, but there were too many dancers in the way for him to be certain.

Slowly, he moved to his right, trying to get a better look, but it wasn't her. Disappointed, he continued to circle the room.

He saw her at last, her face flushed with heat, a wide smile on her face as she stepped through the dizzying pattern of the dance. She moved with an elegant grace that he envied as she followed the complicated steps that Stephen knew he could never master. He would tromp all over her feet.

Still, a part of him wished he could be out there, standing beside her, across from her, looking at her delighted smile as they danced across the floor. Linette was obviously enjoying herself. Something inside of him stirred as he reveled in her pleasure, then it quickly faded.

Seeing her now, amidst the fancy gowns and glittering jewels, only reminded him how different they were. She might work at the Dispensary, and care for the people of the neighborhood, but she belonged to this life. She was as comfortable in society as she was in the tenements of her students and he admired her for that. He could never be comfortable in this world.

But that didn't matter. As a surgeon, he would always be apart from the world. It was more than mere social status; it was the nature of his work. And it was something he had never minded. Until now.

He edged toward the door but she caught sight of him. A wide smile of pleasure lit her face and Stephen forgot his intention to leave.

He couldn't wait to take her down to supper; wanted to watch her eyes dance and her lips curve into a smile as they chatted about innocuous matters. There would be no disease or death discussed at her table tonight. This was a social evening and Stephen vowed that he would make no mention of medicine.

As a new set formed and Linette's partner led her further across the room, Stephen ambled out the door. It would be better out here, away from the dancers. Watching her dance, knowing he could not participate, was too uncomfortable. Crossing the hall, he looked into the card room. Several tables were set up, but they held about as much appeal as the dancing. He had no money to squander on the chance turn of a card.

Bored, he went back into the hall, wondering if he could get something to eat before supper was served at midnight. His stomach rumbled ominously, reminding him he hadn't eaten dinner.

"Mr. Ashworth!" Mrs. Barton hailed him. Stephen walked toward her and bowed in greeting.

"What is a fine young man like you doing out here all alone?" she asked with a twinkle in her eye. "You should be in the ballroom, dancing with an attractive young lady."

He opened his mouth to answer but she took his arm and bent her head close. "There is someone here I should like you to meet. I think he is over—oh, yes, there he is." Without loosening her grip, she firmly drew Stephen behind her.

She halted in front of a portly man with a red-veined nose and balding head.

"Lord Graves, I should like you to meet Mr. Stephen Ashworth, the new surgeon at the Dispensary."

"Delighted, my boy, delighted." Lord Graves shook hands enthusiastically. "Wonderful work you've done at the facility. Helping the poor and unfortunate. A worthy cause."

"Lord Graves is far too modest," said Mrs. Barton. "He was one of our first subscribers and he has done so much for us."

"The medical staff appreciates your efforts," Stephen said.

"I understand you teach at a private school?"

Stephen nodded.

"Have you thought about teaching at a hospital?" Lord Graves eyed him shrewdly.

Stephen quickly readjusted his opinion of the man. He was no fool. "I would very much like to have such a position."

"Come by and have a chat with me next week." Lord Graves gave him a conspiratorial look. "As you know, the London Hospital is planning to create a position for another assistant surgeon . . ."

"I thought the appointment was made," said Stephen, hardly daring to breathe at this opportunity.

"There have been delays and some of the candidates have withdrawn," Lord Graves said. "We are still looking for qualified men."

"I would be very interested in applying," Stephen said.

"Good, good. As I said, come by next week—say Tuesday, at four—and we can discuss the matter." He glanced at Mrs. Barton. "Now, my dear, if you will excuse me—Ashworth—I should like to avail myself of the card room."

He walked away, leaving Stephen staring after him with a mixture of astonishment and elation. He could barely believe his luck. If he could gain the support of a man like Lord Graves, he might even have a chance.

He turned a speculative look on Mrs. Barton. "Did you ask him to talk with me?"

She responded with a vague wave of her hands. "Lord Graves is involved in so many different organizations. We are very lucky to have him supporting the Dispensary. I hope your talk with him goes well." She laid a hand on his arm. "Now, if you will excuse me, I need to look after the guests."

Stephen tried to calm himself. The odds were against him. Lord Graves was probably doing this merely as a favor for Mrs. Barton.

Still, the mere possibility that he might have a chance for the post made his pulse race. He'd given up hopes for the London long ago, but now it looked as if the situation wasn't as bleak as he'd thought. Stephen meant to take full advantage of this unexpected opportunity.

He couldn't wait to tell Linette; she might know more about the situation. But that would be impossible until supper.

Supper. Now that his excitement was tempered with caution, he was hungrier than ever. He'd find something to eat while he waited for her.

After a lengthy search, Stephen finally found the supper room on the ground floor and walked in. His eyes widened with pleased surprise. At the far side of the room, the long serving tables were weighted down with enough food for a dozen banquets. His stomach growled in anticipation. Grabbing a plate, he heaped it with slices of fruit and cheese, and some pastries. It would be enough to take the edge off his hunger.

A footman gave him a disdainful look. "Supper is not ready to be served, sir."

"I've special permission," Stephen replied with an arrogant air and proceeded to eat his food.

He wondered what would happen if, miracle of miracles, he did receive an appointment at the London.

He'd keep his school, of course; the extra work would not be difficult, and it might ease his financial worries. It would take time for a hospital appointment to gain him more paying patients.

The Dispensary was more of a problem, but Stephen honestly hoped he could continue to work there.

And not just because it gave him a tie to Linette.

Stephen shook his head ruefully. No matter the subject, his thoughts always came back to her. Thinking about Linette was starting to be as natural as breathing, despite all his resolutions to the contrary.

He was dangerously attracted to her—dangerous, because he didn't want to be. Yet he was helpless to prevent himself from wanting her. Stephen knew he risked hurt at her hands by admitting his feelings for her. Yet he couldn't erase from his mind the picture of her, at poor Amy's deathbed, when Linette had looked so vulnerable. He'd felt an overwhelming urge to protect her from the hurts of the world, to keep her safe and happy and away from the kind of pain that he encountered every day in his work.

But his feelings for her went beyond that night. He'd had a similar sensation when she'd toppled off the chair in his office and fell to the floor. In those few seconds he'd felt stark terror at the thought that she might have hurt herself.

And when those bullies accosted her, he'd never felt such a white-hot rage, and if he'd been able to get his hands on those men, any oath he'd taken about preserving human life would have gotten short shrift. Murder would have been too good for them.

When the servants moving through the supper room began to give him increasingly unfriendly looks, Stephen decided to leave. Surely, Linette would finish dancing soon. Impatient to be with her, he dashed up the stairs.

It had been a very long time since he'd cared this strongly about anyone, and he knew the danger of that path. It would be better if he forgot all about her.

But when had he ever done what was good for him?

Chapter 17

Linette's face ached from making too many polite smiles, her toes hurt from being stepped on by less than agile partners, and she couldn't wait until supper, when she could sit down and rest.

And be with Stephen.

She prayed he wasn't too bored. Aunt Barton had said she would look after him and make certain that he met some of the important Dispensary supporters. After all, that was why *he* was here tonight.

Linette was here to see Stephen.

At last, the supper dance was only one set away. Eagerly, Linette scanned the room, looking for a glimpse of Stephen. Was he looking forward to their time together as eagerly as she?

She spotted him at last, leaning against the far wall by the door, arms crossed over his chest and a resigned expression on his face. Linette stifled a giggle. He looked like someone waiting for the dentist.

After an interminable time, the music stopped and Linette curtsied to her partner, then hurried across the room to Stephen.

"Are you enjoying yourself?" she asked.

"Would you believe me if I said yes?"

She laughed lightly. "No. But I hope you are not too bored. Have you talked with any of the guests? I promised I would introduce you to some of the Dispensary supporters."

"I had a talk with Lord Graves."

Linette started with surprise. *She* had intended to introduce them. "Oh?"

"Your aunt introduced us."

"He's a very generous supporter—and he's very interested in medicine." She fanned her heated cheeks. "I hope you spoke nicely to him."

"I nearly fell to the ground and kissed his feet," Stephen said. "He's on the appointment committee for the London Hospital."

Her eyes widened in mock surprise. "Really?"

Stephen gave her a suspicious look. "Did you ask him to talk with me?"

Linette toyed with her fan. "I might have mentioned that he should talk with our new surgeon."

"He said they haven't filled the position yet. I'm talking to him next week."

"Really? Stephen, that is wonderful." Linette grabbed his hand. "I'm so excited for you. This is the opportunity you've been waiting for."

"It's only an interview," he said diffidently, but he couldn't suppress his smile. Reluctantly, he released her hand and looked at the dancers. "Your next partner will be looking for you."

"This is the supper dance," she explained. "We can go down now. You may have first pick of all the goodies."

"I was already down there," he admitted, shamefacedly.

Linette laughed. "Stuffing your face with sweet cakes and pastries, no doubt. I have never seen a man so fond of sweets."

"I ate fruit and cheese as well."

"I am teasing you, Stephen." Linette tucked her arm in his. "You can eat as many pastries as you wish."

"I intend to."

Stephen led her downstairs and pulled out her chair, then strode to the food tables and filled their plates.

"I can't eat all of this," Linette protested when he put the plate in front of her. It overflowed with lobster patties, fried oysters, slices of game pie, boiled artichokes, and pickled mushrooms.

"I'll help you," he said with a grin.

Linette darted him an amused look. "I thought you said you'd already eaten."

"Most of this wasn't here earlier," he said, stuffing a mushroom into his mouth.

She took a small bite of lobster. "What do you usually do for meals? Does your landlady cook for you?"

Stephen shook his head. "I eat in one of the neighborhood taverns, or in one of the inns near the school."

"It must be tiring having to dine out every night."

"It's convenient. And I can eat when I please."

"Or forget to eat altogether." She shot him a chastening look.

Stephen shrugged. "A surgeon can't keep regular hours."

Linette picked at the crust of the game pie with her fork. "I hope you were not too bored, earlier. I still wish you had told me you didn't know how to dance. You could have learned a few steps."

"It doesn't matter."

"A surgeon at the London Hospital should know how to dance."

"I'll worry about that *if* I get the appointment." He pointed to her plate. "You're not eating."

Linette pushed his hand away. "Stephen, there is enough food here for an entire table."

"You've been dancing all night. You have to keep your strength up."

She laughed. "I wouldn't be able to dance a step if I ate half of this."

"And I didn't even bring you any dessert."

Linette grinned at the disappointment in his eyes. "Go back and get your sweets, Stephen. See if you can find something with raspberries for me."

He soon returned with several treats—raspberry tarts and a rich custard with a dollop of raspberry jam on top.

"Whoever planned the menu must be equally fond of raspberries," he said with a knowing look. "Or did you know that already?"

Ignoring his taunt, Linette took a bite of the tart. "Delicious. I loved to stuff myself with the neighbors' raspberries every summer."

Stephen nodded smugly. "So you did grow up in the country. I thought so."

"And why is that?"

"You don't act like a city dweller. Most Londoners have a different view of life; they're more unshakable—some would say more cynical. I don't see that in you." He leaned forward, his dark eyes warm, and inviting. "Tell me about the place where you ate all those delicious raspberries."

Linette's hand halted suddenly with the spoon halfway to her mouth. This personal interest was new. Did it mean that he *did* care? "I grew up in Staffordshire."

"Does your family still live there?"

She dabbed her mouth with a napkin. "Yes, they do."

"Why don't you?" He watched her intently for the answer.

The intent look in her eyes made Linette feel as if he could see right through her, to her deepest secrets and desires. To what she felt, in her heart. "Because I prefer to live here in London, where I can do work that I feel is important."

Stephen gave her a sympathetic smile. "They don't approve?"

Linette stared at her plate, stung by a sudden upswell of emotion. Everyone else thought she was foolish. Only Stephen understood.

"They wanted me to do other things. So I chose to live here with Aunt Barton, instead."

"Who allows you to do what you wish."

She nodded and scooped out another bit of custard. "She doesn't always agree with me, but she accepts that I know what I am doing."

He nodded, then looked around the nearly deserted room. "It must be time for the dancing to start again. Should I take you upstairs?"

Linette shook her head. "Not yet. You have time to eat a few more sweets. But you better get them quickly—they are starting to remove the food."

"I'm too full to eat another bite," He leaned back in his chair, arms crossed over his chest. "I'm content to watch you finish your custard."

Linette set down her spoon and gave him an exasperated look. "How can I eat when you are staring at me?"

Stephen laughed. "Will it help if I cover my eyes? I wouldn't want to deprive you of your custard."

Linette pushed the dish away. "I've had enough. If we stay here, my next partner will find me." She gave Stephen a conspiratorial grin. "Shall we find a place to hide?"

She led him to the small anteroom where she'd tied his cravat. She sat on the sofa and patted the cushion next to her. "Sit. We can be comfortable while we talk."

"Are you sure you wouldn't rather be dancing."

She shook her head and Stephen sat beside her. "I'm sorry to disappoint you with my lack of social skills."

"I don't mind. I'd rather sit and talk with you about something more substantial than the weather or the latest *on dit.*"

"It seems to me that we've talked mostly about food," he said with a wry grin.

She laughed lightly. "Ah, but for a ball, that is weighty talk."

"We could talk about other things."

Linette sucked in her breath at the sudden intensity in his gaze. "Such as?"

He took her hand. "Your hand, for example. It is very well formed."

She blushed.

Stephen caressed her fingers and the back of her hand. "Such tiny phalanges and delicate metacarpels."

"What are those?"

"The bones in your hand."

His fingers were tracing patterns over her skin, sending warm shivers up her arm. But she didn't pull away. It felt far too wonderful to have him touching her—like that day in his office. They had been alone together then, as they were alone now.

He ran a hand up the outside of her arm to the elbow. "This is your ulna, the small bone in the arm." Turning her arm over, Stephen ran a finger down the soft skin of her inner arm. "And below here is the radius."

Clasping her hand, he lifted it to his lips, brushing them across her fingers. Then he turned her hand and planted a kiss in the palm, and then the inside of her wrist. Linette closed her eyes at the exquisite sensation.

"Tell me more," she whispered.

His dark eyes gleamed and his hand caressed the nape of her neck. "These are your cervical vertebrae—seven in all." His fingers brushed across her bare shoulder and followed the line of bone across the front. "This is the clavicle—your collarbone. I can tell you're not a laborer."

"How?"

"Heavy labor shortens it, curves it. Yours is long and slender." His fingers hesitated at the hollow of her throat, then lightly touched her skin. "This is the interclavicle notch, where the bones fasten to the sternum, the top of the rib cage."

He traced along the line of her jaw and under her chin. "The inferior maxillary—what you would call the jawbone."

Stephen's breath was warm against her cheek and Linette could barely breathe. As his fingers brushed softly over her lips, she shut her eyes. He was going to kiss her. His hand grasped her chin and turned her head toward him, then he touched his mouth to hers.

His kiss was soft, caressing, and achingly sweet. When

he pulled away, Linette's eyes drifted open and she found herself looking into the dark brown depths of his.

"I shouldn't have done that," he said in a hoarse voice.

"Why?" she whispered.

"Because I want to do it again."

Linette's eyes fluttered shut as his mouth came down on hers again. This time his kisses were eager, demanding, filled with a passion that startled her. Grasping her shoulders, he pulled her closer, his lips hot and hungry.

She was lost. Hopelessly and inalterably lost. Linette wrapped a hand about his neck, caressing his nape, entwining her fingers in the dark hair that fell over his collar. His kisses were beyond anything she could have imagined.

Stephen, oh, Stephen.

His right hand stroked her arm, fingers dancing over her bare skin. A low moan of pleasure sounded deep in his throat and he pulled her closer, squeezing the breath out of her.

Linette shivered, her nerves screaming at his touch. She forgot all else and melted against him, eagerly returning his kisses, wanting him to know that she never wanted him to stop.

Abruptly, he tore his mouth away and pressed her head against his shoulder. Linette listened to their ragged breathing. The blood pounded in her ears, echoed by the equally loud beating of his heart. She took his hand and placed it over the swell of her breast.

"My heart," she whispered. "Beating for you."

There was a noise in the hall and they jumped apart just before the door opened and a round-faced young man in tailored evening clothes stuck his head in. Linette groaned silently. Freddy.

"Ah, there you are!"

Linette prayed that she didn't look as guilt-ridden as Stephen.

"Forgetting our dance?" he asked.

He was right; Linette hadn't given it a thought. "Stephen, this is Freddy Richardson. His mother is a dear friend of Aunt Barton's. Freddy, this is Mr. Stephen Ashworth, the surgeon at the Dispensary."

Stephen rose and held out his hand. "Sorry to have deprived you of your dance partner. We were just discussing plans for staffing the Dispensary during the evenings—for emergencies."

"Yes," Linette chimed in, pleased at Stephen's quick thinking. "Mr. Ashworth thinks his students would benefit from the experience."

Stephen bowed to Linette. "We can continue this discussion at another time, Miss Gregory. Please enjoy the dance."

Linette flashed him a wistful smile and took Freddy's arm, allowing him to lead her out of the room.

A cocoon of warm happiness surrounded Linette as she circled the dance floor. The ballroom, the dancers, even Freddy appeared distant, cloudy. Her mind was still back in that tiny anteroom, with Stephen.

She still felt his arms around her, tasted his heated lips as he kissed her again and again. She'd been lost in his kisses, the touch of his hands, the heated warmth of his body as she pressed herself against him. Desire still coursed through her at the very memory.

A smile came to her lips. He *did* care for her, did want her. She'd finally broken through his wall of indifference, forced him to show her that he was a man with emotion, passion, desire.

And he desired *her*. Linette's blood tingled at the thought.

All her hopes, all her dreams, were coming to pass. She had found the man she could work with, admire, *love*. They would work to make the Dispensary a model facility, a place that the others would look to. Together, they could accomplish everything.

And together, they could be deliciously happy.

*   *   *

Stephen sank down on the sofa.

What in God's name had he been thinking of?

He'd been tempting folly from the moment he'd agreed to come to this blasted ball, but he'd foolishly thought that in such a crowded atmosphere, he would be safe. There wouldn't be any opportunity for him to be alone with Linette. Instead, it was as if the entire evening had been designed with that aim in mind.

And what had he done when he found himself alone with her? Instead of maintaining his distance, he'd touched her at the first opportunity. And when she hadn't resisted, he'd kissed her, caressed her, held her close.

As he'd been wanting to do ever since that afternoon in his office, when he'd first felt her silky skin beneath his fingertips. Tonight, he'd risked all and acted on his impulses.

That was a big mistake. For now he knew what it was like and it wasn't going to be easy to forget the soft touch of her lips.

And forget he must. She was simply too dangerous, a distraction he could ill afford. How many times over the past weeks had he found himself thinking of her, instead of attending to his work? Far too many. And now, it would be worse. Because he would remember how she felt in his arms, how her lips felt beneath his.

He'd thought he'd go mad with pleasure when she'd touched him; the feel of her fingers wrapped in his hair had sent dizzying waves of desire through him.

Desire for someone he did not need, did not want to need, someone who didn't fully appreciate the work he did. That alone should have been enough to warn him to keep his impulses in check. Physical attraction could never overcome that gulf—it was too wide and too deep.

Yet for a few minutes, when he'd kissed her and held her, those thoughts had been far from his mind. Instead, he'd been overwhelmed by the mix of tenderness and desire he felt for her. Linette's eager response posed an even greater danger. It made him think, if only for the moment, that she cared for him; that she actually needed him and wanted him as well.

He cared for her. He wouldn't call it love—that was too strong a word. But caring was bad enough. For he'd learned many years ago that it wasn't safe to care. When you cared, you put yourself at another's mercy. And once that happened, you could never do enough to please them, and they eagerly told you when you failed. They relished the power they held over you.

Stephen wanted to believe that Linette would not be like that; after all, her life was a model of selflessness. She would support him, not tear him down.

But he didn't dare take the chance that he was wrong. Better to control his urges, to keep away from the temptation that she posed. She would only divert him from his goals. And he still wanted them most of all—the prestige, the status that came with a hospital appointment, the opportunity for research, the chance to make a name for himself in the history of medicine. *That* was what he wanted.

Not a golden-haired lady with teasing gray eyes and a kissable mouth.

In the hall, he waited while the footman retrieved his coat and then he stepped outside. The fog had settled, giving the street an eerie, mystical appearance. He stamped his feet to keep warm while he waited for a hackney.

Stephen knew he was being a coward, running away like this, but he had to. He was still under her spell; unable to think clearly. He needed to get home, where he'd be surrounded by his work and the tools of his trade. There, he knew what he was about and what he had to do.

There, he was safe.

Chapter 18

Stephen threw himself into his work on Sunday, keeping his mind and his body so busy that he had no time to think about what had happened the night before.

On Monday, he gave his morning lecture, supervised students in the dissecting room all afternoon, then began the arduous task of recopying the first half of his manuscript, in preparation for sending it to the printer.

On Tuesday, he went to the Dispensary, praying that there would be a lengthy line of patients waiting to see him. As long as he stayed in the examining room, there was little chance of seeing Linette. She never came into that part of the facility.

Except on the day when the resurrectionists had attacked her. And it still filled him with a white-hot anger that anyone would dare to lay a hand on her.

He had to avoid her. She was breaking down all his barriers, all his defenses. They had withstood any number of assaults—until he met her. And after that night at the ball, he knew he was in grave danger of giving in to her, to his feelings for her.

He had fought long and hard to master that weaker side of himself. Medicine had been an ideal choice, for it demanded detachment from the everyday world. Doctors could not care strongly, else they would go mad at the suffering all around them. It was the perfect refuge for one who wanted to hide from his feelings.

He had to keep away from Linette. It was as simple as that. If he didn't see her, he wouldn't be tempted by her sparkling eyes and enticing lips. By avoiding further temptation, it would be easier for him to regain control of himself and his emotions. All he needed was a little time, and he would be safe again.

Stephen had only himself to blame for this. He'd known that he was attracted to her, knew that he looked upon her with a less-than-objective interest. The day he examined her injured elbow had confirmed that. But had he acted sensibly after that? No. He'd allowed himself to be sucked into the emotional whirlwind of her life. At Amy's death, he'd seen Linette's vulnerability, and it had cracked his own defenses. When he'd succumbed to temptation and kissed her, that crack had widened into a valley.

But it was not too late; he knew to stay away from her now, no matter how much he wanted to see her. He had no other choice. If he saw her again, allowed himself to weaken further, he might not be able to escape next time. It was going to be difficult enough as it was.

Stephen could not rid his mind of thoughts of her, the feel of her, the taste of her. He might be able to face the bloodiest procedures in the operating theater without a qualm, but she could turn him inside out with only a smile. He dared not give her another chance to work her feminine magic on him.

The safest course would be to leave the Dispensary, but Stephen was reluctant to take such drastic action. He enjoyed working here, enjoyed treating the wide variety of ailments. As long as he kept out of her way, he was safe enough.

He would stay away from her until he no longer cared whether he saw her or not. Once he'd achieved that degree of indifference, everything would be fine.

Stephen deliberately worked late at the Dispensary, to make certain she would leave before he did. When he could delay his departure no longer, he stepped into the hall, looking quickly to the right and left, then dashed to the door.

On Saturday, after making his regular visit to the Dispensary, Stephen returned to his office. Mathers was waiting for him, ready to review next week's schedule.

When he walked into the office, Mathers tossed the new issue of *The Lancet* onto Stephen's desk. "Hot off the press."

"Anything interesting?"

Mathers slouched on the sofa. "The usual thing. They've collected over two hundred pounds for that surgeon in Exeter."

Stephen gave him a curious look. "The one who was arrested for having a body?"

"The very same."

Stephen laughed. "I'd like to see them try that in London. Could you see the great Sir Astley in the dock?"

"Sitting next to Abernethy? They'd make quite a pair."

"These provincials." Stephen shook his head. "I'd like to be called in the next time one of them takes ill. I'd show them the kind of medicine a medieval barber practiced. Then maybe they wouldn't be so eager to hamper medical research."

He pulled out the schedule, "Now, as for next week . . ."

"I haven't seen our benefactress around recently."

Stephen looked at Mathers. "Who?"

"Miss Gregory." Mathers prodded the books piled precariously on the sofa beside him. "Surely, she must realize it's time to clean your office again."

"Miss Gregory is not a cleaning woman," Stephen said stiffly.

"Have we had a falling out?" Mathers voice was teasing. "And just when I thought she might be willing to put a carpet and curtains in *my* room."

"I imagine she is busy with her own projects." Stephen turned an icy glare on Mathers. "As we all should be. Have you prepared those specimens for Monday's lecture?"

Mathers jumped to his feet. "I can take a hint. But the next time you see her, you might mention the idea. Now that it's winter, it's deuced cold upstairs."

Stephen grunted.

As soon as Mathers left, he dropped his pose of studied indifference.

Staying away from Linette Gregory had become an excruciating torture. Every time he came into his office, he half expected to see her there, calling on some errand or another. And for every sigh of relief he exhaled at finding himself alone, there was a secret sigh he uttered for her absence.

So far, he'd avoided her at the Dispensary for an entire week. But he wondered how long it would be before she sought him out. He didn't think she was going to dance out of his life as quickly as she'd danced in. At some point in time, there was going to be another meeting. She would appear eventually, for she still had several articles she was translating.

He just wanted to postpone it for as long as possible, so that when it came, he would be strong. He didn't dare face her with any feelings of uncertainty, or he would waver. And that would precipitate his downfall. He had to be able to face her without any more emotion than appreciation for the work she'd done.

Linette brushed the hair out of her eyes and bent over the books spread out before her. She was woefully behind in her translations for Stephen, but there had been so little time recently. She was half surprised that he hadn't asked where they were, and felt grateful for his consideration. He must know that with Christmas rapidly approaching, she was busier than ever.

Still, she felt a spark of disappointment that she hadn't had a chance to talk with him even once since the ball. She almost thought that he was avoiding her, but that idea was ridiculous.

Unless, of course, he was embarrassed about those

kisses. But why should he be? She certainly had responded with enough enthusiasm to assure him that his
intentions weren't unwanted. There was no reason for
him to be avoiding her because of that. No doubt he
was spending every spare minute working on his book.

Linette vowed to take him a special treat when she
finished the article she was working on. She'd scour London until she found the richest, creamiest pastry in the
city. That would please him.

Still, a tiny doubt nagged at the back of her mind.
Usually, after a man demonstrated such marked attention toward a lady, he made some effort to see her.
Linette didn't think she'd misinterpreted Stephen's interest. She still shivered as she recalled the feel of his hands
moving over her skin, the husky tone of his voice as
he'd named the bones beneath his fingers. There had
been desire in his face, and in his eyes.

Linette knew that men were adept at displaying feelings they did not feel, but Stephen wasn't that kind of
man. He rarely showed any emotion at all; he would
never display false ones. If he kissed her, it was because
he wanted to.

Perhaps she was attaching too much importance to a
few simple kisses. She was, after all, a country girl and
things were different in the city. Any number of men
would take the opportunity of an intimate tête-à-tête
to steal a few. Stephen could simply have been taking
advantage of the situation.

Still, he wasn't an impulsive man. He always acted
with steady, calculated deliberation. An impulsive kiss
was not in his style. If he kissed her, it meant something.

But what? That he liked kissing? Or that he liked
kissing her? And now, having succumbed to temptation,
was he regretting his action?

Until she saw him again, she had no way of finding
out. She needed to see him in a place where they could
be alone; where he could kiss her again if he wanted

to. If he availed himself of the opportunity, then she would know.

But she wasn't going to have any reason to see him in the near future if she didn't make progress with these translations. With renewed determination, Linette picked up her pen and opened her medical dictionary.

Three days later, on a cold, wet December afternoon, Linette took the finished work to Stephen's school. She could have waited until tomorrow, when he came to the Dispensary, but she preferred this setting.

She wanted to see him alone. Wanted to ask him, point-blank, why he'd made no attempt to see her since the ball. She could no longer accept the excuse that he was too busy with work and research.

He *was* avoiding her. He'd made that clear yesterday at the Dispensary. She'd told him in the clinic that she wanted to talk to him, waited all afternoon for him to finish with his work, then discovered that he'd left twenty minutes after she'd spoken to him.

Linette was tired of this endless confusion and doubt. She would find out today exactly what his feelings were, even if she had to come out and ask him.

No one was in the hall when she entered the school. She rapped lightly on Stephen's office door, but there was no answer. Gingerly, she pushed open the door and peered inside.

Linette knew from Stephen's schedule that he wasn't in the lecture room, so he must be with the students in *that* place. Linette walked into the office and settled herself on the sofa. She would wait here for him.

After twenty minutes passed, Linette grew restless. Stephen's office was in its usual state of disorder. Books were stacked in precarious piles and papers lay everywhere. Sighing, she took off her cloak and rolled up her sleeves. She could accomplish something useful while she waited.

Linette knew better than to move any of his papers,

but she could straighten the rest of the office. There were enough dirty dishes strewn about the room to fill a washtub. She carefully stacked them beside the desk. The one consolation was the evidence that he was remembering to eat. There was probably a sink somewhere in the school, but she had a feeling she knew where it would be. Stephen could wash his own dishes.

His coat was slipping off the back of a chair so she hung it on the wall hook behind the door. She gathered the other clothes strewn about the room and wrapped them in a shirt. Stephen could take them to be laundered.

A thin layer of dust coated every flat surface. Tomorrow, she would send someone over to give the room a thorough cleaning. If he grew accustomed to working in clean, neat surroundings, maybe he'd make more of an effort to keep things that way.

The door flew open and Stephen breezed into the room. He halted in midstride when he caught sight of her, a stunned expression on his face.

"What are you doing here?" he demanded.

"I brought you some translations," Linette explained. "I see you've managed to make chaos of this room again. I'll send someone over to clean it tomorrow, if you like."

"I don't like," he said sourly. "Where are the articles?"

She flinched at his rude tone. "Is that all you are going to say? No 'Hello, Linette' or 'How have you been?' "

He ran a hand through his hair. "I'm dreadfully busy and I don't have time for idle talk right now."

"Perhaps you could come to tea tomorrow?"

"I told you, I'm busy."

Linette's stomach tightened with apprehension. She looked at him intently. "Are you really that busy? Or don't you want to see me?"

The brief flash of guilt in his eyes gave her the answer. With head held high, she walked to the sofa and gathered her things. "Very well, then, I know when I am not wanted."

"Linette . . ."

'Really, Stephen, you surprise me. I had not thought you such a coward. I thought I was being foolish to think you were avoiding me, but I was wrong, wasn't I?"

He looked uneasy. "Why would I want to do that?"

"I can take a very good guess. It has to do with the Dispensary Ball, and those kisses we shared. What I don't understand is who you're the most afraid of—me or yourself?"

"Afraid? Why should I be afraid?"

She took a step toward him. "Because I think you've suddenly realized that you're showing signs of being human. That frightens you, doesn't it?"

He toyed with some papers on his desk. "You're talking nonsense."

"Am I? You've said more than once that you pride yourself on your dispassionate attitude. It must be frightening to find out that you can't maintain it all the time."

His expression darkened. "I don't have time to stand here and listen to these wild ideas of yours. I've a lecture to give tonight."

Linette took another step closer until they stood toe-to-toe. She saw the flicker of fear in his eyes. "Kiss me."

"What?"

"Kiss me. If you aren't afraid, that shouldn't be an imposition. I recall you enjoyed the experience before."

Stephen backed away. "I think you should leave."

"Show me that you're not afraid, Stephen." Linette searched his face, looking for some sign of hope. "Show me that it's merely a trifling kiss."

"I'm not going to kiss you!"

"You want to, don't you? I can see it in your eyes. And you're fighting that impulse." She laughed bitterly. "I had no idea I was such a fearsome creature."

She turned away and put on her cloak. "I feel sorry

for you, Stephen. Someday, you are going to realize that you have a very lonely life."

He held out his hand. "The articles."

Linette pulled them from the bag and slapped the papers into his palm. "Now I know why you like to work with cadavers—you don't have to talk to them."

"I deal with live people every day. Students, associates. I work at the Dispensary, don't I? My patients there are very much alive."

"Ah, but if you had your choice, would you?" Linette pointed an accusing finger at him. "I think you'd prefer to lock yourself up in your dissection room and only cut into dead bodies, because they won't bother you. They won't force you to look at yourself, and what you've become."

He glared at her. "What makes you such an expert on my behavior?"

"I've spent my entire life dealing with other people," she said simply. "And I've seen far too many like you, who profess not to care, when they really do. There is only one thing worse."

"What's that?"

"Professing to care when you do not. At least no one will ever accuse you of that failing, *Mr. Ashworth.*"

She clutched her cloak around her and walked to the door. "Don't bother to show me out. I know the way."

Linette did not look back as she walked through the hall, down the front stairs, and into the carriage.

Surprisingly, she felt no urge to cry. Instead, she was too numb to feel much of anything. Except anger.

How could anyone be such a fool? If he'd rejected her because he didn't want her, didn't care for her, it would be one thing. But he'd rejected her in spite of the longing she'd seen in his eyes. Rejected her because he didn't want to care. And that made him a fool.

She lay her cheek against the window glass, the hard, smooth surface cooling her flushed face. The scene outside passed in a blur.

Why, when so many people in this world were miserably unhappy, would someone deliberately avoid happiness? Why was he so afraid to *feel,* to live? She'd experienced more than one episode of hurt in her life, and yet she still retained her sense of optimism, her sense that she could find some happiness. Stephen acted as if happiness were the plague.

Somewhere, someone must have hurt him very badly. So badly that he was determined to keep himself closed up tightly like a box.

Why did people react so differently to the challenges life put in front of them? Stephen tried to withdraw; Linette reached out to help others. Stephen was afraid to feel; Linette knew she felt too much. Even now, with that humiliating scene fresh in her mind, she still cared enough to feel sorry for him. Wanted to find some way to show him that he didn't have to be afraid of life. That life was to be enjoyed, not fought off.

But she doubted her ability to ever reach him. His mind was so closed to the possibilities, that changing him would be nearly impossible. She suspected it would be easier to change his mind about the value of dissection than it would be to convince him that he needed to care about someone other than himself.

And he had so much to give. In the brief moments when he'd let his guard down, she'd seen the compassionate man who lay behind the facade. A man who could love deeply and strongly if he'd just allow himself. A man who could love her, if he tried.

How ironic that when she finally found a man who would be the ideal companion, a man she admired, whose work so neatly matched hers, he did not want her. No, she corrected herself, he was *afraid* to want her. Afraid to reveal that he had a human side.

Linette could overlook everything else, his brusque manners and deplorable messiness. But she could never bring herself to live with a man who refused to let himself care.

She sighed. For the first time in her life, she realized she had encountered a challenge that was insurmountable. There was nothing she could do to change this part of him. That kind of change could only come from within, and it was obvious he did not care to make the effort.

But oh, she wished he did.

Chapter 19

"I am surprised we have not heard anything from Mr. Ashworth recently." Aunt Barton gave Linette a chiding look as they sat sewing in the drawing room on a chilly December evening. "After all, it's been two weeks since the ball. You did remember to ask him to dine with us?"

Linette pulled her chair closer to the fire, avoiding her aunt's gaze. "I sent him a very polite note, as you asked. Knowing the condition of his office, it's probably buried beneath a stack of papers."

"He will be at the Dispensary tomorrow, will he not? Try to talk with him. He does not plan to visit his family during the holidays, does he?"

"He hasn't said anything about changing his schedule."

Of course, if he had, she would be the last one to know. Linette jabbed her needle into the cloth. She hadn't spoken one word to him since that last conversation in his office, nearly a week ago. Their paths had not crossed at the Dispensary.

Not that she had made any attempt to seek him out. If he did not want to see her, she did not want to see him. It was a pointless exercise. It would only make the hurt worse.

Linette had sent him her aunt's invitation only because she was confident he wouldn't respond, or would decline if he did. She had no intention of reissuing the invitation face-to-face, but for Aunt's sake she would leave Stephen another note in his office at the Dispensary.

It would be too dangerous to see him again. Despite her anger, she still wanted to know how he fared. Was his book progressing? Was he eating regularly? Was everything going well at the school?

Did he miss her, the way she missed him? Or was he content to leave her out of his life?

Linette gave a determined toss of her head. The longer she avoided him, the less she would mind. Already, she found she could forget about him for hours at a time.

It had been a relief when she'd finished the last two French translations last week and sent them to him. It severed the last personal tie between them. Their work at the Dispensary did not overlap; they would have no reason to see each other there.

"Linette?"

She looked up with a guilty start. Her aunt was looking at her, a small smile teasing at the corner of her mouth.

"I asked if you would like to have oysters for Christmas dinner."

"Oysters would be fine." Linette remembered how Stephen had devoured the treat so eagerly at the ball. She doubted he would be eating oysters for his Christmas dinner.

She shrugged. For all she knew, he would be spending a cheery Christmas with his family. Then she remembered his words, how he'd taken up medicine to spite his father. No, she didn't think Stephen would be enjoying a family Christmas. More likely he and Mathers would dine together in some London tavern.

Or Stephen would eat alone in his rooms.

Which would serve him right.

"I am planning a theater party after the new year," Aunt said. "May I count on you joining me?"

Linette forced a smile. "Of course. That sounds very nice."

Aunt smiled. "Good. You have been far too serious

recently; you need some frivolity in your life. I worry that you are still dwelling on the death of that poor child."

"It will be easier to be cheerful with Christmas nearly upon us."

"Come shopping with me tomorrow. You can help me pick out some last-minute gifts and we can stop at Brodie's for a treat. We haven't done that in ages." Aunt's eyes glowed with anticipation.

"That would be fun," Linette said, with a smile at the remembered delights of Brodie's. "I still have some shopping of my own to do."

"I do hope you have picked out my present already," her aunt teased.

Linette feigned astonishment. "A present for you? Oh, dear, I had quite forgotten. It is a good thing I still have time to find one."

Aunt regarded her fondly. "Silly girl. You are becoming a worse tease than I."

Linette appreciated the chance to put her own cares aside and devote the day to escorting her aunt to what seemed like every shop in London. At one window Aunt would see something that cousin Hetty simply had to have; at another emporium, there was the perfect thing for Caroline's boy. And she bought a number of things for unspecified people that Linette suspected might end up in gaily wrapped packages with her name on them.

She didn't complain. Linette had spent so much time at the Dispensary that she'd forgotten how lively the city was at this time of year. Merchants hawked mistletoe and holly on the street corners, the delicious aroma of roasting chestnuts wafted from the street vendors, and small children sold bunches of hothouse flowers.

Making her own few purchases, Linette trailed behind Aunt's wake, carrying more and more packages until her arms threatened to give out.

"Enough!" she cried. "We have to go back to the carriage or I will drop everything."

Aunt looked abashed. "Goodness, I have gotten carried away. Very well, I think I have accomplished enough. We shall have our treat."

After filling one coach seat entirely with packages, they sat down for the short ride to Brodie's. Linette had not been there in an age and couldn't wait to sample the delicious treats.

But she realized her mistake in coming here as soon as she caught sight of the delectable pastries in the window. Stephen would love Brodie's. She could imagine him agonizing over which cream-filled delight he would purchase, and then devour in unseemly haste.

Linette wished he were here with her now. She wanted to tease him over his fondness for sweets, then encourage him to eat as many as he wished.

"What do you want, my dear?" Aunt stood at her elbow.

Blindly, Linette pointed to the first thing she saw. It didn't matter. Whatever she ate would be tasteless.

Linette tried to listen to Aunt's bright chatter as she reviewed her purchases for the day, but her mind was far away.

"I'm not at all sure I should have bought those blue gloves." Mrs. Barton looked critically at her purchase. "Should I exchange them for the yellow ones?"

"The blue ones are fine," Linette reassured her. She didn't want to start another round of shopping. She only wanted to go home, where she could sit alone in her room and berate herself for caring too much—about someone who cared too little.

Aunt took a bite of her cream cake. "This pastry is delicious, isn't it?"

Linette nodded.

"We shall have to come here more often—it can be our special weekly treat. Something to brighten up these dreary winter months."

"You should spend next winter in Italy," Linette suggested. "Think how enjoyable that would be."

"And what would become of you if I went? You would never leave the Dispensary for such a long time."

"You needn't worry about me." Linette smiled. "I would be fine."

"I could not leave you here alone! What would people say?"

"That your niece is of an age where she can look after herself—with the help of a houseful of servants."

Aunt shook her head. "No, it would not do." Then her eyes twinkled mischievously. "I shall merely have to see you married before that time, so I can go abroad with a clear conscience."

"I don't think that's likely to happen," Linette said quietly.

"I had thought . . ." Aunt paused, then took a sip of tea. "Well, never mind. Do you think I should take some of these cream cakes home? They would be delightful with tea."

"I will get them for you." Linette rose and walked to the counter. She placed an order for Aunt's cakes—and a separate one, to be sent to Stephen.

He needed to know that someone was thinking about him at this special time of year, even if he would not appreciate that it was her.

She was wrong about that, however, for a few days later she received a note from him. It was terse and to the point. He thanked her for the cakes and wished her felicitations for Christmas and the New Year. She was surprised he even knew it was the holiday. Then again, it was between terms at the school. Of course he would know.

Early on Christmas Eve, Linette made a quick trip to the Dispensary to take care of some minor matters. Her classes wouldn't meet again until after the new year and she intended to use the time to plan some new projects for her students.

Linette also planned to review the Dispensary ledgers before the annual meeting in January. Even though the

Board of Governors were responsible for financial matters, it had been Uncle's practice to oversee their efforts. Linette carried on his tradition, with her aunt's approval.

Burdened by the heavy ledger books, Linette carefully descended the main stairs. Rounding the landing, she crashed into the male figure bounding up the steps. The ledgers went flying and only his steadying hand kept her from falling. Linette looked up.

It was Stephen.

"Are you all right?" he asked, an anxious look on his face. "I shouldn't have been running, but I didn't think anyone would be on the stairs."

Linette stared at him, her mouth dry, her mind blank with surprise. Regret and delight warred within her at seeing him again. He looked as rumpled and disheveled as ever. And just as handsome.

He bent to pick up the ledgers. "What are you doing with these?"

"I wanted to go over the accounts before the annual meeting in January," she said, unable to take her eyes off him. Did he look thinner than usual? He looked tired, with dark smudges around his eyes. He probably wasn't sleeping enough, or eating properly.

"I see." He hefted the heavy books with ease. "Well, let me carry them to the carriage for you."

"Thank you." Linette fell into step beside him. There was so much she wanted to say to him, so much she wanted to know. But she couldn't form the words.

"It was thoughtful of you to send me those cakes," he said suddenly.

"I'm glad you enjoyed them." Linette gave him a timid smile. "It is between terms at school, isn't it? What do you plan to do with all your free time?"

"I'm trying to get caught up with all the work I didn't have time to finish during the fall."

She darted him a quick glance. "Have you completed your book?"

"Nearly."

"You must be pleased."

He shrugged.

Linette took a deep breath. Somehow, she would wring a detailed response from him. Something that would tell her how he was, if he was happy—or as miserable as she. "Do you have any plans for Christmas? Are you spending it with your family?"

His step faltered for a moment but then he continued walking. "I don't visit with my family."

"Oh."

She saw him glance at her, then quickly avert his eyes. "What about you? Are you going home to your family?"

It must be the strain of seeing Stephen again, or the time of year, for the thought of her family raised an unexpected lump in her throat. "No, I'll be here in London, with Aunt Barton. She prefers to stay in the city and I don't want her to be alone."

They reached the front door and she pulled it open for him. The wind swirled about them and Linette dashed ahead to open the door of the waiting coach. She stood aside while Stephen set the heavy ledgers on the seat.

"Are you going home, or to the school?" she asked brightly. "I can give you a ride."

His expression grew cold. "Thank you, but I have a few more things to do here at the Dispensary." With rigid politeness, he helped her into the coach. "Merry Christmas."

"Merry Christmas."

The carriage pulled away with a lurch. Linette leaned back against the seat and closed her eyes. She was *not* going to cry. Such a pigheaded, stubborn man didn't deserve the honor of tears.

Stephen dashed back into the building, escaping the cold. But the warm interior of the building did nothing to melt the ice in the pit of his stomach. It had been there from the moment he saw Linette on the stairs.

He thought he was succeeding in his efforts to forget her, until those pastries arrived and he realized that nothing had changed. They only reminded him how she had teased him at the ball over his fondness for the creamy delicacies. And how he'd kissed her later that same evening, and held her in his arms. The memory was as vivid as if it had been yesterday.

Avoiding her hadn't done any good. If anything, it made things worse. If he wasn't thinking about her, he was thinking of ways to avoid her. And when each day went by and he'd succeeded in keeping away from her, deep inside he felt a stab of disappointment at his success.

Stephen was surprised that she had given up so easily. He expected her to badger him again about his shortcomings, and his attitude toward her. But except for that package of cakes, she had left him alone.

That should have made him happy, but it didn't. His mood only sank lower. He'd spent weeks trying to convince himself that he didn't need her and had done such a convincing job that she believed him, at least. If only he'd been as successful with himself.

She'd been right when she'd accused him of being afraid of her, afraid of his feelings for her. But admitting the truth didn't make it any easier to live with. Stephen still had to keep away from her. It would be better for both of them.

It would be easier in January, when classes started again. Now, he didn't have enough to do. He could only work on his book for so long before the pages began to swim before his eyes. The drawings were finished; he had no extra work to do in the dissecting room.

Even Mathers had deserted him, visiting some cousin in Norwich or Norfolk or wherever it was that he'd gone. Back to the bosom of his adoring family, who were thrilled to have a surgeon in their midst.

Stephen could go home, of course, but what was the use? He didn't need to torture himself further; he was already doing a good enough job of that already. He could be a surgeon with a reputation like Astley Cooper and they wouldn't care. He'd gone against their wishes and even a knighthood wouldn't placate them.

No, he had no desire to go home.

Linette wasn't going home either. Did she regret not spending Christmas with her family?

Maybe tonight, he'd treat himself to a good dinner— even a bottle of wine or some brandy. No work, just play. He could sit in a smoke-filled tavern and sip his wine and pretend that he didn't have a worry in the world.

Or he could take dinner back to his chilly rooms and eat it in peaceful silence. And he could still have the wine, and not be bothered by the noise and hurly-burly atmosphere of the tavern.

He sighed. Neither prospect seemed appealing. But those were his only choices. Stephen pulled on his coat and headed for the street. Maybe he'd play a game on the way home, counting cats or dogs on his way. If the number came up even, he'd eat out, otherwise he'd stay home.

A light, misting rain began falling before he'd gone more than a few blocks. Stephen cursed the wet but pressed on. There was no point in getting a hackney; he wasn't that far from home.

But he decided to eat in a tavern after all. It was a damn sight easier to dry out there than in his ill-heated rooms. And he admitted to himself that he didn't want to be alone.

Christmas dinner should have been a festive occasion for Linette. Aunt had spared no expense in ordering up every delicacy for this special dinner. The house was full of guests and everyone was filled with seasonal jollity.

Except Linette.

She couldn't help but wonder what Stephen was

doing. Was he having a solitary dinner in his room or was he dining out with a colleague?

He would have loved Aunt's table tonight. In addition to the breast of lamb, boiled salmon, and the oysters, there were vegetable dishes of every description.

But he would have been drawn to the sweets: almond cheesecakes, raspberry cream, apple puddings, cranberry tarts, all manner of fruits, assorted biscuits and candies. He could have gorged himself to his heart's content.

He could have been here, she thought sadly, if he wasn't so annoyingly stubborn. She had given him the chance to apologize, had even sent him a peace offering, but it had done no good. He made them both suffer because he wouldn't admit what he felt.

Why was he so afraid to acknowledge his feelings? This was far more than the need for detachment in his work. He was determined to cut himself off from all human companionship and she desperately wanted to know why. Had he loved once and been hurt? Or was he so afraid because he'd never tried?

Aunt came over and handed her a cup of hot, mulled punch. "You look in need of a cup of Christmas cheer."

Linette forced a smile. "I feel positively satiated after that dinner. I ate far too much. Everything was so delicious."

Aunt beamed. "Yes, it did turn out well, didn't it?" She glanced at the group of singers clustered around the pianoforte. "I'm surprised you are not singing carols with the others."

Linette suddenly realized that she had almost missed her favorite part of Christmas. Stephen Ashworth's infuriating stubbornness wasn't going to ruin her entire Christmas. If he was alone in his tiny rooms, it was his own fault. She didn't have to spend her time feeling sorry for him.

Setting down her cup, Linette crossed the room to the piano. For at least one night, she wasn't going to let Stephen Ashworth ruin her pleasure.

Chapter 20

"We are going to have to practice some strict economies this term."

Stephen paced the length of his office, barely sparing a look for Mathers, who sprawled across the sofa. "The new term starts next week and already it doesn't look good."

"We'll find areas to cut back expenses, I'm sure," Mathers said.

Stephen ran a hand through his hair. He'd spent the morning going over the accounts and knew exactly where he stood. "We need more students, but I'll be damned if I know where to find them. I think half the medical students in England have gone to Paris."

"Maybe we should think of relocating there," Mathers said with a laugh.

"And me with my abominable French." Stephen shook his head. "What a success I'd be."

"You don't think all those students speak French, do you? We could start an English-language anatomy school. We'd have to turn applicants away."

Stephen gave him a withering look. "And how do you propose we find the money to start such a thing? I don't even have a half-interest in this school yet."

Mathers shrugged. "I'm only a surgeon, not a man of business."

"Then stick to your surgery." Pulling out his handkerchief, Stephen blew his nose. "Drat this cold. I feel like hell."

"Pliny advocated tying a caterpillar in a piece of linen, passing a thread around it three times, and knotting it."

Stephen glared at him.

"Or there is another sure cure—the muzzle of the mouse and the tips of his ears, wrapped in a red cloth, worn around the neck."

"Where did you say you acquired your medical training?"

Mathers grinned. "Just trying to be helpful."

"I can treat myself, thank you." Stephen shook his head. "Mouse ears and muzzles. It's a miracle the Roman Empire survived as long as it did."

"Well, this modern man recommends a hearty dinner in a warm tavern."

"Throw in a glass or two of brandy and that's a prescription I can concur with." Stephen stood, then bent over with a fit of coughing. "These numbers will look the same in the morning."

"We can console ourselves with the hope that there'll be a last-minute flood of students next week."

"I'll be content if everyone who registered actually appears," said Stephen as he grabbed his coat. "Otherwise we may find ourselves in the street, giving lectures in the alley."

Mathers slapped him on the back. "Paris, Ashworth, think of Paris."

"I'm trying not to."

"You could bring Miss Gregory along to act as your interpreter."

Stephen clapped his hat on his head. "Now I know you are mad."

If only he could.

As he walked home in the icy rain, he tried not to acknowledge how tantalizing he found Mathers' suggestion. Paris, with Linette by his side.

Any city, with Linette by his side.

But those thoughts were foolish. He'd been all too successful in discouraging her. She would not be back,

not after those last words. It was what he'd wanted, after
all, wasn't it?

Yet Stephen missed her with a deep, burning ache that
distracted his thoughts and disturbed his nights. And the
only cure was for him to admit his feelings to himself,
and more importantly, to her. And that he would not
do. He didn't want to give her that power over him. As
long as she thought he didn't care, he was safe.

Three weeks later, Stephen sat in his office, hunched
over his desk. His head felt like a swollen balloon, and
each breath brought a searing pain to his chest. From
the way he was sweating, he knew he had a fever.

But he didn't have time to be sick. Not so early in
the term, and not with every anatomy school in London
desperate for students. If he missed even one lecture,
a student might leave. And Stephen couldn't afford to
lose any.

Fewer students meant less money. Less money from
which to make payments to Grosse, buy supplies for the
school, pay Mathers, and find something for himself to
live on.

If only the prices for corpses would drop. Everyone
in London was complaining. Eight guineas! The resurrectionists, in their greed, were endangering the very system that supported them. Why couldn't they charge a
decent price and give their customers a break?

Tonight, he'd dose himself and sweat the fever out.
Thank God he'd finished his manuscript last night. It
only needed recopying and it would be off to the printer.

And the way things were going, the book might be
the only thing between him and financial disaster. He
wouldn't survive another year if he had to rely only on
student fees.

Stephen coughed and winced at the sharp pain in his
chest. At the very least, he'd take some laudanum tonight so he could sleep.

"You look like hell," said Mathers with disgusting

cheer when he came in before class. "Why don't you go home?"

"I'm not going to cancel a lecture."

"Better to cancel one now than cancel them all when you're dead."

"I'm not going to die," Stephen said hoarsely. "It's merely a bad cold."

Mathers shook his head. "That's why they say physicians should never treat themselves. What are you doing for it?"

"I'm putting more vile liquids into myself than you can imagine—hyssop, chamomile, and willow-bark tea, all laced with honey, wine laced with honey . . ." Stephen pushed a cup at Mathers. "Here, have some."

"You'd be fine if you just took to your bed for a few days."

Stephen gave him a dark look. "Are you prepared to fill in for me while I do? I'll be fine; I just need a few nights of decent sleep."

As if to refute his words, he was seized with another spasm of coughing that left tears in his eyes.

"Have you willed your body to anyone in particular, or may I have it when you're gone?"

Stephen snorted derisively. "I assure you, Mathers, I'm not going to die. And you're the last person I'd allow to cut me up. If I'm going to be examined, I'd rather have a *skilled* practitioner like Lawrence or Cooper do the honors."

"Then it's in my best interests to keep you alive," said Mathers. "At least until I can get you to change your mind."

Stephen took another sip of the bitter tea. "If it makes you feel better, I'll leave the dissecting room entirely in your hands today and rest in my office until the afternoon lecture. I've got plenty of reading to catch up on."

"I'll bring you some lunch," Mathers promised.

Boisterous laughter and the loud tramp of feet in the

hall told them the students were starting to arrive. Stephen gathered up his lecture notes and crossed the hall.

He managed to get through his talk with only a few coughing spells, soothed by the hyssop tea. But when he reached the privacy of his office, he sank down on the sofa.

Stephen felt miserable. He'd never been this ill in his life; why did it have to come now, at such an inopportune time? Everything would be all right if he could just rest for a while. He swung his feet onto the sofa and leaned his head back, closing his tired eyes. Just a short rest . . .

"Ashworth. Wake up."

Blinking sleepily, Stephen tried to focus his eyes but the man standing before him simply would not hold still.

"I brought you some soup. You've just enough time to eat it before lecture."

Mathers. Stephen struggled to a sitting position. "Good God, what time is it?"

"Half past one."

"You shouldn't have let me sleep so long."

Mathers shrugged. "I was busy in the dissecting room."

Stephen stood and lurched unsteadily toward his desk. The office floor felt like the deck of a ship, pitching and rolling beneath his feet.

God, he felt horrible.

The hot soup soothed his raw throat, but by the time he was finished, he was sticky again with sweat. Stripping off his coat, Stephen flung it onto the sofa, then wiped his face with his handkerchief. He could feel the heat of his skin through the cloth.

At least he didn't need to complain about the cold January weather. The thought of being outside in just his shirtsleeves was appealing.

Mathers bent over him, a concerned expression on his face. "Are you sure you're all right, Ash? I really think you ought to go home."

Stephen shook his head. He was not going to admit defeat. "It's only another hour. I'll give the lecture and go."

"At least sit in the chair this time. The students won't be impressed if you fall flat on your face halfway through the lecture."

"I think I will take your advice." He shook his head. "God, I can't remember ever feeling this miserable. It feels as if an elephant is sitting on my chest."

"Maybe you should consult with someone—besides yourself."

"For what purpose?" Stephen scoffed. "They'd merely bleed me until I was too weak to move. Some cure. I know what I'm doing."

Mathers muttered something under his breath, but Stephen ignored him.

He'd go home as soon as his lecture was finished and crawl into bed. He might even cancel his time at the Dispensary tomorrow. Two days in bed would be long enough to beat this thing.

Stephen stood up, then collapsed back into the chair as his knees gave out beneath him. Closing his eyes against the sickening whirl of the room, he took several deep breaths.

One more hour. He only had to last that long.

Firmly grasping the edge of the desk, he pulled himself to his feet and stood until the dizziness subsided. With unsteady steps, he made his way to the lecture room and perched on the edge of the table, facing the eager, and not-so-eager faces of his students.

Suddenly, Stephen's mind went blank and he couldn't recall what he was supposed to talk about. Grabbing his notes, he scanned the first page, trying to hide his anxiety. The knee. He was giving a lecture on the knee.

Somehow, he managed to give his talk. Stephen had no idea if he was making any sense, but no student walked out, so he must have done all right. His throat burned from talking too long and he badly needed a cup of hot tea.

Yet surprisingly, he felt better when he walked back to his office. A trifle light-headed, but the aching weariness was gone. Maybe the worst was over.

Mathers was waiting for him in the office, Smith at his side.

"I'm holding you to your promise," Mathers said. "There's a hackney waiting outside and I'm sending Smith along to make sure you go home."

"I'm sure Smith has better things to do." Stephen scowled. "Where else would I go?"

Mathers handed Stephen his coat and pushed him out the door. Stephen was too worn out to argue.

When the hack pulled up in front of his rooms, Stephen refused to let Smith out. Did Mathers think he was going to sneak out for an evening of dancing? He'd find something to eat, have a glass or two of wine, and take to his bed.

By the time he reached the second-floor landing, each breath felt like a knife stabbing into his chest. Stephen unlocked his door and sank down onto the floor, gasping for air. He'd be fine in a minute, once he caught his breath. He just needed a little more air....

The room dissolved into blackness.

Early in the evening, Aunt knocked lightly on Linette's bedroom door. "Are you ready to go, my dear? The carriage will be waiting."

Still in her robe, Linette came to the doorway. "I'm sorry, Aunt, but I have a dreadful headache tonight. I don't think I'd find the theater very enjoyable."

Aunt's expression grew concerned. "Are you sure you will be all right? Have you taken some powders?"

"I will."

"Then you lie down now, and rest." Aunt kissed her on the cheek. "There is so much dreadful illness going around the city this winter. I don't want you to overstrain yourself and catch anything."

"That's why I thought it best to stay home. Give my best to Mrs. Longridge."

"I will. But I hate to leave you here alone."

"I don't want to spoil your evening." Linette gave her a wan smile. "Go, and enjoy yourself."

"Well, if you are certain . . . I will come home early, in any event."

"I'll be asleep," Linette promised.

After Aunt left, Linette sat down on her bed. She had not lied—she did have a headache—but it wasn't severe enough to send her to her bed. She simply had no desire to go out tonight. Or any other night.

She should have been excited about the new year. January marked a time of change, of new beginnings, new possibilities. But Linette was more interested in looking back, rather than forward. Looking back to the time when she still saw Stephen

Every time she thought about him, she was filled with regret, wondering if she could have dealt differently with him. She had been too greedy, wanting more than the friendship he offered. If she hadn't pushed him, they would still be talking to each other, at least.

But she hadn't spoken another word to him since their brief encounter before Christmas. Somehow, their paths never crossed at the Dispensary anymore.

Oh, she kept track of him. She knew that he had a miserable cold, and was cranky and irritable with everyone at the Dispensary except the patients.

She wondered how the new school term was going, if all the same students were there. Smith, who'd helped the night Amy died, was, she knew, for he stayed at the Dispensary two nights a week in case of an emergency.

After drinking a cup of tea, Linette felt much better. Taking a book, she went down to the morning room and curled up in her favorite chair in front of the fire.

She must have been reading for over an hour when Mallon appeared at the door.

"There is a young man here to see you, miss. I told him you were unwell but he insists on speaking with you."

Before she could answer, the man squeezed past the butler and dashed into the room. Startled, Linette recognized Smith.

"Beggin' your pardon, Miss Gregory, but Mr. Mathers said I was to come to you. We need to get the physician from the Dispensary—Dr. Wilkins."

"What is wrong?"

"It's Mr. Ashworth. He's collapsed."

Linette jumped to her feet. "What?"

"He's been sick for weeks. Mr. Mathers sent me over tonight to check on him and he looked pretty bad. Thought we should get a physician. Mr. Ashworth keeps asking for the man from the Dispensary."

"Don't go anywhere," Linette commanded as she dashed for the door. "I'll be back as quickly as I can."

She ran into the study and hastily scribbled a note to Dr. Fields, Aunt's personal friend and a noted physician, asking him to meet them at Stephen's rooms. She handed the note to a footman to deliver, then raced upstairs and threw on her clothes.

"Did you come in a hackney?" she asked Smith when she rejoined him in the drawing room. "Is he waiting?"

The lad gulped and nodded.

"Then we can't waste any more time. I've sent for the doctor; he should not be too far behind us."

He stared at her. "You're coming along?"

"You should know by now that I'm no stranger to a sickroom."

"I don't think Mr. Ashworth is going to like it," Smith mumbled.

"If he's as sick as you say, he won't care," she retorted as she stepped into the hack.

Linette was on the edge of her seat for the entire

short journey, filled with worry about Stephen. How sick was he? It must be serious if Mathers was sending for a physician—Stephen was capable of treating himself. The first twinges of fear crept into her stomach.

She didn't wait for the steps to be lowered but jumped from the coach as soon as they reached Stephen's building. Linette raced up the stairs, colliding with Mathers at the top.

"Is the doctor here yet?" she gasped out.

"No. You sent for him?"

She nodded, winded from the steep stairs. "How is he?"

Mathers gave her a considering look, then shook his head. "Not good, I'm afraid. I think it's pneumonia."

He stepped back and allowed Linette to come into the room.

"How long as he been ill?"

"He's had a bad cold for weeks, but it grew much worse in the past few days. He's been working all hours, not getting enough sleep. The beginning of the term is always hectic."

"Can I see him?" she asked.

"He's running a high fever," Mathers said with marked reluctance. "He's not very alert."

She gave him a pleading look and he motioned for her to follow. They passed through the cluttered outer room and into the bedroom.

Even in the dim light, Linette saw how terrible Stephen looked. His face was thin and gaunt, with deep circles under his eyes that looked as dark as bruises. His breath came in horrible, wheezing rasps.

"Can't we do anything until the doctor comes?" she whispered to Mathers.

"I'd like to bleed him, but he won't allow it. You might see if he'll drink some of that tea. He claims it's what he needs."

Linette crossed to the side of the bed and put her

hand on his forehead, then jerked it back with surprise. He was burning up. She turned to Mathers.

"Get me a basin with some water, and some cloths. I can at least wipe his face."

The splash of cool water revived Stephen slightly. He blinked at her through bloodshot eyes.

"Linette?" he croaked.

"Shh." She put a hand on his arm. "The doctor should be here soon. I want you to drink some more tea."

He nodded and tried to raise his head, but fell back against the pillow, too weak to move. Linette spooned the liquid into his mouth.

It reminded her all too much of that dreadful night at Amy's. Linette tried to push the growing fear from her mind. Stephen was going to be fine.

Sounds came from the outer room, and she realized that Dr. Fields had arrived. She turned to greet him but Stephen reached out and grabbed her arm. "Tell Mathers to keep an eye on him. I don't want him doing anything stupid."

Linette nodded and the doctor came in.

"Well, well," he said in a jovial tone. "So this is our patient. Not feeling too well, are we?"

Stephen responded with a weak glare. "You're not Wilkins."

"This is Dr. Fields, Aunt's physician," Linette explained. "I sent for him."

"Don't want—"

Stephen was seized by such a strong fit of coughing that Linette cringed. When he finally caught his breath, he lay back against the pillows, his face white with strain.

"He should be bled immediately," Dr. Fields said.

"No bleeding," Stephen uttered weakly.

The doctor ignored him and placed his bag up on the table. Linette watched with growing apprehension as he drew out an oblong wooden box, flipped open the lid and brought out a sharp blade and a ceramic bowl.

She knew Stephen didn't think much of bleeding, but

Dr. Fields was a skilled man. He knew what was best. Quietly, Linette slipped from the room. She couldn't bear to watch.

Thank God the doctor was here. When she'd first seen Stephen, his appearance had shocked her. But everything would be all right now.

And when Stephen recovered, she would let him know in no uncertain terms what she thought about a surgeon who was so stupid as to allow himself to get this sick. Didn't they say that only a fool treated himself? Knowing Stephen, he hadn't made a single concession to his illness but had worked along at his same break-neck pace until he collapsed.

If nothing else, she would tell him that if he wanted to remain at the Dispensary, he had to set a better example for the patients. It was hard enough to get them to come in for treatment; when the surgeon was equally reluctant, it didn't promote confidence.

Linette paced back and forth across the untidy room, anxious to hear what the doctor would say when he was done examining Stephen. But no one came out of the bedroom. To quell her anxiety, she started to straighten the room, putting books back on the shelves and gathering up the crumpled scraps of paper around his work table. She needed to do something to feel useful.

Then, unable to stand the suspense any longer, she knocked softly on the door. Smith pulled it open.

"What's happening?" she whispered.

"I can't tell. They've been pouring all sorts of medicine down his throat. The bleeding helped, I think; he's calmer."

"Did the doctor say what it is?"

"Oh, there's no question it's pneumonia. They just aren't sure if it's in both lungs."

"Is that bad?"

"I don't think it's good, but I don't know much about the disease."

Linette frowned. "Let me know when I can talk with the doctor."

She tried to make herself comfortable on Stephen's sofa, but it was impossible. Not just because of its worn, lumpy condition, but because she was too anxious and worried.

Pneumonia was dangerous. Linette tried to think optimistically; Stephen was young and strong and would surely recover without too much trouble. Now that he was being treated properly, he would start to improve rapidly.

At last the doctor came out and Linette jumped to her feet.

"How is he?"

Dr. Fields didn't look nearly as jovial as he had when he'd arrived. "That young man's going to take a lot of care. I'll arrange for a nursing woman to come in; he's going to need cool baths to get that fever down, as well as a regular course of purging."

Linette didn't even hesitate. "He can get all the care he needs at my house." She looked around the small room. "Don't you think he'll be better off there?"

The doctor rubbed his chin. "Well, you might be right. But you risk bringing the contagion into the house."

"Pneumonia shouldn't bother us—we're all very healthy. Not a single cold all winter."

Mathers stepped up. "I know a lady who would be willing to watch him during the night."

"And Aunt and I can take turns during the day."

The doctor patted her hand. "Now, Linette my dear, this is no task for a gentlewoman. The man is very ill and needs a great deal of nursing. Best to leave that to those who are experienced. You can visit him from time to time."

Linette held her tongue. Once she had Stephen at the house, no one was going to tell her what she could and could not do.

"I'll stay with him tonight," Mathers said with a faint

grin. "I've got a vested interest in his survival, 'else I'm out of a job." He turned to the doctor. "Write out your instructions and the dosages and I'll see that he takes them."

The doctor scribbled out his orders and handed it to Mathers. "If he shows any more signs of restlessness, bleed him again. I've enough medicines in my bag to leave for the night; you can get more from the chemist's in the morning. I'll look in on him around ten and we'll see how he is doing."

Linette grabbed his hand. "Oh thank you, Dr. Fields. I know Ashworth will be all right, thanks to you."

"Always glad to help your family, my dear. Give my regards to your aunt."

As soon as he'd gone, Linette turned to Mathers. "Did I do the right thing?"

He nodded. "I won't lie to you; he's very, very ill. But from what I hear, you're damn fine help in the sickroom. Maybe together we can pull him through."

A lump rose in her throat and Linette nodded, afraid to say anything. She was dangerously close to tears and that would not do. She had to take care of Stephen. There was no time for her to fall apart.

Moving Stephen to Aunt's house was a nightmare. A chill rain had started to fall and it took all three of them to get the nearly unconscious Stephen into his long coat. With Linette leading the way, Smith and Mathers half dragged, half carried Ashworth down the stairs to the waiting hackney.

The short drive to Fitzroy Square was a nightmare. Stephen started coughing with such violence that Linette feared he would expel his lungs. She squeezed his hand until the paroxysm passed.

"Isn't there anything you can do?" she asked Mathers.

He shook his head. "He has to clear his lungs out."

Stephen slumped back against the seat.

Linette clasped his clammy hand and a fierce determination swelled within her. She was not going to let him die.

Chapter 21

As soon as the carriage stopped, Linette was out the door and running into the house, frantically calling for the butler "Mallon! Help us, quick."

The startled man came into the hall, still pulling on his coat.

"Is the bed in the front room made up?" Linette demanded.

"I believe so, miss, but—"

"Good. Tell Cook to prepare some broth and heat lots of water."

Mallon's eyes widened as Mathers and Smith carried Stephen's semiconscious form through the door. "What is going on?"

"Ashworth is dreadfully ill," Linette said. "I'm going to put him upstairs in the front room."

"Is Mrs. Barton aware of the situation?" Mallon asked doubtfully.

"She will want us to do everything we can to help."

The butler eyed her dubiously, then turned to carry out her orders.

Linette dashed up the stairs, slipping past the three men, and ran to the bedroom to make certain everything was ready. She rang for the maid, then pulled back the bedcovers and plumped the pillows. It was an absurd action, but Linette didn't care. She had to do something.

Mathers and Smith brought Stephen in and dropped him on the bed, then began tugging off his clothes.

"What are you going to need?" Linette asked.

"The largest bathing tub you have," Mathers said. "With plenty of cold water. I want to get this fever down. Some basins, towels." He glanced around the room. "A chamberpot."

Linette scurried about the house, alerting the staff to gather everything Mathers needed and take it to him. She even begged a clean nightshirt from one of the footmen, hoping it would make Stephen feel more comfortable. Tomorrow she would send someone to get his things.

Smith met her outside the door and took the bundle of towels and clothing from her hands.

"Let me know the minute he is back in bed," she said. "Are you going to stay the night, too?"

"I may as well," Smith said.

"I'll arrange a place where you can rest. Shall I have Cook send up something to eat?"

Smith looked grateful. "That would be nice."

Linette hurried back to the kitchen, grateful for the chance to be busy. As long as she did not have to sit, and wait, she would not have time to worry. She helped Cook prepare the meal, slicing bread and cheese, then took the tray to the bedroom herself.

Finally there was nothing more she could do. Linette dragged a chair into the corridor and waited outside the door.

Stephen had to get well, he simply had to.

She jumped up when she heard the front door open. Aunt was back! Linette desperately needed her reassuring voice and smile. Darting down the stairs, Linette reached her just as she was handing her wrap to Mallon.

"Oh, thank goodness you're back." Linette grabbed her aunt's hands. "Stephen is upstairs; he's terribly ill. Dr. Fields says it pneumonia. Oh, Aunt, I'm so afraid. He looks so awful."

Aunt gathered her into her arms. "My goodness. That's dreadful news. What else did the doctor say?"

Linette struggled to remain calm. "He bled him and prescribed enough medicines for an entire household. Mathers is giving him a cold bath to try to get the fever down."

"Come, let's sit and have a cup of tea. You can tell me all about it."

Linette glanced back at the stairs. "I have to go back up. Mathers says I can see Stephen as soon as he's finished with the bath. It will be any minute now."

Mrs. Barton slipped an arm around Linette's waist. "And you are not going to do the poor man any good if he sees you looking this distraught. Take a few minutes to calm yourself."

Linette took a deep breath. Aunt was right. For Stephen's sake she had to keep her emotions firmly under control. He shouldn't see how worried she was.

She had just finished telling Aunt all that had happened when Mathers poked his head through the doorway. Linette jumped to her feet and ran toward him.

"How is he? Can I see him now?"

"I think the cold bath helped the fever," Mathers said. "He's more comfortable."

Aunt reached for the teapot. "Do have a cup of tea, Mr. . . . ?

"Mathers," he offered, taking a seat beside her. "And thank you, I will."

Linette returned to her chair and perched on the edge, impatient to see Stephen. But she wanted to hear what Mathers had to say.

"Such unwelcome news," Mrs. Barton said, pouring. "How does Dr. Fields view the situation?"

Mathers gave Linette an uneasy glance. "I can't lie; Ashworth is very ill. But we're doing all we can," he added hastily. "I appreciate the fact that we could bring him here."

"I knew you wouldn't mind," Linette told her aunt. "I couldn't bear the thought of leaving him alone in his rooms."

Aunt waved a hand. "Oh, tish, tosh. Mr. Ashworth's health is more important than any disruption to my household. Is there anything more we can do to make him comfortable?"

"I will arrange for a nurse to come in tomorrow," Mathers said. "He is going to need constant care for several days. I'll be here as much as I can, but I have to look after the school, too."

Aunt's eyes narrowed. "Is this nurse a respectable person?"

"Oh, most respectable, I assure you. She's a widow who did some nursing during the Peninsular conflict. Ashworth has great faith in her."

Aunt looked relieved.

Linette leaned forward impatiently. "Can I see him, now, please?"

Mathers hesitated. "He's not very coherent. I gave him another dose of laudanum."

"I don't mind if he's asleep. I would just like to see him."

"Very well." Mathers stood. "I'll take you upstairs."

Aunt gave Linette a stern look. "And after you have reassured yourself about Mr. Ashworth's condition, I want you to go right to bed, Linette. You will do no one any good if you get sick yourself. I'm sure things will look better in the morning."

Linette wished she could share Aunt's optimism.

She tiptoed into the bedroom. A single candle stood on the night table, illuminating the bed but leaving most of the room in deep shadow.

Stephen sat propped against a pile of pillows, his pale face nearly indistinguishable from the white linen sheets. Only his dark hair stood out in the dim light.

"He looks uncomfortable sitting up like that," Linette said softly to Mathers.

"It's easier for him to breathe this way," he explained.

Linette walked to the bed and took Stephen's hand in hers. Despite the cold bath and the medicine, his skin still felt unbearably hot. She gave it a gentle squeeze. "I know you will be better," she whispered. "You're far too obstinate to die."

She uttered a silent prayer, then retreated.

In the privacy of the hall, Linette pressed her forehead against the wall. She felt sick and helpless, just as she had during that long night with Amy.

What if Dr. Fields and Mathers were wrong? Everyone tried to sound optimistic, but they continually prefaced their words with a warning of how sick Stephen was.

Should she have insisted that Dr. Fields come back during the night? Stephen might become worse. Mathers was a surgeon, not a physician. Would he know the right things to do?

Linette couldn't imagine what she would do if Stephen died. She flinched at the harsh words she'd hurled at him in December. She shouldn't have pressed him; it was too soon.

And if, in her disappointment, she hadn't avoided him, she might have recognized when he first fell ill, and bullied him into taking better care of himself.

Now, it was too late. All she could do was sit and watch, and hope, and pray.

Linette wasn't sure how long she slept that night; it seemed like only a few minutes. But when she opened her eyes and saw the pale light behind the curtains, she realized it was morning.

Dressing hastily, Linette hurried down the hall and tapped lightly on the door. An unshaven, bleary-eyed Mathers opened it.

"How is he?"

"No worse." He stepped to one side and she walked in.

Stephen was still propped up against the pillows, his head tilted back and his eyes closed. He looked pale as death. His breaths came in hoarse, raspy gasps that made Linette bite her lip.

She turned to Mathers. "I'll sit with him if you'd like to get some rest."

"I can sleep later, but I could use some breakfast."

"Is there anything I need to do?"

Mathers shook his head. "He'll probably keep sleeping. I gave him a good draught of laudanum around dawn. He should be fine until I get back."

Linette told him how to find the kitchen, then took a seat at Stephen's bedside.

She wished she could do something—give Stephen his medicine, or feed him some broth. Anything that would make her feel useful. The sound of his tortured breathing was almost more than she could bear. She felt helpless—and useless.

Linette reminded herself that Dr. Fields would be here soon. He'd be able to reassure her that Stephen was improving.

But the physician was anything but reassuring after he'd examined Stephen. Linette waited anxiously in the drawing room with her aunt, and one look at Dr. Field's face when he came in told her all she needed to know.

"You have a gravely ill young man up there," he said.

Linette's optimism flagged. "But surely he looks better than he did last night."

Dr. Fields shook his head. "His fever is down, but I'm worried about the lungs. I bled him again and that should help."

Linette shivered with revulsion.

The doctor turned to Mrs. Barton. "I understand you will be getting some help to care for the patient?"

"Mr. Mathers says he will send us a nursing woman."

"Good. You'll need an experienced woman to carry out the regimen I've ordered."

"I'll help with anything I can," Linette offered.

Dr. Fields gave her a soothing smile. "I'm sure that

when Mr. Ashworth is better, he will enjoy having you read to him."

Linette clamped her lips closed to keep from blurting out a protest at his condescension. She intended to do everything she could to help Stephen get well. No one was going to keep her out of that sickroom.

"I will come back later this evening to check on him again," Dr. Fields said, and bowed.

When he was gone, Linette looked at her aunt. "You know I intend to nurse Stephen."

Her aunt nodded. "But do remember, my dear, many sickroom duties are distasteful. I do not want you unduly upset."

"You didn't hesitate to take care of Uncle through his illness."

"He was my husband," Aunt replied. "The situation is very different here."

"I will do whatever I have to," Linette said stubbornly.

Aunt clucked her tongue warningly. "Just remember, my dear, that you cannot do everything. And that, despite all your efforts, it may not be enough."

Linette felt the prick of tears. "Stephen can't die, Aunt. He simply can't."

Mrs. Barton nodded knowingly and patted Linette's hand. "If hope alone can bring him through this, I know you will succeed."

Drying her tears, Linette walked slowly up the stairs. Mathers was pulling on his coat when she entered the room.

"You're leaving?" she asked, alarmed.

"I've got to make arrangements for the nurse to come in," he said. "And I could use some sleep."

Linette flushed. In her worry over Stephen, she'd forgotten that Mathers had been here all night. "Of course you do. What do I need to do while you're gone?"

"I hope the nurse will be here within a few hours. I

just gave him his medicine. You really don't have to do anything."

"I'm not helpless," Linette protested.

"Believe me, you do not want to help with his treatment. It's a messy, disgusting business."

Linette eyed him steadily. "You forget I stayed with Amy the night she died. That was not a clean, comfortable experience."

Mathers gave her a sharp look. "The doctor has prescribed both emetics and purges. Do you know what you would have to do? Hold the basin to catch the vomit, then support him while he empties his bowels. Is that really the kind of thing you want to do, Miss Gregory?"

Linette paled at his blunt description, but she preferred his honesty to Dr. Field's patronizing rebuffs.

"If it means that Stephen will get well faster, I'll do anything I can to help."

Mathers shook his head. "You just might be able to handle it, after all." He picked up his case. "While I'm gone, you can clean the room and empty the basins. If that doesn't change your mind, I'll let you do whatever you want."

"Thank you," Linette said.

"You've got an odd notion of favors." Mathers smiled ruefully and headed down the stairs.

Linette made sure that Stephen was sleeping then she set about to clean the room. She grimaced at seeing the stained towels and the blood-filled basin, products of the earlier bleeding. Gritting her teeth, Linette poured the blood into the half-full chamberpot and rinsed out the basin. Then, as a matter of pride, she carried the pot downstairs and emptied it. No task was too distasteful if it helped Stephen.

Her duties complete, she sat by the bedside again, watching him sleep.

After an hour he started tossing restlessly on the bed, knocking pillows to the floor. Linette hastily put them back, making sure that he stayed upright. She thought

Stephen's breathing sounded harsher than before and his face was flushed with fever. Her stomach twisted in knots. She wished Mathers had left more detailed instructions. Just when she was ready to send for Dr. Fields again, Stephen lapsed into a calmer sleep.

The nurse should be here soon, but Linette viewed her arrival with apprehension; she knew the unsavory reputation of most nurses. Linette wasn't going to let a slovenly drunk near Stephen.

A plump, apple-cheeked lady bustled into the room, a cheery smile on her face. "Are you still here, you poor lamb? Gerald said you might be; I came as soon as I could." She took Linette's hand and gave it a comforting squeeze. "I'm Mrs. Plum and you can leave things to me; I'll take good care of him, dearie."

Linette nearly melted with relief at the sight of the gray-haired nurse's calm confidence. She knew Stephen would be safe in this woman's hands.

"He was very restless an hour ago, but he's settled down," Linette said. "I think it is time for his medicine again. I'll help you as much as I can."

Mrs. Plum eyed her critically. "Take yourself off to bed and get some sleep. This lad's not goin' anywhere; he'll still be here when you wake up."

"But—"

"I'm in charge of this sickroom now, and if you want to set foot in it, you'll do what I say." She gave Linette a look that brooked no argument.

Linette hastily revised her opinion of Mrs. Plum. She might appear motherly, but she had a will of steel.

"I want you to send me your strongest footman," Mrs. Plum said as she made a quick inspection of the room.

"What are you going to do?" Linette asked apprehensively.

"Follow the doctor's orders," Mrs. Plum said. "Now, do as you're bid!"

Linette reluctantly obeyed.

*   *   *

She was convinced she wouldn't sleep a wink when she lay down on her bed, but surprisingly, she did. As soon as she awoke, Linette dashed down the hall to Stephen's room. Smith was guarding the door again. He greeted her with an apologetic grin.

"I was told you can't enter until you have eaten a hearty meal."

"How is he?"

Smith shrugged. "About the same. No worse, as far as I can tell."

"I'll just pop in for a minute," Linette said, reaching for the door latch.

The door swung open and Mrs. Plum appeared. "You are going to eat before you set foot inside this room."

"Yes, ma'am," Linette said meekly, backing away.

Aunt met her at the bottom of the stairs. "I'm glad you took a nap, my dear. You look so much better. Come, have a cup of tea with me."

"I have to eat something. Mrs. Plum said—"

"That you may look in on Ashworth when you have eaten. I know, dear. Cook has a cold collation ready for you. Come with me into the drawing room."

Seething with impatience, Linette followed her aunt.

"Dr. Fields was here while you slept."

"What? Why didn't you wake me? What did he say?"

"There's been little change. He said it could stay that way for several days."

Linette searched her aunt's face. "Was he optimistic?"

Aunt nodded. "Ashworth is young, after all. There is no reason to think he will not recover."

Linette gave a small sigh of relief. If Dr. Fields was still optimistic . . .

Aunt handed Linette her tea and shook her head. "I only hope he recovers soon. It is a dreadful thing to be ill and I imagine it is even worse for a medical man."

"That's what is so frightening," Linette said. "Stephen is meekly accepting everything that's done to him. He's too ill to even participate in his own treatment."

A maid brought the food. Linette forced herself to take a few bites of ham, and ate a slice of buttered bread, although the food held no taste for her. But she knew Aunt wouldn't let her return upstairs until she had eaten an acceptable amount.

Aunt watched her with a critical eye, but finally nodded that she'd eaten enough. Linette was out of the room and up the stairs in seconds.

Mrs. Plum sat at the foot of the bed, knitting.

"What did the doctor say?" Linette asked. "Did he change any of the medicines?"

"I'm to continue the same treatments. He seems to think the cold baths are doing the lad some good."

Linette cast an anxious glance at Stephen. "Is he still sleeping most of the time?"

Mrs. Plum nodded. "Best thing for him, so don't you dare wake him up, girl." She set her knitting aside and stood. "I'm going downstairs to have me a cup of tea, since I don't expect much to happen. You can watch while I'm gone."

Linette flashed her a grateful smile.

After the nurse left, Linette felt Stephen's forehead, but it was still dry and hot to her touch. With a sigh, she sat down in the chair and watched him with concerned eyes.

A loud spasm of coughing suddenly shook him and Linette feared he would choke. She poured a glass of water and held it to his lips. He took a few sips, then sank back against the pillows.

"Thanks," he rasped.

"Shh." Linette gently brushed the hair from his forehead. "Don't try to talk."

"What's going on?" he asked in a hoarse croak. "Where . . . am I? How . . . ?"

"You're at Aunt's house. Mathers and I brought you here last night. Her physician is treating you. He says you have pneumonia and . . ."

". . . shouldn't be here. The school . . ."

"Don't be ridiculous, Stephen. I'm sure Mathers is managing things at the school. You need to concentrate on getting well."

"The students . . ."

"Will survive without you for a few days. From what I hear, you nearly collapsed in front of your class yesterday. I'm sure that impressed them."

"Can't close . . ."

Her anger flared at his idiotic stubbornness. "Stephen, you don't have a choice. You should have taken to your bed a week ago. You're sick. Very sick. If you left here, you'd probably be dead within the day."

He struggled to sit up, but bent over with another bout of coughing. This one was so bad Linette was ready to call Mrs. Plum when he finally regained his breath.

"Stephen, please don't worry about anything." Linette grabbed his hand, giving him an encouraging squeeze. "You have to concentrate on getting well."

He nodded briefly and closed his eyes.

She prayed he would sleep again.

How like the foolish man to think he could carry on as usual even when he was sick. Again, she felt overwhelmed with guilt. If she hadn't been so angry with him, and deliberately stayed away, she would have known he was sick. Now, she would have to work twice as hard to make sure that he got well.

Linette refused to consider the possibility of failure.

Chapter 22

"Do you really think Dr. Fields is treating Stephen properly?" Linette asked Mathers when he arrived the following afternoon. "He doesn't seem to be getting any better."

"He's doing all he can," Mathers said bluntly. "It's not like an amputation, when you can just cut the diseased part away. Stephen didn't get sick overnight and he isn't going to get well soon, either.

"But all he does is stuff Stephen with those horrible medicines that makes him vomit until he's so weak he can barely move, then bleeds him. How can anyone get well with that treatment?"

"The emetics are necessary to eliminate the inflammatory fluids." He smiled. "Has Stephen been complaining?"

"No," Linette said. "That's even more worrisome. He's talked a bit about the school and how he needs to get back, but he hasn't protested anything the doctor does."

"You know Stephen; if he had any strength at all he'd try to get out of bed. Believe me, this is for the best."

Linette twisted her fingers together. "Do you think we might want to call in ... a more modern thinker?"

"And let him prescribe a new regimen that will be equally unpleasant?" Mathers shook his head. "Be patient. Ash will improve soon."

Linette said no more, but she wasn't convinced.

* * *

The next two days passed in a blur. Despite Mrs. Plum's protests, Linette emptied chamberpots, carried soiled linen downstairs, and forced foul-tasting medicines down Stephen's throat. She even held the basin while Stephen vomited.

Despite all their efforts, there was little change in Stephen's condition. The doctor came twice daily, bleeding Stephen each time. He still didn't change the medicines or the treatments, which worried Linette.

On Monday, Aunt pushed her out of the house to get some fresh air. Linette took the carriage to the bookshops near St. Barts, and purchased Good's *Study of Medicine*. She would find out for herself what the proper treatment for pneumonia was. When Mrs. Plum went downstairs for her lunch, Linette sat with Stephen and eagerly turned to Good's book. But to her disappointment, Dr. Fields was following the standard course of treatment—purges, bleeding, and cold baths. Stephen was already taking antimony and Dover's Powder, the recommended medicines. Nothing else was suggested.

A cold chill swept over her. They were doing everything they could, and yet Stephen wasn't getting better. What if none of the medicines and treatments helped? It would be like Amy all over again; they hadn't been able to save her and they weren't going to be able to save Stephen either. Linette bent her head, fighting back her tears.

Then she clenched her fists. Linette simply would not allow Stephen to die. Because despite everything, she loved him. And she was determined to force him to admit that he felt the same.

Stephen was never certain when he was awake or asleep. There were times—vomiting over the basin after taking the antimony, or when the sharp lancet sliced his skin, that he knew he was awake. But the rest of his days and nights passed in a confusing haze. People, familiar and unfamiliar, walked in and out of his consciousness and he wasn't sure which were real and which were imagined.

He knew Linette was there, but he saw her so often that he knew it was mostly in his dreams. He still felt her cool hand on his forehead, heard her soothing voice whispering in his ear when he knew she wasn't there. So vivid were his dreams that he even imagined her wiping his brow while he bent over the basin, and he knew that had to be his imagination. She wouldn't be allowed to do that.

But at least the dreams were more pleasant than the reality. Stephen's left arm flamed with pain from the lancing wounds and he thought he might have cracked more than one rib during the violent bouts of coughing.

He watched through a dreamy haze each time he was bled, thinking he should protest, but feeling too weak to speak. Maybe it didn't matter. Maybe it would help.

Something had to. He couldn't decide which part of his body hurt the most; his head, his chest, his stomach, and his arm clamored simultaneously for attention. Stephen welcomed the opium draughts that transported him into oblivion. They dulled everything: the pain, his thoughts, his energy. He simply did not care.

Unless Linette sat with him. Or at least, when he thought she did. In his dreams, she read to him: poetry, stories, even *The Lancet*. He was so delirious that once he thought she was reading to him from some medical book. He suspected that next she'd be talking to him in French—and he'd understand every word.

Stephen had no idea what day it was—or even when it was day or night. Thick, heavy drapes closed off the windows, so even when he was aware of his surroundings, he couldn't tell if it was day or night. Only when the doctor came could he be relatively certain it was day—or early evening. The rest of the time, it could be either midnight or noon; it was all the same to him.

Only a few times, when he feared he was going to slip into the darkness and never come out, did he struggle.

Once, Stephen thought he was falling and he flailed wildly, trying to grab something solid, to save himself. But there'd been nothing to hold on to; he kept falling and falling until he couldn't remember anything more. Was this death?

Stephen was shocked when he next felt the sharp sting of the doctor's lancet. He wasn't dead after all, and he felt a flicker of disappointment. His suffering wasn't over.

Just when he didn't think he could endure anymore, Linette was there again, with her soothing voice and hands, calming him, reassuring him. Even if it was a dream, it was enough. It was then that he realized that he didn't want to die after all. Not until he could tell her how much she meant to him.

Late on Tuesday, Linette waited anxiously for Dr. Fields to arrive. Stephen had been restless all afternoon and she grew increasingly worried as he thrashed about. Then suddenly, he grew still. His breathing, which had once been so raspy, was barely audible. She was afraid to touch him, to wipe his brow, or even smooth the sheets for fear that she would disturb him.

When she heard the doctor's tread on the steps, Linette raced into the hall, grabbed his hand and dragged him into the room. "Something has happened."

The doctor took one look at Stephen's ashen countenance and jumped into action. Ignoring Linette, he barked out orders to Mrs. Plum. Dr. Fields set out his equipment and lit the wick on a tiny torch. Using a towel, he clasped a round, glass cup and shoved the torch inside.

Cupping. Linette cringed. Hot glass applied to the skin, forming a vacuum which raised welts as the glass cooled. He was going to do that to Stephen. Mrs. Plum jerked the bedcovers down and unbuttoned Stephen's nightshirt.

Linette watched in horrified fascination as Dr. Fields put the heated cup on Stephen's bared chest.

"My God," she whispered and turned away, not bearing to look. The pain must be excruciating, but Stephen only uttered a low moan.

Dr. Fields ignored her outburst and proceeded to methodically reheat and apply the cup to Stephen's chest. Daring a glance, Linette winced at the pattern of red circles marking his skin.

"What is this going to do?" she dared to ask.

Dr. Fields gave her an exasperated glance. "It's pulling the blood away from the inflammation in his chest."

"But it must hurt!"

He gave her a frosty look. "Really, Miss Gregory, you shouldn't be here. If you are going to continue these outbursts, you will have to leave."

Linette bit her lip and remained silent.

She heard Mathers' step in the hall and she ran out to him. "He's cupping Stephen's chest. Please tell me that he's doing the right thing; it looks so horrible."

Mathers came in and glanced at Stephen. Linette thought even he paled at the sight of the ugly welts. He gave Dr. Fields a searching look. "Is he improving?"

"Too early to tell, too early to tell." Dr. Fields shook his head. "I plan another round of antimony, then shall apply cold compresses to the head. I have to draw the inflammation away from the lungs."

Mathers himself forced the medicine down Stephen's throat and Linette steeled herself to the inevitable. Stephen was so weak that Mathers had to support him while he vomited. Linette's hands shook so hard she could barely hold the basin.

When he was done, she gently wiped Stephen's face. Glancing over at the doctor, she felt a twinge of unease when she saw him stropping a razor.

"What is that for?" she asked.

"I have to shave his head before I apply the compress," Dr. Fields said, giving her an exasperated look.

Something inside Linette snapped. She'd stood by while the doctor had drained Stephen's blood, and emptied his stomach, and applied hot glass to his chest. Enough was enough.

"No," she said. "I won't allow it. You've tortured him enough. Leave him alone."

Dr. Fields stared at her as if he couldn't believe his ears. "Really, Miss Gregory, I hardly think you're the proper judge—"

"Stephen doesn't deserve to suffer any further. If he is going to die, let him die in peace."

"But the compresses will allow the fever to escape more readily through his head."

She turned to Mathers. "Wouldn't a cold bath be just as effective?"

He glanced at the doctor, then back to Linette, then nodded slowly.

Dr. Fields slammed his instruments into his bag. "I cannot work in an atmosphere where I do not have complete control," he said, his voice quavering with anger. "I wash my hands of this case. Let his death be on your heads." He stormed out into the hall.

Linette put her hand to her face. Dear God, pray that she had done the right thing.

"If you want to keep this man alive, I need your help," Mathers said in a calm voice. "Get that tub filled with cool water, Mrs. Plum. Linette, help me get Stephen out of bed."

Linette draped Stephen's arm over her shoulder while Mathers took the other side, and they dragged the unconscious man to the tub and sat him down. Mathers dumped a basin of water over his head and Stephen's eyes snapped open at the shock.

"Linette," he whispered hoarsely.

She grabbed his hand and squeezed his fingers, her eyes filling with tears. "You're going to be all right," she said, so softly that she didn't even know if he heard. "Please be all right."

Her life became a timeless nightmare of lugging Stephen to and from the bed, forcing medications down his throat, and watching anxiously for any sign of change. Stephen, dosed on quantities of opium and antipyretics, was barely conscious. Linette didn't know if they were making progress or not; she was so numb with exhaustion and worry that she blindly followed Mathers' orders.

At some point during the night, his eyes red-rimmed with weariness, Mathers collapsed in the chair and fell asleep immediately. Mrs. Plum had gone home hours ago, and Linette felt a flash of panic.

What if something happened, what if Stephen's condition took another turn for the worse? A few seconds might make all the difference and she didn't know what to do. Linette wanted to rush over and shake him awake. But she was so bone-weary herself that she couldn't move. Mathers could sleep. She would keep watch over Stephen.

All the work they'd done seemed to have made little difference. She watched him intently, but there was no sign that he was getting better. Instead, his irregular, rasping breathing resounded in her ears like an off-key orchestra. She wanted to stuff her ears with cotton to block out the frightening sound.

At least he was breathing. There had been a time, in between the baths and the medicines, that he'd lain so quietly she'd been terrified he was dying. No matter how horrible they sounded, his torturous breaths gave her a mote of comfort.

She sat beside the bed, his hand clenched in hers. Somehow, Linette thought that he could not die as long as she held on to him. If only she could transfer her strength to Stephen.

Stephen knew he was dreaming again, but he didn't care. Dreams were less painful than reality. He could still feel the searing heat of the cupping glass against his skin.

He imagined Linette was here again, bathing him, tending his tortured skin, whispering encouragements in his ear. Stephen almost wanted to open his eyes, to soothe his fears by gazing on her, but he knew that would destroy the dream so he kept them shut.

Mathers' presence puzzled him. Where was the physician? Mathers must be part of his dream, too. A part he didn't want to think about. The Linette part of the dream was much better. Soft and tender. Like her skin felt beneath his fingertips, like her lips when he'd kissed her.

He wanted to do that again, kiss her and hold her close and let his hands rove over her shapely body. Wanted to see her naked, to touch her and caress her and feel the silky smoothness of her skin. He would kiss her here, and there, and everywhere, listening to her soft moans of pleasure.

Her hands would be all over him, too, stroking, rubbing, making his skin burn with the want of her. They'd roll together, on the grass, the smooth blades cool against their bodies. Down the hill they tumbled, into the pond, splashing and laughing. He lay on his back, feeling the cool water lapping at his sides. Stephen reared up out of the pond and shook his head like a bedraggled puppy, spraying her with water.

Linette laughed and he swam over to her, watching the glistening droplets run down her neck, across her chest. He bent his head and licked a drop from her breast, tasting her sweetness.

A loud clap of thunder shattered the calm and angry waves lapped at the shore. Stephen reached for Linette but she was gone, carried away from him by the foaming water. He tried to swim after her but his arms felt like lead and he could not lift them. The water, thick as treacle, held him prisoner, sucking him down. He gasped for breath, struggling to keep his head above the murky water, but he slowly sank beneath the surface.

Yet he could still breathe underneath the water. Stephen lifted his hand to his face but his fingers were invisible in the darkness. Suddenly, a light appeared overhead.

A golden moon shone down on him as he lay on the hillside again. The odor of crushed herbs was sharp in his nostrils: chamomile, hyssop, mint. He grabbed a handful of leaves and crumpled them between his fingers, then watched the pieces tumble to the ground.

Stephen stood and looked around him, searching for someone, but he didn't know who. Calling loudly, he listened for an answer, but only heard the echo of his own voice. He was alone and the feeling made him sad. Slowly, he sank to the ground.

Two hands covered his eyes. He reached up, clasping the tiny wrists in his hand. A feminine giggle sounded in his ear.

Linette. He'd found her again. And this time he wasn't going to let her get away. Turning toward her, he buried his face in her breasts. She would keep him warm and safe. Forever.

Linette's head jerked back and her eyes snapped open in alarm. She'd fallen asleep.

Horrified, she bent over Stephen, listening to his breathing. To her surprise, it was slow and steady. She touched her hand to his fevered brow, then jerked it back.

It felt cool.

Had the fever broken?

"Mathers!" she hissed loudly. She didn't want to let go of Stephen's hand, not yet.

The young surgeon was still sprawled in his chair. "Mathers," she called, louder. "Wake up."

He sat up suddenly. "What?"

"It's Stephen. Feel his forehead. I think the fever's broken."

Mathers scrambled to his feet and touched Stephen's brow. Linette watched his face anxiously, looking for a sign of encouragement.

"How long has he been like this?" Mathers asked.

She bowed her head, ashamed. "I fell asleep. Not for long, I think, but I'm not certain. Is the fever gone? Is the worst over?"

He frowned. "It's probably too early to say, but I think it's a good sign." He stretched, rubbing the back of his neck. "Why don't you get some sleep? It'll be morning soon. I can watch him."

"I don't want to leave. Not yet. Not until he wakes up again."

Mathers rubbed his stubbled jaw. "How about making some tea, then? I could use a cup."

"There's hot water on the back of the stove," Linette said pointedly. "You'll find the tea things on the kitchen table."

He grinned. "He's not going to wander off if you leave him for a few minutes. I'll stay with him."

"And you aren't incapable of making a pot of tea," she retorted. She wasn't going to leave Stephen's bedside for even a minute.

Mathers held up his hands. "All right, all right. I'll get the tea."

Linette looked over at Stephen's sleeping form, hardly daring to breathe, trying to contain her excitement. Even though Mathers hadn't seemed particularly impressed, she knew that Stephen was better. Lightly, she squeezed his fingers.

"Linette?" His voice sounded distant, sleepy.

"Stephen!" She jumped from the chair and leaned over the side of the bed, tears welling up in her eyes.

"This is a dream," he mumbled. "You're not really here."

"Look at me." Linette took his hand and brought it to her cheek. "I'm here."

His lids flickered open and he looked at her with a bleary, unfocused gaze.

Linette could barely see him through her tears. "See? It's really me. Oh, Stephen, I've been so frightened. You've been so sick."

"Water," he croaked.

Supporting the back of his head, she held the cup while he greedily drank the cool water. Finished, he lay back against the pillows.

"What . . . are you doing here?"

Linette smiled. "Taking care of you."

"Have you been here . . . whole time?" His voice came out in a gravelly whisper.

"A great part of it."

He managed a smile. "Should sleep."

She squeezed his hand. "I'll sleep when I know you're better."

"I dreamed . . . don't know what I dreamed."

"Shh. Don't talk. You're still very weak. Mathers went to get tea and he'll want to have a good look at you when he gets back."

Linette blinked heavily but she couldn't stop the tears from dripping down her cheeks.

Stephen's expression turned sad. "Don't cry. Better."

"I thought you were going to die," she said in a choked voice, burying her face in the blankets.

She felt a touch on her head, a hesitant hand stroking her hair.

"Wouldn't dare. You'd be mad."

Linette looked up and smiled through her tears. "Furious, in fact. Not after everything I've done for you."

"Won't," he said, and closed his eyes again. He sighed deeply. "You were right."

Linette gave him a startled glance. "Right? About what?"

"When you said . . . I was afraid. Of you."

"Oh, Stephen, I was angry when I said that. Don't worry about it now. We can talk about it when you are better."

"Was afraid. Couldn't admit ... wanted you."

She brushed a lock of hair off his brow. "Didn't I say that you were a pigheaded fool?"

Stephen nodded faintly.

Linette leaned over and kissed him on the cheek. "You must rest. You can explain your foolishness in great detail later."

She sat down again, his hand clasped tightly in hers. Linette brushed the wetness from her face.

He wasn't well, that she knew. But for the first time in days she dared to believe that the worst was over.

Stephen would live. Her heart sang at the thought.

Chapter 23

"Well, it looks like the illustrious surgeon is alive."

Mathers' voice was cheery as he walked in, carrying the tea tray and Stephen gave him a wan grin.

"And he's got his hands on the nurse already. A pretty spectacular recovery, if I do say so myself."

Stephen gave Linette a rueful smile. She blushed and quickly slipped off the bed, taking the tray from Mathers.

He reached over and felt Stephen's forehead. "Your fever's definitely down. How's the chest feel?"

Stephen dared a deep breath and winced at the pain. "Elephants. Dancing on it."

"That sounds about right. Your lungs are a mess."

"Where's ... doctor?"

Mathers grinned. "He left in a huff last night when Miss Gregory objected to one of his treatments."

That surprised Stephen. He gave her a quizzical look as she stood at the foot of the bed.

"He wanted to shave off your hair!" she said heatedly.

"Good girl," he whispered.

"And like a good girl, she's off to her bed now." Mathers gave Linette a stern look and pushed her toward the door. "I don't want you back here until after noon."

"Yes, sir," she replied meekly. With a fond parting look at Stephen, she left.

Stephen glanced warily at Mathers. "What day is it?"

"Wednesday. And not another word for a while. You

were nearly on your deathbed last night and I don't want a repeat performance. Take your medicine like a good boy and go back to sleep."

Stephen eyed the cup he held out with suspicion. "What is it?"

"Your medicine," Mathers said firmly. "Drink it."

Grimacing at the foul-tasting brew, Stephen reluctantly complied. Then he lay back against the pillows and closed his eyes while Mathers checked his pulse and listened to his chest.

"Your lungs sound better," Mathers said. "I think the congestion is clearing."

"Don't ... feel better. Chest is on fire."

"That's probably from the cupping," Mathers said in a matter-of-fact tone.

"Cupping!" Stephen tried to sit up but fell back against the pillows, too weak to move. "You let that quack cup me?"

"Quit complaining. You're better now, aren't you? Maybe it worked."

Stephen tried to snort his derision but only managed to start a spasm of coughing.

"I want you quiet or I'm going to double your dose of laudanum," Mathers said warningly. "You're not going to be jumping out of bed for a long time."

Stephen clamped his mouth shut.

His mind was still fogged—no doubt they'd been dosing him with laudanum the entire time—but his thoughts were more clear than they had been in ages. Now he knew where he was, why he was here, and that he wasn't going to die.

And that he would see Linette again.

The thought brought a quick smile. He wondered how much of what he remembered about her presence had been real, and how much the illusion of his delirium. Had she really stayed with him while he was bled, purged, and bathed? It was impossible. Her aunt would never have allowed it.

But then again, Linette usually did what she wanted. It would be just like her to have been here while he suffered through those indignities. He cringed at the thought of her seeing him so helpless.

Yet her devoted attention had probably helped save his life. He owed her a great deal for that.

And for other things.

He knew now that he didn't need to be afraid of her; he didn't want to run from her, or his feelings for her. He needed Linette, wanted her, longed for her. Frightening as those thoughts were, the though of living without her was even worse.

When he'd lain in the bed, not sure if he was dead or alive, he'd realized how much he wanted her. Wanted to always be able to see her sparkling eyes, hear her teasing laugh, feel her soothing hands easing his hurts. He didn't want to be alone anymore. He wanted Linette to care about him; more importantly, he wanted to care about her. Stephen was tired of running from his feelings, running from himself. He trusted her not to turn away when he told her how he felt.

He had so many things to say to her.

Stephen drifted off to sleep.

If Linette had thought the long days of Stephen's illness were hell, the days of his recovery were closer to heaven. Stephen grew stronger every hour. Linette watched his recovery with a growing sense of pride, knowing that she'd had a hand in it. He was still weak, and Mathers wouldn't permit him to leave his bed, but she knew that the worst was long over.

His improvement was so rapid that Mrs. Plum went home several days later and Linette took over most of the nursing duties. It was sheer pleasure to give Stephen his medicine, and bring him his food. When he was awake, she read to him, sometimes poetry, but more often articles from *The Lancet* or some other medical journal.

"Are we ready for lunch?" Linette asked brightly as she followed behind the footman who brought the tray into the room.

"Yes, ma'am," Stephen said, then grimaced as she handed him a cup of arrowroot broth. "Haven't I had enough of this vile stuff?"

"Mathers says this has the nourishment you need."

"That's easy for him to say—he's not the one who has to drink it. When can I have some real food?"

"He says that you might try some beef broth tomorrow." She gave him a stern look. "Your stomach is still very sensitive and he doesn't want to upset it."

"Your stomach would be sensitive, too, if you'd been purged like I was."

Linette shuddered at the memory of the bouts of retching. "You don't have to tell me how awful it was—I was here most of the time."

Stephen shook his head. "I thought I dreamed that. You shouldn't have stayed. You didn't need to deal with that."

She dropped her gaze. "I wanted to make sure you got well."

"You're made of stronger stuff than I am." He took her hand and squeezed it. "Thank you."

Linette bit her lip to keep her eyes from tearing. Even though Stephen was getting better, the ordeal of his illness had left her emotions rubbed raw. She could not forget how close she'd come to losing him. Linette wanted to tell him how worried she'd been, how relieved she was, but she was wary. Despite his words the other day, she couldn't forget how he'd pushed her away before. She set down the cup of broth and grabbed a jar from the table. "Let me rub some more ointment on your arm."

Stephen glanced down at his bandaged arm. "You should have let the man shave my head and stopped him from bleeding me, instead. It would have been a lot less painful."

Linette unwrapped the bandages and gently rubbed the herbal lotion over the lancing wounds. Stephen winced when she touched his tender skin.

"Do you think they are inflamed?" she asked worriedly, peering at the reddened line.

Stephen gingerly prodded his skin. "I hope not. 'Else I'll probably develop gangrene and have to get the whole damn arm cut off."

Linette gasped at the thought. "Could that happen?"

He grinned teasingly. "At least I know you'll be there to offer me comfort. And there'll be dressings galore for you to change."

She set the jar of ointment aside and rewrapped his arm. "If you think I am going to stand and watch while they cut off your arm, you are sadly mistaken."

He grabbed her hand and drew it to his cheek. "Don't worry, it's healing properly. Thanks to your tender care."

Linette blushed.

Stephen continued to improve, growing more and more argumentative as the days passed. He argued with Mathers about his treatment, argued with Linette about the necessity for his medicine, and generally tried everyone's temper.

Linette was never more happy.

She'd brought up his lunch from the kitchen one afternoon and wrinkled her nose at the unfamiliar scent in the bedroom. It reminded her of ... violets? Linette glanced at Stephen, propped up in the bed, and nearly dropped the tray in surprise. With his cleanly shaven face and neatly brushed hair he looked like the healthy Stephen she remembered.

"What have you done?" she demanded anxiously. "Did Mathers say you could get out of bed?"

He grinned at her. "Is it an improvement?"

"Improvement?" Linette carefully put the tray down and stepped closer to examine him. His hair was still damp from the bath and curled in dark swirls around his ears.

She sniffed the air again. "Do I smell violets?"

"I think that was Mathers' idea of a joke," Stephen said, with a wry laugh. "Scented soap." He stretched and rubbed his chin. "Lord, I feel better. Now if I could just get out of this blasted bed."

"That's up to Mathers. And I intend to see that you follow his orders."

When he'd finished his lunch, Linette took a jar from the table and began unbuttoning Stephen's nightshirt, in order to rub ointment over the cupping marks. They were healing nicely, but she still cringed at the sight. Dipping her finger into the jar, she gently smoothed the soothing ointment over his skin.

But today, her composure failed her. Not because of the ugly marks, but because she recognized the intimacy of her actions. As she touched Stephen's skin, her fingers tingled with awareness of the man she touched. She tried to concentrate on putting the salve on the scars, but she couldn't subdue her feelings.

Now that he was no longer desperately ill, Linette couldn't deny the physical attraction she felt. Before, he'd been too ill for her to look upon him as a man. But now ... he was once again the Stephen who'd caressed and kissed her and touching him like this was far too exciting.

She kept her eyes on his chest to avoid looking at him, afraid her eyes would reveal her feelings. He was painfully thin. If she ran her hand down his side she could feel each and every one of his ribs.

She remembered that afternoon in his office, when he'd so carefully examined her arm after she'd fallen, and how his touch had sent shivers of desire through her. Did he feel the same way now, as her fingers stroked across his chest? Was this as disturbing an experience for him as for her?

From the corner of her eye, she dared a glance at

Stephen. He lay back against the pillows, his eyes closed, a faint smile tugging at the corners of his mouth.

She hastily finished her task and set the jar of ointment back on the table before refastening his shirt. Stephen opened one eye.

"Will I live?"

"I'd like to take a cupping glass to Dr. Fields," she said with vehemence.

"I'll hold him down for you." Stephen laughed, then glanced at the clock. "When is Mathers due back?"

Linette straightened the jumble of jars and bottles on the bedside table while she tried to restore her composure. "He should be here soon—he said sometime after two."

"Is he at the school?"

"I have no idea."

He gave her a suspicious look. "No one will say anything. Why won't you tell me what is going on?"

"Doctor's orders," she said blandly. "Mathers doesn't want you to worry about anything until you're well enough to get out of bed."

"I'll be a mass of sores before that time comes," he grumbled and shifted his position.

"Stephen?"

"Hmm?"

Linette nervously played with the medicine bottles. "One thing I realized when you were . . . ill, is that I know nothing about your family. If anything had happened, I wouldn't have had any idea how to get in touch with them."

She saw his expression harden.

"I didn't die so you don't have to worry."

"You could also be run down by a carriage the first day you step outside the house." His sudden anger surprised her. Just how deep was the rift between Stephen and his family?

"I doubt the news would cause them too much distress."

"How can you say that? Of course they would be concerned."

Stephen looked into her soothing gray eyes. He wanted to tell her. Wanted to share with someone the gut-wrenching pain that the years of rejection had brought him. Yet he didn't want to reveal his weakness, his failure before her.

But she'd nursed him through this harrowing illness, performing tasks that the most experienced nurse would blanch at. Didn't he owe her something?

Wasn't this a way to show her that she'd won his trust? He took a deep breath.

"My family—my father, particularly—and I haven't been close for years."

"Is it because of the music?"

He laughed bitterly. "That's only a small part of it. I was always a disappointment to him. No matter what I did, it never was good enough. After a while, I stopped trying."

"But what about your mother? Surely she was more sympathetic."

"One of my earliest memories is of picking some flowers for her. I was so pleased with myself when I brought them home. And she tossed them away because they were only weeds."

"That's terrible! How could she do such a thing?"

"My parents expected perfection. Anything less wasn't good enough for them. No matter what I did, I never was able to live up to their expectations."

"How can they be unhappy with you?" Linette's eyes flashed angrily. "You're a noted surgeon. They can't consider *that* a failure."

"They could care less about my surgical skills. I wouldn't follow the path they'd chosen for me, so I am an ungrateful son."

"What did they want you to be?"

He darted a look at the ceiling. "A clergyman."

Linette let out a peal of laughter. "Oh, Stephen, how

could they even think such a thing? You'd make a terrible churchman."

He gave her a stern look. "You don't think I would have done a good job?"

She giggled. "Not at all."

Stephen smiled at the thought. "Neither did I. But it was what they wanted, and when I balked, they didn't take it well."

"You are still serving people. Can't they see that?"

"Ah, but a clergyman holds a respectable position. Surgeons are only a notch higher than cattle butchers."

Linette wrinkled her nose. "Oh, that's ridiculous. They must have no idea of what you do to think that. Why, being a surgeon is a perfectly respectable occupation."

He shrugged with deliberate casualness. "Not for a gentleman."

She gave him a searching look. "And are you a gentleman?"

"They wanted me to be one." He laughed. "Obviously, they failed."

Linette gave him a hesitant smile. "It is rather ironic. My father *is* a clergyman."

Stephen was taken aback. "You never told me that. It certainly explains a great deal."

"Such as?"

"Your obsession with helping others." He rubbed his thumb across the back of her hand. "You're quite the dutiful clergyman's daughter."

She twined her fingers together in what he'd come to recognize as a sign of nervousness.

"I'm really not."

He arched a brow.

"My family and I had a ... difference of opinion about my future."

He eyed her with new interest. "So you ran away to London."

Linette blushed. "It wasn't quite like that. My uncle

had just died and Aunt was by herself. She wanted me to stay with her. It was the best thing for both of us."

Stephen wondered if that was the entire story but he didn't press her. She was here now, and that was what mattered. "You spend more time at the Dispensary than with your aunt."

"I didn't at first. But when she took up her life again I had to find something to do."

"And charity teas and ladies' improving societies weren't enough for you."

Linette shook her head. "I was taught to help others. And I like to work with people."

Stephen squeezed her hand. "You do a good job."

"I try. But sometimes, it can be discouraging. There are so many people who need assistance; so many things the Dispensary could do to help them."

"I think you've accomplished a great deal," Stephen said.

"Oh, but there's much more that could be done. I want to start teaching the children as well, and find jobs for those who need them. Just imagine what it would be like to expand the Dispensary into a real hospital."

He smothered a grin at her lofty ambitions. "Do you intend to accomplish this single-handedly?"

She gave him a dampening look. "Of course not. But I can make plans, can't I?"

"I, for one, wouldn't wager against your success."

"And I promise to *consider* you for the post of chief surgeon."

He put a hand over his heart. "I'm honored."

"That is, if you take your medicine and promise to sleep." Linette reached for a medicine bottle and spoon.

"Do I have any choice?" he grumbled, but smiled at her determination. Her concern for his health pleased him. When was the last time anyone had really cared what happened to him? He would willingly let Linette bully him all she wanted.

Mathers tapped lightly on the open door, then walked in. Linette gave him a grateful look.

"Thank goodness you're here. I feared Stephen was going to badger me with questions about your whereabouts for the entire afternoon."

"Well, I'm here now." He took a long look at Stephen. "You do look better." He sniffed the air. "And certainly *smell* better."

Stephen laughed. "I'll find some way to get back at you for that," he said with a warning wave of his finger.

Mathers checked his pulse and listened to his chest. "What do you think about going home?"

Stephen eagerly sat up. "Now?"

"Tomorrow, I think. I'm sure Miss Gregory is thoroughly tired of your complaints and will be glad to be rid of your presence."

Linette was no such thing, but she tried to hide her disappointment. She was grateful Stephen was better, but she didn't want him to go home—not so soon.

"Are you sure it's a good idea?" she asked. "I'm not sure he'll remember to take his medicine, or eat properly, or—"

Stephen rolled his eyes. "And to think I survived all these years without your tender care. It's a miracle."

"And you fell sick without any help from me, either," Linette reminded him. She gave Mathers an imploring glance. "Don't you think he should stay here a few days longer? Until we know he will take care of himself?"

Stephen patted her hand. "I promise to follow my physician's orders faithfully."

She gave him a withering look. "Since your physician is a surgeon that gives me a *great* deal of confidence."

Mathers laughed. "Don't worry, I'll keep an eye on him. And you may check on him every day, if you like."

Linette threw up her hands, accepting defeat. "I'll defer to your greater medical wisdom."

Mathers left soon after and Linette stayed with Stephen until he drifted off to sleep, then went downstairs and curled up in her favorite chair, in front of the fire.

She hated the thought of him going home, alone. Despite his assurances, she knew he wouldn't take as good care of himself as he should. But he was determined to go and she had to let him.

As she thought about everything Stephen had said this afternoon about his family, a deep, burning anger filled her. How could anyone have been so cruel to a little boy who only wanted to please his mother?

If Stephen brought *her* a bouquet of cabbage, she would treasure it like the rarest hothouse bloom.

Her own parents had not been happy with the choices she had made, but at least they respected them, and allowed her to do what she wished. They had not held it against her.

She began to understand why Stephen kept such tight control over his feelings. Of course, as a surgeon, he couldn't give vent to every emotion; he would find it impossible to do his work.

But he kept that wall of reserve around him all the time. And now she knew it was his protection against further hurt. No wonder he'd been so frightened after he'd kissed her. He'd shown her that he cared, and he must have been terrified that she would reject him, just as his family had. By denying that he felt anything for her, and pushing her away, he wasn't going to give her the opportunity.

Linette didn't want to pay the price for his family's cruelty. Stephen *needed* her. Although she still opposed his work, she felt confident that she would be able to win him over to her views. Then, nothing could stand in the way of their happiness.

It was more important to show him that he needed her. Needed her to show him that love was not always hurtful, that it could be good, and joyous, and safe. That instead of fearing her, he could love her.

The very fact that he'd admitted his fear was good.

He was confronting his past. Now, Linette needed to reassure him that he would be safe with her. That he was the man she had been looking for all her life, a man who shared her desire to help people. And that she would move heaven and earth to be with him, rather than hurt him.

If he hadn't been so ill, he would have realized that by now. Why else would she have endured the horrors of the sickroom if not out of love?

He would realize it, in time. But she didn't want to wait. Before he could fully let her into his life, Stephen needed to trust her, and the only way he would do that was if she showed him that she trusted him more.

And she knew how she could demonstrate that trust, in a way that would show him that she was irrevocably his.

Linette took a deep breath. What she contemplated went against her principles. But that was the very reason it would mean something to Stephen, would show him how much she cared.

If she dared.

Chapter 24

Stephen lay in his bed that night, listening to the sounds of the household settling down for the night. The lone candle on the nightstand cast flickering shadows on the ceiling. After the dark days of his illness, he felt more comfortable with a light in the room.

He heard a soft step in the corridor, then the click of the latch as the door was pushed open. His eyes widened with surprise as Linette stepped into the room.

She looked as surprised as he.

"I ... I thought you would be asleep." Linette gave him a nervous glance as she came toward the bed.

Stephen grinned. "I slept half the day."

"I know."

He longed to reach out and touch the curling blond hair that swirled about her shoulders, even as he wanted to push her out the door. She shouldn't be here like this, dressed in her night rail and wrapper. She looked too alluring, too enticing.

"Are you here to tuck me in for the night?" he asked lightly.

There was no teasing look in her eyes. "When I thought you were going to die, I was terrified at the thought of losing you." Linette's voice was soft, breathless. "And now that I have you back, I want to show you how much you mean to me."

He stared at her, hardly comprehending her words. She took a step closer, and took his hand, placing it over her pounding heart.

Linette looked at him shyly. "I came to ask ... that is ..." She took a deep breath and her words came out in a rush. "I want you to make love to me. Now. Tonight."

"You don't have to do this," he said, stunned by her words.

"Yes, I do, Stephen. Because you have to understand how much I love you."

Stephen's mouth grew dry as Linette untied the ribbon fastenings at her neck. Her fingers moved with excruciating slowness and it was all he could do to keep himself from reaching out to help her. He had to send her away, for both their sakes.

But he couldn't. Because the urge to hold her was too strong.

Linette slipped the night rail down her shoulders and it fell to the floor. She stood before him, naked, her skin glowing golden in the candle light.

God, she was beautiful.

She took a hesitant step toward the bed and Stephen's breath caught, afraid that she would change her mind. But she came closer and he clasped her hand, pulling her down onto the mattress and into his arms.

He was glad he still wore his nightshirt, because the feel of her satiny skin against his would have been more than he could bear. Already, he fought to control his longing. He ached to touch her, caress her the way he had in those wild dreams during his illness, but he was afraid to. Afraid he would frighten her. Afraid she would leave him if he moved too fast.

Slowly, reverently, Stephen touched her hair, her cheek, her lips with his fingertips, hardly daring to believe this was happening. But she was very real; this was no dream. She loved him, wanted him, was giving herself to him as proof of that.

God, he didn't deserve her. The kind of man who did would resist her entreaties, send her away. But Stephen couldn't, because he wanted her too much.

"Say something," she whispered in a shaky voice. He heard her nervousness and adored her all the more for what she was doing.

"Ah, Linette," he murmured and held her tightly. He put his mouth on hers and reveled in the sweetness of her kisses.

Stephen nuzzled against the side of her neck, breathing in the heady aroma of her rosewater scent. With his fingers, he traced spiraling patterns on her back, feeling the gooseflesh rise.

Ah, she felt so good. And so alive.

He brought his mouth down on hers, his lips insistent and demanding this time. While his tongue teased her lips apart, his hand crept around the back of her neck, lightly stroking her nape, twining his fingers in her hair.

Aching with need, Stephen pulled her closer, tasting her, teasing her tongue with his. She responded, tentatively, then with more confidence, and he uttered a low groan of pleasure.

Suddenly, he wanted his nightshirt off, wanted to feel her silken skin against his heated flesh. He fumbled with the buttons, but with his bandaged arm he was slow and clumsy.

Then he felt Linette's hands at his throat, undoing the fastenings. Stephen struggled to pull his shirt up and she pulled it over his head and he lay back again.

She trailed her fingers across his chest. "I hate what he did to you," she said in a soft voice, then leaned down and brushed her lips against one of the cupping marks. "I want to make them go away."

Stephen's fists clenched at his side. He was in agony, not from pain but from pleasure. If she kept this up, he would be lost. Reaching out, he pulled her to him again.

"You don't know how wonderful you are," he whispered against her neck. He was hard and throbbing and was probably scaring the hell out of her but he couldn't stop, couldn't think about anything else but the feel of her pressed against him.

"I love you, Stephen," she said and he sucked in his breath at her words. He didn't deserve her love, wasn't worthy of it, but he wanted it so badly. Wanted to have this one woman who believed in him, trusted him, needed him.

He ran a trembling hand down her ribs and gently feathered his fingers along the side of her breast. Then he curled his hand around the curving flesh, running his thumb over the nipple, feeling it harden at his touch. Gently, reverently, he bent his head and licked the rigid nub. Linette let out a low moan.

"This is a very sensitive part of the anatomy," he explained softly. "It responds to the lightest touch."

He took her hand and placed it on his chest, sliding her fingers over his own nipple. It hardened instantly and Stephen couldn't restrain a groan of pleasure.

"It is the same on you," she said, in surprise.

Stephen chuckled. "Oh, you have a lot to learn about male and female anatomy. That's not the only similarity."

She buried her face in his neck. "Teach me," she whispered.

He slid his hand down her abdomen, pausing at the top of her pelvis. "This is the pelvic bone. A woman's is smaller and wider than a man's." He traced the curve of her hip. "It makes for a more pleasing shape."

Stephen nipped gently at the delicate tip of her breast while brushing his thumb over the other nipple. He ached with his imposed restraint but knew he must be careful, knew he must move slowly, to cherish the gift she was giving him.

He stroked her leg, teasing along the soft inner surface, inching ever closer to the curling triangle of fair hair that marked the juncture of her thighs. He threaded his fingers through the curls, tickling, teasing. She parted her legs slightly and he caressed the gap between them, then pressed his palm to her mound.

"The mons veneris." Stephen's hand dipped lower and

he touched the outer lips of her vagina. "The labia majora." He traced along the inside edge, feeling her growing dampness.

With his thumb, he brushed against the bud of her pleasure. "The clitoris. It's a *very* sensitive spot." He rubbed against it to prove his point and she arched against his hand, moaning softly.

He moved his hand lower again, probing for the opening to her vagina. She was hot, wet. Slowly, carefully, he pushed his finger in, then drew it out, and in again, imitating the rhythm of what was to come.

"Feel how wet you are? It's the sign of your arousal; your body's way of readying itself." He took her hand and curled it about his throbbing penis, rubbing it along its length. "I get ready in a different way."

Linette squirmed beneath him, pulling him closer. "Oh, Stephen, please."

He shifted her onto her back and nudged her legs apart with his knee.

"Please what?"

Her passion-dazed eyes looked like gray smoke as he looked at her. He bent down and kissed her, and her eyes fluttered closed, a dreamy expression crossing her face. Kneeling between her legs, he slowly guided himself into her warmth.

She was exquisitely tight and he had to stop more than once to catch his breath and dampen the burning fires within him. Murmuring soft words, he inched his way into her snug core.

"Oh, Linette, you feel so good," he groaned, kissing her lips, her face, her ear. "Move with me now, slowly. Let me love you."

Clasping her hips, he pulled her to him and began long, deep thrusts. She caught the rhythm quickly and arched to meet him, fanning his desire. He moved faster, urging her to keep pace, gritting his teeth to keep himself in check.

He pushed a hand between them and rubbed her clitoris, smiling at her shocked gasp against his ear. Her breath was coming in short, ragged bursts and he knew she was close, nearing the edge and it was all he could do to hold back his own release.

"Stephen," she cried out and she writhed with the shock of her climax. He kept moving within her, thrusting, withdrawing, until she stilled, then he poured himself into her as he groaned out her name.

Linette twined a lock of Stephen's hair around her finger as he lay cradled in her arms.

"Are you still afraid of me, Stephen?"

He laughed, a low, rumbling sound that reverberated through her body. He lifted his head and looked into her eyes.

"Petrified," he said. "You are obviously trying to kill me."

Linette examined his face anxiously. "I didn't think . . . Are you all right?"

He grinned. "If I die right now, it will be from pleasure."

She felt relieved. "I . . . I wanted you to know that you are loved, and wanted, and needed by someone, Stephen. That despite what your horrid family thinks, you are a good, courageous, wonderful man."

He remained silent for so long that she feared her words had displeased him.

"I've been afraid to have any feelings for so long," he said in a soft voice. "I decided it was much better not to care, than to suffer the hurt and pain that goes with caring." He ran a hand over the swell of her breast. "But I can't fight against what I feel for you, Linette. I tried, but I can't."

He raised his head again and she saw the anguish in his dark gaze.

"I was miserable without you." He grinned crookedly. "Just ask Mathers. Now, I wonder why I put up such a fight."

Tears stung her eyes and she hugged him to her, wanting to protect him from everything, even himself. "For a trained surgeon, you have so much to learn about some things."

"Oh?"

"Living. Loving. The world outside of medicine."

He sighed. "I didn't think there was one ... until now."

"I'll show it to you."

Stephen rolled to his side and raised himself on one elbow. With a finger, he traced the line of her jaw and Linette shivered at the gentleness of his touch.

"I don't know if I'm capable of loving anyone," he said quietly. "Not the way you mean. But I want to try. I know my life hasn't been the same since I met you. And I know I don't want to be without you." He kissed her with a tenderness that made her heart ache.

He made love to her again, this time with a fierceness that left her panting and drained. His intimate knowledge of her body brought her a pleasure she found unimaginable, and when he cried out her name again in his moment of release she felt a deep satisfaction in her power to please him.

When he slept, she watched him. It was such a relief to see him sleeping so peacefully after those long, terrifying nights. Sleeping now, beside her.

Linette snuggled closer to his sleeping form.

A hot warmth crept over her at the memory of their lovemaking. There had been something wonderfully exciting about having him explore her body with a surgeon's eyes, surgeon's hands. She was already familiar to him; he knew how she would respond when he touched each special place.

For her, it had been a dazzling education in the secrets of her own body. And she wanted to learn more. Wanted to learn how to touch him, to bring him the same pleasure he brought her. Linette smiled to herself. She thought Stephen would be a very willing teacher.

As her eyes drooped and she grew drowsy, Linette knew she should leave. She didn't dare fall asleep in his bed, but she was reluctant to leave its cozy warmth, the delicious feel of his warm body pressed close to hers.

But she didn't want to be found in his bed, not like this. No breath of scandal was going to be attached to them. If anything was to come from this night, if they were going to be together, it had to be Stephen's wish.

Reluctantly, she slid out from under his encircling arm. Shivering in the chill air, she donned her night rail and robe. Then Linette bent and kissed Stephen on the cheek before she slipped out into the hall, a smile on her face.

"Good morning."

Mathers' booming voice jolted Stephen awake. He stretched lazily, until he caught the faint aroma of rose petals lingering on the sheets.

Linette.

Stephen's arm shot out and he groped among the bed-covers, breathing a sigh of relief at finding himself alone. Smart girl; she'd known enough to go back to her room.

Although he would have liked to have awoken beside her. He imagined the feel of her curled up against him, envisioned the pleasure he would feel as he made love to her again.

Mathers came over to the bed. "You look like you had a good night's sleep," he said cheerfully. "Sit up so I can listen to your lungs."

Stephen sat patiently while Mathers applied the stethoscope to his chest.

"They sound better every day," Mathers said, putting the hollow tube back in his bag. He put a hand to Stephen's forehead. "Did you feel feverish during the night?"

Stephen shook his head. "No."

"You usually wear a nightshirt."

Stephen strove to keep his tone casual. "After this

many days in bed, it was a treat not to have my legs tangled up in the blasted thing for a while."

Mathers gave him a suspicious look but said nothing. He unwrapped Stephen's bandaged arm and examined the lancing wounds. "These are looking good, as well. The scarring should be minimal." Then his face took on a funny expression and he sniffed the air. "What have you been putting on these sores? It smells like roses in here."

Stephen choked, then covered his outburst with a cough. "Must be something in the salve," he said.

Mathers rebandaged the arm and gathered his instruments. "I can't see that you look any worse. You're certainly well enough to go home."

Stephen threw back the covers and sat up. "It's about time. Another day in bed and I would have gone mad."

Mathers picked up the discarded nightshirt and tossed it at Stephen. "Not so fast. This afternoon will be soon enough. I'll be back after the last class."

"And then will the good jailor release me from prison?"

Mathers laughed. "Some prison, with a pretty girl to wait on you hand and foot. We should all be so lucky."

Stephen grinned with smug satisfaction at the remembrance of last night. "Well, I suppose it hasn't been all bad . . ."

"I imagine she's managed to keep you entertained."

Stephen's eyes narrowed suspiciously. "And what is that supposed to mean?"

"She'd make a damn good doctor's wife," Mathers said with an innocent look. "Any woman who can cheerfully hold the basin while you vomit has a stronger stomach than I do."

"You should have kept her out of here," Stephen said. "She shouldn't have been allowed to do that."

"And risk my life and limb by saying no to her? Not me. I wouldn't dare to refuse her anything."

Stephen sank back against the piled pillows, knowing

he was equally helpless against her entreaties. "Yes, she can be persuasive."

"If you want my advice—"

"Since when have I *ever* asked for that?" Stephen demanded with a grin.

"I'd snap her up quickly before someone else does," Mathers said. "She thinks the world of you, Stephen. Why she does, I can't imagine, but she does. If you could have seen her in here, hour after hour . . ."

Stephen closed his eyes, trying hard to suppress his satisfied grin.

"She knows I'm grateful."

"She deserves more than gratitude," Mathers said.

"Oh? What do you suggest?"

"Marry the girl, dammit. Lord knows, you could use her looking after you."

Marriage. Of course he would marry her. Stephen had no intention of letting her go. "I just might do that," he said.

"Right, and I—what did you say?" Mathers stared at him.

Stephen sighed loudly. "But I can't think about that until I know how the school is faring."

Mathers busied himself rearranging the medicine bottles on the nightstand. "There's no point in worrying about it until you're well enough to go back."

"I want to know. Now."

"About half the students are gone," Mathers admitted.

Stephen groaned.

"It's not that bad. The ones who stayed are working hard; they'll be better surgeons because of it."

"Did they demand their fees back?"

Mathers nodded. "But I made sure to charge them for each day they were there. You didn't lose it all."

Stephen looked away. He might as well have. If he'd lost that many students, he'd be hard-pressed to make the next quarterly payment to Grosse.

The quarterly payment that was due in a few weeks.

Grosse might be willing to postpone the payment, allowing Stephen to make it up at a later date, but it would only be a temporary reprieve. Stephen wouldn't have any more income until the fall term started.

He wondered what he was going to live on until then. And how would he ever be able to support a wife—to support Linette?

Mathers clapped him on the shoulder. "Cheer up. You're recovering much faster than I expected, seeing how sick you were. You could be back to work as early as next month."

"Next month! It better be next week if what you say is true. I can't afford to be away any longer."

"What does it matter now? The students who have left aren't going to come back, and the ones who are still here will stay." Mathers smirked. "I think I've been doing a halfway decent job of giving the lectures, if I do say so myself."

"Great," Stephen muttered. "I'll lose the school *and* my job."

Mathers measured out some medicine. "By this fall you'll be teaching full-time at the London Hospital and begging me to handle your other classes."

"That's about as likely as me being made a Fellow of the Royal College."

"Stranger things have happened."

After Mathers left, Stephen thought about his dismal financial situation.

Somehow, he had to find a way to earn some money. Fast. He could take on some private students. That meant he wouldn't have time for his own research, but he could endure that for a period. Stephen was more worried now about whether he'd even be able to find any students. He wouldn't be able to board them, which was the usual arrangement. Most men who took private students were married, with homes and families. Stephen had neither.

He could provide them with a room—at the school. That might be appealing—they would have full access to all the facilities whenever the classroom students were gone. In fact, that could be a distinct advantage.

That was, if he still had a school for them to stay in.

But even with some private students, his financial situation would still be desperate. What was he going to do? He needed Linette's presence like a drug, but he was leaving here today. Once he was gone, he wouldn't be able to take her to his bed, to explore the secrets of her body, to teach her the mysteries of his.

He felt a deep stab of longing. How was he going to live without her until he could afford to take care of her?

Stephen brought the bedsheet to his nose, breathing in the faint scent of rose that still clung to it.

God, he loved her.

Chapter 25

For the first delicious moments after she awoke, Linette could almost imagine herself in Stephen's bed, clasped in his arms. But the moment she opened her eyes, she knew she was back in her own room, alone. Yet his scent clung to her, a musky, masculine smell that mixed with her rosewater.

Grinning widely, Linette stretched. All those things people said *were* true. She *did* feel different. More alert, more alive, more like a woman. A woman who knew what it was to love a man.

Did Stephen feel this same giddiness? This delicious urge to laugh and dance for joy?

And now that she knew all this, he was leaving the house, going back to his cold, dark chambers. No one would make sure he ate regularly, and rested, and regained his strength so he wouldn't fall ill again.

Linette wanted to go with him, to live with him, to be the one to look after him. But until—unless—he asked her, she could not.

But she would do what she could. Linette threw back the covers and jumped out of bed. She would send him home with plenty of food, at least.

And she would visit him, whether he wanted her to or not, to make certain he was doing all right. If she took him food, tidied his rooms, and made sure he had enough coal to keep warm, she would feel better. Linette knew he was worried about money after being ill for so long. She would do everything she could—everything he would let her—to help.

Linette rang for the maid to bring the bathwater. She had a great deal to accomplish and not much time. Once Mathers gave Stephen his official release, he wouldn't linger here, even for her. She needed everything to be ready in time.

And if she kept her mind busy with plans and lists, she would have less time to think about how empty the house would feel when Stephen was gone.

Stephen slept after Mathers left, for when he awoke, Linette was sitting in the bedside chair, sewing. He watched her for a few minutes through half-closed lids.

She looked composed and self-assured, but he thought he noticed a slight flush to her cheeks. An awareness of her newfound womanhood? The knowledge of the physical power of her body?

Desire surged through him as he watched her delicate hands guide the needle in and out of the cloth. He clenched his fists. It was excruciating torture to be this close to her now, knowing he couldn't take her with him when he went home. And that it might be a very long time before they could be together.

Stephen opened his eyes. "Good morning," he said.

A wide smile lit her face. "Afternoon," she replied.

Stephen glanced at the clock. "Mathers must have slipped laudanum into my medicine this morning. I can't believe I slept this long." He reached out and brushed her cheek with his hand. "Then again, I'm not accustomed to such active nights."

Blushing, Linette glanced away.

"Look at me, Linette."

Slowly, she turned to face him and he saw a new, endearing shyness in her soft gray eyes. He leaned over and kissed her gently.

"I wish you'd been here when I awoke this morning," he said. "I missed you."

She regarded him steadily. "I thought it would be best if I left."

Stephen took her hand and twined his fingers in hers. "I ... I don't want you to have regrets ..."

Her smile widened, revealing that enticing dimple. "There is nothing to regret. I love you, Stephen."

He leaned over and kissed her again, than sank back against the pillows.

"I talked with Mathers about the school this morning." Stephen sighed deeply. "He says half the students have left. I don't have much of a school anymore."

Linette gave him an arch look. "Then we will just have to find you new students to replace them."

He laughed and squeezed her hand. "Unfortunately, it's not that easy. There won't be any new students until the fall term. I couldn't have picked a worse time to fall ill."

"I don't want you to waste your energy worrying." Linette gave him a stern look. "Your first job is to get well. Consider that an order."

"Yes, ma'am."

Linette giggled. "I can't believe that you're actually agreeing with me! The illness must have affected your brain."

Stephen reached over and put his arm around her shoulders, pulling her close.

"I don't think it was my brain that was affected," he said with a wicked grin. "Some other part of my anatomy, perhaps."

"Stephen!" Linette turned scarlet.

He leaned over and kissed her, a long, searing kiss that left them both breathless and Stephen wishing that it was night again, and the rest of the house was asleep. Left him wishing once again that he could take her with him when he left today.

But he had no place to take her—no place that he would allow her to live. His own rooms were totally unsuitable. With a groan, he released her, cursing the fate that had brought such joy into his life at a time when he was powerless to do anything about it.

A step sounded in the hall and Linette hastily settled back into her seat. Mrs. Barton peered through the doorway.

"Ah, Mr. Ashworth, you are awake. I hope you are feeling well today."

"Very well, thank you." He smiled broadly at Linette. "Thanks to your niece's efficient nursing."

Mrs. Barton beamed at Linette, then turned back to Stephen. "Mr. Mathers informs me that he is going to send you home today."

"That is my hope, ma'am. I have intruded on your kindness for too long."

"Oh, nonsense." Mrs. Barton waved away his apology. "I am only glad we were able to play a part in your recovery."

"I will be forever in your debt," Stephen said, then gave Linette a fond look. "And yours."

"Linette, Mrs. Branby is arriving soon. I thought you might like to join us. She does so wish to see you."

Stephen arched a brow. "What? Abandoning me already? Shame on you."

"I have no intention of abandoning you."

Aunt Barton shook her head. "Nonsense. You've spent far too many days cooped up in this room. You're beginning to look as peaked as Mr. Ashworth."

Stephen gave Linette a long, searching look that brought another flush of color to her face. To his eyes, she looked the picture of health, with her rosy cheeks and sparkling eyes. "I think perhaps your aunt is right. A change of scene would do you good."

"I am perfectly content to remain here, but if you are so insistent, I will be glad to leave." Linette rose and put down her sewing, and followed her aunt to the door.

"Have a nice visit," Stephen called after them. "Bring me back some tea cakes."

Linette turned, a mischievous look on her face. "I'm

terribly sorry, but your physician insists that it would be most dangerous for you to eat anything that rich. I can have someone bring you a nice bowl of beef broth if you are hungry."

Stephen resisted the temptation to toss a pillow at her.

He was torn between relief that he was going home, and regret at leaving Linette. But after last night, it was best for him to leave. It wouldn't take long for her aunt to suspect that something was going on—not when he couldn't keep his eyes off her. Yes, he had to leave, to preserve her reputation.

Stephen stepped out of bed and began to dress. He wasn't going to give Mathers the chance to change his mind about letting him leave.

It felt odd to wear clothes again. Their restricting tightness was uncomfortable after the loose freedom of a nightshirt. He had no intention of putting on a cravat. The mere thought of that long cloth wrapped around his neck made his throat feel tight.

When he finished dressing, Stephen sat down to rest. Even such a simple task left him tired. He must overcome this lingering weakness as soon as possible. He had to, if he and Linette were going to have a future together anytime soon.

Mathers walked into the room and Stephen smiled at his look of consternation.

"Not taking any chances, are you?" Mathers gave him a rueful look.

"No." Stephen laughed. "I've merely to pack my things and I'm ready to go."

Mathers placed a cool hand on Stephen's brow. "Hmm. No sign of fever."

Stephen brushed his hand away. "I feel fine. Fit as a fiddle."

"Just remember, you need to take it easy at first. You can't jump back into your old habits or you'll find yourself flat on your back again."

"Believe me," said Stephen as he tossed the last of

his things into the bag, "I have no intention of suffering that indignity again."

He looked up and saw Linette at the door.

"You're getting ready to leave."

The dismay in her eyes tore at him, but he pushed the feeling aside. "Mathers says I may."

"I had Cook prepare you a basket, so you will have something to eat tonight." She took a deep breath. "I'd like to bring you some food every day, to make sure you are eating properly."

Stephen smiled at her concern. "I'd like that."

Mathers grabbed Stephen's bag and started out the door. "I'll take this downstairs."

When he'd gone, Linette walked up to Stephen and wrapped her arms around his waist. "I am so glad you are better. And so sad you are leaving."

He stroked her hair. "It's for the best. After last night . . . I want to be with you all the time. And this is not the place."

She nodded.

Stephen wrapped her in his arms. "But I expect you to look in on me to make sure I am taking care of myself. And to bring me all sorts of delicious foods."

Linette laughed. "Now I know you are better, for all you are thinking about is food."

"That's not the only thing I'm thinking about," he said softly, and kissed her gently. "Ah, Linette, I owe you so much."

"Can I come with you and Mathers? Just to see that you get settled in?"

He shook his head. "It's better this way." He took her arm and led her down the stairs. Mathers waited by the door, with Mrs. Barton.

Stephen shook her hand. "Once again, I cannot thank you enough for your wonderful care."

Mrs. Barton beamed at the praise, then gave Linette a sly look. "I really think the credit must go to my niece. She is the one who worked so hard."

Stephen took Linette's hand and brought it to his lips, his eyes never leaving her face. "I hope she is aware of my gratitude."

Dropping Linette's hand, he turned to Mathers. "Shall we go?"

Stephen resisted the impulse to lean out the carriage window and stare at the Barton house until it disappeared from view. It was hard enough leaving Linette behind; he didn't need to prolong the agony. He must think of the future, and all he had to do before he could be with her.

Leaving Mathers to deal with the luggage, Stephen slowly climbed the stairs to his room. He put the key in the lock and pushed the door open, then walked around his front room, analyzing it with the eyes of a stranger.

Someone had cleaned it while he'd been gone—Linette obviously had arranged that. His medical equipment, papers, and books still littered the room, but every surface had been scrubbed clean. New draperies hung at the windows. Draperies.

He grinned ruefully. She had already invaded every corner of his life, why not his rooms as well? And just knowing she had been thinking about him made him feel less lonely.

Winded from the long climb up the stairs, Stephen sank into a chair. Mathers was right—he was still weak. But after last night, Stephen knew he had to leave the Barton house. He could not trust himself to stay away from Linette and he didn't want to risk scandal.

No, it was better this way, away from the temptation of her sweet kisses and willing body. Those pleasures would have to wait until they were properly married.

But seeing his shabby furniture, his tiny rooms, and his meager belongings, Stephen grew acutely conscious of how little he had to offer her. He couldn't give her a life even half as comfortable as the one she enjoyed now.

He couldn't ask her to move from a house full of servants into these two cramped rooms.

Somehow, he had to earn some money. It was all well and good to talk about finding more patients, recruiting more students for the fall term, or the Dispensary board deciding to pay the staff. But he needed money now, to keep him from losing the school and to enable him to work toward those other things.

But short of sitting on a street corner and offering his medical services to each and every passerby, Stephen didn't know how he was going to increase his income fast enough to help. He would need a steady stream of well-heeled patients to make any difference. And they weren't going to appear overnight.

Somehow, he would find a way. He had to. He needed Linette with him, wanted her by his side. Needed her more than he'd ever needed anyone, anything in his life. She'd given him hopes for the future—a future they would share.

Now he only had to find a way to fund it.

Mathers staggered in, weighted down by the enormous hamper of food. "She must have thought you were living with a small army," he complained. "I see you survived the hike up the stairs."

"I'm doing well enough," Stephen growled.

Mathers circled around, examining the room. "Looks like the fairies were in here cleaning while you were gone. It's certainly an improvement.

"Since you're so worried about my health, start the fire and make us some tea." Stephen shivered. "It's damn cold in here."

Shaking his head, Mathers started the fire. "Why you wanted to leave your plush accommodations for this hovel is beyond me. I suppose some men don't feel they deserve to be comfortable."

"I didn't want to wear out my welcome. Besides, if you keep giving my lectures, I'll have to pay you more money," Stephen said, only half joking. "I can't afford it."

"You can't afford to have a relapse, either. I don't want to see you set foot in that school for a week. You have to regain your strength."

"I'm not going to be moving furniture," Stephen protested. "I'm merely talking for two hours. I could have done that last week."

Mathers shrugged. "It's your life. Just don't say I didn't warn you."

"Believe me, I'm not stupid. I won't do any more than I'm able to. Giving a few lectures isn't going to kill me. Besides, Monday's two days away. Plenty of time to rest up."

Mathers looked unconvinced.

Linette lay in her bed that night, staring at the ceiling.

Had it only been last night that she'd lain in Stephen's arms? Already, it seemed longer. Yet whenever she closed her eyes she could conjure up the image of his face bent over hers, seeing the dark passion in his eyes.

He loved her. He hadn't said so in words, but he'd shown her with his hands, his mouth, his body. She hugged herself at the thought. She'd sought to give him the gift of trust, and in return, he'd given her something equally precious.

Himself.

Now, she had to make certain that he didn't try to hide from his emotions anymore.

Linette smiled into the darkness. How wrong she'd been about him, from their very first meeting. He was a caring, compassionate man, merely hiding behind his impassive attitude. But she had finally seen through his charade and drew him out, forced him to admit that he cared. As terrible as his illness had been, it had brought them together again. And this time, she wasn't going to let him slip out of her life again.

If only she could have gone home with him today. But

they would be together soon, she had no doubt. Stephen worried about his school, and money, but Linette wasn't concerned about that. They could easily live here with Aunt until they could afford to have a place of their own. Stephen could still work at the Dispensary and teach at his school.

That is, until Linette convinced him that he didn't need to concentrate on anatomy and dissection anymore. With Aunt's connections, it wouldn't be long before Stephen had established a profitable surgical practice. Then he wouldn't have to bother himself with dead bodies.

And together, they could work together to improve the lives of those around them, turning the Dispensary into a model institution that would be their special pride. There was no end to the good they could do once they began working together.

Linette rose early the next morning. Already she missed Stephen and couldn't wait to see him again. But before she visited him, there were several things she needed to do.

It was past noon when the hackney finally pulled up outside Stephen's building. Her arms overflowing with packages, Linette carefully made her way up the stairs.

She knew he couldn't have eaten all the food she'd sent yesterday, but there were other things he needed. New shirts of the finest lawn, several pairs of the warmest socks, and a thick woolen scarf to wrap around his neck.

And a box of pastries from Brodie's.

At the top of the stairs, she stopped a moment to catch her breath, then tapped on the door with her foot. It swung inward and she smiled at Stephen's surprised look.

"What are you doing here?"

Linette walked past him and dropped the packages on the sofa. Stripping off her gloves, she turned to face him.

"I told you I planned to visit. To make certain you were taking proper care of yourself."

He gestured at the packages. "But all this ... You sent more than enough food with me yesterday."

"Oh, this isn't food. Just a few things you needed." Linette picked up one of the packages and tossed it to him.

His expression was doubtful as he tore off the wrappings and pulled out the scarf.

"This will help keep you warm on your way to work." Linette put the scarf around his neck.

Stephen fingered the soft wool. "Thank you."

Linette gathered the ends of the scarf and slowly pulled Stephen's head down until their lips met.

She only intended a simple kiss. But the jolt of electricity that shot through her said otherwise. Stephen's hands dropped to her waist and he pulled her against him. Linette dropped the scarf and wrapped her arms around his neck.

"Oh, God, how I've missed you," Stephen murmured as he feathered kisses across her brow.

His tongue softly flicked over her lips, teasing, pleading until her mouth parted beneath his. Linette's whole body tingled with the intimacy of the kiss.

She wanted him to love her. Wanted to feel his naked body against her, atop her, inside her. And wanted him to know how much she needed him.

Linette curled her fingers in the hair at his nape and pressed her body against his. "Take me to your bed, Stephen," she whispered. "Please."

Chapter 26

Stephen's hold loosened and he gave her a searching look, his eyes dark with what she hoped was passion. "You know I want you, but—"

Linette pressed a finger to his lips. "Don't say anything, Stephen. Just love me."

He slowly lowered his mouth to hers, brushing her lips with a touch as light as a butterfly's wing, then crushed her against him. She leaned her head back as he trailed kisses down her neck, pausing to nibble her ear before he once again claimed her mouth with hot kisses. Her body felt on fire.

"If I were a gallant gentleman, I would sweep you into my arms and carry you into the other room," he said with a quick smile. "But I think you'd be safer with your feet on the ground."

He took her by the hand and drew her toward the bedroom.

Their clothes landed in a jumbled pile on the floor, but Linette did not care. She could not wait to hold Stephen against her again. In moments they were in the bed, their bodies pressed close, tongues meeting, dancing, teasing.

With newfound boldness, she caressed his back, running her fingers down the bumpy ridge of his spine. His hand cupped her breast and it hardened instantly, sending deep shivers of anticipation through her. Linette arched against his hand while his mouth and tongue burned a path of liquid fire across her breasts.

Stephen's fingers brushed the curls between her legs, and Linette moaned softly at the delicious feeling he evoked. His probing fingers slipped into her, stroking her in a rhythmical pattern that sent her body into flames. White-hot fire flooded her body, then she twisted and arched with shuddering tremors.

Stephen nudged her legs apart, slipping a hand under her hips as he brought her to him and slowly pushed into her. Linette sucked in her breath as he filled her completely, binding their bodies together. He began a slow, careful thrusting, slipping one hand beneath her buttocks to hold her closer, moving her with him in a smooth motion.

Linette hugged Stephen tighter, wrapping her legs around him as she pulled him deeper, their bodies meeting again and again. She heard his labored breathing in her ear, felt his warm breath against her neck. His hands and mouth seemed to be everywhere, caressing, stroking, suckling.

The pressure grew unbearable and Linette cried out his name, overjoyed to hear her own torn from his throat.

The sky was darkening when Stephen reluctantly bade her goodbye. He was loath to see her go, but knew that she must.

And knew also that she should not come here again. Apart from the risk to her reputation, there was the very real risk of pregnancy. Once they were married . . .

But with his finances in such a precarious position, that wasn't going to be soon.

Clenching his fists as he watched the hackney roll away, Stephen vowed that he would do everything he could to rectify the situation. She had completely, thoroughly, stolen his heart. It was up to him to make a life for them.

As he walked up the stairs to the school on the following Monday morning, Stephen felt a deep swelling of joy in his chest. He was alive, and back where he belonged. Everything would be better soon.

Linette's cleaning hand had extended to his office, for there wasn't a speck of dust anywhere. Stephen sat down in his chair and put palms on the desktop. The feel of the solid wood beneath his fingers gave him an intense pleasure.

The building was still deserted this early in the morning and he wandered through the halls, reveling in the joy of being back. Even the dissecting room looked inviting after being away for so long.

He didn't realize how much he'd missed this place until now. All the petty annoyances: the inattentive students, the joking in the dissecting room, even the constant, cloying smells of dead flesh faded with the sheer joy of being back.

Stephen realized how much he enjoyed teaching here. Only one thing mattered more—Linette. But it was clear to him that the school would have to be part of the plan he developed for them.

He was back in his office, sitting at the desk, when Mathers came in.

"Time for lecture." Mathers darted Stephen a warning look. "Are you sure you feel up to it?"

"I've had such a trying morning," Stephen drawled sarcastically. "I think I can manage to entertain a bunch of harebrained students for an hour."

"I'll be in the dissecting room if you need me."

The usually noisy students fell silent when Stephen walked into the lecture room. He scanned the faces of the hushed students, noting who was still here, relieved to find a few faces gone. Stepping up to the lectern, he shuffled his notes, savoring the joy of being back. Then he cleared his throat.

"The ligaments of the wrist are ..."

Stephen didn't want to confess how exhausted he was when he returned to his office. He sank down on the sofa with a long sigh of relief. How could mere talking tire him so? Linette would be furious if she could see him.

But she couldn't, and Stephen vowed that she wouldn't find out. She would fuss and complain and probably find some way to drag him back to his sickbed if he wasn't careful. He had two hours to rest before the afternoon lecture, plenty of time to restore his strength.

Stephen stretched out on the sofa and promptly fell asleep.

The delicious aroma of hot meat pies woke him from his sleep. Stephen blinked in sleepy confusion and saw Linette sitting at his desk.

"I should have known," he said with a rueful grin, swinging his legs around and sitting up. "You didn't trust me to take care of myself, did you?"

"Not at all," she replied with a smile that belied her tart words. "I wanted to make sure you ate a decent lunch."

"I feel like I can eat an entire ox." Stephen stretched. "I hope you brought enough."

Linette handed him two meat-filled pastries. Stephen wolfed down the first one, then sat back to savor the second. He felt Linette's eyes on him, assessing his condition.

"Mathers said you gave the lecture this morning," she said.

"I did. And as you can see, I then took a nap. I'm being a good boy."

She scrutinized him carefully. "I wish you had waited another week. You are still so thin."

"I'll be fine." Stephen liked the idea of Linette worrying about him, even if it wasn't necessary. "I promise to stay away from the Dispensary until you give me leave to return."

"When you can deliver both daily lectures and maintain your normal schedule without having to take a nap, I *might* consider it."

"You're wasted teaching sewing to the ladies," he said, grinning fondly. "You'd be happier bullying a regiment of soldiers about."

She smiled back. "You need as much care as a regiment of soldiers."

Mathers walked into the office. "That smells good. I hope you brought enough for me!"

"Go find your own," Stephen said.

"I have enough." Linette unwrapped another pie and handed it to Mathers.

"I'm keeping a close eye on him." Mathers gave Stephen a chastising look. "He was sleeping like a babe only a quarter hour ago."

"I know. He was still asleep when I arrived." Linette rose and brushed crumbs off her skirt. "And I must leave. I just wanted to make certain that you hadn't overtired yourself."

Despite her warning frown, Stephen stood and walked her to the door.

"Thank you for coming," he said softly. "I've missed you."

He took a quick glance to assure himself the corridor was empty and gave her a swift kiss.

"I will be back tomorrow."

"I'm counting the hours."

After seeing her safely into the carriage, Stephen walked back into the school, a wide grin on his face. But by the time he'd returned to the office, his grin had faded.

However was he going to support her?

"This is bloody unbelievable!"

In the early hours of a Friday morning, Stephen stood, hands on hips, in the hallway at the Howard Street School. He'd been rousted out of bed at midnight and dragged over here by the student on night duty, only to find that his troubles with the resurrectionists were not over.

"Eighteen guineas! They must be mad!" He glared at Mathers, who'd initially handled the situation. "Are you sure that's what they said?"

Mathers nodded.

"And what did they say when you refused?"

"The man just laughed and said they'd be back in a few more days—after you had time to think about it."

Stephen swore under his breath. He didn't need this, now, of all times. He couldn't afford to pay those prices; he would have to pass them on to the students. Yet already he'd lost too many of them. How many would remain when he informed them that they were going to have to pay over twice the going rate for their dissection subjects—if they were able to get any at all?

Damn the resurrectionists.

He turned to the student porter. "There's nothing more that can be done tonight. Lock up and go back to bed." He motioned to Mathers to follow him into the office.

Stephen poured them each a glass of brandy and then perched on the edge of his desk.

"How are we going to find a way out of *this* mess?"

"Oh, that's easy enough to manage."

Stephen looked skeptically at Mathers. "How? I can't afford to pay those prices. Unless you've found a way to turn base metal into gold, I'm finished here."

"Think, Stephen. Where do the corpses come from?"

"The resurrectionists."

Mathers leaned forward eagerly. "And where do they get them?"

Stephen looked at him with dawning awareness. "The churchyards. But you don't mean . . . ?"

"I think we should go into the resurrection business ourselves."

Resurrecting. Stephen's thoughts whirled. It had been many years since he'd made a midnight foray to a grave-yard. He remembered his first trip, during his appren-ticeship. A long, cold drive in a wagon—it wasn't politic to raid the nearest churchyard—then the backbreaking work with the shovel, and the even colder drive back to the surgeon's.

Stephen hadn't stopped to look at the body when they'd hastily trundled it into the wagon, but when it lay on the table in the back room, he had his first look at a corpse. He was overwhelmed with curiosity, couldn't wait until his mentor began the dissection. He'd never been bothered by working with dead flesh.

"I haven't skulked around a churchyard since my student days," Stephen said, thinking aloud.

"I'm not exactly in practice either, but I doubt the process has changed much." Mathers grinned. "All we need is a few shovels and a cart and we're in business."

"If the gangs found out they'd do a lot worse than dumping a cow carcass on the front steps of the school."

"What have you got to lose now?"

He was right. If the body trade refused to deal with him, Stephen might as well close down the school. He really didn't have much choice.

"It's a mad idea," Stephen said slowly. "But I think you're right—it's the only thing we can do."

"Besides, the term is almost over. We won't need to go out more than a few times. And by fall, I suspect the whole fuss will have blown over."

"We'll need another helper—we can't do it by ourselves."

"Smith would be willing—he's a bright lad."

The key difficulty was in keeping the resurrectionists in the dark about their plan. They would be furious to find someone threatening their hold over the London body trade and Stephen knew that he'd feel the full force of their wrath if they discovered what he planned to do. He would have to be very, very careful.

His breath caught. Linette. If she ever discovered what he was doing . . . Stephen tried to push that worry out of his mind. He was doing this for her, after all. If he couldn't keep the school running, he couldn't ever hope to wed her. There were just some things about his work that she didn't need to know.

They approached Smith the next morning, before class.

"You want me to what?" Smith looked shocked.

"You look like a virgin who's suddenly been told how babies are made." Stephen tilted back in his chair. "Where do you think the damn things come from?"

"But I thought ... I mean, that's what the resurrectionists are for."

"The resurrectionists don't want to sell bodies to us," Mathers said. "We have to do this."

"But won't they get mad? They might dump something unpleasant on the front steps again."

"We won't be doing this long enough for them to find out. We only need a few bodies to keep us going until the end of term. It should be easy."

Smith gulped. "Well, I guess ..."

"We might even be able to let you have a body of your own—one that you won't have to share with another student."

Stephen smiled as Smith's expression changed at the thought of the tempting bribe.

"I guess I'm willing."

"Good."

It took several days to organize their plans. But late the following week, Stephen thought they were ready.

The students had gone home for the day and Stephen and Mathers sat in the school office, sipping mugs of hot mulled wine.

"There's not much of a moon this weekend," Stephen said. "Have you found a cart yet?"

"We should be able to get it tonight," Mathers said.

Stephen cupped his hands around the warm mug. "Then the only thing that can stop us is a hard frost, and it hasn't been that cold."

"I still say you should stay home this first time—you shouldn't be exposing yourself to the damp this soon."

"It can't be much damper at night than it is in the morning with that blasted fog. Besides, that's to our advantage."

"We're more likely to bump into one of the resurrectionist gangs, too—I can just see us showing up at the same churchyard."

"I doubt that'll happen. We won't be using their usual haunts."

Mathers grinned. "I thought my resurrecting days were over when I sat for my license."

Stephen laughed loudly. "I've known of men in their sixties who still enjoy a late-night trip to the graveyard once or twice a year. Reminds them of their student days, I guess."

He raised his mug. "To our new endeavor—may it be quick, profitable, and without snags."

On Saturday, Stephen ate dinner at a tavern near the school, then went to his office. He spent an hour or so dealing with some paperwork, then stretched out on the sofa for a nap until Mathers came back.

"Everything ready?" Stephen asked when Mathers shook him awake.

"Smith'll meet us in the alley with the cart."

Stephen pulled on his heavy boots. "What did he learn today?"

"The usual winter ailments are keeping the undertakers busy. There are two fresh subjects waiting for us."

"Good. That's even better than I hoped. I assume he made the necessary arrangements so we won't be bothered?"

Mathers nodded.

Stephen donned the shabby greatcoat he'd bought yesterday at the secondhand clothiers and they slipped out the alley door, walking the three blocks to their rendezvous with Smith.

"Anyone asking any questions?" Stephen asked as he climbed into the cart beside Smith.

"Not a one," Smith said. "No one's come past in the last half hour."

"Good." Stephen folded his arms across his chest and kept a sharp watch as they followed a deliberately winding route to the churchyard.

It was nearing five when Stephen stumbled up the stairs to his rooms, damp, muddy, and tired.

He chuckled when he shut the door behind him. The whole process had been laughably easy. The ground had been soft and easily removed and only his lingering weakness prevented him from working the entire time.

Yes, it had been easy. But he hoped he wouldn't have to do this too many more times. London was far too dangerous a place for disinterring bodies. They'd been lucky tonight, but he couldn't expect their luck to hold. Too many churchyards were too well guarded—either against or in collusion with the resurrectionists.

Stephen still worried about Linette, and what she would think if she found out about his nocturnal activities. He knew she wouldn't approve. But he didn't have any choice, not with the resurrectionists trying to put him out of business.

If only England had a system like that in France, where indigent bodies were turned over to the teaching schools. The resurrectionists would be put out of business, English students would stay at home, and he wouldn't have to worry about keeping his school open.

Stephen scheduled their second graveyard foray for the following weekend. It was a risk, going out again so soon. But he'd weighed his options and decided it was worth it. He wasn't going to let the resurrectionists destroy his school. Once they saw he couldn't be bullied, they would tire of the game and leave him alone.

And he'd spoken with Lord Graves again yesterday.

It wasn't an official meeting; the man had been at the Dispensary and ran into Stephen in the hall. But he'd sounded encouraging about the situation at the London Hospital.

Stephen didn't want to think about what he would do if he didn't get the appointment. It could be years before there was another opening at a hospital in London. And he didn't want to wait years.

He pushed those concerns to the back of his mind. Tonight, he would only think about the job at hand.

Heading out to meet Mathers, Stephen walked down the alley behind the school with a jaunty air. He almost felt like a new man: no cough, no shortness of breath, no pain in his chest. It was hard to believe that he had been so ill such a short time ago.

Fog drifted slowly through the streets while he stood at the corner, waiting for Mathers. Smith was sick and they didn't need a sniveling, coughing assistant to attract unwanted attention.

"Should be another easy night," Mathers said as he drove the cart toward their destination. "A fresh grave."

"I just hope the bastards will back down after this," Stephen said, pulling his coat tighter against the clammy chill. "Skulking about churchyards is rapidly losing its appeal."

"What did you hear at the Chirurgical meeting tonight? Are they squeezing anyone else?"

Stephen shook his head. "I talked with a few people and no one else is having trouble. They're only after us."

"This fog should make things easy enough tonight."

"We'll be lucky if we don't get lost on our way home," Stephen said, eyeing the mist-shrouded buildings around them.

"Maybe we should leave a trail of crumbs to follow," said Mathers with a laugh.

They soon reached the small churchyard on the far edge of the city. Stephen tied the horse to the gate while Mathers retrieved the shovels from the rear.

"It should be off to the left, in the far corner," Mathers said in a low voice as they unfastened the gate. It swung open with a high-pitched squeal.

Stephen froze, hardly daring to breathe while he listened for any reaction. Then he unshuttered the lantern and guided them along the wall to the new grave.

Their destination was clearly discernible even in the fog-shrouded yard by the dark hue of newly turned earth. Stephen grabbed a shovel and shoved it into the dirt.

Despite the cool air, sweat was dripping down his face when his shovel hit the wooden lid of the coffin.

"It's all yours." Stephen took the lantern from Mathers and shone the light into the hole. Mathers took a pry and attacked the lid of the cheap wooden coffin.

"Wait!" Stephen hissed. "Did you hear something."

Mathers froze, listening. No sounds penetrated the fog-drenched churchyard.

"Probably some animal." Mathers shrugged and turned back to his work.

Stephen felt uneasy. He'd rather be working under the full moon than in this blasted fog. If anyone was coming, he wouldn't see them until they were right on top of them.

The fog protected them too, but didn't do much to muffle the noise of Mathers' work. Stephen urged Mathers on, wanting to get away from here as quickly as possible. Once the body was free, Stephen quickly refilled the hole, then the two of them lugged the heavy bundle to the cart and shoved it in the back.

Stephen breathed a huge sigh of relief when they were done. While Mathers went back for the shovels, Stephen untied the horse and took the reins, ready to drive away.

A loud whistle broke the night silence.

"We've got 'em, boys."

Chapter 27

Running footsteps echoed through the fog. Before Stephen could tell from which direction they came, he was surrounded by a motley crowd of workmen.

One man stepped forward. "It's like I told ye, boys. The filthy doctor's stealing bodies."

Stephen felt an icy chill race up his spine, but he was determined to brazen this out. He turned a disdainful look on his accuser. "*You* are interfering in a private matter."

"Diggin' up graves is a crime," a stout man said. "We intend to see that you're properly punished."

Stephen's hands tightened on the reins and the horse danced uneasily. Was he to be a victim of mob justice? He prayed that Mathers had heard the commotion and remained hidden in the churchyard. Someone had to report what went on.

He tried to smile. "I'm not trying to cause any trouble. Let me drive my cart home and we can all go to our beds."

A man jumped forward and grabbed the harness. "You're not going anywhere with this load."

"Yeah. We've got a magistrate coming and he's gonna see wot you got in the back."

Stephen realized with a sudden shock that this was not a chance encounter. Someone knew he was going to be here tonight, and had waited until he'd unearthed the body before moving to stop him.

Anyone concerned with the moral issue of grave robbing would have stopped him long before. Only those who knew the value of the cargo he was carrying would wait until now—when all the work was done.

"Who sent you?" he asked boldly. "Bill Wilkins? Sam Arnold?"

He saw from their uneasy looks that they recognized the names of the resurrectionist leaders.

Stephen tried to look unconcerned. "Look, I don't want to cause any trouble. If this is a dispute about my cargo, you're welcome to take it. I don't think anyone wants to get the law involved. It could be awkward—all sorts of strange stories could come out."

If he'd been dealing with the leaders, his words might have had some effect. But these were the underlings, who were only going to do what they'd been told.

"We're waiting for the watch," the man at the horse's head said.

Stephen sighed and dropped the reins. It was going to be a long night.

Thank God they hadn't caught Mathers as well. Stephen could rely on him to get him out of this fix. It was a pity that all their work had been for nothing.

In short order, the watchman arrived and gave Stephen a stern look. "Caught ya thievin' a body, did they?" He spat. "Bloody doctors."

"This is a ridiculous waste of everyone's time." Stephen's anger grew. "This is London. No one prosecutes surgeons for disinterring bodies."

"That's up to the constable," the watchman said. He gave the contents of the cart a swift glance and grimaced. "Into the hack with you. I'm taking you to the watch house."

"What about my cart?" Stephen demanded.

"These men will bring it to the lockup."

"Those men," Stephen said with growing bitterness, "are themselves resurrectionists. They'll steal my cart and you'll never see that body again."

The watchman shrugged. "It's not my concern."

Stephen ground his teeth in frustration. "At least tell me where you're taking me. I have a right to know." If Mathers was listening, he'd learn where to find Stephen.

"You'll find out when you get there," the watchman said and pushed Stephen toward the coach.

The constable at the lockup was equally indifferent to Stephen's protests.

"So, Mr. Ashworth, you were found with a body stolen from the churchyard at St. Agatha's." He looked sternly at Stephen. "This is a very serious charge."

"And one that has no meaning," Stephen argued. "Half the surgeons in the city could be charged with that."

"They should be," the man said with a nasty sneer and glanced down at his notes. "To that is added the charge of trespassing, creating a public disturbance—"

Stephen glared at him. "What disturbance? If anyone caused a disturbance, it was those louts who called in the watch. And what about my cart? They've stolen it, just as I predicted. Are you going to charge them with theft?"

"I might, if I find them."

Stephen wearily shook his head. He wasn't going to get any sympathy from this man. "I'm tired. What do I have to do in order to go home?"

The constable smiled. "Are you prepared to make bail?"

"How much?"

"Twenty pounds."

"Twenty pounds!" Stephen glared at the man. "That's ridiculous."

"That is the cost. These are serious offenses."

"I don't have twenty pounds with me."

Shrugging, the constable made a note on the paper before him. "Then you'll have to wait until the magistrate sees you."

"And when will that be?"

"Monday."

"Monday!" Stephen looked around in disbelief. "You can't hold me here that long on this trumped-up charge."

The constable's smile widened.

Sitting in the tiny prisoners' room, Stephen tried to regard this as an educational experience. He'd never seen the inside of a lockup. But the thought gave him little cheer. He couldn't believe they would keep him here until Monday.

Thank God he had his warm coat; it was blasted cold in the watch building. Unlike the other tenants, Stephen hadn't warmed himself with copious quantities of alcohol this night.

He shook his head at his plight. He, a surgeon, shut up for a day and a half with a bunch of disorderly drunks. The situation would be laughable if it weren't happening to him.

Stephen pulled his collar closer and settled in a corner. He'd use his anger to keep warm.

His attempt to thwart the resurrectionists had certainly gone awry. Stephen was amazed at the lengths to which they'd gone to have him caught red-handed. Now he was in custody and they had the body. Things couldn't have gone more wrong.

The stupid thing was, it was all so pointless. Stephen would see the magistrate on Monday and the whole thing would be cleared up in a matter of minutes. This was London, after all, not some provincial city. If they started arresting people for possessing corpses, half of the Royal College would be in jail.

No, he'd be out of here as soon as he spoke with someone who had an ounce of sense in his head. He'd lost the body, but that didn't matter.

He was more worried about Linette.

Stephen tried not to think about what she would say if she found out he'd been taken up by the watch. She wouldn't understand.

He clung to the hope that Mathers had followed him here, and would be able to pay the bail, but after an hour had gone by, it was obvious Mathers wasn't going to come to his rescue right away. Stephen hoped he'd gone back to the school to keep watch, instead, in case the resurrectionists had more mischief planned. No doubt he would turn up tomorrow and free Stephen.

Sometime, near dawn, he dozed off.

In the morning, the captain of the watch brought his prisoners a thin, watery gruel. Then, to Stephen's fury, his drunken companions were freed.

"Why are you releasing them and not me?" Stephen demanded.

"Oh, we just lock them up long enough to sleep it off."

"You mean if I'd been drunk, you would let me go?"

"Not with all the other charges against you."

Stephen was so mad he wouldn't have posted bail even if he had the money.

Dejected, he sat on the floor. Where in God's name was Mathers? Even if he'd had to search every lockup in the city, surely he would have come here by now.

Then Stephen sat up. What if something had happened to Mathers? The men who'd turned him over to the watch weren't fools; they knew he wouldn't be working alone. What if they'd gone into the churchyard after the watch left, and found Mathers?

Stephen refused to believe his assistant was dead. That was going too far, even for the resurrectionists. But they might have roughed Mathers up; enough that he wasn't capable of going out to rescue Stephen.

At least the thought was more comforting than thinking Mathers wasn't even trying to win his freedom.

By Monday morning, Stephen was exhausted, dirty, and starving. He couldn't wait to see the magistrate and get this farce over with.

When he heard, to his disbelief, that the magistrate

had no intention of dropping the charges, Stephen's temper snapped. It was a parody of justice and he wasn't going to play along with them anymore. If they wanted to imprison him for refusing to post bail, let them.

Stephen maintained an aloof silence during the short drive to Tothill Fields. He could only hope that someday the men of the watch house would need a surgeon's services—and he would be the one called in.

Linette looked up with surprise as Mallon hesitantly came into the drawing room at nine. It was far too early for morning callers.

"Mr. Mathers is here to see you, miss."

"Mathers!" Linette jumped to her feet. He wouldn't be here unless something had happened to Stephen. She dashed toward the door, nearly careening into the surgeon as he walked in. He held out an arm to steady her.

"It's Stephen, isn't it?" Linette anxiously searched his face for a clue. "What's wrong? Is he all right?"

"He's fine," Mathers said. "I mean, his health is fine. But he's in some trouble and I need your help."

"Of course I'll help. What can I do?"

Mathers took a deep breath. "He's in jail."

Linette's mouth dropped open. "Stephen is in jail? Where?"

"He's in Tothill Fields."

Linette's alarm grew. "Whatever for? Are you sure he's all right?"

Mathers gave her an uneasy look, and crammed his hands in his trouser pockets. "I believe the charges are trespassing, disorderly conduct, and disturbing the peace."

Her brow wrinkled. That didn't sound at all like Stephen. "What on earth was he doing?"

"You don't want to know."

Mathers' discomfort made her instantly suspicious. "I'm going to find out sooner or later. If you want me to speak to Stephen, you're going to have to tell me."

"We were . . . exhuming a body."

"Exhuming a bod—You mean you were digging up graves?"

Mathers nodded.

Linette felt as if she'd been slapped. Stephen knew how she felt about the resurrectionists and their methods. How could he have done such a thing? He deserved to be in jail.

He had blatantly disregarded her feelings, showing how little he cared for what she thought. Confusion, hurt, and anger warred within her. Stephen had betrayed her; betrayed the love she'd given him. He'd gone out and deliberately violated a grave.

He could not love her and do something like that.

Mathers' voice broke into her thoughts.

"There's a problem . . . that is . . . Stephen's being his usual stubborn self and I need you to talk some sense into him. He's refusing to post bail."

"Idiot." Linette gave an angry toss of her head.

"Will you help?" Mathers' voice was hesitant.

Linette whirled about and glared coldly at Mathers. She had no sympathy for his discomfort. He'd been a part of this, after all. "Why should I?"

"Stephen shouldn't be in jail. His health . . ."

"He should have thought about that earlier," she snapped.

"I'm not asking you to accept what he did; I'm merely asking you to convince him to post bail."

"So you can both go out and do it again?" she asked icily.

"That was our last time, I assure you," he said glumly.

That was small comfort to Linette. The damage had already been done. Her trust in Stephen was gone.

But she still worried about him. Jails were full of disease. The longer he remained inside, the greater the chance he would contract some vile illness. Having pulled him back from the brink of death once, she didn't relish having to do it again.

"I'll go," she said finally. "But only because I'm worried about his health. As far as I'm concerned, he belongs in jail for what he did. As do you."

Linette rebuffed Mathers' every attempt to start a conversation in the carriage. Her temper wasn't improved when they were forced to queue up outside the entrance to the prison while they waited to be admitted. Finally, the turnkey let them in, and they entered the narrow hall that led to the prisoners' rooms.

Linette shivered at the dismal surroundings. She had never been in a prison. No wonder so many people were calling for reforms. The large, unheated building, dank, dripping walls and overcrowded rooms were a health menace.

Not the place for a man who'd barely recovered from pneumonia.

As they climbed the stairs to the first floor, she tried to gather her thoughts, concentrating on what she would say to Stephen. Right now, she couldn't think of anything strong enough to convey her displeasure.

But when the turnkey pushed the door open and she first saw Stephen seated on the narrow bed, her anger momentarily faded. He looked exhausted. Dark circles lined his eyes and with his unshaven face he looked far too much like the desperately ill man she'd nursed back to health. She reached out to touch him, then snatched her hand back.

This was his own fault. He was here because of his own incredible stupidity. Her initial sympathy dropped away.

Stephen glared angrily at Mathers. "Why did you bring her here?"

"Because you're acting like a fool, Stephen," Linette said. "Pay your bail and go home. You don't need to be here."

He compressed his lips in a thin line. "I have no intention of acknowledging these ridiculous charges by posting bail."

She put her hands on her hips and glared at him. "I didn't spend endless nights nursing you back to health only to watch you catch jail fever."

Mathers stepped forward. "She's right, Ash. Besides, you've got a school to run and you can't do it from in here."

Stephen took a deep breath and gave Linette an apologetic look. "Mathers had no business dragging you into my problem this morning. I'm sorry."

"Sorry for what you did or sorry that you were caught?"

"Sorry that you became involved. I don't regret what I did—it was necessary." His eyes darkened. "If it wasn't for some overzealous magistrate, I would have been sent home with nothing more than a stern lecture."

"It is a *crime* to disinter a body," Linette said scathingly. "Or does the law mean nothing to you?"

"Who am I offending in the process? Once someone's reached the churchyard, they're past caring." Stephen ran a hand through his hair. "The resurrectionists are insisting I pay double the going price for a body. I can't afford to do that."

"If you are so desperate for money, why didn't you come to me? Aunt would gladly loan you what you need."

"I don't want to borrow the money from your aunt—or anyone else."

Linette wanted to stamp her foot in frustration. "Stephen, why do you have to be so maddeningly stubborn? You'd rather go to jail than ask anyone for help. Why can't you see that you don't have to do everything by yourself? There are people who want to help you; let them."

"I can manage my affairs on my own," he said stiffly.

She twisted her fingers together, trying to push back her anger. "You aren't alone anymore, Stephen. We're not like your family; we care about you. *I* care about you."

"If you cared, you'd be more sympathetic to my position." He gave her a long, searching look. "The work I do saves people's lives. Teaching girls to sew can't prevent them from dying. My work can."

"At what price? Are you happy that you can dig up a grave and not be bothered by what you're doing? That you don't trust your friends enough to let them help you?" Linette sighed wearily. "I feel sorry for you."

"Sorry? For me?"

"You are losing your humanity, Stephen. I really thought you'd seen the value of caring, recognized that it could make you a better surgeon, a *compassionate* surgeon. But you don't want to be that kind of man, do you?"

"I *am* a surgeon. A damn good one."

"And you hide behind that label as an excuse to avoid dealing with your life, with your feelings. You don't want to change, do you? You really think you're better off this way."

Linette abruptly turned away, fighting her tears.

How could she have been so wrong about Stephen? She had thought he wanted to change, thought he wanted to care about the people he treated.

But he didn't. To him, it wasn't that important.

And she realized that she wasn't that important to him either. Medicine and research would always come first with him—before human feelings. Stephen would never change his ways. And Linette could not accept that.

She had hoped, prayed that he cared for her enough to listen to her, to consider what he was doing as well as why. But he didn't want to.

And she was not going to take second place in his life. As long as he was determined to pursue his own goals, to the exclusion of her feelings, there was no hope.

But oh, to think what Stephen and she could have done together.

*　　*　　*

Stephen stared at Linette's rigid back and swallowed an angry retort. She wasn't going to listen to him, wasn't even trying to listen to him.

The thought struck him like a blast of icy air.

She didn't understand. For if she did, she wouldn't be so damned persistent in insisting that she was right. He'd been a fool to think that she accepted his work. That she understood *him*.

Stephen looked from Linette's icy stance to Mathers' embarrassed expression, and then back to her again.

"All right," he said wearily. "I'll post bail. But I'm going to make sure that every surgeon in the city hears about this. They can't arrest me for trying to do my job."

Linette slowly turned around. "Do you have the money?" she asked quietly.

"Yes." Stephen sighed wearily.

"You won't have to pay it," Mathers said. "Several people have already made donations for your legal costs. There's more than enough for bail."

The news surprised Stephen, then he uttered a mocking laugh. "I suppose I'll be reading all about my adventure in the next issue of *The Lancet*."

"I think Wakley is aware of the situation," Mathers murmured.

Stephen darted a glance at Linette, whose pale face and frozen expression made her look as if she'd turned to stone.

Yet even in her anger, she was beautiful. He wanted to tell her that, wanted to tell her that he loved her and pull her into his arms and kiss her anger away. But he knew that it wouldn't be enough for her. She expected too much from him—more than he could give her.

She expected him to give up his work for her, and that he could not do.

Mathers edged toward the door. "I'll see to the bail. You should be out of here in an hour or so."

With one last cold look at Stephen, Linette followed Mathers out the door.

"Linette?" Stephen called after her but she did not turn around.

Stephen wanted to smash his fist into the wall, venting his anger at her, himself, the entire world. But he didn't dare risk injuring his hand.

He consoled himself with a torrent of profanity.

Once Mathers arranged his release, Stephen went directly back to his rooms. He immediately threw off his clothes and settled in the bath, where he wearily scrubbed the stench of prison off his body.

Linette was furious and he was going to have a devil of a time dealing with her.

He thought he'd convinced her that anatomy study was crucial to medical study. Yet her anger today showed that she still wanted to hold back medical progress because the method of obtaining cadavers offended her. Hadn't Amy's death showed her how little they knew, how much more they had to discover?

Stephen shook his head. He didn't think he would ever be able to understand Linette's reasoning. He respected her dislike of anatomy study; most people didn't find it a pleasant subject. But he wasn't asking her to venture into the dissecting room, merely to let him go about his work in his own way. Was that too much to ask?

Apparently, she thought it was.

How could he have fallen in love with a woman who felt so strongly that his work was wrong?

But judging from her reaction today, he wasn't going to have to worry about it. She might never speak to him again.

Chapter 28

Stephen refused to make any attempt to talk to Linette that week. He knew she would want him to beg for her forgiveness, but in his mind, she had nothing to forgive. *She* was the one who was wrong, the one who was trying to change him, to force him into her vision of what he ought to be. And as long as she thought that way, there was nothing he could say to her.

He wished there was. He still needed her, wanted her, with a fierce ache like nothing he'd ever experienced. Was this what love was? This desperate need to be with her, talk with her, touch her? To have her approve of and encourage his work?

If so, he was in deep trouble. Because she had told him that his work was unacceptable. She'd lied to him. She didn't love him after all.

The thought hit him like a blow. He'd taken a chance with her, trusted her, relied on her. And she'd betrayed his trust. She wasn't willing to accept him as he was, but wanted to change him. And when she discovered she couldn't turn him into the man she wanted, she'd tossed him aside.

Just like his family had.

And he wouldn't change, couldn't change, even for her. It went against everything he believed, everything that had drawn him to medicine in the first place. She was asking him to give up his teaching, his research, his life. He couldn't do that and the fact that she'd asked showed him that she didn't love him after all.

Best now that he tried to concentrate on his work. Now that she had found him wanting, it was the only thing he had.

Stephen told himself that, but it wasn't easy. Now, when he knew how much he loved her, had planned for a future with her, it was impossible to chase her from his mind. There were too many memories. Memories of how she'd tenderly nursed him while he lay ill. Memories of how he'd made sweet love to her those three glorious times.

Days were not so bad; he had work to occupy his mind and his hands. Stephen spent long hours at the school, giving his lectures and personally guiding the students through their dissections. They were going to be better surgeons for it, but that wasn't what motivated him. It was easier not to think about Linette when he was explaining the delicate tracery of veins and muscle and nerves to a student.

And it was easier not to think about her when he was lecturing, or tending patients at the Dispensary, or discussing the latest articles in *The Lancet* with Mathers.

It was only at night, when he was so tired he was ready to drop from exhaustion, that he couldn't keep the thoughts away any longer. And no matter how much he needed to sleep, he would lie awake in his bed, staring at the ceiling, thinking of her and all the plans he'd made. The plans that she'd so unceremoniously destroyed.

"You look even more miserable than usual." Mathers made himself comfortable on the office sofa. The last students had left for the day and they could both go home.

"You're so observant," Stephen said acidly.

"Oh, she's bound to forgive you eventually."

"Thanks for the vote of confidence." Stephen shoved his papers into a messy pile. He wasn't going to get any more work done now.

"You need a challenge. She's a strong-minded woman."

Stephen scowled. "I *know* that."

"Go see her. Act as if the whole thing was your fault—"

"She already thinks that," Stephen snapped.

"Well, try to pretend as if *you* believe it too. Take her a present. Women like presents."

Stephen rolled his eyes. "Sounds more like a bribe to me."

"It is," Mathers agreed cheerfully. "But it's expected."

Stephen didn't want to admit how appealing Mathers' suggestion sounded. He wanted to do *something* to restore his relationship with Linette. Being without her was too damn painful. "What do I take?"

"Flowers. Simple but effective."

Stephen gave him a skeptical look. It sounded far too easy. "Maybe I shouldn't worry." Stephen paced the floor. "She's bound to realize how unreasonable her attitude is. Eventually, she will apologize to me."

Mathers laughed. "How long are you prepared to wait? Forever?"

Sighing, Stephen sat down. "All right. I'll talk with her. But the only thing I have to apologize for is being stupid enough to get caught."

"That would be a start," Mathers said under his breath.

Stephen glared at him.

The following day, Stephen prepared for his visit to Linette. He took extra pains with his dress, even struggling to tie a presentable knot in his cravat.

Stopping at a flower seller's, he purchased some exorbitantly expensive blooms, then walked with an uneasy air to Fitzroy Square. What if she wouldn't agree to see him?

What if she did? Could he convince her that he had to carry out his work? That without it, he would never be content?

And that without her, he couldn't be content either.

"Miss Gregory is not at home," the butler informed Stephen when he stood at the front door.

Stephen shifted uneasily from foot to foot. What was he to do now? Was she deliberately avoiding him, or was she really not at home? Finally, he shoved the flowers into Mallon's hands. "See that she gets these," he said and walked slowly down the stairs.

He took a circuitous route back to the school, discouraged by the failure of his visit. Mathers was supervising in the dissecting room; there was no need to hurry back. It had taken all his nerve to go to the Barton house today; finding Linette gone had been a disappointment. Had he reacted too hastily? Should he have waited until she returned?

No, he'd left the flowers; that was good enough. Hopefully, she would see them for what they were—a peace offering.

Several hours later, he finally returned to Howard Street. He walked into the office and halted, suddenly, at the sight of what lay on his desk.

The flowers he'd left for Linette. Returned.

Stephen tossed them into the wastebasket without bothering to see if there was a note attached. The mere fact that they'd been returned said enough.

He stomped out of the office and strode back to the dissecting room.

Mathers glanced up when he walked in and Stephen gave him a warning look. He traded his good coat for the stained one hanging on the hook and walked between the tables, examining the students' work.

Stephen leaned over a student's shoulder. "That's a rather wobbly cut."

"Sorry, sir," said the student. "The scalpel was dull."

"Well, sharpen it then," Stephen snapped. "Your instruments should always be in top condition."

"Yes, sir. Right away, sir." The student backed away.

Stephen felt the tension rise in the room but he didn't

care. He wasn't going to tolerate sloppiness and any student who didn't understand that didn't belong here.

With a critical eye, he examined the other students' work, but found nothing more to complain about. Frustrated at having no more outlets for his anger, he left the room. Shoving his hands in his pockets, he marched down the corridor and shoved open his office door.

The scent of flowers permeated the room.

He picked up a trephine and threw it across the office. It hit the wall with a satisfying thunk and clattered to the floor.

Why couldn't she accept him for who he was, what he was? He thought she was different, thought she was one of the few who could understand how important his work was to him. But she cared more about herself.

Ironically, he'd been right all along. He didn't need a woman in his life. Particularly *that* one.

He only had himself to blame. He had dared to care, and been burned. It was his own damn fault. He'd fought a long battle to keep his feelings in check, and he'd almost succeeded. But in a moment of weakness he'd succumbed, and had given her power over him. And she'd turned around and slapped him in the face.

A knock sounded on the office door and Stephen jumped, irritated at the interruption.

"Come in," he growled.

Lord Graves walked in. "Ashworth."

Stephen whirled about, embarrassed to be seen in his stained dissecting coat. They shook hands and Lord Graves took a seat on the sofa.

"I've a favor to ask of you, Ashworth."

"Of me? What is it?"

"Some of the farsighted men in Parliament realize that the situation regarding anatomical studies cannot go on as it has been. They are holding hearings on the subject and many of the London medical men are speaking. I came to ask you to speak before the committee."

Stephen laughed hollowly. "Am I considered the latest expert on the problem?"

Lord Graves waved a dismissive hand. "That was an unfortunate incident."

"I wish *you'd* been the sitting magistrate," Stephen said with a touch of bitterness. "I tried to tell him that but he wasn't having any part of it."

"That matter has been taken care of," Lord Graves said. "We can't have one of our leading surgeons treated like a common criminal because of his work."

Stephen couldn't help but be flattered by the man's words. "I appreciate that."

"Good." Lord Graves rose. "The hearings begin next month. Sir Astley Cooper is to be the first witness. They will let you know when they want you to appear."

"What are they going to ask me?"

"Oh, the usual. The necessity for dissection, the difficulty of obtaining bodies. You will want to talk about your recent experience. Give them any suggestions you may have for improving the situation."

"That's easy," Stephen said. "Give us the unclaimed bodies from the hospitals and the workhouses, as the French do."

"I think you'll be a good witness." Lord Graves shook Stephen's hand again. "I'm sure the committee will be interested in hearing your views."

Stephen wanted to ask if there was any news about the position at the London Hospital, but he held his tongue. If the news was bad, he didn't want to know.

"Thank you again," Stephen said. "I'll do my best."

After he saw Lord Graves out, Stephen thought about the committee hearings. They probably wouldn't do any good; Parliament usually moved with glacial slowness. But it was a good beginning—and a poke at the men at Surgeons' Hall, who hadn't done anything about the problem.

Stephen crossed the room and picked up the trephine he'd tossed. What would Linette think when she heard that he had testified? Would she acknowledge that he was doing something to change the situation? That he was trying to find another way to supply the medical men with the bodies they needed without having to depend on the resurrectionists?

But even if she did find out that he spoke, would she care?

Linette stared morosely at the walls of the empty bedroom—the room where she'd fought for Stephen's life, cared for him, tended him. Made love to him, for the first time.

Her fingers curled around the bedpost. Now, everything had changed.

Turning him away this afternoon had been a cowardly act, but a necessary one. Linette knew she couldn't face him. Her resolve would weaken.

Like it almost had when she saw the flowers he'd left. Flowers. From Stephen. It was such a totally unexpected action that her heart had wavered for a moment. But then reason had reasserted itself. Flowers were no substitute for caring.

She sent them back because she couldn't bear to have them in the house as a constant reminder of what might have been.

And the gesture would also discourage Stephen from making another attempt to see her.

Linette turned and surveyed the room again. She could not regret the time she had spent with Stephen, even if it had been a mistake. He'd showed her the power of love, the physical joy, the emotional thrill. She would always cherish those memories.

Slowly, Linette walked out of the room and shut the door behind her. She would keep those memories shut up in that room. It was best that way.

Even though she knew they were locked away in her heart as well.

*   *   *

Several weeks later, Stephen sat in the rear of the committee hearing room, listening to Richard Grainger of the Webb Street School testify. Now that it was nearly time for him to speak, he wasn't at all sure he wanted to do this. Did the committee members really want to hear his opinions, or were they just going through these hearings as a formality? Was it possible that real change could come about?

At least he could consider himself in good company. So far, the witnesses before the committee read like a list of the country's leading surgeons. Stephen was pleased that he'd been included. He'd spent the last two days preparing facts and figures to present. He wanted to make sure the members understood how desperate the situation was, and how it could be solved.

Linette, of course, wouldn't be satisfied with his solution. She wouldn't allow the Dispensary to give up bodies for dissection; she would oppose the French plan as well.

It wasn't fair. He had thought he'd found a woman he could share his life with, one who admired the work he was doing, supported it, wanted to help. But because she could not accept this one part of his work, she had rejected him.

Grainger finished and Stephen prepared to take his place.

"Ashworth!" The teacher at the Webb Street School walked up to Stephen. "Heard you were going to talk to the committee. You're name's heard everywhere since your recent adventure with the law."

"My fleeting moment of fame," Stephen said drolly. He jerked his head toward the committee. "Are they receptive to what we have to say?"

"Oh, very," Grainger replied. "They want to see things changed as much as we do. Tell them all your horror stories."

"I've got enough of those," Stephen said with a wry laugh. "Between the resurrectionists and the antiresurrectionists, my last six months have been full of excitement."

"Trust you to antagonize both sides." He clapped Stephen on the back. "Let me know how your legal troubles turn out. I know everyone will want to help."

"Fortunately, someone stepped in and the whole matter was dismissed."

Grainger raised a brow. "Friends in high places, eh? Good for you."

A clerk stepped forward. "Mr. Stephen Ashworth is called before the committee."

Grainger held out his hand again. "Good luck, Ashworth. Come by the school sometime. I have a few interesting specimens you'd appreciate seeing."

Stephen nodded his thanks and followed the clerk to the front of the room, bemused by Grainger's interest. They hadn't exchanged more than a few words in passing in the past; now Grainger treated him like a valued colleague.

Ironic that it had taken getting arrested to bring him to everyone's notice. That, and Lord Grave's influence. Stephen knew that was why he was testifying here today—and suddenly realized that this simple act had catapulted him into a new world. Only a fraction of the surgeons in London were here; nearly all of them with quite larger reputations than his own.

Lord Graves had done him an enormous favor. By being one of the men who testified, Stephen's name would be in the papers. His opinions would be talked about, discussed. It would only help his work, and his reputation.

If only it would help him win over Linette.

He sat down and nervously faced the committee.

The chairman gave him a friendly smile and began the questioning. "Mr. Ashworth, you are a teacher of anatomy and surgery in the school at Howard Street?"

"Yes I am."

"What is the importance of dissection with regard to these fields of study?"

Stephen took a deep breath. "Dissection is absolutely critical. One cannot learn either anatomy or surgery without extensive examination and practice on the bodies of the dead."

"Are there great difficulties in obtaining the bodies needed for study?"

"There is a great deal of difficulty." Stephen grinned wryly. "The other speakers have detailed many of the reasons for the shortage of bodies. Because we medical practitioners are forced to rely on the resurrectionists, they enjoy a monopoly and can manipulate prices to suit their own purposes."

The chair leaned forward. "You have been a victim of this price manipulation?"

"Yes." Stephen sat up straighter. "The resurrectionists suddenly doubled the prices of the bodies they brought to me. I had either to pay their demanded price or go without."

"To what effect?"

"I couldn't afford to supply my students with materials for dissection at those prices. My livelihood was threatened."

"Thus, you were forced to find other ways to obtain the bodies you needed."

"Yes."

"What was the result?"

Stephen eased back in his chair, relaxing slightly. "After exhuming two bodies on my own, the resurrectionists learned of my activities, alerted the authorities, and I was arrested."

"What would have happened had you not sought to obtain these bodies by your own initiative."

"I would have been forced to close the school, to great personal and financial disaster," Stephen answered evenly.

"If bodies were more readily available for dissection, would this problem have arisen?"

"Not at all." Stephen looked directly at the committee chairman. "The resurrectionists obtain their power from the scarceness of the commodity. A well-regulated supply would put them out of business."

"Do you agree that a system like the one followed in Paris would be useful?"

Stephen smiled. "Yes, for two reasons. It would guarantee an ample supply of bodies for the schools and private practitioners, and would also encourage English students to remain at home to study. Everyone would benefit."

The questioning continued for a short time, then Stephen was thanked for his efforts and allowed to go.

Would it do any good? Had he, or any of the other men who testified, made any difference? Or would things go on as they had been?

He hoped for his sake that they would not. Then maybe, he could talk with Linette, convince her that his work shouldn't come between them. If the resurrectionists could be eliminated, if bodies could come to him without having to be disinterred, maybe she would reconsider. It was the fact that he'd gone digging that had made her so angry, wasn't it? If that became unnecessary, there was a chance—a chance—that she could accept his work.

If he ever had the opportunity to see her again.

Chapter 29

Linette gazed out the window at the dreary streets outside the Dispensary. It was spring in London, but here, one couldn't tell. There were no trees or flowers to relieve the bleakness of the scene. Just as there was nothing to relieve the bleakness of her spirit.

It had been nearly a month since she had last spoken with Stephen, but the pain in her heart hadn't gone away. If anything, time made it worse.

Aunt had sensed her unhappiness and suggested they take a holiday, but Linette declined. She needed to be here, working at the Dispensary. Here, at least, she was needed.

Stephen didn't need her, or want her.

But she couldn't forget him, or all the reasons she loved him. Linette remembered the aching anguish on his face as he'd watched Amy's life slipping away, helpless to save her, and the comfort Linette had found in his arms afterward. She remembered the warm light in his dark, piercing eyes the night he'd kissed her at the ball. And she remembered the times he'd loved her, his dark eyes bright with passion, his hands gentle and enticing as he explored her body.

Yet that all seemed so far away now. Far away and in another life.

Oh, how she missed him.

But the same hands that caressed her also held the knife as he cut into human bodies. How could one man be so tender at one moment, and so coldly clinical at another?

But wasn't it that dichotomy that made him the man he was? He was a contradiction, a compassionate man lurking behind a wall of studied indifference. Once, she thought she had broken through that wall, seen the vulnerable side of him, seen the man that needed to be loved. For a brief moment, he'd said that he needed her, wanted her.

But it wasn't true.

A soft rap sounded on the door. Linette opened it, surprised to find Mary outside, her arms full of magazines.

"Come in," she said. "This is a surprise. What are you doing here today?"

"I wanted to bring these back to you," Mary replied in a low voice, handing her armload to Linette. "Seeing as I won't be needin' them anymore."

Linette glanced at the magazines. "But, Mary, these are the embroidery patterns. You're not giving up your sewing?"

"I'm gettin' married, Miz Gregory."

"Married?" Linette could hardly believe her ears. "You're too young to be getting married."

Mary drew herself up. "I'm sixteen, Miz Gregory. That's plenty old enough."

"You're just a girl. What about your sewing? You were making real progress."

Mary tossed her head. "There won't be time for that now. He's got kids already, see, so I'll be busy with them."

"You're marrying a widower?"

The girl nodded.

Linette shook her head doubtfully. "Mary, I thought you wanted to get a job, to earn your own money and be independent."

Mary shrugged. "From what I see, takin' care of kids

is a mite easier that toiling in some fancy ladies' dress shop."

"Who is this man? He sounds like he merely wants someone to look after his children."

Mary gave her a fixed stare. "And what if he does? He's got a good job, 'e does, layin' bricks, and he's promised to take care of me mam as well."

"But ..." Linette's dismay left her speechless. This was Mary, her prize pupil, the girl who was going to prove to everyone the value of education and training. And now she wanted to throw it all away. "What about all our plans?"

"Miz Gregory, I'm grateful for what you've done, showin' me how to sew and all." Mary gave her an uneasy glance. "And maybe I would 'a liked workin' in one of them dress places. But I got a man to take care of me now. I don't need that."

"Well, Mary, if this is what you want to do ..." Linette made no attempt to hide the disappointment in her voice.

"Learnin' how to sew fancy stitches ain't gonna put food in my mouth tomorrow," Mary said. "I've got Mam to think about, too."

Linette struggled to hold back her anger. "What's the point of learning anything, then? Reading or writing or figuring isn't going to be of much help then, either."

"Look, round here, it's more important that we got a roof over our head and food in our bellies. And if marryin' this man is gonna give me that, I'd be a fool to say no."

"I hope then, for your sake, that the marriage will be a happy one." Linette could not bring herself to sound pleased.

Mary gave her a saucy grin. "'E's a 'andsome one, 'e is."

Linette sighed. "You will let me know when the wedding is?"

Mary nodded and left.

Linette looked at the magazines in her lap.

What was the use? Maybe it was pointless to try to help these people. They didn't have the imaginations to see where they could go; they only worried about the here and now.

A tiny voice nagged at the back of her mind. When life was a daily struggle, the here and now was important, and anything that would make it better was a godsend.

But Mary . . . Linette had held such plans for her and now they were ruined. How could the girl be so ungrateful? She had tossed Linette's hard work back in her face, rejected it as unimportant. She wasn't interested in Linette's plans for her.

Because they didn't mean anything to Mary. They were a step into the unknown, a departure from the life she knew. Could Linette blame her for clinging to the old ways, for grabbing what stood for security in her life?

In fact, how many other women married for the same reasons? Security, familiarity, a sense of being needed. Who was Linette to say that Mary was wrong in doing this? She was thinking more of herself than Mary; Linette was more concerned about what *she* wanted than what Mary wanted. And ultimately, it was Mary's life. She had to make the best choice for herself. No matter how much she wanted to, Linette couldn't rule her life.

She sat back in her chair.

Wasn't that what she had tried to do with Stephen? Force him to conform to her desires, and not his?

Then when he hadn't, she had walked away from him.

Linette moaned softly and buried her face in her hands. She'd treated him the same as his family had, expecting him to accede to her wishes.

She had rejected him because he wouldn't do what she wanted.

Dear God, what had she done?

And she remembered the anguish in his voice as he'd called after her in prison, and she had not replied.

Would he ever listen to her again?

Could she accept that Stephen would not change his views on anatomy, that she was the one who would have to compromise if they were to be together? The thought troubled her. All her life she'd had a firm sense of right and wrong. But since meeting Stephen, those beliefs had been challenged. Could some evils be acceptable because of their ultimate benefit to mankind?

Stephen thought so.

Linette let the papers fall from her fingers.

It was wrong of her to try to change him. She had to accept him as he was, for what he was. A surgeon. A teacher. An anatomist. A man who cared deeply and sincerely about the work he was doing and the value it held for humankind. A man she admired, respected, and loved.

He wasn't perfect. But did she love Stephen more than she hated dissection, and all its attendant evils?

Her heart answered yes.

She had to tell him that she'd been wrong, that she could tolerate his work. Because she loved him. Loved him enough to accept what he did, because it was what he wanted, what he needed to do. She had no other choice.

But after the way she'd treated him, would he believe her when she told him?

Now that Linette had admitted what she wanted to do, she was nervous. Stephen *might* not be willing to see her again. She'd struggled so hard to get past his rigid indifference, and then when she finally succeeded, she'd informed him he wasn't worthy. He must despise her.

Somehow, she had to show Stephen that she was the one who wasn't worthy of him—and convince him to accept her anyway. She had done it once. Could she do it again?

The same plan that had worked before just might work again.

Linette spent the next two days dashing around London, talking with students and booksellers, buying every French medical work that she could get her hands on.

Stephen wouldn't be able to read them, but she could. It might take longer to win back his trust this time, but she had to show him that she really, truly loved him.

Stephen leaned his forehead against the window glass in his office, watching rivulets of rain streaming down the pane. A typical spring day in England. Cold, damp, and miserable.

Just like he felt.

Every time he thought about Linette, it was with a mixture of sadness, anger, and regret. Sadness, because for a short while he'd thought he could be happy with her. Anger, that she demanded perfection of him. Regret, that he couldn't be the man she wanted him to be.

And regret that he'd allowed himself to fall in love with her. He'd known the danger, taken the chance, and lost. He wasn't good enough for her.

He'd never been good enough for anybody.

Well, it wouldn't happen again. If he didn't allow anyone to come close, they couldn't reject him. Never again would he allow himself to feel anything for a woman. Living alone was infinitely better than the hell of these last weeks.

He couldn't even feel much satisfaction in the new developments since his committee testimony. Suddenly, his services were being sought by a number of people. Stephen seriously contemplated setting up an examination room here at the school to deal with his new patients. Patients who paid for his services. If this continued, his financial situation would be rosy by the fall.

Surprisingly, there had been no more trouble from the resurrectionist gangs. Whether it was due to the summer lull in the body trade, or that they'd considered his jail-ing warning cnough, Stephen didn't care. There might be problems when school started again in the fall, but if they wouldn't trade with him, he knew that every teach-ing surgeon in London would come to this rescue.

Even his new book had achieved a modest success.

He'd been sorely disappointed, of course, when he didn't obtain the appointment to the London Hospital. The hospital board had decided not to hire another assis-tant surgeon after all. Stephen consoled himself with the knowledge that by merely being considered, his name had come before a number of powerful and influential men. They would remember him.

And this way, he could go ahead with his plan to take on some private students. And they would pay him, something the London Hospital would not.

Still, he was miserable. Miserable because he missed Linette, missed her teasing smile and laughing eyes. He wanted her here with him. Wanted her as fiercely as he'd ever wanted anything in his life.

What did it matter if his financial situation was im-proving? It meant little to him; he'd only wanted more money so he could support her. The new patients and new connections he'd gained didn't seem very important anymore. He was doing well and he didn't care—because he couldn't share it with her.

Even Mathers noticed his gloom when he stepped into the office this rainy May afternoon.

"You're looking glum today."

Stephen gave him an exasperated look. "It's raining, there's a draft in the lecture room, and I can't find the issue of *The Lancet* that I'm looking for. Who has a reason to be cheerful?"

Mathers laughed. "Sounds like you need a night out. After a good hot meal and a few glasses of brandy, you'll feel better."

"Is this another one of your ancient prescriptions for

health?" Stephen asked. "What learned Greek physician recommended that?"

"As a surgeon, I'm trained to excise diseased tissue. But that's a bit too drastic for what ails you."

"And what ails me?"

Mathers flung a hand across his heart. "Alas, the man has suffered a reversal in love."

Stephen snorted derisively and continued rummaging through the tumble of papers on his desk, trying to find the missing journal.

"Yes," Mathers continued, "I think that our learned, respected surgeon is pining for his lost love."

Stephen ignored his comment. It was too accurate a description. "When are you off to Scotland?"

"Next week. Are you sure you don't want to come?"

"And give up the modest comfort of my own rooms for the nonexistent comforts of the Highlands?" Stephen laughed derisively. "I've no inclination to sleep under the stars and tramp through wet heather and sheep dung, thank you."

Mathers gave him a knowing look. "You don't want to leave town in case she comes back."

Stephen glared at him, not wanting to admit how close to the truth he'd come. "I don't want to leave town because I'm finally going to be able to undertake some research without any disruptions. Until fall term starts, my time is my own."

"Aren't you still working at the Dispensary?"

"Apart from that," Stephen added.

"Well, I'll think of you when I'm breathing that fresh, clear Highland air."

"And I'll think of you when I'm in the middle of a complicated surgery, practicing a new technique I've developed while you were gone."

Mathers rose and shook hands. "I should be back in a month. Don't hire another assistant while I'm gone."

"I'll *think* about it," Stephen said with a laugh.

Stephen stifled the urge to run after him and tell

Mathers he would go to Scotland with him after all. He should leave London, the Dispensary, and the school for a time. Maybe, in the wilds of the Highlands, he could forget.

But he feared that forgetting Linette was about as impossible as giving up medicine. And if he couldn't have one, he could at least throw himself into the other. Even with his new patients and his days at the Dispensary, he had had ample time to pursue his own interests.

Stephen already had some ideas for new articles. Wakley at *The Lancet* had expressed interest in a few of his projects. No doubt there would be an interesting case or two at the Dispensary to write up. He would have ample time over the summer to pursue his own ends. There were no lectures to prepare, no students to supervise.

And far too much time to think about Linette, and how she'd left him. And why.

Stephen pushed back his chair. Dwelling on his misery wasn't going to make him feel any better. Mathers was right. Maybe a good dinner and a glass or two of brandy would make him feel better. He could stop at his favorite tavern on the way home and enjoy a leisurely meal.

Before he returned to his cold, lonely room and spent the night dreaming about a woman who did not want him.

Chapter 30

The hackney stopped in front of Stephen's building, but Linette was reluctant to leave the security of the cab. She put her hand on the package of books beside her, seeking reassurance that she was doing the right thing. Now that it was time to face Stephen, she was overcome with nervousness. What if he refused to see her?

What if he did see her but remained unmoved by her apologies?

Linette screwed up her courage. She had to talk with him eventually and she might as well get it over with. At least she would know where she stood, and whether she had a chance to convince him that she loved him without reservations or conditions.

After paying the driver, she walked into the building. The same shabby carpet stood in the entry hall, the stair railing still needed a coat of paint, and the stairs had not been swept for days. Yet she would live here gladly, if Stephen would only ask her.

She hesitated again, outside his door, before she reached up and knocked softly. Then, not waiting for a reply, she pushed the door open and stepped inside.

Stephen was hunched over his work table, scribbling furious notes.

Linette cleared her throat. "Hello, Stephen."

She saw his shoulders tense. He set the pen down with deliberate care and slowly turned around to face her.

"What are you doing here?" he asked hoarsely.

Linette took another step into the room. "I brought

you a present," she said, holding out the package of books.

He took it from her and set it on a chair.

"Open it." She gave him an encouraging smile.

His face expressionless, he rummaged around on his table until he found a scalpel, then slit the string.

"It was an interesting adventure, seeking these out. You could not guess the number of shops I visited, or the strange looks I received when I asked for these."

Linette knew she was babbling but she couldn't help herself. She was too nervous about talking with Stephen, wondering how he would react, what he would say.

He unwrapped the paper and stared at the pile of books and pamphlets.

"They are all the latest publications," she said quickly. "I tried to get a mix of surgical and medical materials."

He gave her a withering look. "You know I can't read these. They're all in French."

She studied him carefully. "But I can."

Stephen picked up the top volume and thumbed through it, pausing to examine some of the engravings. "Why," he said at last, "would you want to?"

Linette nibbled her lower lip. "Because I . . . because I had no right to be so angry with you over those disinterred bodies. I was wrong."

He uttered a bitter laugh. "How generous of you to accept fault."

"I saw the *Times* last month; I read about your testimony before the committee. I was proud of you for speaking out."

He didn't answer and Linette twisted her fingers in the fabric of her skirt. "Stephen, I want to apologize for all the things I said. I was wrong to think that you had to agree with me on everything. At the time, I couldn't imagine how you could have done such a thing, knowing how I felt about it." She gave him a wan smile. "I know I was being foolish. I realize now that the whole incident had nothing to do with me."

"It had everything to do with you," he said quietly.

She looked at him, puzzled.

"I was desperate to save the school. I needed every penny I could save. For the school and . . . for you."

"Why me?"

He gestured at his cluttered room. "It was bad enough, knowing that I could never ask you to live in a place like this. Then the school was teetering on the edge of disaster. I would be ruined financially and there'd be no future for us."

Linette's mind was still back on his first words. "You wanted me to live with you?"

Stephen glared at her. "Did you think after taking you to my bed that I planned to leave you? Of course I intended to marry you."

"You might have said something!"

"What could I say? That in a year or two, if I was lucky, I might have enough money to support you?"

"I didn't expect you to marry me." Linette watched him carefully. She didn't want him to act out of a misplaced sense of obligation. "I came to you willingly. I wanted you to know that you were loved."

"Well, you succeeded in that. I really believed you— for a time."

She hung her head. "Stephen, I can't take back what I said or what I did. I thought that I could change your views about dissection, about admitting your emotions." She smiled sadly. "I was wrong to think that. Love isn't about changing people, but accepting them for what they are, who they are."

Linette reached out and put a hand on his arm. "I can't change you, Stephen, and I don't want to. If I did, you wouldn't be the man I fell in love with."

She looked down; his fingers were white where he clenched the book and she knew her words affected him. But she had to break through that wall of reserve one more time, to force him to admit that he still cared, that he still loved her.

"It will take me a long time to translate all these books," she said. "By the time I'm finished, I hope you'll be more certain that I love you, and that I want to be with you." She saw a muscle throb in his cheek and she traced the line of it with her finger. "Because I do, Stephen. More than anything else I've ever wanted.

"Stephen." She looked into his cold, dark eyes and a shiver of fear ran through her. "Please tell me that it isn't too late, that you can forgive me." Her voice broke. "Please say that you love me."

The heavy French medical book fell to the floor with a thud and he pulled her into his arms, crushing her against his chest.

"Oh, God, how I've missed you."

Linette wrapped her arms around him. "Hold me, Stephen, please hold me."

He held her tightly, and neither of them moved for several long minutes. Then he cupped her face in his hands and touched his lips to hers.

It was a long, exquisitely tender kiss that Linette wanted never to end.

Stephen lifted his head at last and looked into her eyes. Her heart ached at the anguish she saw in his.

"I wish I could be the man that you want me to be, but I can't, Linette. Medicine is too important, too much a part of my life. I won't give up my anatomical studies."

She put her hands on his shoulders. "I'm not asking you to give up anything, Stephen. I don't want you to. Don't you see?" She looked at him with pleading eyes. "I know how important it is to you. And even though I don't like it, if I have to choose, I choose you."

He pulled her against him, tucking her head beneath his chin.

"I swore that I wouldn't care about anyone ever again," he said, stroking her back. "But it's too late for that. You stole my heart a long time ago. I don't think I could stop loving you if I lived to be eighty."

Linette snuggled against him. "I won't mind. As long as I can be there with you."

"Oh, you will be." He hugged her tightly. "I'm not letting you out of my sight again."

Linette grinned. "Aunt Barton will be shocked when I don't come home tonight."

Stephen kissed her again, gently, tenderly. "Well, maybe out of my sight for a *very* short while. But never out of my heart."

He took her hand and placed it on his chest, letting her feel the rhythmical beating of his heart. "As a surgeon and an anatomist, I shouldn't believe what you've just done. But somehow, you've managed to repair a damaged heart."

Linette stood on tiptoe and kissed him. "Sometimes love can heal where medicine can't," she whispered.

Stephen smiled at her. "Just don't expect me to mention that in my lectures."

"It will be our secret. Forever."

Also Coming in October

I wonder why it is that my mistress is so ignorant, Lord Ragsdale thought as he took a sip of morning brandy and gazed at the heavily scented letter spread out before him on the breakfast tray. Could it be that no one ever taught her the difference between *there* and *their*—and what on earth is this word?

He held up the paper closer to his good eye. Hm, it appears that I am either thoughtless, thankless, reckless, or feckless, and I don't think Fae knows that word.

He felt a tiny headache beginning from all that scent, so he crumpled the letter into a ball and threw it across the room toward the wastebasket by his desk, which was overflowing with other correspondence. As usual, he was wide of the mark. "Fae, why so much musk on one letter? Do you think I am an otter?" he asked her miniature, which resided, smirking, on his night table.

He took another sip, then slid down to a more comfortable level in the bed. Of course, you didn't take on Fae in the first place because she was a grammarian, he reminded himself. You acquired her services because of her other splendid talents. Fae Moullé might not be able to string a coherent sentence across a page, but she knows her way across a mattress.

It was a thought that only a week ago might have propelled him from his own bed on Curzon Street and into hers only a brisk walk away. As he closed his eye, he asked himself what had changed in so brief an interval. Perhaps it was the rain. That was it; too much rain always made him restless and dissatisfied, even with the prospect of making love.

Making love. Now, there is an odd phrase, he thought as he opened his eye and stared at the ceiling. "Fae Moullé, I do not love you," he told the plaster swirls overhead. "You provide a pleasant jolt to my body, but so would another. No, Fae, I do not love you."

Lord Ragsdale sighed and jerked the pillow out from behind his head. He lay flat on the bed and almost returned to sleep again. The room was cool and silent, but some maggot was burrowing about in his brain now and wouldn't let him doze. Of course, it was well past noon, too.

Perhaps it was time to send a letter to Fae, severing all connections. He could sweeten her disappointment with a tidy sum, and offer to provide excellent references. The thought made him grin in spite of his vague discomfort. Any woman who could perform such magic between sheets ought to have no trouble snaring another marquis or earl. Lord knows England is full of dilettantes, he thought, and we recognize what we like.

He thought back to Fae's letter, and the one the day before, teasing him for a new wardrobe to peacock about town in. While he liked the way she looked when she strolled about town with him, her hand resting lightly—but so possessively—on his arm, he was already dreading the mornings that would be taken up with modistes and models. Fae would not buy anything he did not approve of, so he would have to accompany her to the salons. She would coo and simper over each dress trotted out on display, then look at him with her big blue eyes. "Whatever you want, my dear," she would ask.

"Whatever you want, my dear," he mimicked. She even said that when they were in bed. Damn, Fae, don't you possess a single stray thought of your own? What do *you* like? Do you know?

He sat up then and left his bed, thoroughly disgusted with himself. He glared into the mirror and pointed a finger at his night-shirted facsimile. "Johnny Staples, you are a spoiled son of a bitch," he told himself. "You pay Fae's bills and she must jump through your hoops. You should be ashamed."

He regarded himself another moment, then looked about for his eyepatch. No sense in disturbing the maid, who was due in here any moment with his shaving water. He found it and grinned to himself again, wondering how loud she would scream if she came into the room and found him leering at her with his patch over his good eye.

Too bad it was the Season now. He would have happily traded it all for a week or two on a friend's estate, if he'd had any friends left. He could take off that stupid patch and let the cold winds blow across his dead eye, too, as he rode the land. But this was London, and really, his eye didn't look too appealing, all milky white, perpetually half open, and with that nasty scar. I could scare myself if I were drunk enough, he observed as he pulled his robe about his shoulders and gave the coals in the fireplace a little stir.

He grunted when the maid knocked, and she entered with his hot water. When she left, he sat at his desk, staring glumly at all the correspondence before him. This was the overflow from the book room, too, he considered, wondering again why he had fired his secretary last month. He ruffled through the letters, many of them invitations that should have been answered weeks ago. "Well, Johnny, maybe it was because your secretary was robbing you blind," he reminded himself. Which was true, but Lord, the man could keep up with my business and knew how to write letters that sounded just like I had written them. What a pity the wretched cove could also duplicate my signature.

Ah, well, the little bastard was cooling his heels in Newgate now, waiting transportation. Maybe if he survived the seven months in the reeking hold of a convict ship, he could find someone to bamboozle in Botany

Bay. Lord Ragsdale sighed and looked at his frazzled desk. *I suppose now if I want to cancel my liaison with Fae through the penny post, I'll have to write my own letter.*

Nope, no letters to Fae, he reminded himself as he took off the patch again and lathered up. *She thinks I'm thoughtless, thankless, reckless, or feckless. And besides that, it's too much exertion. I suppose a new wardrobe won't kill me. It's a damned sight easier than explaining to Fae that I'm tired of her.*

Lord Ragsdale was not in a pleasant frame of mind when his mother knocked on the door. He knew her knock; it was just hesitant enough to remind him that he paid her bills, too. He tucked in his shirttails and buttoned up his pants, wondering at his foul mood. *Maybe I should pay Fae a quick visit,* he thought. *I'd at least leave her house in a more relaxed frame of mind.*

"Come in, Mother," he said, trying not to sound sour. It wasn't his mother's fault that he was rich and she was bound to him by his late father's stupid will. *I really should settle a private income on her,* he thought as he reached for his waistcoat. *I wonder why Father didn't? He had never done anything wrong.* Lord Ragsdale sighed. And death had come too suddenly for him to say, "Oh, wait, I am not ready."

As his mother came into his room on light feet, he felt his mood lifting slightly. How dainty she was, and how utterly unlike him. She didn't look old enough to have a thirty-year-old son, he thought as he inclined his head so she could kiss his cheek. True to form, she patted his neck cloth and tugged it to the left a little.

"Am I off center again, ma'am?" he inquired. "Funny how one eye gone puts me off, even after ..." He paused a moment. "Let's see, is it ten years now?"

"Eleven, I think, my dear," she replied. "Oh, well. Two eyes gone would be worse."

He nodded, wondering at her ability to cheer him up. She was so matter-of-fact. Why couldn't he have inherited that tendency, instead of his father's leaning toward melancholy?

"I suppose," he agreed as he allowed her to help him into his coat. "Damn the Irish, anyway."

She frowned at him and he took her hand.

"Yes, Mama. That was rude of me," he said before she could. "Didn't you teach me not to kick dogs? For so they are. I apologize."

He kissed his mother and she smiled at him. "Accepted. Now hurry up and put on your shoes. They are belowstairs."

He looked at her, then rummaged for his shoes. "Mama, who are you talking about?"

She sighed loud enough for him to pause in his exertions. "What did I forget this time?" he asked.

"Your American cousins, John. They have arrived."

He paused a moment in thought, embarrassed to have forgotten something that obviously had meaning for his mother. "My cousins," he repeated.

"John, you are the dearest blockhead," she said and took his arm, pulling him toward the door. "My sister's children from Virginia! Don't you remember?"

He did now. In fact, he remembered a winter's worth of bills to refurbish the ballroom and downstairs sitting rooms. And wasn't there something about Oxford? "Let's see if I remember now, Mama," he teased. "Someone is going to Oxford, and someone else is attempting a come-out under your redoubtable aegis."

"Excellent!" she commended him. "Sometimes you are the soul of efficiency."

"Not often, m'dear," he murmured as they descended the stairs. "Will you begin reminding me on a regular basis that I must engage a secretary, and soon?"

"I have been," she said patiently. "And I've been reminding you about a valet, too, and while we're at it, a wife."

He laughed out loud at the seriousness of her expression. "Which of the three do I need worse, madam?" he quizzed as she steered him toward the gold saloon, reserved for unpleasant events, formal occasions, and, apparently, little-known relatives.

"A wife," she replied promptly as she allowed Lasker to open the door for her. "Ah, my dears! Heavens, are you drooping? Let me introduce your cousin, John Staples, Lord Ragsdale. John, here are Robert and Sally Claridge, your cousins from Richmond, Virginia. Come forward, my dears. He won't bite."

Of course I will not bite, he thought as he came forward to shake cousin Robert's hand. He thought he might kiss Sally's cheek, but she was staring at his eye patch as though she expected him suddenly to brandish a cutlass and edge her toward a plank. He nodded to her instead. "Delighted to meet you," he murmured automatically, wondering how soon he could escape to White's and bury his face in a pint of the finest.

He had to admit that they were a handsome pair as he stepped back and allowed his mother's conversation to fill in any awkward gaps before they had the chance to develop. Sally Claridge had his mother's ash blond good looks. If the expression in her blue eyes was a trifle vacant, perhaps a good night's rest on a pillow that did not pitch and yaw with an ocean under it would make the difference.

On the other hand, Robert's dark eyes seemed to miss nothing as he gazed about the room, looking for all the world like a solicitor totaling up the sum of each knickknack and trifle. I certainly hope we measure up, Lord Ragsdale thought as he cast an amused glance in Robert's direction, indicated a seat on the sofa to Sally, then turned his attention to the fifth person in the room.

She should have taken up no more than a moment's flick of his eyes, because she could only be Sally Claridge's servant, but he found himself regarding her with some thoroughness, and his own interest surprised him.

Lord Ragsdale was an admitted breast man. It was the first feature he admired in all classes of women, and this female before him was no exception to his time-honored tradition. She was still covered with a rather shabby cloak, but the slope of it told him that she was nicely, if not excessively, endowed. Ordinarily, his glance would have lingered there as he contemplated her suspected amplitude, but his attention was drawn to her regal posture. She stood straight and tall, her chin back, her head up, as poised a lady as ever favored the gold saloon. Her air fascinated him.

He knew she must be tired. Sally Claridge had sunk onto the sofa with the appearance of one destined never to rise again, while Robert leaned heavily on a chair back. The servant before him made no such concession to exhaustion. She bore herself like a queen, and he was intrigued in spite of himself.

"And you are . . ." he began.

Robert threw himself into one of the dainty chairs, and he heard his mother suck in her breath as it creaked. "That's Emma, Sally's waiting woman. Emma, I wish you'd take my cloak. And see here, there's Sally's, too. I don't know why we need to remind you."

Without a word the woman came forward and took the cloaks. They were both much heavier than the one she still wore, but she draped them gracefully over her arm and retreated into the background again, her back as straight as a duchess.

Lord Ragsdale looked around at his butler, who stood in the doorway. "Lasker, take the cloaks. Yours, too . . . Emma, is it?"

She nodded and showed the barest dimple in his direction.

"Lord, Emma, you are such a dunce! Can you not at least say, 'Thank you, my lord'?" Robert burst out.

"Thank you, my lord," the woman whispered, her cheeks a flame of color.

"That wasn't necessary," Lord Ragsdale replied mildly to his cousin.

There was an awkward pause, which his mother filled adroitly, as he knew she would.

"Robert, Sally, tell me how my sister does. I know you are both tired, but I must know."

With a shy look in Lord Ragsdale's direction, Sally murmured a response to his mother, and Robert rummaged in his waistcoat for a letter. Lord Ragsdale clasped his hands behind his back and took another look at the waiting woman, as Robert called her.

It was a quaint expression, one he had not heard before, but it fit her exactly. She stood patient and still as his mother forged ahead with conversation, looking like someone used to waiting. He thought her eyes were green, and her expression told him that her mind was miles distant. For a brief moment he wondered what she was thinking, and then he laughed inwardly. Really, Johnny, who cares what a servant thinks? he told himself. I am sure I do not.

"Well, son, is it agreed?"

Startled, he glanced at his mother, who was observing him with that combination of exasperation and fondness he was familiar with.

"I'm sorry, m'dear, but I was not attending. Say on, please. Tell me what it is I am about to agree to."

It was the merest jest. Out of the corner of his eye, he noticed that fleeting dimple again. Sally registered nothing on her face, and Robert just looked bored.

"John, sometimes I think you are certifiable."

Sally goggled at that. "Aunt Staples, he is a marquis!" she gasped.

"A title never gave anyone brains," his mother remarked, her words crisp. "Bear that in mind, Sally, as you begin your own adventure here this season." She looked at him again. "My dear, I was merely suggesting that we all drive down to Oxford to install Robert. It will give your cousins the opportunity of seeing their Grandmama Claridge, whom they have never met."

"Then brace yourselves," he murmured, wondering

what the waiting woman was making of this family talk. "I think it an excellent idea. Once you have met the family Gorgon, you will only be too grateful for Charon to row you across the River Styx and into the quad of Brasenose."

The blank stare that Robert returned made Lord Ragsdale sigh inwardly and long for the comforts of his liquor cabinet. Obviously his alma mater would be suffering one more fool gladly.

"Provided Mr. Claridge can find the coin necessary for the boat ride."

It was said in a such a low tone that he doubted Emma's words carried much beyond his own ears. He grinned appreciatively. "A hit, a palpable hit," he whispered back, and was rewarded with that fleeting dimple again. What have we here? he asked himself. A servant who knows her Greek mythology and Shakespeare, too?

But there was something else about her softly voiced reply that set off a bell in the back of his brain. He knew the lilt in her voice.

"Emma, where are you from?" he asked suddenly, his voice too loud in the quiet room.

He knew his question was inappropriate, and a rude interruption to his mother, who was saying something to Sally about Grandmama Claridge. Besides that, he could not think of a time when he had ever asked a servant anything that personal. And here he was at his most strident, demanding an answer.

She was as startled as he was. The dimple disappeared, and she looked in dismay from Robert to Sally, as though waiting for a reprimand.

"Come now. It's an easy question," he said, egged on by some demon that seemed to be amplifying his voice until he sounded almost as though he were commanding troops again. He could see his mother coming toward him, alarm on her face. He held up a hand to stop her. "I want to know where you are from and what is your name."

The servant's face had drained of all color now. She swallowed several times; then, if anything, her carriage became even more regal. She looked him right in the eye, something he had never seen before in a servant, and spoke quite distinctly.

"My name is Emma Costello, sir, and I am from County Wicklow."

"Well, damn you, then, you and all your bog-trotting relatives," he said, turned on his heel, and left the room. In another moment he slammed out of the house, ignoring his mother, and hurried down the sidewalk. He was too upset for Fae. It would be White's and a bottle of brandy. Maybe two.

From *Reforming Lord Ragsdale*
by Carla Kelly

Have you read a Signet Regency lately?